I0730352

# LENA GIBSON

Black Rose Writing | Texas

©2026 by Lena Gibson
All rights reserved. No part of this book may be reproduced, stored in a retrieval system or transmitted in any form or by any means without the prior written permission of the publishers, except by a reviewer who may quote brief passages in a review to be printed in a newspaper, magazine or journal.

The author grants the final approval for this literary material.

First printing

This is a work of fiction. Names, characters, businesses, places, events, and incidents are either the products of the author's imagination or used in a fictitious manner. Any resemblance to actual persons, living or dead, or actual events is purely coincidental.

ISBN: 978-1-68513-693-2
LIBRARY OF CONGRESS CONTROL NUMBER: 2025942456
PUBLISHED BY BLACK ROSE WRITING
www.blackrosewriting.com

Printed in the United States of America
Suggested Retail Price (SRP) $22.95 / CA $25.95

*The Right Time* is printed in Garamond Premier Pro

*As a planet-friendly publisher, Black Rose Writing does its best to eliminate unnecessary waste to reduce paper usage and energy costs, while never compromising the reading experience. As a result, the final word count vs. page count may not meet common expectations.

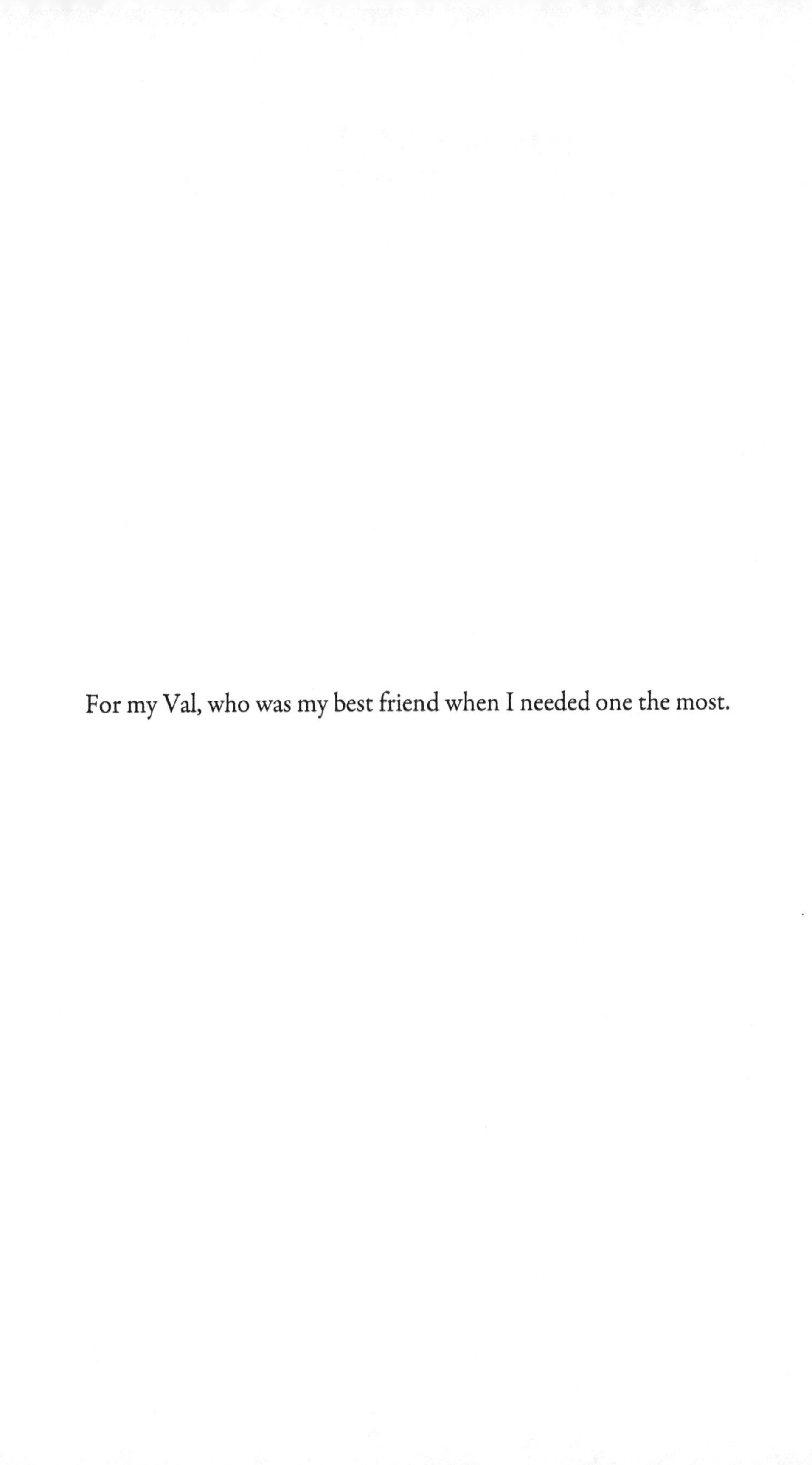

For my Val, who was my best friend when I needed one the most.

# PRAISE FOR
# *THE RIGHT TIME*

"A heartwarming, slow-burn time-travel romance–like *Outlander* imbued with the '80s nostalgia of *Ready Player One*!"
–Cam Torrens, award-winning author of the Tyler Zahn suspense mysteries

"Gibson's time-slip novel brings back the 80s with wonderful simplicity and characters you will root for from the very start."
–Lucille Guarino, author of *Elizabeth's Mountain* and *Lunch Tales: Suellen*

"How far would you go for a second chance at a happy ever after? In order to escape her abusive husband, Andie is willing to sacrifice everything and start over almost 50 years earlier. Timing is everything in this gripping time slip romance."
–Gail Ward Olmsted, best-selling author of the *Miranda Quinn Legal Twist* series

"In *The Right Time: Back to the 80s*, Lena Gibson deftly blends women's fiction, romance, and magical realism to craft a can't-miss story of love and identity."
–Travis Tougaw, author of the *Marcotte/Collins Investigative Thrillers*

"*The Right Time* is an emotional tale of growth and survival as Andie looks to begin a new life in a past she barely recognizes."
–Gary Gerlacher, author of the *AJ Docker* series

"Gibson has done it again! This is another unputdownable book that had me hooked from the first page. With her unquestionably excellent writing skills she has created another genre-defying novel that has something for everyone."
–A.J. McCarthy, author of the *Charlie and Simm Mystery* series

"Lena Gibson is at her best in this novel. It's a love story that isn't possible, but then again, who's to say?"
–Karen K. Brees, best-selling author of the *WWII Adventures of MI6 Agent Katrin Nissen* series

"Lena Gibson has done it again! Her new romance, *The Right Time*, reeled me right in from page one with her wonderfully drawn characters and clever plot twists, and kept me going all the way to a very satisfying ending."
–Diane Hawley Nagatomo, author of *The Butterfly Cafe* and *Finding Naomi*

"The nostalgia of this simpler era shines through in this retro, charming romance not to be missed."
–Anna Daughtery, author of *Outside Grace* and *Reaching for Grace*

"Lena Gibson has done it again. *The Right Time: Back to the 80s* is an engaging trip from the near future to a fondly-remembered past that will have you yearning for those days gone by."
–Bill Schweitzer, author of *Doves in a Tempest*

"There's a gentle power in this book—its slice-of-life moments are tender and real, and the way it ties together is nothing short of elegant. Lena Gibson has a gift for crafting beautifully written, deceptively clever stories."
–Michele Amitrani, author of the *Omnilogos Singularity* series

THE RIGHT TIME
BACK TO THE 80S
A TIME SLIP NOVEL

# CHAPTER 1
## ANDIE

"I just want them to know they didn't break me"
—Andie, Pretty in Pink (1986)

For her ninth birthday, Andie received a castle—not a fancy one with turrets and crenellations, but a fortress. It might not have looked like anything special to most people, but it contained a bed she didn't have to share with her younger sister, plus a built-in bookcase to fill with her favorite books. The room gave her the high ground in her house, and she imagined it would be the perfect place for dreams, tucked into the highest point of the vaulted ceiling.

What a fool her nine-year-old self had been.

Twenty-one years later, as Andie drove up to the curb outside her new rental and parked, she realized her expectations of that long-ago bedroom and this place had both been too high. A sinking sensation filled her stomach and rested like a stone-hard lump as she took stock. When would she learn to be realistic?

She couldn't take her eyes off her new accommodations. What a dump. Still, what could she expect for somewhere that hadn't requested references and had been available on fourteen hours' notice? Who knows how long it had stood vacant.

The compact house hadn't appeared so run-down in the pictures online—just cozy. Its faded mottled brown exterior, sagging front porch, and overgrown lawn were a stark contrast to the pristine white house next door. The neighbor's residence had a wrap-around porch and a well-maintained lawn, which looked professionally cared for—every blade of emerald grass even. A round turret rose from the rear, giving it more of a castle look, which must be what triggered her memory. Tulips and daffodils blossomed in orderly rows. Unlike her new yard, which just sprouted scraggly weeds—not even dandelions, which would at least be cheerful.

Still, anywhere was better than staying at her old apartment in a fancy high-rise, where Dylan would soon return. She just needed to adjust her attitude and view things as they were instead of turning everything into a story.

The Seattle area was expensive, so this place was all Andie could afford to rent at short notice on a public-school teacher's salary. With a deep breath, she spoke to herself. "Come on, living alone and starting over isn't so awful. You did it before. You can do it again." She glanced at the indented band on her left hand, where, until an hour ago, her wedding ring used to live. Her barren finger seemed naked, but she couldn't stay married to Dylan after the last beating.

His anger had always been terrible. The first time he'd hit her, he'd apologized, but last night, he'd pummeled her again. She wished she'd left after the first time, and she wasn't staying for a third occurrence. Her whole life, she'd promised herself she wouldn't put up with physical violence—not from anyone. No matter the circumstances. Yet, here she was, doing damage control. Her mind had replayed the latest incident a thousand times since it had happened yesterday. She'd forgiven him once, but never again.

If she hadn't moved out, she wouldn't have respected herself. Tears welled up at the memory, but she blinked them away. Dylan wasn't worth it.

Two fingers returned to her tender cheekbone with the livid eggplant bruise.

That's where the first blow had landed.

Andie bit her lip and stopped. If she wasn't careful, she'd give herself cold sores, a side effect of stress and chapped lips—a deadly combo. The tight sensation in her chest persisted. This morning, she hadn't spoken to Dylan, who'd returned after she'd gone to sleep. She hadn't told him she was moving out. Instead, she'd gotten up, pretending to get ready for work, and waited for him to leave before packing.

She glanced at her phone. In eight hours, he would arrive home. When he didn't find her there, he would call, demanding to know where she was. They had another political event on the schedule tomorrow, and he'd have to go solo—which would irk him. Like the first time he'd hit her, Dylan would be contrite today and buy flowers. He would expect forgiveness. She took a deep breath and held it for several seconds before exhaling. Such a move wouldn't sway her, and she didn't intend to divulge her new address. Let him fume; she was across town and safe.

She swallowed. What if he showed up at her school? She couldn't leave her job; she owed it to her students to stay. Plus, she'd never get a reference for another teaching job if she abandoned this one. Andie couldn't dwell on her fear right now. She had more immediate concerns.

Lifting her chin, she opened the car door and stepped out into the brisk morning air. This rental would have to suffice, at least for a while. When Dylan had stormed out of the condo for his usual session at the gym last night, she'd arranged new accommodation and logged her absence online to request a substitute for today. She planned to get settled in her new place while he was busy at work.

Andie examined both sides of the quiet street. Most of the houses were like the white house, large, clean, and well-kept. Her eyesore of a rental stood out—sending her mind back to places she'd lived growing up. Why had the neighbors allowed it to remain in this condition? She'd make a stab at improving the exterior and the garden because it seemed to be a decent neighborhood, and she didn't want to live in a place that screamed poor or neglected. Her family had done enough of that in her childhood. She thrust those thoughts from her head and got moving.

Slinging her backpack over her shoulder, she popped the trunk and grabbed her suitcases before heading up the cracked and pitted walkway to the rundown house. The top two boards of the stairs rocked, but she could fix them. While she strode toward the door, she continued her list of what she'd need to buy—a few basic tools, like a hammer and a screwdriver. The weathered planks of the porch seemed sturdy enough. Her acquaintances from work seemed to think it unusual she took care of odd jobs on her own, but she always had.

Andie unlocked the front door with the key she'd just picked up from her new landlord down the street. She wrinkled her nose at the first step inside and restrained her gag reflex. Perhaps rotten garbage had been left behind or a rodent had died. But she could handle something like that. No wonder the landlord was willing to take anyone. Steeling herself, she continued exploring, stopping in the kitchen to scrape open the window over the sink, letting in a blast of fresh air. She added cleaning supplies to her mental shopping list.

Andie glanced around the cramped living room and dirty, sun-faded kitchen, her chest tightening as her anxiety over all the changes that day spiraled. The description online said "furnished," but was a generous claim. The faded, brownish-red couch cushions had worn thin and displayed a suspicious gloss, while the sagging upholstery also sported half a dozen cigarette-sized burn holes. She'd have to cover the whole thing with something pretty. Maybe a crocheted afghan. Only two chairs sat at the stained, uneven kitchen table—one leg of which was an old broom handle.

She'd left behind an upscale apartment and new furniture, but everything there belonged to Dylan. Honestly, she didn't mind leaving it all behind. Andie had grown up with nothing, and she could make do for a while—the familiarity of her history adding to the feeling of safety and of returning to herself. It wouldn't be the first time she'd started over. Or the second.

Biting her lip again, Andie headed into the bedroom, not expecting much. To her surprise, she found a bookcase, a bedside table, and a matching bed courtesy of IKEA. They looked solid. The bookcase had room for her favorite books. The tightness in her chest relented somewhat. At least this space she could make her own. She'd likely be hanging out in here most of the time.

She poked her head into the bathroom to find a bland, cramped bathroom with a shower-tub combo featuring black spots on the caulking and grout, while a faint scent of mildew pervaded the air. A massive spider web strung across the far corner, its inhabitant dangling from the middle, lurking. She'd deal with it later. The ceiling sported several vintages of brown water stains. Perhaps she'd ask her landlord about painting. She didn't think he'd mind, if she completed the work herself.

Andie closed her eyes and took a deep breath. If she lived here for a while, she could save money for an upgrade next year. She was still searching for a forever home. Maybe she could beat her record and live here longer than three years.

She yawned as her energy waned. The argument last evening had thrown her for a loop and left her awake long into the early hours. Four hours of sleep would need to suffice, because she had a lot left to accomplish today. With a little elbow grease, she could transform her rental into a new and improved castle. One where she'd feel protected.

# CHAPTER 2
# ANDIE

"We're all pretty bizarre. Some of us are just better at hiding it."
–Andrew, The Breakfast Club (1985)

Hours later, Andie glanced up from her cleaning, using the back of her rubber-gloved hand to swipe the wisps of hair from her sweaty forehead. Instead of rot and mildew, the scent of lemon-fresh cleaner filled the kitchen. She'd been scrubbing and disinfecting for several hours, and she needed a break.

Now that she was paying attention, her body ached, and not just from her cleaning efforts. She checked her phone again. Two more hours until she expected Dylan's call. After another trip to their apartment to fill her car with plants, her old dishes, her original bedding and linens from storage, and some groceries she'd bought last weekend, she had enough for a fresh start.

Peeling off her yellow work gloves, she draped them over the edge of the now spotless stainless-steel sink where she stood. She prodded the sore patch on her cheek, the tender bruise reminding her why she was moving. She shuddered. Dylan would be furious to find her missing and no dinner prepared. When he called, he would yell. While she was dreading the call and feared talking to him, she wanted the satisfaction of saying their relationship was over.

After one conversation, he could deal with her lawyer.

For the tenth time during the last twenty-four hours, she wished she hadn't moved across the country for a man she barely knew and a shot at stability. She'd married him and had to deal with the consequences. Still, the Seattle area had its charm, and with no family, she had no reason to return to the East Coast.

At least she had a decent job.

Andie huffed out a breath and stretched with a wince, surveying her handiwork as she rotated her hips and shoulders. Every surface gleamed, and the grimy kitchen floor had proved to be an attractive off-white linoleum—older and worn but still serviceable. She'd worked hard today. Perhaps she should get outside and go for a walk to loosen her tight muscles.

She peeked out the kitchen window with its repurposed yellow curtains. Inside now had a cheerful look, contrasting with the gray sky outside—layers of billowing clouds, often the case in the Pacific Northwest in spring. Still, it wasn't raining right now. Exercise and fresh air would do her good. Plus, she'd better be able to determine if she'd eradicated the stench in her house if she left and came back.

She grabbed her lilac-colored, waterproof jacket and stepped out. At the sidewalk, she turned left, past the gorgeous white house, and strode down the walkway, excited to explore the neighborhood. While lots of the homes were beautiful, the castle-feel of the house next door made it her favorite.

Andie walked for an hour before turning back toward her new place, a spring in her step after discovering trails in a nearby park where she could run another day. The rain had held off, but dark clouds were rolling in, so she picked up her pace. Her hood blew off twice as the wind gusted while the trees along the boulevard swayed in the strong breeze.

Just before she turned up the path to her rental, an unexpected voice interrupted her return.

"Hello. You must be Jake and Susan's new tenant."

Andie spun. She'd been lost in her own world and missed the slim older woman standing near the blushing pink, dark purple, and sunny yellow tulips of the house next door to hers. She had dark brown eyes which flashed with interest and a cheerful smile. Two thick braids, one over each shoulder, adorned her long gray hair. She reminded Andie of an elderly Anne of Green Gables—from her favorite childhood story.

Andie's tense feeling leached away, and her shoulders dropped. Not Dylan.

"I was curious when I saw your hatchback out front this morning," the woman said. "There hasn't been anyone living in that place for three or four months." That explained the musty, rotten smell. The woman stepped forward. "My name's Andie."

On the sidewalk, Andie did a double take, her eyebrows shooting upward. "Nice to meet you." She tried to match the other woman's smile and manner. "Surprisingly, my name is also Andie. My mother was enamored with an 80s movie star named Molly Ringwald who played a girl named Andie who loved pink in the movie *Pretty In Pink*. I think my mom hoped I'd love pink too. It was her favorite color." Andie clamped her lips shut. Her deceased mother had been on her mind a lot today. Why had she volunteered so much unnecessary information to a stranger? It just proved she was off her game—usually, she was more careful.

There was something familiar about the other woman which set her at ease, but over-sharing was a common error Andie used to make when she'd been younger. She'd learned better. Most people weren't interested in the truth when they asked questions. They wanted polite, generic answers, like, "fine," "okay," or, "I'm great. How are you?" They all meant nothing.

"Two Andies. What a coincidence," said the older woman with another friendly smile, not seeming to notice Andie's mistake. "I've never met another woman Andie. Most are boys or men. My husband always makes up different names for me, saying Andie must be a nickname. Right now, he calls me Andromeda."

"It will be odd to hear my own name, even inside my head," the younger Andie said. She bit her lip. "Would it be strange for me to call you by a reverse nickname, too?" Was her request weird? She held her breath, waiting.

Her new neighbor smiled. "I'd love it. Why don't you call me Andrea? I've always liked that one." She half-turned toward her house. "Say, it's about teatime. Could I interest you in a cup?" When Andie hesitated, the older woman tilted her head. "I'd love the company."

Though a classic introvert, Andie wanted a fresh start with new expectations. It wouldn't hurt to get to know her new neighbor. The woman seemed harmless. Plus, if Dylan called, being with someone was an acceptable reason to let it go to voicemail. Anything to delay the inevitable argument.

"That would be nice, thanks." Andie would stay long enough that perhaps Dylan would calm down enough to have an actual conversation. Her chest tightened. What would he say after he found her note and wedding ring on the kitchen table?

On cue, her phone vibrated in her pocket, and her throat constricted. She snuck a peek. His name lit up her screen. Her lungs squeezed all the air outward, leaving her short of breath. She should have guessed he'd leave the office early today, with flowers to buy. He might have to pick up his tuxedo too with the fancy dinner they were supposed to attend tomorrow.

With a clenched jaw, she jammed her phone deep into her jacket pocket and strode along the sidewalk until she came to a gate in the white picket fence.

Andrea opened it and led the way toward the lovely house next door. Andie's phone buzzed again. A glance showed a barrage of texts from Dylan. She opened the first, and it knocked the wind out of her. She stumbled.

*"Andie. What are you doing across town in Redmond?"* She could have kicked herself. So forgetful not to have turned off location sharing. With shaking hands, she deactivated the app from her phone, hoping it wasn't too late. Maybe he wouldn't realize this was where she was staying. She shoved her phone into her pocket as her neighbor entered the white house.

Bright hues decorated the interior; a rainbow of colored glass was set near the windows, and jewel tones on accent walls added personality to the open-concept main-level rooms. Tall windows looked out over the stunning gardens. This place, especially with the turret at the back, was like a traditional castle, though more modest.

"Come, have a seat. We can sit in here." Andrea put a kettle on the stove and bustled around the kitchen preparing loose-leaf tea in a china teapot covered in delicate pink and bright yellow flowers. She removed two different floral teacups and saucers from a cupboard and set them on the counter. One was covered in lilacs and violets with tiny yellow flowers, while the second had blue forget-me-nots. "I love an excuse to use my wedding china." She shot another smile at Andie, who perched on her chair at the small round table, her hands in her lap. "Most people choose dishes of all one pattern. I chose eight different pairs of beautiful cups. If I have company, I mix and match."

Andie was about to comment on the teacups when several packages, each with five $100 Visa gift cards, caught her eye. Together, they must be worth several thousand dollars. Why would her neighbor need so many? She tried to get a more accurate count.

Noticing her interest, Andrea said, "I know that looks like a lot of gift cards. I got a voicemail yesterday from an old friend's daughter, asking for help. She was specific about what she needed. It's just a loan for a month until she sells her house and gets some cash."

Andie frowned and bit her lip. At first glance, the cards appeared to be worth close to five thousand dollars. She'd heard of AI scams of this type, but was unsure if she should interfere. Though they weren't friends, her new neighbor seemed like a nice person. "Um. Did you speak to your friend after you got the message? To confirm it was from her?"

The kettle whistled as steam billowed out of the spout. Andrea poured the water into her teapot on the counter. When she returned her attention to Andie, she wore a frown.

"I can't stand the idea of a young woman dealing with hardships alone. I couldn't reach Emma to ask more about the gift cards. I tried, but the phone number I had was out of service. It was an old landline number, from before cell phones became the thing. I have no idea where she lives or how to reach her. I was surprised to get the message from her daughter. It arrived out of the blue, but I didn't want to chance it wasn't real."

Andie rubbed her empty ring finger. "I hate to tell you this, but it sounds like a scam. I've heard of this happening. People, especially caring people, are taken advantage of. Because it's a lot of money, I wouldn't send the gift cards until you can verify the person who asked is who they say. Scams use AI all the time now." She looked down, afraid she'd overstepped. After all, they'd only just met. Heat flooded her cheeks. What would the older woman think?

"I appreciate your candor. You're right. I'll follow up tonight. Thank you." She pivoted toward the counter. "How do you take your tea?" Andrea rummaged in a drawer, coming up with a teaspoon.

Andie hesitated. "Sweet, please. Stevia if you have it. Sugar if you don't."

Andrea nodded and returned with a green container of Stevia, the same brand Andie bought. "I hope you don't think I'm foolish for not doing more to check about the gift cards. The voicemail sounded so real. Even the way she signed off sounded like something Emma would say. It hadn't occurred to me it might be a scam." A deep crease remained between her brows, and the lines across her forehead looked more etched than they had outside. Maybe Andrea was older than Andie had guessed. She'd lived a full life.

"Hopefully, it's nothing. That kind of scam can seem so real." Andie hoped she'd said enough.

Andrea carried the teacups and teapot to the table and poured two steaming cups. The scent of orange spice filled the air. The purple floral cup clinked on the saucer as Andrea pushed them across the table.

"I love your china. It's beautiful," Andie said, taking a cautious sip of the steaming liquid after adding Stevia. "My grandmother used to have assorted cups like this, too. The variety reminds me of her." A wave of nostalgia hit. Her grandmother had been gone for many years.

Andrea smiled. "It reminds me of my grandmother, too. When I was first married, I used to only take them out for special occasions. One day, I realized they spent most of the time in the cabinet. I'd hardly ever used them—which was a shame. I chose them because they were beautiful, so I changed my policy. No more saving things for someday or for special occasions. I use the good china, the new candles, and the special soap." She laughed. "Sometimes I dress up fancy for dinner, even when it's just myself and my husband."

Andie looked around. "Is your husband here too? Does he want tea?"

Andrea checked her silver wristwatch, a motion which caught Andie's attention, as did the device—an old-style one with Roman numerals. So few people still wore watches, unless they were linked to their phones or were for tracking exercise. "He's in his eighties and is having an afternoon lie down in his office. It's filled with audio equipment. He calls it his 'listening time.'" She laughed. "He'll have tea when he wakes up in an hour or so. We've been married almost fifty years, and I still like teasing him about his naps." She smiled fondly.

The watch was a reminder that Andrea was part of a different generation. Andie couldn't imagine what would it be like to be married to the same person for so long. Today was Friday, and during her free hours this weekend, she would check into how long it would take to get a divorce.

"So, tell me about you," said Andrea as she sipped her tea. Her dark eyes seemed interested in more than polite answers.

"I teach fifth grade," said Andie. "In my spare time I write."

"Anything I might have read?" said Andrea, peering over her cup.

Andie shook her head. "I haven't published my writing yet, but maybe someday." She wasn't sure what else to say about her writing. She'd never shown it to anyone. Writing something worth publishing was a distant dream.

Her pocket buzzed again, this time continuing for several rounds before it finally stopped. Dylan was relentless. This time, she chose not to look and ruin her calm mood. She would pretend he didn't exist. She sipped her tea, letting the scalding liquid warm her as she and her new neighbor talked. Not once did the older woman inquire about the bruise on Andie's cheek, but her neighbor's eyes strayed to it more than once as they chatted.

Andie didn't stay long because she didn't want to overstay her welcome. Plus, putting off the conversation with Dylan too long would make it more difficult, and she might lose her courage. When her cup was empty, she stood. "Thank you for the tea. It was lovely to meet you, but I should get home. We both probably need to make dinner."

Andrea stood and followed her to the front door. "I hope you'll come by again soon. I appreciate your advice about those gift cards. I had my doubts, but I'll try harder to find out if the request was a scam." She hesitated, her gaze flicking to the buzzing phone in Andie's pocket. "It looks like you've made a tough decision. I have a long-time friend who is a counselor. If you'd like to speak to someone who specializes in listening, let me know."

"Thank you." Andie's cheeks burned again as she left. It was true she might need someone to talk to. She didn't have many options in her life. Her mother had passed away two years ago, she didn't know how to locate her sister, and she'd never known her father. Andie had few friends, and the majority were across the country. Here in Seattle, she wasn't just on her own—she was alone.

# Chapter 3
# Andie

"I just want to be happy. Is that so much to ask?"
–Mystic Pizza (1988)

Andie splashed back to her house next door, the rain descending in a pale torrent that bounced off the street and the sidewalk, soaking her shoes, socks, and pants. In less than a minute, she was drenched to the skin.

Once back in her place, she changed into dry clothes and headed into the kitchen to cook. She hadn't taken more than a dozen steps when her phone vibrated again. Dylan wouldn't stop calling until she spoke to him. She couldn't put this discussion off any longer. She didn't owe him anything, but for herself, she wanted to do more than leave a note and run. Andie hoped talking to him would give her closure.

"Dylan," she said, trying to maintain her composure despite her heart pounding like a jackhammer.

"Andie. Where the hell are you?" He wasn't yelling yet, but the irritation in his voice made her stomach churn and her hands clammy.

Good. He might not know her location. "Did you read my note?" Her voice quavered. Shit.

"I hoped you'd come to your senses since you wrote that rubbish. You're my wife. We can work this out. Come home."

She closed her eyes. "I don't live there anymore. I've moved out." She was proud of her even tone this time.

"I mean it, Andie. Get your ass home and discuss this like an adult." His voice had become a growl.

She remained silent, her jaw clenched so hard her teeth ached. If she spoke, she would cry, and she didn't want to give him the satisfaction. He'd be all over it like a shark with blood in the water. She had to stay strong.

"I bought you roses. Red ones cost a fortune. Come home so we can talk." His voice dropped. "I'm sorry about what happened last night. It wasn't all my fault, but I promise it'll never happen again. Please, baby. Come home." Met with silence, he switched to wheedling. "Pretty please."

"That's what you said the last time you hit me." The words slipped out, and she winced. Her head replayed his lousy apology. How was hitting her not his fault? She'd done nothing wrong. How dare he try to offload the blame? Typical.

"I. Said. It. Won't. Happen. Again. Be reasonable. Come home." He bit off each word, his volume rising.

His face would have become a familiar mottled red.

Anger gave her strength, though her vision blurred. "No. I've moved out. My lawyer will contact you in the next week or two about an official separation agreement until we can get a divorce." She'd said the words. Her fist shot upward in victory. She could stand up to his bullying. Take that Dylan.

"Your lawyer? Get a fucking grip." His last words blasted through her phone, the sound skewering her brain. There was the yell. "I'm not signing anything. You're my goddamn wife."

"Please don't contact me again," she said. "If you come to my work or fight this, I'll call the police. I've taken pictures and documented the bruises." She hadn't, but that was the next step. She should have done it already. For a second, she panicked about logistics. Andie didn't have a decent mirror to get pictures of her back. She inhaled. She would ask Andrea to help as soon as she got off the phone.

"Andie. Stop this, baby. Why are you doing this to us? You're breaking my heart."

She hung up before he said anything else. Not wasting more time, she blocked his number so he couldn't call back. She rotated her neck, trying to loosen tense muscles. Then she got on social media and blocked him everywhere, so it would be like she'd disappeared. To be safe, she also unfriended and blocked his snobby family. She'd gotten proficient at the vanishing routine. Best to keep this a clean break.

Next, she set up her laptop on the table. She didn't have Wi-Fi yet, though she had an appointment with the installer tomorrow. She changed the settings on her phone to make it a hotspot.

With trembling hands, she googled, "affordable divorce lawyers in Seattle." She scrolled through the top ten names, clicking links for each. After reading the descriptions, she chose three women. After continued research, including finding a picture, she chose one who looked to be a few years older than herself who looked smart, kind, and professional. Scanning the reviews, they were positive.

Andie wrote an email.

*Dear Ms. Clark,*

*I've left my abusive husband and am seeking representation for a divorce and an immediate separation agreement. I'm not claiming anything except what I came into the relationship with less than a year ago. I'm also hoping to file a restraining order to keep him away from me at work and home.*

*If you are available to take my case, please call my cell after three p.m. on weekdays or email any time.*

*Sincerely,*

*Andie Marks*

She read it over and added her contact information before she hit, *Send.* Soon, she could use Sterling again, her maiden name. Dylan Marks and his name would be erased from her life forever.

There was one more thing she needed. Proof of his physical abuse. Proof which, if leaked, would ruin his political career. She'd make him think twice about chasing after her.

Andie donned her rain jacket and boots, collected her phone, and ventured into the rain to ask for Andrea's help. While she could take decent pictures, the ones on her back would be tricky. Plus, she didn't want to see them more than necessary. She bit her lip as she knocked on the sky-blue door of the white house. A tall man with silver-gray hair answered wearing sweatpants and a black and teal Seattle Kraken T-shirt. This must be Andrea's husband. For a second, neither of them spoke.

"You must be the new Andie," he said, a spark of curiosity in his eyes.

She said, "You must be Andrea's husband." She hadn't caught his name.

The handsome older man grinned, causing crinkly lines to appear around his blue eyes. "I called her Andrea for a long time. It's a good name." His kind face looked like one she could trust. "We've been married forty-seven years this fall and counting. Why don't you come inside, and I'll get her."

Andie nodded and stepped into the house, now filled with the delectable aroma of melted cheese and tomato sauce. "I'm sorry if I'm interrupting your dinner. I didn't think." If her mission hadn't been important, she would have left.

He waved away her words. "You didn't interrupt. My Andromeda popped a frozen pepperoni pizza in the oven and is making a salad. She won't mind if I finish chopping while you ladies talk. No worries at all." He winked as he left her standing in the front hall.

So Andie didn't drip water all over their clean tile floor, she toed off her polka-dot rain boots, standing them upright by the door. She fought her tears. She didn't want to make a big deal of taking photos, but she felt vulnerable tonight and didn't have anyone else to ask.

Andrea emerged from the kitchen almost immediately, wiping her hands on a blue and white checked tea towel. "I'm glad you came back," she said. "I put two pizzas in the oven, hoping you might. You'll stay for dinner, won't you?"

Andie couldn't believe the other woman's generous offer. "That's very kind. I actually came back for a different reason. I was hoping for some assistance." She kept her chin up and her voice even as she spoke. "As you might have guessed, I left my husband this morning because he hit me." She took a deep breath. "I'm afraid he'll contest the divorce unless I have proof of his wrongdoing." Her words sped up. "Could you please take a few pictures to document my bruises? I have some on my back and ribs, where they're awkward to photograph."

Andrea nodded. "Come with me."

Andie was grateful there'd been no questions or sympathetic noises. Just business. Empathy might bring her to tears, and she didn't want to fall apart, especially in front of a new acquaintance.

The other woman led her down the bright hall into what appeared to be a guest bedroom, where she closed the door behind them. She stretched out her hand for Andie's phone. "If it keeps him away from you, I'm happy to help. Good for you. Leaving him is brave."

Andie shivered as she turned, lifting her shirt to expose the bruises hidden by her shirt. After the backhand to her face, Dylan had punched her in the ribs several times. He'd done more than hit her. He'd administered an actual beating. When she'd crumpled to the floor in tears, he'd kicked her twice, marking her back. Those bruises were deep and hurt like hell. None of the violence had been accidental. It had started because she'd repeated something one of her male colleagues had mentioned at work about the local hockey team. He didn't enjoy hearing about other men she interacted with, even colleagues.

She took a deep breath. Dylan was just a jealous creep with anger issues. She deserved better.

Andrea took several pictures before handing back Andie's phone. "I wanted to thank you for telling me to look into the gift card situation," she said once Andie had lowered her shirt. "I called another old friend and mentioned the message with the emergency request. She put me in contact with Emma. Turns out, Emma's daughter lives in Japan and is happily married. She didn't contact me for help. Emma mentioned three other people contacted her about con artist voicemail messages pretending to be her daughter."

"I'm glad I could help." Andie tugged her sweater down and smoothed it with a deep breath. "I have an update too. I did a little research and emailed a lawyer this evening. I also found out it'll take a minimum of four months to get a divorce. One for the separation agreement and an additional ninety days as a cooling-off period." A few tears escaped, streaming down her burning cheeks. She pressed the back of her icy hand against them, trying to dispel the heat. "I wish it could be over now, so I didn't need to see him or talk to him again." Something about Andrea invited confidences Andie wouldn't usually share.

Andrea took one step forward but didn't touch Andie. "I was in a similar situation once when I was younger. I'm going to give you my friend's number, even if you didn't ask. She's a terrific therapist, even if a smidge unconventional," she said as they left the guest room. "And I insist you stay for a few slices of pizza. If you were emailing a lawyer and doing research, you didn't cook. You must be starved. Moving is grueling work, and you've had a lengthy day."

Andie's stomach rumbled. "If it isn't too much trouble, I'd love to stay. Thank you." She followed Andrea into the kitchen, where Andrea had sliced both pizzas into six pieces and had left an array of salad dressings on the counter beside a gorgeous, polished wood salad bowl.

Andrea's husband dished up several pieces of pizza and a small bowl of salad, and with another wink, he disappeared into the living room, where a hockey game was playing on the flat screen.

"I hope I didn't drive him away," said Andie.

Andrea laughed. "You saved me from watching another hockey game. This is a win-win." She handed Andie a plate.

While neither of them spoke much, Andie enjoyed the warm, peaceful space with the sound of the game's commentary in the background. At the end of their meal, Andrea grabbed a notepad and scrolled through the contacts on her phone. She wrote a name and number, then slid the paper across the table.

*Dr. Maeve Fossey, (206)-555-2595*

Andie bit her lip as she took the number. Would she call the therapist? Maybe. At least having another resource was comforting. "Thanks for dinner and the help," she said, lifting her phone. While she hoped Dylan wouldn't put up a fight, she had the photos in case she needed to prove Dylan Marks wasn't a decent human.

Andrea waved it off. "It's what I'd do for anyone. Especially if they're on their own. I have a feeling things will be successful for you." She smiled and escorted Andie to the door. "Come back anytime."

Andie left, giving a wave from the gate as she fastened it behind her with a click. The rain had stopped, and she glanced up at the dark sky. Clouds obscured the moon—they were in for more rain overnight. Her neighbor remained on the porch until Andie unlocked her front door and entered her new house. She hadn't finished dealing with Dylan, but for the first time all day, the overwhelming pressure eased.

# CHAPTER 4
## ANDIE

"I'll be back."
–Terminator (1984)

Andie awoke twice that night, a strangled scream escaping each time. Vague flashes of Dylan's face lingered as she lay in the strange dark room, gasping while his dream words lingered, *"You're nothing and nobody cares about you."* The anger in his face sent chills through her, and she made a decision. She wouldn't continue like this, frightened of her nightmares. She would call Dr. Fossey on Monday to set up an appointment. Andie hated talking about her past, but she suspected getting to the bottom of her feelings now would show them rooted in her childhood.

That's when things had first gone awry, and she'd first felt alone.

She spent the weekend unpacking her few belongings from the half dozen boxes she'd brought. When she examined the house, she no longer saw a stinky, run-down rental, but a place where she could get her life back in order, a life free of Dylan. With her personal space in order, she attacked the never-ending mountain of schoolwork that needed marking. Plus, the new, complicated report card program took a level of tech savvy, which made her want to scream. All the menus had moved, and squinting at the size eight font made her eyes ache.

Monday morning, Andie drove to work as usual, fighting grid lock traffic. Though her school was twenty minutes away, the drive took over an hour and left her a soggy wreck, as she was always only one accident away from arriving late. Once inside the building, she found the ordinary and predictable routine of school soothing to her overwrought nerves and battered pride from her failed marriage.

While she excelled at pretending to be fine from living a double life as long as she could remember, a tightness remained in her sternum and her jaw. Though she'd warned Dylan not to come to her work, she expected him to ignore her wishes. It was just a matter of time. Nobody at work would understand. To her co-workers, Dylan Marks was a catch, someone to be admired for his handsome face, his charm, and his political clout.

She got through Monday on adrenaline. At lunch, she called Dr. Fossey's office and made an appointment for the following Monday after work. She also booked an appointment with her new lawyer for after school next Tuesday—the first available time. With the appointments booked, the rest of the day became a little easier and by Thursday, Andie took breaths without feeling like a car had parked on her chest. Plus, after school, she had plans she was looking forward to.

Though Andie often stayed after school for several hours, at a quarter to four, she drove to the Starbucks down the street. Once there, she ordered a chai tea latte and squished two tables together to make room for eight. She inhaled the distinctive coffee aroma and let the peaceful feeling of being there wash over her. She'd set this up a month ago, and she'd been looking forward to this gathering all week—anything to take her mind off the stress of waiting for Dylan to make a move.

Andie stared out the window toward the busy parking lot. It was so easy while teaching to only interact with children because she spent most of her time at work teaching and preparing lessons in her classroom. This would be an excellent chance to interact with adults. Though she'd been at the current school since September, there were several teachers she'd never spoken to, other than in passing. She'd overhead talk of a book club, but it didn't seem like it was open for new members. Still, she wanted to connect with her colleagues and after school tea might be the ticket.

Two teachers had replied saying they couldn't make the gathering, and a few others had said they would try. Four said they'd be here at four p.m. The rest hadn't answered, but she hoped more might join since everyone always had a Starbucks cup in hand. Who couldn't use an extra hit of caffeine before fighting traffic on the way home?

Not daring to take more space, as Andie felt conspicuous enough already, she scoped out extra chairs they might steal if their group became too crowded. Some of the "maybes" might join them, and she wanted there to be enough seats.

She sipped her chai tea, letting the hot sweet liquid and caffeine chase away some of her stress. Perhaps the other intermediate teachers would come. They were the ones she interacted with the most. Without being too obvious, she positioned herself where she could watch the door, so she'd be able to make eye contact with her colleagues as they arrived.

She glanced around the busy coffee shop. Another group had staked a claim to a long table. Two small round tables were occupied by lone occupants on their laptops, while couples and groups of three filled the bar seating and other tables. The line at the counter was only two deep. Starbucks was always a popular place for meet ups.

A large group of teachers had met at the pub for happy hour at the same time last month—a loud and boisterous outing from which Andie had escaped early, too overwhelmed to speak to anyone. Small talk and chit-chat were nightmares, but with coworkers, at least they had common ground with which to break the ice. Perhaps tonight, she would make a friend or two. She needed one at work. In her second term evaluation, the principal had commented that Andie was anti-social and needed to make a greater effort to jell with the rest of the staff. Which brought her to this, planning a gathering for her peers.

At the counter, the barista called names and drink orders while time passed. Refusing to check the time on her phone again, Andie's throat tightened. The other teachers were late. A sinking sensation spread from her shoulder blades as her table remained empty instead of filling with potential friends.

At her old job, she'd had a friend to rant to when the pressure became too much. They'd helped each other muddle through the technological worries and expectations of learning new software. Andie hadn't grown up with iPads and technology like most of her peers; she'd been too poor to afford a phone until after she'd left home at eighteen. Then, she hadn't needed one through the first years of university because she'd had no one to call. Eventually, she'd gotten one for email, research, and documenting writing ideas.

Time ticked on. At four twenty-five, she was still alone. With speculative eyes surrounding her, she slipped her Kindle from her purse and tried to read. With each successive entrance into the coffee shop, she glanced up, heart racing, but each time the newcomer was a stranger. Her chest grew tighter. When she could no longer take the suspense, she slid her phone out and checked her messages. Her heart sank. Two of the confirmed attendees had sent texts.

*"Can't come. We have a cat emergency at home."*

Another read, *"Caught up at work. Can't make it. Another time perhaps."*

Andie's stomach churned as she finished her lukewarm tea. How long was too long to wait for the others? She checked her messages again. Nothing.

At five, the table remained empty.

"Can I slide this table over?" Someone stood over her, holding a cup in each hand. His hand rested on the second table she'd shoved against hers. "You aren't using it, are you?" His words jarred Andie back to the moment.

She blinked. "Of course." Her face flamed and her mouth became parched. "I was expecting some co-workers." As soon as the words left her mouth, they tasted like a lie. Had she expected anyone to show? She'd wanted them to come, but deep down, she'd known it could go this way. They didn't know her. Why would they bother?

The young man motioned to a woman behind him, who held their cups while he scraped the table a foot and a half to the right. The couple sat next to her, holding hands across the table, oblivious to anything and anyone except each other. Andie's heart hurt to see them. Even before she and Dylan had trouble, they'd never been that kind of cute couple. She wanted someone to share her day with, someone to hold her hand and forget about the busy world.

Andie waited another agonizing half hour before she gave up. Tears pricked at her eyes, but she ignored them. She would wait to cry when she wasn't in public.

Nobody was coming.

It was the same old story. People didn't understand how much she craved friendship. She'd tried social media, but the barrage of negativity had made her deactivate the apps on her phone. From time to time, she checked in from her computer, but it seemed pointless. She hadn't made friends online. It was difficult enough in person.

With co-workers, she often didn't know what to say, but she was here. Her awkward conversation skills didn't mean she wasn't interested in their lives, just that she was at a loss for what to ask when trying not to babble. The aching loneliness had grown up with her, continuing at university when she'd struck out on her own. She'd found no one to connect with on a deeper level. She never seemed to fit in and had always been different.

The years after graduation had been lonely, so she'd moved across the country at the first sign of interest from Dylan. She'd married a stranger, but she didn't belong here either.

This non-gathering was a reminder of her biggest fear. Andie didn't belong anywhere.

The reminder of her bone-deep loneliness was the last straw. Though she'd tried to connect with others at work again, she'd failed. She swallowed and, blinking back her tears, she stood, tucked in her chair, and left. She wouldn't attempt to organize something social again. The hope of companionship wasn't worth the inevitable disappointment. Was she going to spend the rest of her life alone?

Fighting the constant busy traffic, Andie returned to her run-down rental, finished reading a romance novel over a microwave dinner, and started another book, reading until her eyes couldn't focus. Only then, did she close her Kindle and go to sleep.

On Friday morning, she parked in her regular parking stall and entered the building by eight a.m., using a side door so she didn't have to face anyone who'd stood her up last night. Classes didn't start until nine, but she enjoyed arriving early enough to play her music and run through the day before her students arrived. The time ticked by slower than usual.

Soon it would be the weekend, and she wouldn't have to fear an unwanted drop-in by Dylan. It hadn't happened yet, but she knew him. He would come through the school's main doors and pretend he was welcome. Waiting for it kept her on edge. Every male voice in the hall raised the hair on her arms and she didn't know how much longer she could live with fear hanging over her like a blade.

She focused on work. At eight-forty-five, she'd posted the schedule for the day, arranged the student seating, and checked her materials for class, when the intercom chimed in her classroom.

"Mrs. Marks, please come to the office. You have a visitor."

Andie's face grew warm and sweat trickled from her armpits. She wasn't expecting anyone else, so it was probably Dylan. What would happen if she ignored the summons? The hard lump in her stomach expanded, tamping down the urge to be sick.

He would make a scene and come back another time. She wished she had the restraining order. Next week, she'd have to inform the office staff when she obtained the document. She wasn't looking forward to explaining how her life had gone to hell. Still, in the future, the document should keep him away. As a politician, he was careful not to get in trouble with the law. Proof of wrongdoing on his part could make it difficult to get re-elected.

She turned off her music and hurried down the stairs. A minute stretched to an eternity as she approached the main office. Her steps grew shorter. Dylan's fake good-humored laughter reached her before she turned the corner. He must be schmoozing with the secretary. After all, his interactions were all about getting votes and maintaining popularity. She braced herself, taking three calming breaths before continuing. She rounded the final corner and came into view of the front door and main office.

"Andie, darling. I wanted to surprise you. I brought you flowers," said Dylan, rushing toward her, seemingly oblivious to her lack of enthusiasm about his presence. His charm was often calculated to throw her off balance. He could be disarming and magnetic when he wished. That's what had gotten him into office and her into this mess.

She held her ground and clenched her hands behind her back. "I'm sorry, Dylan. I can't accept those. You need to leave." She was proud her voice didn't waver.

"Baby, I don't know what's wrong with you," he said, shoving the massive bouquet of crimson roses in her face. She wrinkled her nose at the thick floral scent and leaned away. Roses might look lovely, but she didn't enjoy the cloying smell.

She took two steps backward. "You can't be here. I'm at work." Why couldn't he respect her place of business? "Class starts in less than five minutes." She turned and headed for the stairs, her heart pounding. She could feel his eyes drilling into her back, and it was difficult to walk normally and not stumble. Her mind flashed to another time Dylan hadn't respected her profession.

Two weeks after Dylan and Andie returned from their honeymoon in Mexico, they'd attended a political function. An attendee had asked Andie about her career.

"I'm a teacher." She'd always been proud of doing something that made a difference.

Dylan had taken over the conversation, smooth and polished. "Just until we have a family. One of these days soon. Then Andie will stay home with the children." He announced it like her job didn't matter and was just to kill time.

"I hadn't planned to be a stay-at-home mom," said Andie, her forehead growing tight. "In my spare time, I write."

"Until she met me," said Dylan, pulling her closer and kissing the top of her head. "Now she has more important things to concern herself with."

She'd been fuming but hadn't pushed back. At least today she'd spoken up. She continued down the corridor, trying to figure out what else she should have said. Today was the first day she hadn't caked on make-up to cover the bruise on her face. Now, she wished she hadn't all week, then perhaps her co-workers would understand why Dylan wasn't welcome. She sighed. She also hadn't wanted questions from her students which would be uncomfortable to answer.

"Andie, don't go." Dylan's heavy footsteps raced to catch up.

She walked faster, her throat closing. She needed to get away. He wasn't listening and her emotions were leaking through. He had to go.

She whirled around. "I'm at work. If you need to meet with me, please wait for my lawyer to contact you and we can set up something. You should receive a letter from her office any day." She paused for his reaction, keeping her distance.

"No lawyers. We're not getting a divorce." He looked in both directions. With no one in sight in the hall, he lunged, grabbing her by the arm. She tried to pull free but couldn't. Tears welled up in her eyes. He squeezed harder, to the point of pain.

She let out a small gasp, the noise covered by the beeping of the warning bell.

"I need to get back to class." Her voice had a shaky, breathless quality she despised. "We can't do this now."

He smiled a nasty smile and tossed the flowers to the floor. She stared at the blood-red blossoms scattered across the clean, polished floor. His firm hold on her arm remained, and he yanked her into the alcove outside the library. Where was everyone? Security must be outside waiting for the students to enter. Students would flood the hall in a matter of seconds. She needed to get loose.

"You're going to pay for what you've done. Nobody leaves me," Dylan hissed in her ear. His hot breath set her heart galloping, and she broke out in a cold sweat. She hoped he wouldn't hurt her where the children might see. She cowered, knees shaking, though she couldn't escape his iron grasp.

"You need to go." Her voice shook and her legs barely held her upright. She hadn't believed he would go as far as hurting her in public, but she had been fooled like the others. She had no idea what he was capable of. The deep bruises on her body still hurt, though the one on her face had faded to a hue like the leftover smudge from a dandelion. She almost sagged in relief when adult footsteps neared their position—probably the office staff.

Dylan dropped her arm, though the reddened imprint remained around her biceps. That was going to leave a lasting mark, too. The bell for students to come inside buzzed—the sound blaring three times. The exterior doors at the far end of the hall crashed open and several dozen primary students flooded the lower hall. Wave after wave of children entered, their voices filling the hall with cheerful sounds. Teachers stood at most of the open doorways to greet their students while older children headed up the stairs. Witnesses.

Dylan shifted out of the alcove and, in the middle of the hall, fell to his knees, his hands clasped together. "Please Andie, don't do this to me. I'll do anything to win you back. I swear you mean everything to me. How can you be so cruel as to abandon me and not even explain why? Have you met someone else?" He projected his voice so everyone could hear.

In the background, several of the teachers' heads swiveled in her direction.

Andie's cheeks blazed and tears filled her eyes. She glanced skyward to keep them in check.

Many of the incoming students faltered in the hall, wide-eyed, listening. She tried not to make eye contact with anyone. Several teachers tried corralling their students and directing them into classrooms, but they must have found the Dylan show difficult to step away from because they also stopped to stare.

Andie trembled, her muscles paralyzed and her feet frozen. Her mouth was parched, and her clothing drenched with sweat. This couldn't be happening. This scene was worse than she'd imagined. Everyone's eyes bored into her, and Dylan gave her a private smirk, probably acknowledging how such a public display would hurt. He'd done this to embarrass her; he must realize it would never work to change her mind.

"Andie, you're breaking my heart. I'll do anything to win your love. Just don't leave me." He broke down sobbing in the middle of the hall, bowing his head toward the floor.

Andie's cheeks flamed hotter, if that was possible. She turned away, glancing toward the office.

The principal strode toward them, her high heels clicking on the floor, and the students scattered. Mrs. Green raised one pencil-drawn eyebrow. "Mrs. Marks. Shouldn't you be upstairs in your classroom? The bell has gone." She flicked a haughty glance toward Dylan.

He stopped acting and stared at Andie, a faint smile playing about his lips again, his back to her boss. The bastard.

The principal's rebuke broke Andie's paralysis. She scooted for the stairs, hurrying toward her classroom and the cluster of ten-year-olds waiting for their teacher.

All morning, she kept her head down and concentrated on teaching her lessons and the morning routine. One big question remained, lurking at the back of her brain. What would be the fallout from this morning's encounter?

Just before lunch, Andie's phone buzzed. She glanced at the incoming text from the principal.

*"Please see me at lunch. Bring your personal items. We've found a substitute for your class. You'll be going home for the day."*

Andie bit her lip and straightened the top of her desk, writing a few quick notes on Monday's day plan. She reached the office at 12:15, carrying her purse, her heart racing. No one had ever summoned her before as if she were a student, leaving her embarrassed and feeling small and insignificant.

The secretary made a sympathetic face. "Mrs. Green will see you now." She pointed to the open door.

As soon as Andie entered the cluttered principal's office, her throat closed.

"Close the door and take a seat," said her boss, not looking up from a pastel notebook where she'd been writing. "I take it that was Mr. Marks," she said as she removed her reading glasses. "He looks different in person than on his campaign signs." She folded her glasses and placed them on the desk, making eye contact with Andie for the first time.

The lurking anger in the principal's eyes made Andie's sweat glands work overtime. She folded her icy hands in her lap and tried to keep from crying.

"The scene this morning, when you should have been working, was unacceptable. I'd like you to go home early today. Take next week off too. You need to get your... affairs together." When Andie opened her mouth to explain, the other woman's hand rose like a traffic cop. "I don't want to hear any excuses. We can't have that kind of drama here. It's bad for the students and for the school."

"Am I fired?" said Andie, tears leaking from her eyes though she struggled to keep them contained.

"No, but I need a counselor's report stating you are safe to have at school. In my opinion, you don't seem stable. Until I receive one, consider yourself on medical leave." Mrs. Green leaned back in her padded swivel chair. "I sympathize with your situation on a personal level, but I can't allow that sort of disturbance in the workplace. There are children here." Her watery blue eyes didn't look sorry. All her boss cared about was image, and a "lovesick," abusive husband in the hall was negative publicity.

Andie stood to leave.

But the principal wasn't finished. "Mrs. Marks, during your time off, I would also like you to evaluate if our school is the best fit and consider your options. We don't plan to renew your contract for next year. I've noticed you haven't joined committees, created clubs, and don't speak up at meetings. Unfortunately, you're not our kind of team player." Mrs. Green turned toward her computer. "That will be all."

Reeling from her boss's words, Andie went to her car and left the premises. Several blocks from school, she stopped at the side of the street. She banged the steering wheel with the heel of her hand and then covered her face. Without her job, she had nothing to fill her days, leaving her far too much time to ponder all the things she should have done differently. Even if she returned, her employment ended in a couple of months.

Once again, she was alone.

# CHAPTER 5
# ANDIE

"The only winning move is not to play. How about a nice game of chess?"
–WarGames (1983)

Once Andie composed herself, she headed to the grocery store. Her hands still shook as she drove and planned. She would stock up and stay home for the weekend. She had the meeting with Dr. Fossey on Monday and one with Sarah Clark, her lawyer, the following day. Perhaps she'd feel better with a couple of tubs of her favorite gourmet ice cream.

Fifteen minutes later, Andie stood in line at the checkout, self-conscious about shopping at midday instead of being at work. What if she ran into the parents of her students? She kept glancing over her shoulder and wasn't paying attention to the clerk scanning her groceries.

"Excuse me, miss." The clerk's voice brought her back to the present. "That'll be twenty-seven dollars and twelve cents. Cash, debit, or credit?"

Andie fumbled with her wallet and scanned her credit card. She should have shopped somewhere farther from the school and closer to home. Maybe then she wouldn't be so anxious about attracting attention. Most of the shoppers were seniors at this time of day. She just hoped she could get away before she was spotted by anyone who recognized her.

As if she had summoned someone with her thoughts, Mrs. Anderson, the president of the Parent Advisory Council, pushed her cart into the same line. The only times Andie had seen the woman, she'd been with the principal. They'd seemed like friends.

Andie faced the front. Shit. How long was this transaction going to take? The cashier held out her hand and gave an impatient shake. Perhaps Andie had scanned her card wrong, so she passed it to the cashier.

"Mrs. Marks. What a surprise," Mrs. Anderson said. Her booming voice seemed too loud. "Cutting out early on a Friday?" She eyed the trio of ice cream pints and Andie's outstretched hand.

Andie's cheeks flamed. "I have an appointment this afternoon." She did. With her ice cream and Netflix.

"Excuse me, do you have another card?" The cashier grimaced. She glanced around and lowered her voice. "When you scanned your card, I got a message to take this one and cut it up. It's been deactivated. I could be fired if I don't follow the rules."

"Pardon?" Andie said, her attention swinging from Mrs. Anderson back to the transaction at the till. "I must have given you the wrong card." She swallowed a lump that sank like a stone. Dylan must have canceled their credit card, and she hadn't used her separate one in ages.

With trembling hands, she searched her wallet, hoping she'd kept the old card with her maiden name. She fumbled with the hidden slots, pulling out a handful of plastic. There were so many damn cards for things she seldom used. Nope. She kept trying. This was taking an eternity. Her breathing seemed too fast as she tried a fourth or fifth pocket, at last producing another credit card.

The cashier motioned for her to scan this one. Andie did, this time watching the screen. Declined. Expired. Blood pounded in her ears and the room felt too hot. She looked back at Mrs. Anderson, witness to her embarrassment. The line behind her seemed enormous.

While Mrs. Anderson had pretended not to watch Andie's difficulties, the backward glance seemed to grant permission. Mrs. Anderson said, "Is something wrong?"

Andie worried the woman would think she'd wasted her money.

She shook her head and stepped away, no longer wanting the ice cream after all. She could live with the food already at home until she talked to the bank to clear up this misunderstanding. One positive thing about leaving school early—at least she had time to call during business hours. The banks should still be open for several hours after she got home. Hurrying to her car, she got in, slammed the door, and left, gripping the wheel tight enough her arms ached.

She wouldn't get anywhere in this state, so she stopped at a park and went for a long walk, allowing the fresh air and light exercise to calm her overwhelmed brain. She couldn't remember the last time she'd had time to relax, to wander and let the stress from her hectic life drain. This time, she'd been so close to melting down in public. Just after two-thirty, she drove home, stopping for a tea at a drive-thru Starbucks where they scanned the stored card value on her phone.

Once home, Andie ran inside and opened her laptop, searching for a number to call her bank. There were several email options, but it took some digging to find a customer service number. At last, she located a toll-free one. It rang forever before the call went through. With the first words on the other end, her elation crashed—only a recording.

She looped through the menu options, listening twice. None of the choices seemed to be what she needed. She pressed zero, hoping it would take her to a person. Instead, the line clicked, hanging up. Gritting her teeth, she tried again. This time, she chose a different option. She glanced at the clock. It was already after four.

A new artificial voice took over. "Please state the nature of your call. For example, if this is regarding billing, you can say, 'my bill.' If this is regarding an ongoing promotion, say, 'current promotions.' If this is regarding customer service, please say 'customer service' and remain on the line."

With her fingers tapping against the tabletop, Andie said, "Customer service," and waited while faint music played in the background. At last, there was a click on the line. She held her breath, hoping to launch into the story of what happened to an actual person, when yet another voice recording started.

"Your call is important to us. All agents are currently busy. Please stay on the line and a customer service representative will be with you as soon as possible. Estimated wait time, forty-five minutes." The artificial voice sounded almost sincere, but she wasn't fooled.

Andie placed her phone on the charger and left it on speakerphone while she attempted to login to her online banking with her laptop. As suspected, her joint account with Dylan was empty. She took a long breath and held it to let out slowly. There hadn't been much, as he seemed to spend money as fast as they earned it. Then, she tried to login to her old bank account, only to discover her passwords were no longer valid. Everything was so complicated.

She wracked her brain, trying to think of the last time she'd used her secondary Visa or the bank card with her maiden name. She hadn't used them since she'd been married. Was the problem because her name had changed? Perhaps there had been a company-wide reset because of security threats. That had happened to her mobile account a few months ago, and it had taken several tear-filled calls to regain access to her online account. She took another deep breath. The reason didn't matter. She couldn't access her money on her own.

In the background, the customer service hold music continued. Andie clenched her jaw; the repetitive music drilling into her brain as it cycled through for the thousandth time. Gripping her pen like a dagger, she gestured toward the screen, seconds away from another meltdown. With several deep breaths, the impulse passed. For now.

Just like on the phone, the website guided Andie in circles while she tried to access her account. In the interval since she'd last used this online banking system, the bank had switched to two-factor verification. Her previous personal verification questions would no longer work, and she needed a specific app.

Since she didn't have an authenticator app, she couldn't access her account. When she tried to load an authenticator app, her panicked attempts were unsuccessful. One company charged by the week and needed a valid credit card number, which she didn't have, while another required a code from the bank from her internal bank messages, which she couldn't access. Around and around, she went, unable to progress. It was all she could do not to scream. When had everything become so difficult?

She slammed shut her laptop lid and got up to pace while she waited for her call to connect with a person. Maybe then she'd have better luck. By the time it was her turn to speak with the agent on the phone, an hour had passed, and Andie had cried out of frustration twice. As soon as she spoke, it took everything not to sob into the phone. The poor customer service agent. The system wasn't her fault.

"I tried to use my Visa and couldn't because my soon-to-be ex-husband may have frozen all our accounts. Plus, he cleaned out our joint account." The words poured from Andie in a torrent she couldn't stop. "I tried to use my old credit card with my maiden name, but it was declined. I need access to my money."

"I'm very sorry, ma'am. I'd love to be of assistance, but before we begin, I need to verify your identity. What is your banking PIN?"

Andie closed her eyes. "I don't think I have one anymore. Or if I do, I don't remember it." Her voice trembled as tears threatened once more. She must have set one up, but at the moment, the memory was irretrievable.

"I see." The agent plowed on. "Then, in order to verify who you are, I'll have to ask you a series of questions about your accounts." There was a brief pause. "What is your bank card number?" Andie recited her old number from memory. "Thank you. Let me pull up your information." There was another pause. "What is the location of your home branch for our bank?"

Andie bit her lip. She had no idea. "Boston?"

"Can you be more specific please, ma'am?" The customer service representative sounded bored, with no inflection in her voice.

Had she set up this account while she was at university? Or was it from after she finished school? She'd moved so many times. Her mind scrambled, but nothing came to her rescue. "Near the university in Boston." She was grasping, unable to remember the street. "It's been so long. At least ten years. I don't remember the address. Can you ask me something else, please?"

"What is your current zip code?" The agent's tone remained flat.

Andie rattled off her new one, though, the bank wouldn't have it on file yet. Flustered, she tried to think of her previous one. She mumbled the first numbers which came to mind, fumbling as she blanked.

"I'm sorry, that's incorrect."

"I just moved a week ago. This is the one which should be on file." Andie exhaled and rattled off the zip code where she'd lived with Dylan.

"I'm sorry, that's still incorrect. Can you verify your mobile phone number?"

Andie's face grew hotter than ever, and her voice strained. "I got a new phone a year ago when I moved to the Seattle area. You won't have this number on file." Already upset, she blanked on her old number. She rattled off two options with a sinking sensation. Those would be too old.

The voice confirmed her struggle was no use. "I suggest you try to access this information online. If you don't remember your password, try the 'Forgot Password' option." The woman now sounded frustrated. She must be losing any belief in Andie's story.

Andie's eyes flooded. She'd already tried that option, but no longer had access to the email where the recovery code had been sent, as it was her through her old job back East. "Can you please ask me something I'll know, like my driver's license number or my date of birth?"

"I'm sorry, ma'am. You need to answer questions which are not easily known by others. We require secure verification."

"Can you look for me by my current name, Andie Marks? Maybe I changed it with the bank when I first got married." It was a last stab of desperation.

There was a long pause. "I'm sorry. We don't have anyone with that name in our system. Would you like to speak to my supervisor?" It seemed like the woman wanted to get rid of Andie.

Andie sniffled, her nose running. "Yes, please." She waited several minutes, the dreadful hold music battering her brain until the supervisor came on the line. With each minute passing, Andie's face grew hotter. Why couldn't she handle routine calls like this without becoming distraught? Why couldn't it be straightforward? Sometimes all this hassle with identity and security seemed overwhelming. When had the world become so distrustful?

The supervisor arrived at last and asked identical security questions. While her voice sounded sympathetic, she couldn't verify Andie's identity either.

"I've written your name and phone number, and I promise to investigate next week. It's closing time tonight. I'll contact you no later than three business days from now. Thank you for choosing our bank. Is there anything else I can help you with?"

Near tears once again, Andie said, "No, thanks." She hung up her phone and slumped in her chair. She was on her own with no funds until at least Wednesday.

Everywhere she looked, technology, which was supposed to make things easier, didn't. Identify theft, gift card scams, online AI assistance that went in circles, and frustrating two-factor verification. She needed a different app or card for everything. Even with an excellent memory, it was impossible to keep track of everything. Not to mention the climate crisis, fake news, and political unrest throughout the world. When you added Dylan to the situation, no wonder she'd been placed on stress leave.

Her boss wasn't wrong—sometimes things seemed like too much to handle. Andie shoved her chair back, gripping the edge of the table as her hands turned to ice.

Without access to her money, she wouldn't be able to pay for a lawyer.

# CHAPTER 6
# ZACK

"Sonny, true love is the greatest thing in the world, except for a nice
M.L.T. A mutton, lettuce, and tomato sandwich when the mutton is nice
and lean and the tomato is ripe."
–Miracle Max, The Princess Bride (1987)

Zack stared at the snow-filled TV screen and stretched to the accompaniment of low-volume static. He'd fallen asleep in front of a late-night movie after his shift again. His back protested as he sat up and rotated his neck, trying to work out some of the early morning stiffness. Standing, he reached over and switched off the TV. Ambulance dispatch had been busy last night, keeping him and his paramedic partners hopping from one call to another for their entire twelve-hour shift. He'd been too keyed up to sleep when he'd gotten home after four a.m.

He staggered to his bedroom down the hall and collapsed, fading into sleep again.

Some time later, he woke to daylight streaming in through the blinds. He yawned and checked his watch—ten a.m. Today was April seventh, so starting today, he had four days off. While his body needed a break, he preferred the action of work. He didn't always know what to do with himself on his days off besides the obvious, exercise. His job was demanding and physical, requiring him to be fit.

As he moved about, something about today's date nagged at him. April seventh. It hit like a stab to the solar plexus that he'd almost forgotten. His parents' anniversary. Despite his mom's death when he was eight, each year his dad held a family dinner to commemorate the occasion. Mom was gone, not forgotten.

Zack took a shuddering breath, trying to regain his equilibrium. His father had never quite recovered from her loss, and neither had Zack and his sisters. His mom had been the most vibrant and beautiful woman he'd ever seen. She and his father had been the best of friends, always holding hands and dancing together in the kitchen. Zack took a breath. Many years after her loss had been rough.

After the car accident, she'd just been gone—a gaping hole in the fabric of their family, one that had taken years to stitch back together. He shook his head, refusing to dwell on her death, preferring to think of happy memories. These days, he enjoyed spending time with his family and remembering little things about his parents being together.

His oldest sister, Val, had organized the get-together for the first few years when his dad had been so broken, but as he dragged himself together, the anniversary had once more become an occasion for the family.

Zack sighed. Today was also Easter Sunday, which meant everyone in the extended family would be in attendance. He rolled his shoulders to loosen his tense muscles. His aunts would all attend the dinner. Could he beg off this year? Not a chance. Val knew he didn't work today, and he didn't have a valid reason not to go, so avoiding questions about his sorry relationship status would be impossible.

It wouldn't just be his immediate family, but both of his mom's sisters and his adult cousins. Not to mention his dad's aunt, another well-meaning busybody. Didn't his aunts understand work was more important than breeding up a new generation? Everyone except Val and him were in a long-term relationship—and they didn't bother her. His sister was lucky. Well, she'd lost her fiancé years ago in a tragic accident, so not so fortunate in that respect, but at least the aunts didn't harass her about dating. Her loss had been a sobering second reminder of how devastating it was to love and lose your soulmate.

Zack jumped into his exercise routine, eating a granola bar and stretching in the living room of his sparsely furnished apartment before heading out into the spring rain. His run was refreshing and after a quick eight miles, he returned home, feeling lighter inside after the flood of endorphins.

Tossing his keys onto the kitchen counter nearest the door, the blinking light of the answering machine beckoned. He ignored it, heading for the shower. Time enough afterward to check in with the outside world.

After cleaning up, he ate lunch and checked his messages.

He punched the play button, and his cousin Xander's voice emanated from the box *"Yo. Zack. You're probably running or at the gym again. You free for an hour this afternoon before we head north for dinner? Call me back."*

Before Zack left for the gym, he called his cousin.

Xander answered after the third ring, typical for a Sunday when he often puttered around his place. "Hey. I hoped you'd call me back. You have time to meet at the house site before dinner tonight? I want to make sure everything's set for the concrete pour tomorrow."

"Sure." Zack couldn't remember the weather forecast, but as a contractor, his cousin kept up with the details. Zack could squeeze in a meetup with Xander before the family dinner.

"How's three o'clock? If we hurry, maybe we can sneak in a beer before facing Great Aunt M., Aunt Jen, and my mom. Bets on which one will corner you this time?" Xander chortled.

"Dick." Now that he was engaged, they left him alone. "My money's on Auntie M. Family matriarch and all that." Zack sighed again, then remembered he hadn't answered the original question. "Three works. See you then."

"Later," said Xander, before hanging up.

The rest of Zack's day went as planned. His off days tended to be the same, one bleeding into another. Whenever someone at work asked about his time off, he was hard-pressed to remember what he'd done. He surveyed the mess in his apartment—more clutter than dirt. Since he often came home exhausted, his stuff landed wherever. He might find time tomorrow to run a vacuum and do laundry. Wahoo.

Tomorrow he'd tidy the place, stock up on groceries, run, and work out. That's pretty much how the cycle went—lather, rinse, repeat. There was a sameness to it all. At least the anniversary dinner would break the monotony. A voice in the back of his head, which sounded suspiciously like his aunts, reminded him having plans with friends—or a girlfriend—would also be less boring. He didn't want just sex, though; there had to be someone out there he could laugh with, spend time, somebody he could see as a partner. Not someone flaky or false, not again. No thanks.

He grabbed his keys and headed out.

Zack arrived at the construction site five minutes early and waited for Xander. The usual hive of activity was quiet. Today was Sunday, so the construction crew had the day off. The soon-to-be-house had been a gamble. Each of his siblings had inherited a piece of land from their grandparents—held in trust until they turned thirty. All their lots had been on the same street because, once upon a time, his grandfather's family had owned the entire area.

Val had fixed hers up and moved in years ago since she was ten years his senior. His sister Yolanda had sold hers, pocketing the money to buy a fancy condo in downtown Seattle with her husband. That was when Zack decided to get off his ass and do something with his property. His section had a decrepit house on it which had sat vacant for several years. One trip through the place had made him decide to rebuild. It was practically falling down.

He'd recruited Xander to help with the teardown and had been surprised when his cousin had presented him with blueprints for a new place. Something he'd drawn up in his spare time, in advance. Zack hadn't decided yet if he'd sell the house or live there after it was finished. Moving into a whole new house on his own seemed daunting and unnecessary.

Perhaps building the house would get his aunts off his back, buying him some time.

He seldom dated and had only had a couple of girlfriends, the most notable being in university. He was too busy with work. Plus, he often picked up extra shifts, covering for buddies who wanted holidays off. The women he'd dated had been pissed he hadn't wanted to spend holidays, like the Fourth of July or Memorial Day weekends, with them. On his end, it had only been casual.

They'd been nice enough, but not worth more effort. After the last one had been bugging him about the lack of intimacy in their relationship, he'd called it quits. He hadn't been in love and after seeing a close relationship like his parents', he wasn't interested in less.

Zack seldom felt the lack, despite the odd, lonely moment. Unless he was talking to his aunts. Then, not having a girlfriend seemed like a sin. Of course, their argument was he wouldn't meet anyone to fall in love with if he was always working. He shoved the thought down. Whatever.

When Xander's dusty gold pickup pulled up, Zack headed for the walkway to the work site, meeting Xander partway.

"Hey. Thanks for meeting me," said Xander.

Zack glanced back at the hole in the ground. "No problem. I wanted to check the progress, anyway."

Up close, the forms for the foundation made the house look big. Grander than he'd ever need on his own—two floors with four bedrooms, three bathrooms, a workshop, and a library, for crying out loud. Why the hell did he need a library?

"Remind me again why you've designed a house big enough for a large family?" He narrowed his eyes. Had Aunt M. been involved with the design? He hadn't asked before, but it was probable. She had her fingers in a lot of pies. Still, the finished house would be gorgeous, so Zack had agreed. That had been last summer. Since breaking ground this spring, the pro and con list had started in his head once more—keep or sell.

Xander laughed. "If you sell it, you'll make a mint. If you decide to stay, you have room for whatever you want. Even a family. Odds are three to one you sell."

Zack wished his family would stay out of his life. He worked hard and was there for them. Wasn't that enough? He wasn't a guy who did things just because it was expected.

He clenched his jaw. "We going for a drink or what?"

•   •   •

At five-thirty, Zack parked his blue truck outside his dad's house outside Snohomish, the same house he and his siblings had grown up in, and headed inside. He couldn't tell who else was already here besides Val, Yolanda, and her husband. His sisters had planned to come together. Val's car sat in the driveway behind his dad's white locksmith van.

The aroma of tomato, basil, and cheese met him on entry. He inhaled, filling himself with the scent of lasagna. Val always used mom's recipe, and the smell brought memories cascading back.

The last time his mom had cooked her lasagna had been six days before the accident. He remembered her long dark hair tied back in a ponytail, wisps escaping in the heat of the kitchen while she chopped garlic, onions, and mushrooms. She'd swayed back and forth to the Beatles on the kitchen radio, the rich aroma of sauteed food filling the room.

After adding the tomatoes, he'd helped her with the spices, stirring them into the sauce—basil, oregano, and her "secret" ingredient, ground anise. She'd always saved that job for him, the youngest. He couldn't think of Italian food without thinking of his mom and cooking with her. He shook his head. The last time he'd helped her, he'd gotten bored and ran off before they were done. If only he could get that time back.

Behind him, as Zack toed off his wet shoes, the doorbell rang, jolting him back to the present.

He opened the door, smothering a grin. His Great Aunt M. stood on the porch. She'd redyed her wild curly hair—a color she referred to as Sunset Glow. She appeared unchanged by the evening light. Most of the time she looked old enough to be a grandmother, then she'd smile, and the years would drop away. He had no idea how old she was—a family secret. Sixty? Seventy? Today she wore five or six necklaces she'd probably made herself from semi-precious polished stones and bits of shell. Her loose turquoise pants billowed in the breeze. He'd met no one else like his great aunt—she was one-of-a-kind.

"Aunt M., come on in," he said, standing aside. "I just got here."

"I saw you park," she said. "I was waiting for you."

He smiled. Though she gave him a hard time sometimes, his dad's favorite aunt was Zack's favorite, too. She didn't have children but acted like a godmother to his siblings and their cousins Xander and Wanda.

"You didn't bring anyone again." She pursed her lips, tapped his cheek with one finger. "Maybe next year. I have a proposition for you."

"Not a setup." He groaned. Aunt M. meant well, but she was the worst at meddling in his personal life.

She smiled as she sailed past him and into the house, her floral perfume trailing in a cloud. "I brought my own wine." She passed him a bottle. "Be a dear and pour me a glass when you grab yourself something. I'll be in the living room, waiting for our chat."

She wouldn't take no for an answer. As usual.

Zack ran the gauntlet into the kitchen. "Happy Easter," he said to his dad and sisters.

"Was that Aunt M. I heard coming in, too?" said his dad from where he stood with a navy-blue apron wrapped around his slim frame. The front read, "Lives to Grill."

Zack lifted the bottle of red. "I'm to get her a glass and deliver."

His dad chuckled. "Better not keep Aunt M. waiting. It just makes her feisty. We can catch up in a bit." He went back to chopping vegetables for the salad.

Sitting at the small table in the eating nook, Yolanda laughed.

Zack turned to see the younger of his sisters whispering to Val. No sign of Mike, Yolanda's husband. He must be traveling for work again. Seeing Zack's glance, Val and Yolanda broke into gales of laughter. He winked and turned away. He didn't want to know what was so amusing. They were probably in on whatever Aunt M. was cooking up. He poured the wine for his aunt, got himself a Coke, and headed to the living room. He'd already had a beer with Xander and didn't need another, after all, he had to drive home later.

Zack set Aunt M.'s drink on a coaster beside her and settled into a comfy chair beside her. He had to at least be polite and listen to her proposition.

"I think I've found someone for you. Your soulmate," she said. Holy shit. She got right to the point—not wasting a second. "I have an excellent feeling about this one. She has an appointment with me next Monday." His aunt's eyes gleamed, and she got a stubborn set to her jaw while she stared him down.

"Aunt M., I'm not looking for someone right now and I don't believe in soulmates. My job keeps me so busy. What woman is interested in someone who works crazy hours and picks up shifts on holidays?"

"You aren't working today." Her green eyes bored into him.

He laughed. "If I'd stayed home, everyone would have kicked my ass and then I'd be the one calling the paramedics." Dammit. He rubbed the back of his neck. If she organized a blind date with this woman, he'd have to go. He shifted in his seat and sipped his Coke, thinking of another tack to take. "Wait. If your appointment is next week, you haven't even met this woman yet. What makes you think she could be the one for me?"

"It doesn't matter." Her deep green eyes seemed to expand as she spoke. "Sometimes I just know." She tapped her temple.

Goosebumps raised on his arms, and the hair on the back of his neck stood up. It was true. Sometimes Great Aunt M. knew things she shouldn't. Her predictions were usually spot on. She'd set up Xander with his fiancée, as well as Yolanda and Mike. Her track record was excellent. Sweat dripped down his forehead.

"I wish," he hesitated. "I wish it was easy to find someone, but it's not." Zack took another swig of Coke, almost choking on the bubbles as they rose. "Not like my soulmate is going to fall to the ground at my feet." If only it would be that simple.

Aunt M. patted his back. "At least keep an open mind. You never know when your luck is about to change."

Unable to help himself, Zack wondered if his aunt could be right. Maybe it was time to consider dating again. But he'd rather find someone on his own than endure more blind dates.

# CHAPTER 7
## ANDIE

"There is no escape. Don't make me destroy you."
–Darth Vader, The Empire Strikes Back (1980)

Monday afternoon arrived and Andie stood outside the brick building with Dr. Fossey's office in the April drizzle. She shivered as she checked the address before entering, unsure why she was so unsettled over going in. Her leg twitched. Maybe she should postpone this for another day. She bit her lip. Over the phone, the receptionist had mentioned the doctor alternated weeks between Portland and Seattle. If Andie hadn't taken this appointment, she would have had to wait another two weeks to speak to the therapist.

Until she'd spoken to someone, she couldn't return to work. She'd never talked to a psychiatrist before, and procrastinating here on the sidewalk had butterflies flapping around her stomach. Many people swore by therapy. How difficult could it be? Andie was more of a problem avoider and hadn't spent much time thinking about the past. There was no point. Everyone had a history and memories they wished to forget. She sighed. That sort of thinking may have led to this snarl of repressed feelings and nightmares.

She took a deep breath and then opened the glass door. The directory in the polished lobby listed a dozen doctors' offices in the four-story building—showing Dr. Maeve Fossey in room 213 on the second floor. Andie preferred the stairs to the elevator for climbing a single flight, so she entered the stairwell.

The chemical stench she'd always associated with the dentist filled the enclosed space as she ascended to the next level, making her skin crawl. Despite the listings downstairs of various medical professionals, the scent was unexpected. There must also be a dentist's office nearby. Her shoulders tightened—the distinctive smell brought the discomfort of cavities and needles rushing back.

She turned a corner, looking for 213. Seattle's Smile Dental was in 212 and Dr. Maeve Fossey was across the hall.

Andie wanted this appointment over with. She pushed into the therapist's office and stopped just beyond the threshold. The inside wasn't what she expected. The dentist office smell was gone, and she inhaled, filling her lungs with fresh air. A water fountain trickled in the corner and green plants grew everywhere, like an indoor jungle. The counter partitioned off a small reception area with three deep armchairs. A large plate of chocolate chip cookies and a bowl of Granny Smiths sat on the table.

"You must be Andie," said the perky young receptionist with pierced eyebrows from behind the counter. At Andie's nod, she said, "I'm glad you're a few minutes early. I'd like you to fill out these forms."

Andie's chest clenched. She'd trusted Andrea enough to step through the door, but every little thing left her more off-kilter. Andie stretched out her hand for the clipboard, expecting insurance or payment forms she wasn't sure how she'd pay. Should she have gotten more information over the phone, like the cost?

Instead, the woman passed her a piece of mauve paper with standard questions about her age, her job, and her marital status. It also asked her to list her last three jobs, three relationships, and three addresses, and then to rate her health from one to ten. On the back was a section about bests and worsts, such as houses, relationships, pets, and jobs. Andie wished she'd checked online for an intake form, wishing Dr. Fossey wasn't so old-fashioned. If she'd seen these questions in advance, she would have bailed.

Andie extracted a pen from her purse and scanned both pages before starting. She hesitated, chewing on the end of the pen when she got to the section about her family. Father... Unknown. That wasn't quite true, but she'd never met him. Mother... Deceased. That was true, but it was such a tiny word to contain the mix of guilt and relief she'd experienced after reading her mother's obituary online. Cancer was never pretty. The next question was the worst. Siblings. Andie hesitated, tapping the pen against her lips.

She hadn't spoken to her sister in ten years and wasn't even sure where Jess lived anymore. Andie started to write, Unknown again. She scribbled out the U, leaving a thick blotch on the paper. It was simpler to leave her sister out of the equation, so she wrote "None" in the remaining space provided. Marital status... Separated. She winced, glancing at her other answers. She'd left several thick blobs of ink, almost screaming, "lie."

Andie listed a cousin ten years older than her mom from the Boston area as Next of Kin. During her university years, she had sometimes met up with extended family for Thanksgiving. They weren't close, but at least they'd know who she was if contacted. When Andie completed the form, she handed it in at the counter, the woman taking it with a polite smile.

"Dr. Maeve will be with you in a few minutes. Help yourself to a cookie or some fruit." She waved a hand toward the cozy waiting area. Interesting that the doctor preferred to be called Dr. Maeve, instead of Dr. Fossey. Perhaps the doctor thought it made her more approachable.

Andie headed for one of the comfy chairs in the office, snagging one of the Granny Smiths on the way. She bit into the apple as she sat, the tart juice filling her mouth. The crunch of her bites seemed loud in the small space, but eating provided an excellent distraction.

She'd just tossed the core in the garbage bin when a smooth voice said, "Andie Marks." Andie turned. "You must be the young woman referred to me by my old friend Andie. She said she'd passed on my number. Come in, come in." The woman's voice was soothing, though her appearance differed from what Andie would have expected from a medical professional. She also had to be in her seventies. Maybe older.

Dr. Maeve wore a fringed rainbow sweater shawl, which fell past her knees, lace-up black boots with high heels, and faded ripped jeans. While her face resembled a storybook grandmother, her wild red hair was a shade that could have only come from a box. She turned, retreating down a short hall while Andie followed in her wake, trailing through a cloud of a faint spicy smell lingering where Dr. Maeve had stood.

Once in her office, Dr. Maeve shut the door and waved Andie to the closest of a matched pair of burgundy leather recliners. "Take a seat, please. How can I help you today?" She took the other. Between them and off to the side on a low table was a tray of polished, spherical stones—a fantastic variety of colors and sizes.

Andie's eyes were drawn to one with silver flecks and toffee-colored swirls. What a cool collection. She wrested herself back to the present and sat facing Dr. Maeve in the matching chair. Andie's hands clutched the ends of the armrests. Dr. Maeve held Andie's checklist, her eyes roaming downward as she scanned. Her eyes stopped a few times. Would the lies register?

Andie wiped her palms on her jeans. She hoped she didn't look as nervous as she felt. Her stomach was tied in knots and her mouth dry. "I should have asked about the price and whether my insurance will cover the cost of our session." Her voice sounded scratchy and harsh. Best to get that weight off her chest in case they couldn't continue.

"Don't worry about the fee," said Dr. Maeve, waving her hand with crimson nails. "Someone special referred you to me, so I hadn't considered charging you for our talk today. If we move forward with regular appointments, we'll figure something out."

Andie swallowed. "Like a payment plan?" That might be okay. Maybe she wouldn't need many sessions.

Dr. Maeve leaned forward, her eyes seeming to expand. "On your worksheet, you listed the same house as your favorite place and your least favorite. Tell me about it."

Andie looked up, her gaze caught by Dr. Maeve's intense stare. She wasn't sure where the question was going, but answered anyway. "When I was eight, we moved into my mom's boyfriend's house. At first, I had to share a room with my younger sister. Our bed was on top of a playhouse inside our room. When I turned nine, Garry built me my own room for a birthday present. I'm not sure why I listed that place. We only lived there for a year and a half, and I've barely thought of that house in years."

As soon as the words left her mouth, they felt bitter, like another lie. Many nightmares brought those days back. So much for not mentioning her sister. She'd brought her up in the second sentence emerging from her mouth.

Dr. Maeve didn't comment, the look in her eyes willing Andie to continue.

Andie pushed on. "I moved just over a week ago into a real dump. I'd like to change my answer. It's my least favorite place now." She clamped her lips shut. She'd been babbling. Something about Dr. Maeve's wide green eyes invited confidences. Andie would have to watch herself, or she'd say too much—a constant hazard. She was here to talk about Dylan, not dredge up the past.

Dr. Maeve tapped her finger against her pursed lips. "Tell me more about how this bedroom from your childhood compares to your new accommodations. I'm not quite seeing the connection, but we're going somewhere interesting."

Andie didn't want to talk about the long-ago bedroom, but it was better than sharing information about her sister. Still, why had she mentioned anything about it, or her first impression of the rental? Now, at thirty, Andie had a different perspective about her bedroom at Garry's. Had she known so many nights would become nightmares, she might have refused to move her clothes, tattered books, and her fuzzy-leafed African violet into her new loft bedroom. She'd have insisted the three of them move out. Not that her mom would have listened.

Andie fidgeted in her seat and cracked her knuckles, the popping sound loud in the otherwise quiet counseling office. She didn't talk about those days very often and always detoured conversations headed in that direction. Still, perhaps talking with a professional would be fruitful. "My castle bedroom was a loft above my younger sister's room." She paused. The doctor raised an eyebrow and made a quick note. A second mention of her sister was too much. Shit.

Andie pushed onward. "The only entrance into the room was a hole in the wall above a ladder fastened against Garry's son's bedroom wall." She pictured the handmade, sanded ladder with round wooden rungs stuck to

Lionel's wall. He'd been five when they'd moved in—a petulant, spoiled brat. His early years wouldn't have been easy, either.

"That's a mouthful," said Dr. Maeve with a lilting laugh as she pushed her dyed locks away from her expressive face. "Go on, the ladder was located in another kid's room. That's three children in the house, correct?" Without waiting for Andie's answer, the doctor made another quick note on her paper.

Andie nodded, her throat tightening. "To enter, I climbed through a rectangular hole cut in the wall in whiny Lionel's room. I loved my room on sight, even if it was plain. It was the first time I'd ever had my own bedroom, but it had three drawbacks. My little gray Mo-cat scritched and clawed up the ladder to sleep with me—but Garry's lovely collie couldn't. Auggie slept at the base of the ladder for over a year, the perfect sentry on guard."

"And Garry was your mother's boyfriend?" At Andie's nod, Dr. Maeve made another note. She peered over the rim of her dark-rimmed glasses. "Maybe we'll delve into your relationship with your younger sister another time."

Damn. Or maybe not.

Andie craned her neck but couldn't see what had been written. The image of Garry's fake-kind face and sleek, long hair flashed behind her eyes. He'd seemed nice at first. Then they'd learned what lurked within him. She shuddered and continued. "My new room also didn't have a door, so I hung a blanket over the opening. This allowed me to sneak-read late into the night without alerting the adults to my illicit well-past-bedtime reading. The pale glow of my reading light seeped into my sister's bedroom room along one narrow edge, but Jessie seldom tattled."

Andie leaned back and crossed her arms, ready to be finished with this conversation without discussing the third fault. "My current rental is at least clean now. But you should have seen it when I moved in." She shook her head, as if disapproving of dirt and mess.

"That's only two problems," said Dr. Maeve, not allowing Andie to shift the topic. She angled forward in her seat, her emerald eyes intent on Andie, reminding her of a bird—an egret waiting to spear its dinner.

Andie took a deep breath and braced herself. This part was the worst. "The room had very thin walls." She cracked her knuckles, focusing her gaze on her hands instead of the doctor. "No blanket or guard could help with that problem."

She felt haunted by the violent sounds from so long ago. Those sleepless nights in her tower stained her soul, leaching fear into her for years. Even now. The violence downstairs was why she'd left Dylan. She couldn't let her younger self down—an odd thought and a new one.

"We'll come back to the guard and why you think you needed one. Why were thin walls a problem?" Dr. Maeve made another few marks on her paper. All this follow-up might cost a fortune.

"Unfinished walls and rooms without proper doors couldn't block the distinctive smash of a fist crashing through drywall." Andie's voice came from far away as she replayed the worst night. The reminder of the hollow *thunk* took her straight back to long ago. Her voice shook. "Half-height walls, loft bedrooms, and high ceilings captured sound from the open living space below." She pictured the smooth reddish brown of the stained log walls and the L-shape of Garry's kitchen, where many fights had occurred.

"Whose fist," said Dr. Maeve. "Garry's?"

Andie nodded, a lump in her throat.

"What else did you hear?" said Dr. Maeve. Her voice continued—soft and encouraging.

"Shouted obscenities, splintering furniture as it smashed against the floor, and the thud of fists on flesh." Andie shivered. "The sounds carried to where I huddled under the eaves with my Mo-cat and whatever I was reading." She winced. "His voice wasn't always loud, but it dripped with anger and menace. I was ten and he terrified me."

Her voice shook and she stopped to catch her breath. "Not only that, but he also used to kick my cat, and he gave my pet rabbit to the neighbor— to eat. Cruelty to animals should have been our cue to leave, since it happened before the beatings." Her voice was no longer fearful, but angry. Those heinous crimes had made Garry into Andie's enemy.

"Did nighttime incidents like this happen often?" Dr. Maeve's voice remained quiet. "Did you ever talk to your mother about them?"

Andie wanted this conversation to be done and didn't answer the questions. Her mother had never wanted to discuss those days. Neither had Andie. Not that the next situation had been a vast improvement. Her childhood had been a series of unfortunate decisions.

"I'm not here to talk about my relationship with my mother." Andie shut the hot rush of feelings down and took a breath. She had to do something. Her voice cracked as she forged ahead. "On subsequent nights, I read with one ear cocked, waiting for the violence to erupt. Sometimes it exploded, sometimes there was silence. I couldn't sleep because I was afraid he'd go too far and injure my mom. The last three months we lived in that house were excruciating. Even at ten, it was clear to me that Jessie, my mom, and I needed to escape."

"Why do you think your mother stayed? Do you ever resent her for failing to keep you safe?" Dr. Maeve leaned back. "How did your sister handle the situation?"

Though Andie wasn't offended, she remained silent, her thoughts whirling. If she was honest, she'd always been jealous of and resented her sister's ability to leave the past behind. Andie had left home at eighteen, heading to a distant university. She'd never gone home or talked to her mother or sister again. Sometimes the guilt had threatened to eat her alive. She'd left her sister behind to cope on her own. Andie locked those thoughts up tight and turned her mind back to Dr. Maeve's original question, the details of their final days living there flooding back.

In June, Garry gave her mom a black eye. She'd tried the story about falling and hitting a doorknob, but even to ten-year-old Andie, that was clearly untrue. No one else had bought that version either.

"My mom was too scared to leave. It took a black eye she couldn't hide from her friends at work before we moved out. Her entire staff showed up in trucks on the last day of the school year to help us move."

Andie shivered at the memory of terror on the frantic move out. Garry had helped, putting on a pleasant show of helping for the sake of her mother's friends all while Andie had waited for further violence. But Andie was no longer a child; she shouldn't fear the dark and arguments. She'd left Dylan behind, and he couldn't hurt her, but like those sleepless nights so long ago, helplessness infused her bones. The circumstances leading to Andie's sleeplessness should be different now—she lived alone—but she didn't know how to escape the terrors her mind spun, as if the past and present violence had converged.

Throughout her life, when exposed to yelling or confrontation, like with Dylan, she relived the nightmare sounds—the stool smashing against the floor, her mother's name, the thumping fists, and the cracking walls. On those nights, Andie kept an arm's length between herself and sleep until the pounding of her heart subsided. She needed time to convince herself she was safe, and the broken furniture and bruises were ancient history.

Maybe if she had someone else to share her fears with, the feelings would dissipate. That's what had brought her to therapy and Dr. Maeve. Andie had more to talk about than Dylan—much more if she included her feelings about her mother's decisions. The idea was a revelation that blew her mind. Too bad she didn't have anyone close to confide in, but with long hours at work and few friends, it was challenging to make connections. She'd have to thank her neighbor again for leading her to Dr. Maeve.

Andrea had done her an incredible favor.

Dr. Maeve interrupted Andie's thoughts. "Before you leave, I'd like you to select a worry rock. Stones have unexpected properties which can ease anxiety and help change how you think, or even bring comfort. Choose something from the table that speaks to you." She picked up a purple stone from the tray, rolling it between her hands, before returning it to the selection with a faint clacking sound. "Next time, we'll talk about your mother and your anger." Her eyes seemed to dare Andie to return.

Depending on the cost, there might not be a next time. Still, without further thought, Andie reached for the round stone she'd noticed at the outset, the one with amber swirls and silver bits which caught the light. The cool, smooth shape fit in her palm and had a solid weight that seemed satisfying. She covered the stone with her other hand. An odd gleam of light from the flecks pulled her attention as she examined the stone. She didn't expect the worry rock to succeed, but she liked how it looked and felt.

●  ●  ●

After her session with Dr. Maeve ended, Andie returned home. Unwanted flashes of her tough childhood intruded on her thoughts for the rest of the day. Her mother's drinking had ensured that Andie had to be the adult in the house. She'd often been the one to buy food, cook, and take care of things, even before high school. Thrusting those details from her mind again, she finished the book she'd been reading and watched an episode of a new show, which did little to hold her interest. She clicked it off before it was done.

Though it wasn't late, she went to bed. Lying still, the busy events of her emotional day caught up to her after her quiet evening. She reached for another book, one of her favorites, to soothe her restless mind. Rereading familiar stories was often an excellent distraction as well as comforting. When midnight rolled around, she flicked off the light and stared into the darkness.

It was clear it was one of those nights—perhaps because she'd dredged up the source of her fear to Dr. Maeve and Andie's nerves were raw. Her current bedroom wasn't a castle, but there were similarities to that childhood loft, such as its refuge status. Stacks of books were piled by her bedside, and she maintained a watchfulness toward the dark, the shadows pressing against a tightness in her chest, squeezing. They made it difficult to breathe, and she gasped for air. She closed her eyes, concentrating on her breathing, trying to regulate.

A pounding intruded on her efforts. She froze, waiting. A few moments passed, then the sounds repeated. Was that in her head? A dream about fists?

Andie sat up as the pounding returned a third time. The noise was real, not part of her imagination. Someone was thumping on her front door. Her blood chilled. Only one name came to her—Dylan. He'd found her. He must have used the last address he'd found on the Find My Phone app, and then her car out front had done the rest.

Maybe she should have parked around the block. This place was supposed to be safe. Heart racing, she swung her bare feet to the chilly floor and padded toward the main living area, leaving off the overhead lights. The banging grew louder and more insistent.

Did he know she was awake?

Her hand trailed across the wall, the glow from the streetlights outside enough to help her navigate. Deep down in her gut, she didn't need to see Dylan to know it was him; she only wanted confirmation. She snuck into the kitchen and peeked outside. The sight of Dylan's car, though expected, hit like a gut punch, knocking oxygen from her lungs.

He must have noticed her shadow near the window because he shouted, "Andie, let me in. Come on. I just want to talk." His words slurred together, and her blood ran cold. He'd been drinking, probably the reason he dared to make a scene in public. That and the anonymity of darkness; the neighbors wouldn't recognize him. The banging on the front door grew more forceful. "You made me track your phone by refusing to speak like a reasonable person. Open up."

Andie wished there was someone to call, but there wasn't—except perhaps the police. Should she get her phone? Having *the* Dylan Marks brought in for questioning would have repercussions. Other than Andrea and her husband, Andie hadn't met her other neighbors, and she didn't want to bother the nice older couple in the middle of the night. Besides, they'd done enough already.

Hands shaking, she backed away. Dylan shouldn't be able to get inside— she'd checked the locks on the doors and windows as part of her rounds before going to bed. If she ignored him, he might tire of yelling.

She swallowed and retreated to her room. A stray gleam of light caught her eye, causing her to pause. She instinctively grabbed her new stone. Flinging herself into bed, she tugged the covers over her head, making a dim cave underneath. She rubbed the sphere between her palms for comfort until it grew warm, almost hot. Even with the heat, she kept it clutched tight, watching the strange flecks of light which seemed to emanate from within.

A tear slid down Andie's cheek. More followed since it was dark and there was no one to see. No one to hide them from. Maybe she should call the police. She didn't have a restraining order yet. They might make Dylan leave, but it wouldn't solve anything long-term. She took a shuddering breath. Best to let the visit run its course on its own. He'd be less likely to return if he left of his own volition. She covered her head with her pillow and squeezed her eyes shut, trying to block all traces of Dylan's violent outburst outside.

Eventually, his pounding stopped, but still, she held the warm stone, pressing it close to her chest with both hands.

With her anger resurfacing and Dylan outside, this ranked as the worst day in a long time. "I wish life wasn't so complicated. If only I could go somewhere Dylan couldn't find me. Somewhere I could have a simpler life." The words hovered in the air like a comic book. If only there was such a place.

After waiting for what seemed an eternity in the ominous quiet, Andie flung off her covers, shuffled across the cold floor, and went to the bathroom. She took a deep breath and returned to bed. She still couldn't hear Dylan. Had he gone? She didn't dare check lest it encouraged him to resume his efforts. Inhaling, she focused on her breathing again. She needed sleep. To help relax, she ran through the list of names of all one hundred forty-four episodes of *Buffy the Vampire Slayer*, her all-time favorite show. She'd watched the series dozens of times and practiced this recitation so often the names were rote.

The occasional glow from her charging phone lit up the far side of the room like a childhood nightlight, while the blue glow of the clock's numbers burned their way into her brain. Three a.m. Her jaw creaked as she yawned, at last finding it difficult to focus as she fumbled for the names of the season six episodes after Seeing Red. Villains, Two to Go, and Grave. Season seven could wait. She flipped onto her side and yawned again before sinking into sleep between one breath and the next.

# CHAPTER 8
# ZACK

"Bueller...? Bueller...? Bueller...?"
–Economics Teacher, Ferris Bueller's Day Off (1986)

The conversation with Aunt M. regarding her mysterious setup played over in Zack's mind several times in the following days. Her words grated like an annoying song stuck in his head. What was Aunt M. up to? Would she really ask one of her patients about going out with her nephew? That seemed like an enormous conflict of interest. Not to mention a horrible idea. It would give the poor girl the wrong idea from the beginning. It wasn't fair.

He'd told M. he wouldn't cooperate, and she'd ignored him, telling him all the ways he was cutting himself off from life with excessive work. He'd told her he'd rather just meet someone on his own. She'd laughed and said if it was going to happen that way, he'd have done it already. She wasn't wrong, galling as it was to admit. It had been years since he'd followed up on anyone interesting with more than a single date. It had been too long since he'd been laid.

On his first day back at work, Zack awoke early as his shift started at four a.m. Despite the hour, he welcomed the return to his routine. This early in the year, it was still pitch dark, which made it even more difficult to get moving. He rolled out of bed at the first note of the alarm, dressed in his uniform, added cream and sugar to his coffee, and was out the door on time. The ambulance dispatch center where he worked was less than a ten-minute drive away at this time of the morning—no traffic, unlike a four p.m. shift.

He'd only been at work more a few minutes when they received the first call of the day.

They left the station at a run and hopped into their rig.

"Code 3," came over the radio.

Responding to the Code 3 signal, Zack flipped on the sirens while Cole, his usual partner, drove. Cole was a decent sort and wouldn't bother him to talk until later when the caffeine kicked in and they were more awake. The first call was at an old age home, where an elderly resident had had a heart attack when getting up in the night.

By the time Cole and Zack arrived, it was too late. Zack's spirits sank. They couldn't save them all, but this was someone's father and grandfather, and a death was a rough start to the shift.

The second call was similar, a nursing home emergency. This one, they rushed to the hospital, giving the patient aspirin, nitro, and oxygen. They called it in as a Code Red so the ER would have doctors waiting on the other end. Zack was optimistic about the patient's chances because the elderly man woke in the back of the rig. He'd been dazed at first, then seemed more coherent saying he'd been fishing. Fishing must be his happy place.

Their third call was a car accident in the morning commute, and they were one of two ambulances called to the scene. Zack braced himself, as he always did for traffic calls. The gritty bits of glass shards, blood, crumpled metal, and the smell of rubber always brought images of his mom's accident. He took a quick breath, bracing himself before exiting the ambulance, dealing with his personal demons. He hadn't been there when she'd died, but he'd been to so many, and they always smelled the same.

This one had been a five-car collision, a domino effect situation. The front car had stopped without warning, the next had rammed into it from behind causing them to stop, and a chain reaction ensued. He and Cole cleaned several lacerations, triaged the occupants, and transported two to the hospital—one for concussion, the other for serious whiplash.

Other than the early morning heart attack, there had been no additional deaths today and nothing life-threatening. Pretty routine so far. The next several hours passed in much the same way—non-stop calls and lots of action, just enough to make his shift fly and keep his brain in the present.

The next call made his heart drop.

"Mount Washington Elementary. Eight-year-old girl seizing. No previous known condition. Code 3." The call came in on the radio just after noon.

Zack glanced at Cole who grimaced. "Copy." Zack spoke into the two-way radio. Sick or injured kids always ripped out his heart. Sometimes there was nothing they could do.

With sirens blaring, the traffic clearing in front of them, they arrived at the school seven minutes later. Someone on staff had removed a metal pole which normally blocked vehicle access to the tall, brick building of the private school and waved them toward the front walkway. The playground was filled with white and navy uniformed children playing.

At the ambulance's approach, most of the kids stopped and stared, curiosity rolling off them in waves. Zack scanned the area and couldn't see anyone down outside; their patient must be inside. Adults outside kept the children at bay as his partner parked as close to the front door as possible.

Zack switched off the siren but left the red lights flashing. He grabbed his kit as they hopped out. Working together, he and Cole opened the back, grabbed the stretcher, rolling it toward the front doors where a stocky man in a blue suit waited.

The older man stepped forward. "Thank heaven you were quick. We've called Casey's parents. We're to let them know which hospital to meet you at. She's inside." He must think it serious enough she'd be transported for certain. With kids and seizures, without knowing anything more, it was the safe plan.

Zack's heart drummed faster. "You're the principal?" he said as they followed the man into the school.

"Yes. Bryan Williamson," he said. "She's just over here, down the hall. We extended lunch to keep everyone else away."

Smart. Best not to have an audience. Zack's chest tightened. He wouldn't relax until he knew the girl's condition. However, nerves didn't affect his work. He remained functional and calm—lives often depended on this skill to compartmentalize.

He and Cole stopped near the girl lying on the floor at the end of the hall. Her skin was the color of chalk and she looked too tiny to be eight, lying motionless on the floor covered from the neck down by a blue blanket. With her eyes closed, she could have been sleeping.

Two women attended the patient. They'd propped her head on a pillow, turned the little girl onto her side, and covered her. They'd done that well. He gave them a nod.

"I'm Zack," he said, smiling a professional greeting-type smile. "This is my partner, Cole. We're here to take over." He tossed his chin at Cole, who crouched down.

Cole knelt on the floor beside the girl and checked she was breathing. Their first assessment was always ABC—airway, breathing, and circulation. Her translucent skin was traced with faint webs of purple lines, but her chest rose and fell. So far, positive signs. Her eyelids fluttered open at Cole's first touch.

"I don't feel so good," she said, her voice weak. "Where's my mommy?"

"You're okay, honey," said Zack, squeezing her ankle through the covering. "Cole and I are paramedics. We're going to help you feel better and get you to the hospital. We'll give you a ride in our ambulance and your mom will meet you there." Her brown eyes filled with tears and her bottom lip trembled, but she nodded.

"Breath sounds are good. No SOB," said Cole as he tucked away his stethoscope. No continued shortness of breath was another positive sign.

"Skin's clammy," said Cole, "and her heart rate is ninety-five."

Fast but not serious. Zack glanced between the women. "Did she lose consciousness? How long was the episode? Do we have a timeline?"

"Casey headed out to play for lunch but lagged behind her friends. She said she was feeling weird," said one of the women. "That was at 12:15."

"Are you her teacher?" Zack zeroed in on the woman with the information.

She shook her head. "I'm the teacher's aide in her class. I was waiting for another student I work with, but Casey stopped here. It looked like she was dizzy and tried to regain her balance with her hand on the wall. I wasn't close enough to hear anything, but she stumbled and then fell to the floor twitching. I sent her friends outside." She checked her watch. "We cleared the hall, and I sent Maxine," she indicated the other woman, "to tell the office to call 911. Her first seizure lasted about two minutes. The second was more than five. Casey lost consciousness and was confused upon waking and is weak."

Zack nodded as Cole continued to check the patient's other vitals. "You did the right things." That wasn't always the case. His shoulders loosened. "How long ago was the first seizure?"

The principal interrupted. "Twelve minutes. We did our best to keep her comfortable." He glanced at the clock. "How much longer until you move her? Her parents are extremely concerned and some of her friends will be too." The principal glanced at his watch. He was probably concerned about how long she'd been on the floor. Plus, he'd want to be sure she was on her way before allowing the other students back inside after lunch. He seemed brusque, but taking care of everyone and their education was his job, and it was obvious he cared about Casey and her family.

Cole flicked a glance at the principal as he spoke. "I'm almost done here. We'll load her onto the stretcher in a minute."

"Is she allergic to anything?" said Zack.

"No food or medication allergies listed in her file," said the principal, his eyes concerned. "We don't know what caused her seizure."

"We're ready," said Cole, as he tucked his penlight back into his med kit. "Pupils are equal and reactive. She's stable enough to transport. We'll monitor her on the ride."

Zack lowered the stretcher and he and Cole worked together to shift Casey onto it, fastened the safety straps, and raised the stretcher. The little girl kept her eyes on Zack. He gave her arm a squeeze of reassurance.

"She'll be at Bellevue Memorial," said Zack to the principal. He turned to Cole as they shouldered their bags. "Let's roll."

The principal once more led the way and activated a button on the wall to open the automatic door. Outside, their audience had grown but remained at a distance on the gravel field.

Zack and Cole loaded Casey into the back of the ambulance and Zack hopped in with her to watch her while they drove. Her chin trembled again with her efforts not to cry. Once more, he squeezed her ankle and shot her a smile. Hopefully, she wouldn't seize again, but if she did, he'd be close at hand. The TA from her class hovered near the door, wringing her hands.

"I'm to meet you at the hospital and stay with her until her parents arrive. I'll take my car." She pointed to a blue sedan.

Zack nodded. As the ambulance rolled out and left the parking lot, the school bell rang, and the onlooking children ran toward the building.

Cole radioed in their report. "Unit Two. Transporting female. Eight years old. No SOB. LOC before we were on the scene, NKDA, coming in Code One. ETA five minutes. Parents called and en route. Code Yellow. Over."

"Copy Unit Two."

As Casey didn't seem in further danger at this time, they left without the wail of sirens until they reached the main streets, where they turned them on to cross busy intersections.

It wasn't until they reached the Emergency Room of Bellevue Memorial without any further seizures and Zack relinquished his patient, that he breathed deeply. Casey should be okay. If she had a previously unknown seizure disorder or epilepsy, going forward, she could be medicated and get the help she needed. Successful saves like this made the job rewarding.

After they dropped her off, they headed back to the dispatch center and the rest of the calls on their twelve-hour shift, grabbing a bite for a late lunch at about 1:30 p.m. between calls.

That afternoon, dealing with what was probably his last patient of the day, Zack revised his earlier opinion. While car accidents had the potential to ruin his day and children were the hardest on his emotions, patients like the current one were the worst.

"When's your shift over?" the thirty-something woman said, stroking his arm.

Zack lowered his arm, making it harder to reach. "Ma'am, you need to remain seated while we check you over. You collapsed at work and fainting can be serious. Your boss was concerned."

"I probably just forgot to eat," she said, waving off his concerns. He clenched his jaw. She remained standing and stepped forward, resting one hand on his chest, and running a finger across his name tag while she leaned in. Ick. "Zack. That's such a strong name."

"What time was your last meal?" He inched backward and tried to keep an even tone while Cole tried to suppress a grin. Cole was middle-aged and a little heavier, though still fit, and seldom a target for flirting. He also made sure to flash his wedding ring near patients like this. These moments made Zack wish he'd taken Val's advice and worn a fake one to work. Some women were ridiculous flirts because he wore a uniform.

"If you're off soon, we could share my next meal," she said, almost purring.

Zack removed her hands and shot a glance at Cole, who smirked.

"Ma'am, please sit. Have you fainted before?" She could have an underlying condition, such as heart trouble. She should take this more seriously.

"No," she said. "There's nothing wrong with me. My manager over-reacted, but I'm glad he did." She batted her eyelashes.

Zack refrained from rolling his eyes as he helped lower her to a chair. She clearly wasn't about to lie back down but he wanted her stationary to answer their questions. Plus, it would be easier to fend off her busy hands. What a waste of time and money. There could be real emergencies elsewhere. Some people didn't consider what else was happening to anyone else. He hoped there were no actual emergencies they should be attending. This woman was annoying. She'd also be on the hook for the bill. Maybe that would make her think twice.

"Any continuing dizziness?"

She huffed out a breath of air. "No." She pouted like a child when he wouldn't engage beyond professional questions.

"What was your water intake like today? Could you be dehydrated?" Her lips were pale and cracked. Low blood sugar and or dehydration was likely the cause of her fainting. "Have you been drinking?"

"Of course I haven't," she snapped. "I'm working." Her eyes narrowed. "Did my boss say I was intoxicated?"

The manager had indicated it was a possibility. It was more likely she was hungover and dehydrated as they hadn't found a problem with her heart or blood pressure. She was also a pain in the ass. Zack glanced at his watch. He couldn't wait to get off and go for a bike ride before picking up something for dinner.

He'd crash by eight as he had three more early shifts before he switched to nights—usually more traffic incidents, overdoses, and victims of violence on those shifts. Still, less annoying than this misguided flirt. She was barking up the wrong tree. His aunt's words about the set-up played in his head. Maybe it wouldn't be all bad because her track record of finding great matches was impeccable. At least he wouldn't have to date someone he met on the job.

# CHAPTER 9
# ANDIE

"Remember, best block, no be there."
–Mr. Miyagi, The Karate Kid (1984)

The blare of Andie's alarm startled her awake with a jolt. Though she couldn't recall setting it, she clicked off the alarm on the odd-looking digital clock beside her bed. It must have come with the rental—perhaps she'd turned it on while cleaning. She yawned. It was Tuesday, but with her leave, she didn't need to be up for work, and her appointment with her lawyer wasn't until four p.m. Without work, that would be a lengthy wait. Maybe she should run—it would kill time.

Daylight seeped in through cracks around the blinds and she lay there for a minute longer. Somehow, she'd survived another harrowing night. The events during the wee hours were a little hazy pre-caffeine. Had Dylan been here? Or had that been a dream?

Andie sighed. She was quite sure the whole door-pounding scene was real. Leaving him had clearly been the right decision. She sat up, rubbed her gritty eyes, and took stock of how she felt. She glanced at the clock again. Less than four hours of sleep. Ouch. She could function on that little for a day or two at most. Experience taught her less than three hours and her heart would gallop, thumping too hard.

She groaned, swinging her bare feet to the floor. Better to run tomorrow, provided she was better rested. This afternoon, she would meet with the lawyer, though she wasn't sure how she'd pay the retainer. Thankfully, today's consultation would be free of charge. She tried to not dwell on the cost if they moved forward.

A peek outside confirmed it was raining—the cold, dismal kind she'd been told settled into the Pacific Northwest in November and sometimes stayed until the end of February. She'd expected better for April—though maybe she shouldn't, there was an expression about April showers. She yawned again, slid into her waiting slippers, and shuffled over to the living room window to check the street through bleary eyes. Dylan's car was gone.

On autopilot, Andie trudged into the kitchen to make tea, leaving it to steep while she hopped in the shower. Refreshed from the soothing heat and steam, she searched for clothes. She found next to nothing in the dresser. Nothing familiar at least. Her forehead tightened as she removed an unfamiliar white T-shirt. She dug in the drawer where half a dozen T-shirts had been stacked. She'd never seen any of them before. In the next drawer, her new jeans were missing. In their place, she found two pairs of faded jeans and a pair of khakis.

What had happened to the clothes she'd unpacked yesterday? The idea Dylan might have come into her house while she slept sent snaking chills cascading down her spine. She reached for her phone on the bedside table to find it missing too. Her stomach roiled at the idea of him lurking while she slept. She'd add this to the list to discuss with her lawyer. If he'd been able to get into her place, she might need to move again—perhaps somewhere with a security system.

She stalked to the kitchen, intending to email her lawyer, but she couldn't find her laptop. She'd been certain she'd left it on the table and had a moment of panic. Everything important was on her laptop, including passwords, her photos, and her writing.

With her jaw clenched, she scanned the kitchen again, not finding the device. Her fists tightened, and she began to sweat. With limited belongings, it should have been easy to locate. She opened a few cupboards—in case she'd stowed it in the wrong place when tired. She ran back to her bedroom to check again. Spinning in a tight circle, her eyes scanning the strange room. Everything looked different. She ran through the list of missing items. Her clothes, the laptop, and her phone as well as the charge cords.

Her chest constricted. Clothes she could purchase again, but a missing laptop was awful. She didn't have the funds to replace it. But the absence of her phone was a catastrophe—it was as essential as another limb or an appendage, like a thumb. What the hell was happening?

Dylan must have been inside and taken her things while she'd slept. Her blood turned to ice and her breath grew ragged. Her vision grew dark at the edges. Recognizing she was letting her emotions take over, and a meltdown was imminent, she stopped. Get a grip, Andie. She closed her eyes and took three deep breaths before starting her search over, moving methodically from room to room retracing her steps from last night. She found no sign of her belongings. They must have been stolen.

Andie peered out the window. The rain had ceased but there was still no sign of Dylan. Perhaps she'd imagined the glow of her phone in the night. Perhaps she left her laptop and phone in her car yesterday after the difficult appointment with Dr. Maeve. She'd come home unsettled and more scattered than usual. She'd spent the evening with books and TV, not using either portable device. She stepped outside into the gray day to investigate.

She reached the curb before she stopped. A lump filled her throat as she spun, turning to look up and down the street. Her used white Civic was nowhere in sight. Had it been moved? Friends had once pranked her mother in high school and moved her car to the back of the building. Andie didn't understand how that could have happened in this case. Who would do that to her now? This seemed odd, even for an angry Dylan.

She frowned, replaying yesterday's events. Had she parked somewhere different and walked home? No. Andie was certain she had parked here and walked inside.

Andie rubbed her temples. Had her car also been stolen? On the verge of tears, she turned toward the house. She scanned further up and down the street to no avail. She couldn't afford to replace the missing possessions. If she'd lost one item, it could be a mistake, but there was no way she'd lost them all. Someone must be messing with her. Everything vanishing simultaneously wasn't coincidental. It must have been Dylan.

A red haze descended and supplied her with a burst of renewed energy. With her jaw set, Andie stormed into the house, slamming the door. The walls shook. Details she hadn't noticed earlier in her single-minded search became clear as she surveyed the interior. On the near side of the living room, an array of packing boxes had been stacked—hadn't she already unpacked her half dozen smaller boxes?

Where had these come from? They weren't hers and she didn't want to open them, unnerved by what she might find. The plot thickened. Was Dylan trying to make her think she'd gone crazy? Or couldn't live without him? Moron.

He could think again. There was nothing he could do to regain her trust. Forgive and forget? He was unhinged. Not a chance. They were done.

Andie flicked on the overhead light and stomped further into the living room, her forehead bunching tighter. She halted, taking in the view. The couch looked almost new without cigarette burns and the crocheted blanket covering was gone. An old tube TV sat on a stand across the room, its rabbit-ear antennae seeming ridiculous and old-fashioned. The convex screen looked warped and tiny, while the unit seemed fat, compared to modern flat-screen TVs. The rotary dial phone on the end table below an unfamiliar lamp was similarly antiquated.

She closed her eyes, backed out of the living room, and turned off the light with shaking hands. Had he taken some items and left props behind? Nonsense. That couldn't be the explanation—even for Dylan, the changes seemed too elaborate and impossible to accomplish while she slept.

Frantic to make sense of the differences, she returned to her tea. Though not a solution, maybe drinking it would help settle her frayed nerves. Now that she was paying attention, the kitchen was no better. The table had all four legs and appeared different than it had last night—more rectangular than square. Plus, it had four chairs instead of two. The yellow curtains she'd installed were gone in favor of pale blue sheer ones. None of these changes made sense either. She squeezed the sides of her head and swallowed a scream. Was she losing her mind?

With her heart racing, Andie checked to see if anything else was different. She looked inside the remainder of the kitchen cabinets. Dishes only and no food. She removed a plate. It had a different pattern than the ones she had brought. She slammed the wooden cupboard.

Next, desperate for something to be the same as when she'd gone to bed, she opened the fridge. Her shoulders slumped. The only contents, a six-pack of bright red Coke and two slices of Hawaiian pizza; typical moving-day fare. She straightened a crumpled receipt from the counter. Someone had bought the pizza yesterday. Where were the groceries she'd purchased?

Knees wobbling, she plunked onto the nearest vinyl-covered chair. Her tea now partially cooled, she picked it up and finished it, taking several calming breaths between sips. Everything in the house was wrong, and she needed an explanation. Maybe she should try to eat, though her appetite had vanished.

Half-heartedly, she checked the pizza—the only food in the house. Without alternatives, pizza would have to do for breakfast. It seemed fine, so she ate half a slice cold, as there was no longer a microwave on the counter. When she couldn't choke down more, she tossed the crust to the plate. She'd have to buy something else.

In her bedroom, Andie grabbed her purse and dug everything out. She sat cross-legged on the bed and flipped open her wallet. At least this wasn't lost. Inside it, she found cash and a credit card from a different bank than her norm. She slid it out, noticing it had her old name, Andie Sterling. She unfolded a yellow piece of paper, discovering a temporary driver's permit which would expire in August. She tossed it aside.

Her purse also contained an unfamiliar ring with three keys, including a strange old car key with no buttons to press and no fob. She pulled out a small dark blue booklet, thinking it might be a passport. Instead, it was a bank book for an account with less than five dollars.

A flash of white in what should have been her empty purse caught her eye. Tucked along one side was an envelope which she removed. The paper gave her goosebumps as she turned it over in her hands. Her name was written on one side in handwriting which seemed almost familiar. She bit her lip, setting the key ring aside on the bedside table to investigate later. Frowning, she tore open the flap of the envelope and removed a single sheet of paper.

*Dear Andie,*

*If I remember correctly, you find this letter after a long sleepless night and a confusing morning. I'm sorry Dylan arrived and scared you to death in the night. You don't deserve the fear and pain he caused. You've had a difficult morning; the contents of your house have changed, your car is gone, and your computer and phone are missing.*

Difficult. No kidding. The morning had her questioning her sanity. Andie's eyes scrolled to the bottom. The note was from Andrea. How did her neighbor know these details? Had she been the one to pull a prank? It didn't seem likely. Andie returned to the mysterious letter, her heart thudding in erratic beats that made her feel unwell.

*There is an explanation for all these changes. I suggest you sit down, if you aren't already, because you are going to have difficulty believing what I am about to tell you. I sent you to my therapist, Dr. Maeve, because she has unconventional means to help people. (Btw, she tucked this letter into your purse for me yesterday.)*

*Please keep an open mind and accept the help being given. Allow her therapy to run its course before you measure its failure or success. When she helped me, I was angry at first, but soon came to see she had method to her madness.*

*Here goes. You're no longer in the year 2033 but in 1985. It is April 16th, and you have traveled back in time. Dr. Maeve granted your wish to escape from Dylan and to live in a simpler time where he'll never find you. Don't ask how I know this; you'll just have to believe me. Life might be simpler in 1985 and could make you happy. Only time will tell.*

*You were a perfect candidate for Dr. Maeve's therapy as you have no close family ties and no one who will miss you for long, though I would have enjoyed getting to know you better and being your neighbor. I'm rooting for you.*

*Be on the lookout for another note. The cash accompanying this one is all you have and the credit card only has a $500 limit. Be thrifty in your spending and best of luck finding a summer job.*

*Take care,*

*—Andrea*

That was the end of the letter. Andie crumpled the paper and threw it at the wall—where it bounced and fell to the floor, landing beside a pair of unfamiliar clunky running shoes. She wanted to tear the note to shreds and scream. Being in 1985 was impossible. She didn't believe in ridiculous notions like time travel, even if she enjoyed reading about it in novels. Besides, wouldn't this qualify as a time slip, not time travel? After all, she couldn't return at will.

She shook her head. Why was she even considering the possibility Dr. Maeve had sent her to the past? It was ludicrous. Even if she did believe it, why would she be sent back to 1985? This whole thing must be a dream. The idea gave her some comfort despite being unlikely. It seemed like she was awake. If she'd truly gone through a time slip, she was terrified. Even with Dylan and all its frantic problems, at least 2033 was a known quantity.

Here, she would never belong.

1985 was her mother's time. It's not like Andie could use this time to understand her mother better, though she'd often envied the straight-forward seeming life of the 80s portrayed in her mother's stories. If Dr. Maeve had this incredible power, why hadn't she just sent Andie to a time before she'd dated Dylan? That would have been safe. Or before she'd abandoned her sister and gone to university twelve years ago? Sometimes she wished her choice then could have been different.

If the therapist could have chosen any time, what was Andie supposed to see or learn in 1985? That was a strange thought she'd have to return to later when she was calmer. Andie propped her chin on her knees, clutching them hard. Not sure why she was entertaining the idea of being in 1985, it brought more questions, including how to prove the date without her phone. She glanced around the room for answers.

She dove for the clunky old box TV on its wooden cabinet. After fumbling with every unfamiliar dial and switch, she managed to turn on a grainy picture with horrible clarity. This was TV? She clicked the largest dial and changed the channel to another with equally poor definition and static-filled sound. She scanned for a remote and, finding none, rotated the knob again.

After twisting the dial clockwise, she found only a dozen channels—two of which were static-filled and without a picture. She located the channel guide on Channel 2. Crouching on her heels, she stared. The numbers and letters with the date and time scrolled across the top of the screen. Tuesday, April 16th, 1985. She slipped back, landing on her ass as her eyes remained fixed on the screen.

This should be impossible.

In 1985 she was alone, without any help. She didn't know anyone. Even if she could get a hold of her, Andie's mother would be thirteen years old. Plus, she lived near Boston, far from Seattle and the West Coast. This had to be a joke—or perhaps a hallucination? It was like *Stranger Things*, minus the kids and the monsters. Was this the Upside Down? Andie stared at the date, her vision blurring. However, there was no way this could be a trick, and everything seemed genuine.

It must be true.

Maybe she should run and ask Andrea about the letter. Demand answers. Andie started for the door, only to pull up short, her hand reaching for the knob. Her stomach bottomed out. In 1985, Andrea probably wouldn't live next door. Forty-eight years ago, she wouldn't have been married yet. Her husband had mentioned they'd been married for forty-seven years. They could have lived anywhere in 1985, separate or together. Plus, how would she explain this to a young Andrea when Andie didn't understand either?

The blood drained from her face. If this was real, not only was she trapped in the past, but she was also on her own. Tears filled her eyes. She'd never felt more alone. Not during her misunderstood and lonely childhood. Not the interminable teenage years taking care of her alcoholic mother and younger sister before university had given her respite. Not the teaching years in the East when she seldom spoke to anyone, other than her students. Not even married to Dylan or the first days after. Here and now, she had no one.

Her jaw flared and her tears evaporated. How dare Dr. Maeve make this decision? She'd taken away Andie's control and set her adrift. If she located the woman, she would demand answers. The question was, how to find her?

Andie closed her eyes and took a deep breath. She would have to rely on herself.

To do that, she'd have to determine more about her surroundings. She glanced at the unpacked boxes. If she opened them, she felt like she'd be admitting she might stay in 1985. Her eyes burned and her stomach clenched. She exhaled. Time to pull herself together. Ten minutes later, with her hair in a tight ponytail and her sneakers on, she returned outside.

At least the rain had slackened in favor of fast-moving billows of dark cloud. She scanned for details she may have missed in her single-minded panic when she'd discovered her car missing. She stood on the sidewalk and spun in a slow circle, taking in the location as she hadn't before. The houses looked newer, with brighter colors, but the neighborhood hadn't changed much, except for one notable difference.

Instead of the beautiful white house next door, there was a gigantic hole in the ground and an active construction site. Her knees wobbled. Andrea didn't live there.

What the hell was Andie going to do in 1985?

# CHAPTER 10
# ANDIE

"E.T. phone home."
–E.T the Extraterrestrial (1982_

Andie stared at the giant muddy hole and stacks of lumber next door. She could cry and feel sorry for herself, or she could deal with the situation in front of her. It didn't matter if she believed in wishes and time slips or not; she wasn't in 2033 anymore. The world was different, and she needed to learn as much as she could about her existence here and now. She would operate as if she believed this ridiculous time travel idea and carry on, for now. She would seek Dr. Maeve in this time, so Andie could demand she be returned to the future.

She spun on her heel and stalked back to her house.

Inside, she collected her new wallet and gave the contents a more thorough inspection. Most of the never-ending membership and points cards she owned were gone. Score one for 1985. Like her credit and bank cards, the name on her temporary driver's license read Andie Sterling. That was something. She ran her fingers over the raised numbers and letters on her cards. She enjoyed having her real name back. Tucked in the wallet, she found three hundred dollars cash. She pursed her lips. That was new. It wasn't much, but it should be enough for essential groceries, so at least she wouldn't starve.

She reached for her phone to look up the location of a nearby grocery store, only to stop. No cell phone. No laptop. No Wi-Fi. She slumped back in her chair. No internet of any kind. In 1985, it wasn't publicly available yet. How was she supposed to find anything? Not having her phone left her even more unsettled than the lack of her wedding ring the first days after she'd left Dylan.

Andie's gaze returned to the squat, black rotary phone in the living room. It sat like a toad, perched on a thick book—some pages were white, others yellow. Her eyes narrowed. How many times had she watched old movies where the protagonists ripped out pages of the phone book for addresses and phone numbers?

Andie moved the clunky corded phone, grabbed the book, and flipped through the flimsy newsprint pages of the directory. She found a section at the back with yellow pages and business listings. There was nothing listed for Dr. Maeve Fossey. Damn. She'd have to think of another approach to find the woman. Chills shot through her. Dr. Maeve might be too young to have a license or be practicing. Then what?

Rather than give in to despair, Andie moved on to the next pressing matter. Next, she looked up grocery stores, discovering one in the same location as the store where she'd shopped last week. At least she knew the route.

Oh. Her car. If her phone and computer had disappeared, a 2026 model of car would also be gone. Perhaps there was a replacement, like the clothes, shoes, and wallet. She raced to the bedroom, scooping up the set of keys from her purse. Marching outside, she examined the car key. It was plain silver with a black hard plastic top emblazoned with the standard H logo.

It was still a Honda key but had no fob. Her heart sank. She couldn't just click it to find her vehicle.

She'd have to do this old-school and try the door locks. There were two Hondas parked nearby on the street. A silver-blue Accord, which seemed to be in decent shape and possibly a newer model, caught her eye; yet, upon closer examination, she noticed all the cars looked strange, with unusually dull paint and unfamiliar, squared-off shapes. The second Honda was a dented sunflower yellow Civic hatchback—probably older than the first.

Holding her breath, Andie walked to the Accord, her purse slung over her shoulder. She would act like she belonged, though she felt like all the neighbors must be lurking in their houses, ready to call the cops because of her suspicious loitering at the curb. Nothing unusual to see while she tried to match the key to the car. She glanced in all directions when the street remained empty, trying the key in the lock.

It didn't go in. Strike one.

She bit her lip, glanced up the street again, and moved to the second car. The curtains twitched in the house across the street. She might have an audience. To the neighbors, had she just appeared? Who did they think lived in the little house she'd rented? Feeling conspicuous, she jiggled the key into the lock. It was tight but fit. She pushed harder and turned.

Through the car window, she spied a metal cylindrical post popping up. Opening the unlocked door, she hopped into the front seat, where she searched the interior for clues about this time. There wasn't much in the car's interior other than three cassette tapes in the glove box. She'd heard of music in this format but had never used them. Their plastic cases rattled when she shook them. She held them in a stack, flipping through the assortment. Tears For Fears' *Songs From the Big Chair,* Cyndi Lauper's *She's So Unusual,* and Bryan Adams' *Reckless.*

Had Dr. Maeve made the selections? It was impossible to know how much power the woman had. Perhaps this was random, or Andie was taking someone else's life. Was she a replacement? She laughed at herself. The idea was too much like fiction. Her breath caught. Dr. Maeve's emerald eyes had seemed like someone with purpose. Andie had to believe there was a reason she'd ended up in 1985. Did the albums have a hidden meaning? Their names were at least familiar though, thanks to her mother, she recognized the artists—though they were not what Andie usually listened to.

She gripped the wheel, taking stock of her discoveries. There were so many questions. She would concentrate on what was in front of her, one thing at a time. She had wheels and the means to get the groceries she needed. Leaning over, she searched for the button to start the car. Nothing.

Right. She spun the key ring on her index finger, then jammed the car key into the ignition and closed the door. She held her breath as she rotated the key and started the engine. As it roared to life, it seemed such an odd way to start the car. After she figured out how to adjust the seat and mirrors manually, she pulled out. Driving the small vehicle felt like operating a go-kart; it was low and the steering stiff.

Not wanting to reach for the cassette tapes, she clicked on the radio, and the station blasted an enthusiastic male voice. She cringed and fumbled with the dials to turn down the volume.

*"And the former number one song slips from fifth to eighth this week on our top twenty countdown."* One of her mom's favorite songs came on—*Can't Fight This Feeling* by R.E.O. Speedwagon. A thrill raced through her. Thanks to her 80s obsessed mother, Andie should recognize a lot of music and movies. The next song was familiar as well, *We Are the World* by U.S.A. for Africa. She'd never heard of the supergroup or the song, but hummed along to the chorus as she drove.

Maybe it wouldn't be horrid to be stranded in 1985, at least for a while. She'd have to view it as an adventure.

At the grocery store, Andie couldn't help but catalog the differences between this time and her own. She didn't need a coin to get a shopping cart; they were loose. Perhaps people were more trusting here in the past. Or fewer carts were stolen. Perhaps homelessness was less of a problem. In her time, the cost of living was so high, the streets overflowed with the homeless with nowhere else to go. She removed a shopping cart from the line outside the door, wheeling it inside.

The grocery store seemed small and dim on first impression—a little run down. She was used to modern, big box grocery stores and this one, with fewer lights and crowded shelves, created a unique, almost quaint atmosphere.

As she shopped, the prices seemed shockingly low at first, about a third the cost of what she was used to paying for bread, cereal, and fruit. Her three hundred dollars might stretch even farther than anticipated. She grabbed a couple of bananas, some apples, and a few vegetables for snacking. She hadn't considered dinners or a list, which wasn't like her. Maybe she'd tour the store and check out her options for what to cook, then make a second pass to fill her cart.

The convenience sizes, pre-packaged cut vegetables, and salads Andie was used to weren't available, but that wasn't a bad thing. Less packaging was better for the environment. The selection of fruit was different as well. The standard apples, oranges, and bananas were there, but no dragon fruit, fresh pineapple, or mangoes. Maybe their availability was seasonal. The middle class of 2033 ate like royalty, and most of them didn't even realize. Like her, they took the fabulous variety at the stores for granted.

The more Andie looked, the bigger the differences were between her version and 1985. No tofu. No gluten-free options. Good thing she wasn't vegan or celiac. If she'd been vegetarian, she would also have to be creative, or have a difficult time finding anything to eat except fruit and vegetables.

In the meat department, she couldn't believe the quantity and variety of cuts of beef. In 2033, the prices of meat were sky-high. She'd seldom been able to afford red meat. Even when she was young, it had been a luxury item. Her mouth watered and her eyes wandered to the other selections. She grimaced. The best price on chicken was for whole or half chickens. None of the pieces were boneless or skinless. She didn't have a clue where she'd start if she had to cut up her own chicken.

After checking the prices, aware she was on a limited budget because she didn't have income, Andie grabbed a couple of packages of cheap ground beef and an "On Sale" tray of pork chops before returning to the produce department for a bag of potatoes, a few tomatoes, a cucumber, lettuce, and a bundle of celery. She added a loaf of whole wheat bread, a few buns, a box of macaroni, another of Hamburger Helper, several cans of Campbell's soup, a package of bacon, and a dozen eggs to her cart. She added a few other items, including tea and sugar, because she couldn't find Stevia.

When Andie arrived at the checkout, instead of a narrow lane and straight counter to place her groceries, she unloaded her wares onto a round disc that rotated toward the cashier. The scanner looked different but seemed to function the same way.

She monitored the running total above the till and was relieved at the end when a week's worth of groceries came to just over fifty dollars. She hesitated when she opened her wallet. Though she had cash, she might need it for other purchases. It was limited, so she handed over her credit card, holding her breath. The cashier grabbed an odd metal and plastic device, inserted Andie's card flat, and shoved something back and forth with a clacking sound.

The woman removed several almost translucent paper slips in a pile with an impression of the credit card numbers. She handed back the card and set down a pen beside Andie.

"Just your autograph, please." The cashier slid across the postcard-sized stack of Visa papers.

Andie stared at the woman for a moment, then gripped the pen too tightly with her sweaty hand. Feeling almost like she was committing fraud, she signed her name at the bottom on a line. The cashier passed her a copy and returned the pen and machine to a shelf underneath the till. The process seemed slow and unwieldy compared to 2033, where Andie either tapped her card or scanned it herself, sometimes on her phone. This process also seemed more personal and accountable. The process might make her pay more attention to what she was spending.

When would she be billed? How would she make money? Paying this way didn't seem smart financially. More questions for another day—the list growing in her mind was becoming unwieldy and distracting.

She turned to collect her grocery bags.

A second cashier had deftly packed the groceries into filmy white plastic bags while Andie paid. With the ban on single-use plastics years ago, she hadn't seen bags like this since she'd been a teenager. She scanned the other two open tills. A bent little old woman with short gray hair in the far lane carried cloth bags with faded flowers that looked homemade.

Maybe she could look for some to buy so she didn't contribute to future landfill problems, even if in 1985 that didn't seem to be common. She added reusable bags to her mental list and pushed onward. Focusing on loading her car, she headed home.

While she'd taken care of business so far this morning, all the changes to everyday things left her shaken. The world was real and so different. The jury was still out on if it was simpler. People who lived through all the rapid changes might be disconcerted sometimes, but for her, it was jarring. Her grandmother had complained from time to time, as had her mother. They'd struggled with technology.

Andie struggled to process the differences. She hoped she could cope with all the changes here. She needed to write a list. That might make everything more manageable.

When Andie parked in front of her house, she spied a woman in a white golf shirt and faded blue jeans sitting on the front stairs of Andie's place. Andie's muscles tensed as she stepped out of her car and the woman stood to greet her. She was terrified she might be called out as a thief.

"Hello," the woman called, trotting out to the curb, speaking before Andie could reply. "You must be Andie. Such an unusual name for a young lady. I'm sorry I missed you earlier. I'm Susan, your landlord. I spoke to your aunt before Easter when she answered an ad and rented the place for you, but I wanted to introduce myself. I didn't like not knowing who was living in my rental property." She gushed, leaving no room for Andie to speak.

Andie's stomach bottomed out. Weeks? She hadn't even met Dr. Maeve at the time she'd planned this time slip. Three weeks ago, Andie was married and living on eggshells, in 2033. This was another thing to add to her list of impossible questions.

Susan stopped talking to breathe.

Andie didn't know how long the silence would last, so she seized the opportunity.

"Hi. Nice to meet you." She shook Susan's hand and collected her bags from the trunk, using the time to calm her shaking hands. She just needed to make it a few more minutes before she broke down. When she gathered her groceries, her new landlord reached in to grab the last few bags.

"Let me carry these for you, dear." Susan followed Andie toward the house, still chatting away, though Andie wasn't listening. Her aunt had rented the house. Susan must mean Dr. Maeve. It seemed the therapist was in this time, and nearby, after all. She would just be younger. Andie filed away the thought. Was there another place to search for the doctor besides the phone book? She'd have to find one. Andie deserved an explanation and, hopefully, a trip back to her own time.

In the house, she set her groceries on the kitchen table and Susan added the final three bags. "Thanks for helping," Andie said. Her stomach growled at the thought of lunch. Could she ask the other woman to leave without seeming rude? Probably not. She'd have to keep chatting, even if she'd rather be alone.

"You're welcome. Oh. Your aunt mentioned you were looking for work and I've got a lead for you. It doesn't pay much, but since I understand you've got a teaching job arranged with that fancy new private school for the fall, this would just be until September."

Andie's head reeled with this new information. Clearly, Dr. Maeve assumed Andie would still be here in the fall. This was just about the last straw. Dr. Maeve had gone too far, but there was nothing Andie could do right now. She would have to watch for paperwork or a contract. There might be something in the still-packed boxes. She added that to her mental list of things to accomplish. Breakdown. Eat. Make a list of questions. Find Dr. Maeve. Unpack.

"That sounds great," said Andie, her tight muscles unclenching. It seemed Dr. Maeve had planned for everything. With this influx of information, anything seemed possible. Perhaps Andie wouldn't have to stress so much about money if she had to stay in this time for longer, even if she'd rather go back to her actual time.

Susan passed her a red business card with the name West Coast Video typed on it. "Call them any afternoon. They should still be hiring." She pulled a slim, flip-style notebook from her back pocket. "Your first month's rent is paid, and I'll write you a receipt before I leave, so you have the correct contact information for me. Your copy will also have your new address in case you need it for something official, though I had the power turned on already since utilities are included. I hope your aunt mentioned the amount. Your next $300 rent is due on the first of May."

Andie nodded, relieved she hadn't spent the cash in her wallet. Unbelievable that $300 would cover rent for an entire house. It wouldn't pay for a room in a shared place in 2033. It also meant she had two weeks until the next installment of her rent was due. Hopefully, in that time, she'd either have returned to the future or have secured employment. She flipped the card over. Video store. Did that mean VHS tapes? In 1985, those weird, clunky tapes and VCRs were new technology. It was a strange thought since, in her time, videos and VCRs were ancient and obsolete.

Susan tore off a piece of paper from her receipt book and handed it to Andie. The landlord's address was across the street. Susan tapped the top with her pen where her phone number was listed. "You need anything or have any trouble, either my husband or I will get back to you right away."

"Thanks." Andie's voice shook. Overwhelmed by the changes, she needed some quiet time to regroup. "I hope you don't mind if I finish putting my groceries away." As much as Susan seemed kind, so much had happened that Andie needed to process. She needed to figure out her next move and eat a proper meal. As if on cue, her stomach gurgled again.

"Don't mind me," said Susan, waving her hand. "Do what you need to do. Make your lunch." She kept chattering about the neighborhood, the weather, and where to find the garbage pick-up schedule.

Andie only half listened as she stowed her purchases in the cupboards. A sandwich would be quick. She left out the bread, ham, cheese, and mustard.

A change in Susan's voice brought Andie back to attention. "If that's all," the older woman said, "I'll let you settle in. Good luck with the job hunt. You'll have to let me know how it pans out."

At Andie's nod, Susan said, "Enjoy your lunch and see you later. I'll let myself out." She smiled and departed, the door banging behind her a few seconds later.

A large breath whooshed out of Andie at the silence that followed. She rotated her shoulders to release the tension. Susan was a fast-talking whirlwind, and Andie had barely kept up with her sleep-deprived brain. Still, the woman had provided solid information and suggested a potential job.

# CHAPTER 11
# ANDIE

"I don't want to sell anything, buy anything, or process anything as a career. I don't want to sell anything bought or processed, or buy anything sold or processed, or process anything sold, bought, or processed, or repair anything sold, bought, or processed."
–Lloyd Dobbler, Say Anything (1989)

Andie ate her sandwich and returned to what she'd been doing. After putting away her groceries and squashing the bags for reuse under the sink, she lifted the archaic phone. She tugged on a long cord that disappeared behind the couch and attached to a plate in the wall. She gave herself enough slack to sit on the couch while she figured out how to dial the number on the business card. The only way to make the numbers move was by sticking her fingertips in the proper number hole, rotating a clear plastic disc around to the end, and releasing it. What a pain.

Twice she messed up with the rotary dial as she got the hang of the odd motion. Gritting her teeth, she started over, getting the numbers correct on the third attempt. No wonder this technology had been replaced. She wasn't sure she'd get used to something so cumbersome.

With the bulky corded receiver pressed against her ear for the call, the phone rang twice on the other end.

"West Coast Video," someone with a masculine voice answered. He sounded bored.

"Um, yes," Andie's tongue grew thick and awkward. "I'm looking for a job." She winced at the abrupt sound of her voice. "I heard you might have an opening."

"Yeah. Bring a resume to this location in Redmond on Saturday. Rick, the boss, should be here between eleven and noon. I'll schedule you for 11:15. What's your name?"

"Andie." She didn't bother providing the spelling.

"See you Saturday."

The line went dead, so she hung up. While she was thrilled to get a chance at a job nearby, the interaction had seemed odd and abrupt.

Today was a Monday, meaning she had a few days to put together a resume, but without a computer, how was she going to type it? Would a handwritten one be acceptable? These questions made her head hurt. Despite her limited funds, maybe she should rent a couple of movies, test a VCR, and investigate what titles were available on VHS—like a scouting mission.

As homework, she could have a movie marathon for the next few days. She could borrow a bunch of the 80s movies she and her mom had watched when she was young. They might make better sense than they had when she was younger. She could put off unpacking the mystery boxes a little longer. She couldn't solve all her problems or return herself to her own time, so instead of dwelling, she would do what she could to fit into this time.

A concrete plan for the afternoon helped. She grinned for the first time since arriving in 1985. Research was important.

Andie threw together a second sandwich. After all, she'd skipped breakfast. While she ate, she checked a map from the back section of the phone book, using it to make a list of directions to drive to the movie store. It appeared close, down a few blocks, along two sides of an extensive park, then across a few more blocks. While close enough to walk, today, she would take the car, since she wanted to rent a VCR and didn't want to carry a heavy machine back.

A summer job would pay for gas and groceries and alleviate some of her worries about limited cash. Still, the low credit card limit meant she had to be careful. She sighed. There would also be rent from June to September that she had to come up with before she received a teaching paycheck—if she remained in 1985. She caught herself. She wanted to go home.

Rather than dwell on the unknown and give herself a headache, Andie hopped in the little yellow car and drove the short distance, finding the video store without difficulty. It seemed odd not to have her phone and its GPS when driving somewhere new, but arriving where she wanted was easier than expected. She just had to pay attention to street names and the route she'd planned.

After parking in front of the strip mall with the video store, she exhaled and wiped her damp palms on her jeans. Unable to see much inside the store's interior, she checked for the hours. The pink neon Open sign glowed in the window and below it, a placard listed the store hours.

West Coast Video had opened at eleven, about fifteen minutes ago. Andie went inside and took a minute to acclimatize herself to the dingy store with glaring fluorescent overhead lights, faded and worn carpet of indeterminate color, and scuffed paint.

A life-size cut-out of Arnold Schwarzenegger as the Terminator took up considerable floor space. Movie posters covered the windows and many of the walls, including sun-faded ones for *Indiana Jones and the Temple of Doom*, *Ghostbusters*, *The Karate Kid*, *Footloose*, and a dozen for unfamiliar 80s action movies with actors she'd never heard of, like Charles Bronson, Chuck Norris, and Michael Dudikoff. Whoever they were. She would have to get used to calling them just movies. She would get odd looks for referring to them as 80s movies.

A boxy TV mounted in the corner near the ceiling played *Star Wars Episode 6: The Return of the Jedi*. Princess Leia had just fallen from her speeder on Endor before meeting her first Ewok. Like all the Star Wars movies, Andie had seen this one at least half a dozen times.

"Can I help you?" A short, roundish young man sprang up from behind the counter. The sound tugged Andie's eyes from the screen. The clerk had greasy hair, which was short and spiky on top, while long and stringy in the back. He wore a thin-lipped smile that didn't reach his eyes. He held a chocolate bar in his hand—perhaps noting her glance, he set it down behind the counter. The young man reminded Andie of a grouchy hobbit, though he was probably too tall to fit the type. She calculated it would be several years before Peter Jackson's *Lord of the Rings*. More than a decade. If she was stuck in 1985, his movies were something to look forward to. Tears pricked her eyes once again.

She blinked them back, then nodded toward the screen. "I like *Episode 6*."

The clerk frowned slightly. "You mean *The Return of the Jedi*?" His know-it-all tone got under her skin.

She nodded, flushing at her obvious error. The original trilogy would be the only Star Wars movies at this time; the prequels and sequels were still years away. Perhaps there was still a way to undo Jar Jar Binks. Maybe he didn't need to exist. Her nervous smile was faint.

"Would I be able to rent a VCR for the next three days?" Her eyes roamed to the sign below the counter listing the prices. A machine rental with two tapes would be $20 for three days. If she rented additional movies, as it was mid-week, they'd be two for $5. She would put it on her credit card. Though money would be tight, she justified this expense as a learning experience.

The young man behind the counter shifted toward the back, shuffling his feet. "You're in luck. We had a machine returned first thing today. Usually, you need a reservation." He shot her a pointed look she couldn't interpret. "We don't have many machines anymore. Most people are buying their own VCRs," he said as he typed something onto the bulky computer on the counter. "Do you have an account?" His flat voice sounded bored, like it had on the phone.

She shook her head. "I'll need to open one of those too, please."

He sighed. "I'll need to see ID and something with your current address."

For a second, Andie panicked, then she remembered the rental receipt in her back pocket and the paper driver's licence in her wallet. She nodded. "I just moved into the area." She hesitated. "How does your store work?"

"Pick out some movies, then I'll ring you up," he said, his attention drifting away from her and back to the movie.

She hesitated, biting her lip.

Perhaps noticing her pause, he sighed. "Grab the tag off the movie box and bring it to the counter. If there's no tag, the movie is rented." His impatience was evident as he returned his gaze to the movie once more.

Andie wandered the store. It was going to be difficult to keep her list to four shows. Perhaps if she watched them all, she could bring them back and restock. Five dollars for two movies seemed impossibly cheap. She paused. Or was it expensive?

She frowned. In her time, streaming services were three times the cost, but for unlimited TV and movies. Still, juggling who was showing what, was difficult to keep track of, so she'd always limited herself to one platform at a time. It didn't matter. Without a job, she'd need another hobby besides watching old movies. Maybe she could find a public library. That wouldn't only be cheap, but free.

Eventually, she stepped up to the counter with her choices, a stack of tags clutched in her hand—the original *Terminator*, *Indiana Jones and the Temple of Doom*, *Sixteen Candles*, and *Footloose*. Molly Ringwald and the movie posters had helped her to decide what to watch first. Her selections were all new to her this time, though she enjoyed rewatching movies. She flicked a glance at the overhead screen. Another time, she might have a Star Wars marathon.

Andie had a moment of panic when he carried out the VCR in a padded case, like a soft suitcase. What if she couldn't figure out how to hook it up to her TV? She hadn't considered that issue until now.

She took a breath. "Does it come with the required adapters and cables?" She had no idea what was needed, nor was she confident she could just figure it out. She already missed the idea of being able to watch a YouTube tutorial.

"I'll throw in a set of instructions," the clerk said, grabbing a laminated piece of paper and slipping it inside the machine case. Though he'd been helpful, everything he did made her feel like her presence was intrusive. What was his problem?

With her fingers drumming on her thigh, Andie paid with her credit card again—the same type of archaic plastic and metal slider making an imprint of the numbers, producing a copy for her to sign. She was shocked at how insecure it all seemed. Anyone could steal a card and use it without a PIN—maybe for any amount, unlike a tap. Did anyone even check the signatures? How would they know it was her card?

She lugged the heavy machine out to her car and loaded it in the trunk before retracing her route home to watch movies. While today had been messy and unnerving, the evening was looking brighter.

# Chapter 12
# Andie

"No one can stand being alone. The minute you stop thinking there's
someone out there for you, it's over, you know."
–Keith, Some Kind of Wonderful (1987)

Andie awoke to the sun streaming in around the edges of the bedroom
curtains of her 1985 room. She'd slept in later than she had in ages. In part,
it must have been because she'd stayed up late watching movies. It wouldn't
have hurt to pace herself more, but with little to occupy her brain, movies
had felt comforting. She glanced toward the wall where, if she had a phone
and charger, it would be plugged in. Still nothing.

An unexpected and odd thrill raced through her at the prospect of
another day, safe in 1985. She stretched luxuriously in bed, feeling better
rested than at any time since she'd left Dylan. Perhaps knowing he couldn't
find her had enabled her to get a proper rest.

By the time she ambled into the kitchen for tea and breakfast, it was
10:00 a.m.

After munching on a piece of toast, she jammed her feet into her
running shoes and headed out. She jogged toward the nearby park with the
trail she'd discovered on the far side. The unpaved trail wound through an
upscale neighborhood, which seemed like a safe place for a woman to run
alone.

It took a while for her muscles to warm up, perhaps because it seemed
peculiar to run without her AirPods and music. Perhaps she should check

into what alternative there was available in this time for portable music. In a movie last night, a character had headphones with a tape box on their hip. She sighed. Something like that would probably cost too much money.

Despite the lack of music, once she hit her rhythm, she seemed more in tune with her body and her surroundings. She enjoyed the surrounding birdsong, something she'd likely missed out on before. Maybe she could get used to running this way.

Andie ran perhaps three or four miles out, though without her phone she couldn't track her distance or the number of steps she'd taken. She would need to get a wristwatch so she could monitor the time, if not the distance. She didn't miss all the tracking devices and reminders to use apps for everything.

Exercise would also help her sleep. She'd have to be sure to make running a regular part of her routine this spring and summer. She hadn't run much since moving to the Seattle area, but prior to that, she'd always been a runner, finding it cleared her head more than most activities. Her brain was a busy place, and she often needed a respite.

She slowed to a brisk walk, catching her breath and considering her options. If she went further, she might not have the energy to run back, so she turned around to return home. By the time she neared home, sweat dripped from her forehead and her legs felt rubbery, but the strenuous workout left her exhilarated. She gave one last push, sprinting the last hundred yards towards the edge of the park.

Andie dropped to a jog once more before the crosswalk, her legs shaking. Without warning, a boat-like navy-blue muscle car screeched around the corner, thundering onto the street by the park. As it roared past, the car blasted its horn, and Andie stumbled. For an instant, the driver's profile resembled Dylan, but with long poofy 80s hair.

Off-balance and unable to wrest her eyes from the car barreling up the street, she crashed, falling toward the pavement. Time slowed as she smashed onto the asphalt, making a jarring impact with both hands and both knees. Pain shot through her hands, knees, arms, and shoulders. She sucked in a breath as she tried not to burst into tears.

Perhaps winded or in shock, she remained on all fours at the edge of the street for a couple of seconds, unable to move. She tried to stand and took a deep breath. The sound of a bicycle bell ringing jolted her out of her frozen state. First faint, then louder. At first, it seemed the cyclist might hit her. She scrambled out of the way to assess her injuries.

Back on the sidewalk, her knees shook as she fought the tears. Bright red blood streamed down her legs from both knees. One shredded knee contained tiny bits of gravel, and both burned with a fiery sensation that spread. She'd also scraped both hands—the right considerably more than the left, which was scuffed with a few bloody punctures. A larger patch on her right hand looked deeper and openly bled instead of oozing. She squeezed her hand into a painful fist to slow the bleeding.

The slowing cyclist passed, and Andie dropped her gaze. She stared at her injured hands as her ears roared. Why couldn't she move? In the distance came a hissing, scraping sound.

"That looked like a nasty fall. Can I help?" The man on the bike had stopped. The noise had been his brakes. Her brain seemed to have trouble processing the world.

Her face flamed as she met his gaze—his pale blue eyes intent as he waited for her answer. Not that she didn't appreciate the help, but of all the times for someone to stop. She looked like an extra from *The Walking Dead*. She blinked a few times and swallowed as she looked away, afraid her tears would erupt and scare him.

Andie took a shuddering breath as she stared at the cracked sidewalk, her throat aching from the effort not to sob. "Thanks for stopping. I'm such a klutz. I live close by, so please don't worry about me." Despite her intentions to sound okay, her voice shook.

While avoiding his gaze, she checked for traffic and, with the street empty, she crossed with several limping steps. She grit her teeth and continued along the far sidewalk, turning onto her street. Tears welled up in her eyes anew. Every footstep hurt. She cradled her right hand with the back of her left, pulling it closer to her chest. What a mess. She glanced toward the blue sky as if searching for answers and opened her hands again.

"Those scrapes look deep. Do you have disinfectant at home?" The man's concerned voice remained nearby. He was pushing his bike just behind where she walked. She'd concentrated so hard on getting home, she hadn't noticed he'd followed.

Andie shook her head. "I just moved in. All I have is soap and water." It would have to do. She wasn't going out for bandages until she changed out of her damp, sticky running clothes and showered. Plus, she didn't have any money with her—no Apple Pay in this time and her wallet was at home. She snuck another peek at the man with his bike.

He was tall, slim, and broad-shouldered. His dark wavy hair also wasn't tucked into a biking helmet. Clearly, they hadn't yet enacted helmet laws. Would she ever be able to switch off the part of her brain that cataloged all the differences between this time and her own?

"My sister lives near here. Why don't we go to her place for first aid? I should check those cuts." The man remained nearby. While she appreciated his concern, she just wanted to get cleaned up at home. Then stay there. Forever.

"That's a kind offer, but I think I'll just go home." She sounded ungrateful for his offer of help, but she was in a lot of pain. She glanced down. The tops of her socks had turned dark red, soaked with blood, which continued to course downward. Her lip trembled. Below one wrecked knee, a piece of skin flapped over a swath that looked raw, like something had grated her skin. She averted her gaze and kept hobbling, both knees and shins hurting even worse than her pride.

"Wait a second," he said, scrambling to get ahead of her. "Please let me help."

She stopped and gave him a thorough stare. He didn't look like a creep, but neither had Dylan.

His pale blue eyes twinkled, probably because of her long appraising look. "My sister's place is so close, and she has a proper first-aid kit. I gave it to her as a Christmas gift the year before last." His voice took on an authoritative note that somehow made Andie less off-balance. "I'm a paramedic and I can't let you go home without looking at those gashes. You might need stitches."

Andie paled. She couldn't afford a trip to the hospital. In this time and place, that could be awkward and outrageously expensive. She didn't have insurance in 1985. She shoved the thought down. Rather than spill that information, she kept her mouth pressed flat, so she didn't overshare with another stranger.

"Okay." Her words came out blunt and cold, but she didn't have the energy for polite chit-chat.

His slight frown shifted to a friendly smile, softening it into a kind face that made her feel safe. "Val lives three houses over." He pointed to an attractive yellow house with white shutters. "Can you make it that far?"

She nodded, hobbling along the sidewalk, wincing with every step. This was her street, but her place was at the opposite end. Good thing his sister lived a couple of blocks closer than Andie's house. She wasn't sure how much further her wobbly legs would take her. She wanted to get off her feet.

When they reached their destination, he parked his bike, looping the chain lock around the bottom railing of the front stairs. "Don't worry. If Val's not home, I have a key."

He stayed beside her on the short flight of stairs, supporting her upper arm and giving her a boost when she faltered just before the top step. Instinct and experience made her suspicious of his nice guy behavior. This might be a bad idea. She considered turning back, but he seemed harmless.

The man knocked on the front door, but without waiting for an answer, he unlocked it. He nudged it open with his shoulder and poked his head inside. "Val, you home?"

His voice echoed in the empty hall. There was no answer. He opened the door wider and entered, flicking on a light in the front hall.

"You can sit here," he said, patting a bench inside the door for putting on shoes. "You should get off your feet. Wait here. I'll be right back."

He bounded upstairs while Andie stepped inside, awkward at being in someone's house when they weren't home. The house smelled clean and had the same basic layout as hers, though it was two stories. In typical 80s fashion, oak trim decorated the globe-like light fixtures and spindles on the stairs. Warm, pre-LED incandescent lights reflected off the light-colored blocks of tile that made up the flooring. Soothing hues of light brown and sky blue decorated the entryway and living room.

Gingerly, she sat on the padded wooden bench and leaned back against the wall, closing her eyes. She concentrated on slowing her breathing. From above, a cupboard banged, then another.

She opened her eyes as the man returned, skipping alternate stairs on the way down. He carried a folded towel and a white box under his arm. This must be legit. Her shoulders released an infinitesimal amount.

"I'm sorry I've been so rude," she said. "I appreciate your help."

He smiled, lighting up the entryway to his sister's house. "I'm just glad you're okay." He hesitated and gave her a direct look. "It isn't any of my business, but you looked startled by the car. Maybe even scared. Did you know the driver?"

Andie shook her head. He must have seen the accident from further away. "He resembled someone I used to know, but it wasn't him." She clamped her mouth shut. She'd said enough. Besides, she didn't want to talk about Dylan, and it would be impossible to explain being in the wrong time.

"By the way, I'm Andie. With an 'ie,'" she said, the need to clarify bubbling from within as he set down the white metal box with the red cross logo on the floor.

"Andie's an unusual name for a girl," he said with a flash of a smile as he lifted supplies from the medical kit, preparing to set to work on her wounds.

She drew a blank about what else was safe to say about her name. She couldn't mention the character from *Pretty in Pink* as she had when she'd introduced herself to Andrea, as it would be released in 1986, and the reference wouldn't make sense. Andie didn't want him to think she was delusional.

"I'm Zack," he said, as he stood up. "Soap and water are actually the best place to start with cleaning you up. A couple of these cuts are deep. Maybe I should just take you to the ER." He waited for her answer. "We could borrow Val's car once she gets back."

Andie shook her head. "My insurance doesn't start until September." She said, hoping it was true. She bit her bottom lip at the concerning thought. A hot stab of pain radiated from the place her tooth had touched.

She found the place with one finger. It tingled. Right in the middle of her bottom lip, a raised patch of tiny blisters had formed. In a few hours, her whole lip might become a swollen mass.

Injuries all over and fever blisters on her lip. She was going to have a huge cold sore. Part of her wanted to sink into the floor and disappear. Her day had sucked so far, other than meeting the gorgeous paramedic. She prodded below her lip, noting where it seemed numb. The blisters hadn't reached the stage yet where she'd feel the odd tingling sensation in other places. Fever blisters played havoc with the nerves of her face, and in 1985, she didn't have prescription medication or a way to obtain any. With the latest discovery, her day had gotten so much worse, despite the wonderful run.

Soon she'd be hideous. At least once her knees were patched up, she could go home. Maybe tonight would be perfect for another movie, followed by a week of hiding while she read books until the worst of everything passed. She would talk to a pharmacist about something topical for her lip and delay dropping off her resume until the cold sores had passed.

But money was so tight, she couldn't afford to be vain. She needed to organize the job as soon as possible. Not knowing how to find Dr. Maeve meant Andie might be here a while, and it was difficult to live without money.

"I'll be right back," Zack said. "Cleaning those cuts and scrapes might hurt like hell."

Andie met his blue eyes again and her stomach flipped. What was wrong with her? This wasn't the time to be attracted to anyone. She didn't belong here. "They already do." Her truthful words surprised her—so much for trying to be tough, but she didn't have the energy to mask.

Zack returned with a bowl of soapy water and a dry cloth. He spread the navy-blue towel on the tiled floor, she lifted her feet, and he slid the towel underneath. He gently lifted her left leg, holding her calf. Thank goodness she'd shaved her legs last night. His large hands were warm. She tried to focus on her injuries rather than the sensation of his hands. This shouldn't be sexy.

"It looks like the bleeding has mostly stopped on this one." He wet the cloth and squeezed water onto her leg, washing away the worst of the blood.

Zack did this several times before washing the scrapes more directly with the damp cloth, blotting her wounded leg to remove most of the dirt. He used a set of tweezers to remove several additional pieces of gravel embedded in her wound.

After he finished, he changed the water and repeated the process on the right. She clenched her jaw and suffered through the painful cleaning. Before he finished, he trimmed the loose flap of skin from below her mangled right knee.

Andie sucked in her breath at the sting.

"I'd leave the flap, but if it traps dirt inside, I worry there will be more chance of infection than having the skin open to the air." With a featherlight touch, Zack slathered clear ointment on both knees and the rest of the scrapes. She glanced at the tube. Neosporin—much like the Polysporin in her medical cabinet at home. Or had been in 2033. She'd bought it for emergencies, though she'd never skinned her knees so severely as this, not even as a child.

Perhaps noticing her interest, he said, "It's just antibiotic ointment."

She nodded. He seemed capable. The right knee continued to weep from the rawest scrape, even through the Neosporin. He laid a non-stick pad on her wound, then taped on a thick chunk of gauze and a covering bandage. "I think you should try leaving the other one open to the air. It'll heal faster and isn't as likely to leak. It should scab over nicely." He winked. "Barring further accidents."

Her cheeks warmed. "I'm thinking next time I run, I should wind myself in bubble wrap first," she said, wincing at the road rash mess of her uncovered legs. The wounds would leave scars.

He laughed, his eyes crinkling at the corners. His easy-going presence kept her relaxed. He looked like someone who laughed often.

"Let's see those hands too." She spread them out in front of her. Dealing with them was quicker, but still painful. He trimmed the loose skin on her right palm, applied more ointment, and bandaged that one, too.

Zack was cleaning up his mess when the front door opened, and a woman with long, dark hair entered carrying several heavy-looking bags. She was slim like Zack and had similar pale blue eyes—the chestnut hair and blue-eyed combination striking, even more so with the few long silver threads streaking her hair. This must be his sister, Val.

"Zack," she said, her face lighting up. Her eyes flicked toward Andie. "I see you found a use for my first aid kit, after all." She filed past toward the kitchen with her load of groceries. Over her shoulder, she called, "Back in a sec." She returned empty-handed a minute later, leaning against the doorframe of the opening leading to the kitchen. "Do you need anything else? It looks like you're nearly done."

"I didn't think you'd mind if we used your place to patch her up," he said. "This is my new friend Andie. She was running and tumbled off a curb, about a block and a half from here. She was kind of a mess, so I figured this was the closest place to tend her injuries." He turned to Andie. "This is my sister, Val."

Andie pasted on her polite smile, holding up her bandaged hand. "I'd shake your hand, but it would hurt too much right now."

"Did my brother at least get you something for the pain? Like Tylenol?" Val raised her eyebrow.

Andie shook her head. "He's been great, though. If he hadn't stopped on his bike, I'd have hobbled home still bleeding and be crying alone in my kitchen about now." She snuck a peek at him to see how he took her statement.

He winked.

Val groped inside her purse, removed a travel-size container, and produced two tablets for Andie. Val ducked into the kitchen, returning in no time with a tall glass of water.

Andie took it and swallowed the tablets. Thirsty from her run, she drained the rest.

"Don't let her fool you," Zack said to his sister. "She's been a trooper. It was a gnarly fall. I give it a solid ten."

"I bet I know what we all need," said Val, tilting her head to one side. "Lunch. Then tea and homemade cookies."

Andie's stomach growled. Despite the kind offer, she didn't want to overstay her welcome or be a burden. They must have had plans. She'd taken enough of Zack's time today. "I appreciate the invitation, but I should get home." She got to her feet. Her rubbery legs wobbled.

"On no," said Val, stepping forward. "Stay and eat here. Please." She clasped her hands together and appealed to her brother. "You'll stay. Right?"

Zack nodded. "I'll even help make lunch. I make a mean BLT."

Val smiled at Andie, infusing it with warmth. "He's never turned down free food in his life. My plan this afternoon was to make soup and sandwiches, then bake cookies." When Andie hesitated, Val continued. "It's no trouble and I'd love the company. I have homemade soup in the freezer and can whip up the rest in no time. I love to have people to feed."

"It's okay," Andie said, stepping toward the front door. She didn't want to impose on her neighbor. She flexed her legs, one at a time, swinging one, then the other. Both knees still stung with fiery pain. The unscraped portion of her knees had turned pale purple with dark red blotches. No surprise. She'd landed hard enough to give herself bruises to go with the cuts and scrapes. When she took another step, the room spun. She thrust her hand to the wall to support herself, closing her eyes.

"She would love to stay and eat," said Zack, his voice close as he wrapped an arm around her waist for support. A slight crease appeared between his brows. "You okay?"

"I just got up too quickly," she said. "Head rush. I'm fine." She didn't feel fine, but she would power through.

Andie should be annoyed at his invasion of her personal space, but she wasn't. His arm seemed like it belonged, and his assistance seemed like genuine concern. She reminded herself he was a paramedic. His concern for her was that of a medical professional, not personal, and she couldn't help the surge of disappointment. Despite her physical attraction to Zack, she sensed no trace of another agenda from him. She also couldn't summon the energy to be annoyed at his presumption. Someone looking after her was a pleasant change.

"If I'm not mistaken, you're my new neighbor," said Val, directing her gaze back to Andie. "Aren't you? You moved into the rental house at the end of the block and have a little yellow car." Val smiled, perhaps at Andie's nod and for connecting the dots. "I was certain you looked familiar."

Zack grinned. "Then you're going to be my neighbor, too." His smile widened as he stepped away, taking his warmth and support. Andie was surprised to find she wished he'd stayed. Still, the dizziness had passed.

She quirked an eyebrow toward him. He lived here too. She hadn't gotten that impression earlier. Wasn't this his sister's place?

He must have seen her puzzled look. "I'm building a house on the lot next to yours, though it will be a while before it's ready for me to move in."

Score another point for 1985. She might get to see more of Zack.

# CHAPTER 13
# ANDIE

C-3PO: "Sir, the possibility of successfully navigating an asteroid field is approximately 3,720 to 1."
Han Solo: "Never tell me the odds."
–The Empire Strikes Back (1980)

After delicious BLTs on fresh bread, Andie watched the siblings interact as Val whipped up the promised batch of chocolate chip cookies in her warm, inviting kitchen. The scent of melted chocolate mingled with the lingering background smell of bacon.

Andie perched on a stool at the island near the action. The humorous scene of sibling teasing in front of her keeping her mind off the pain from her fall, mostly. Heat burned in her cheeks at the reminder of the embarrassing incident. She hadn't had such a fall since she'd wiped out on her bike at thirteen and rolled down an embankment. That time she'd limped home and patched herself up.

"Zack," said Val, her tone one of exasperation.

Andie's lip twitched. Zack kept stealing chocolate, two or three chips at a time. Never from the package, but always picking them out of the batter. He'd wait until Val's hands were busy and covered in cookie dough as she spooned globs onto the baking sheet or turned to set the timer.

She swatted at his hand with the spoon, missing, though she'd hit him once before. Andie winced, the last time Val had made contact had Andie anxious to figure out if the siblings were joking or serious. She couldn't imagine smacking her younger sister's hand, but they'd had an unconventional relationship, one which had ended in their teens.

Though apart from the fun, she enjoyed their antics even if it reminded her of how alone she was; she felt more like an observer than a participant. Andie had been away from her sister for a long time, and they'd never had this type of easy, teasing relationship. She longed to be part of their group one day.

"Zack. Stop it." Val's voice sounded irritated, but her eyes danced. She must like the challenge. She missed smacking his fingers for the third time in a row and rolled her eyes. "Do you have siblings?"

Andie shook her head. "Yes, and no." She seldom spoke about Jess, but now seemed like the proper time. "I have a sister, but I left home a long time ago, and we lost track of each other. When my mom passed two years ago, I only found out because I came across the obituary. I tried to reach out to my sister, but none of her contact information was current." She kept the tremor from her voice that often went with talking about her family. She'd already resigned herself to her sister's absence, after all, it was Andie's fault they weren't closer as she was the one who'd left.

She glanced at Val's face. Something about the look in her neighbor's eyes encouraged Andie to share more. "It's been more than ten years since I've seen Jess." She swallowed. Would they judge her? She watched their faces for clues to their reaction.

"I can't imagine not seeing my family." Zack's face had become serious.

"I can." Val sighed and faced her brother. "It would be so peaceful." She turned to Andie. "All joking aside, I'm sorry. Not knowing where your sister is must be difficult and lonely."

With Andie's move across the country, then her name change, Jess faced an impossible task to find her, especially given Andie wasn't even living in the same year now. If Andie returned to her time, she would make it her mission to find out what had happened to her younger sister. If she was trapped here, she might never know. That line of thinking was too dark to contemplate right now, so she pushed it from her mind.

The creak of the oven door returned her to the present.

The scent of crispy butter, sugar, and melted chocolate filled the air as Val removed one cookie sheet from the oven and slid another onto the rack. Andie missed baking. It used to be something she did on Saturday afternoons to relax. She hadn't had the leisure to bake since getting together with Dylan. Between her job and his political events, there'd been no time. That was something she could change now she was here.

"Do you have other siblings?" she asked in return, focusing on a more pleasant topic. "Or is it just the two of you?"

To Andie's surprise, Zack and Val laughed and shared a conspiratorial look.

"Not only do we have siblings, but we also have double cousins about our age," said Zack.

"Double cousins?" said Andie.

"Our mom and her sister married brothers, which means all the cousins have the same grandparents on both sides," said Zack. "That makes us double cousins."

"Not only that, we are the alphabet family and Zack's the youngest," said Val. "Everyone in our dad's family has a specific letter for their first name, running through the alphabet in order, and we finished it."

"Alphabet family?" said Andie. "That sounds interesting." She'd met a couple of families where everyone had names with the same letter, but not a large group with twenty-six names in a row. A bunch of siblings and close cousins sounded like quite the family. Her family gatherings had always been small. Her immediate family and the odd great-aunt or second cousin. Nobody close. She'd never met her father or anyone from his family, even if she'd Googled them a few times.

"Val is the oldest of our generation. The next is Wanda. Then there's Xander, our sister Yolanda, and me." Zack reached for another clump of dough filled with chocolate and Val stopped him with a spatula rap to the knuckles.

"What happens if you have children? Do you have to restart the alphabet?" Their names sounded like they belonged in the Bridgerton series, but Andie couldn't say that. The romance novels hadn't been written yet, let alone the TV series. The Sue Grafton alphabet mysteries might be older, but the series wouldn't go back this far either. She'd borrowed several of those from her mom's bookshelf in her teens.

"If you two ended up together," said Val, "You could use any letters you like because you're already A to Z." Val was busy making a third tray of cookies, setting it near the oven—out of Zack's long-armed reach. Perhaps she didn't realize the significance of what she'd said.

Andie's face warmed, and she shot Zack a glance, but he wasn't paying attention. Once more, he seemed intent on the cookie dough, his hand hovering close enough to pilfer more chocolate chips as Val turned to lift her first batch from the cookie sheet onto the cooling rack.

Zack popped some chocolate into his mouth with a devilish grin.

Val sighed and picked up the bag of chocolate chips. She shook another handful into the batter, stirred, and picked up her spoon to make the last round of cookies while the second batch baked.

"You take more, and I won't send any cookies home with you." She shook her rubber spatula in his direction. This time, her irritation seemed genuine. Perhaps she'd had enough.

Zack stuffed his hands behind his back, as though to remove temptation. "That's all you had to say." He shook his head and stage-whispered to Andie. "She plays dirty. Hitting below the belt like that. Nobody who smells applesauce chocolate chip cookies baking could resist." He sighed and stared at the fresh-baked cookies like a puppy waiting for a treat.

"Fine. Go ahead," said Val. "The ones on the rack are fair game. Dig in." She picked up one of the baked goodies and bit into it. Her eyes fluttered closed. "Melted chocolate is the best."

Zack grabbed two and ate them in quick succession while Andie nibbled one in small bites, savoring the combination of cinnamon and chocolate. The cookies were soft and had a texture like cake, probably from the applesauce. She couldn't remember the last time she'd eaten warm, fresh cookies. They were amazing, so she helped herself to a second.

Val packed half a dozen cookies into a Ziploc bag and left the top partly open. She passed the package to her brother. "Shouldn't you be going?"

He glanced at his wristwatch. "Shit. Yes. I have a shift at four. Thanks for the reminder. I lost track of time." His eyes flicked to Andie and her cheeks flamed again.

Andie had been here for a couple of hours, much longer than expected. "I'm going to head home, too." Despite her care, her lip, knees, and hands still hurt with a throbbing heat. She'd need more Tylenol in a couple of hours and should stock up on bandages and supplies from the pharmacy.

"You don't have to leave," said Val. "Your cookies are the next batch."

Andie hesitated. "They're delicious," she said. "But you don't have to give me more. I ate a couple already."

Val shook her head. "You'll be saving me from eating them all. I made a double batch so I could share."

"You're okay to get home?" said Zack from the hall by the door. "No more dizziness."

Andie slid off the stool and moved to see him out. "I'm good. Food helped. Thanks again for picking me up and patching my wounds."

"What was I going to do, ignore you while you bled on the sidewalk?" said Zack. "Not a chance." He glanced at his watch and then at the door. "Hey. Can I stop by your place on Saturday?" He lowered his voice. "Maybe we can go to a movie or something."

Andie's face flushed, and her tongue tied in knots. It would be fun but might not ideal if this was meant as a date. She fumbled for words to express she wasn't ready and had just gone through a nasty breakup, but the silence lingered too long. This was complicated.

The tension became awkward, and she glanced at the floor. If she was in 1985, was she still married? Dylan hadn't even been born. Of course, she might leave soon if she found Dr. Maeve. She'd searched the house for the special rock and come up empty. She might need a different wishing rock.

She'd taken too long to answer. "I like movies," Andie said at last, her voice half strangled while she stared at Zack's shoes.

"I want to watch a movie too," said Val, moving up beside Andie. Val shot her brother a look Andie couldn't interpret.

He must have received her message, though. "Of course. All three of us. Saturday. See you two later. I'll check the movie listings in the paper on

Friday and let you know what's playing." He left, banging the door closed as he exited.

Andie exhaled. She almost grabbed for her phone to check the listings. Some habits were harder than others to break, and not depending on her phone was the worst. When she was used to having information at her fingertips, patience was difficult.

"He's a terrific guy," said Val, "But I ran into Susan just after your aunt rented your place for you. I guess your aunt mentioned to her you'd just gotten out of a relationship. I hope you don't mind my interference. My brother might not appreciate me third-wheeling, but if I come, it removes the pressure."

Andie grimaced, thinking of Dr. Maeve, who must be the mysterious "aunt." "My aunt is a meddler. But since I panicked and froze when Zack asked, you made it easier. Thanks." They returned to the kitchen and Andie slid back on her stool while Val bustled around, tidying up the baking ingredients. "I hope my aunt didn't tell all my secrets for Susan to spread around the neighborhood." She was certain Dr. Maeve wouldn't mention crazy ideas like time travel, but she barely knew the woman. She had no clue what her "aunt" might have shared.

"Oh, nothing like that," said Val. "I planned to bake welcome-to-the-neighborhood cookies and drop them off at your place this afternoon. While I've lived here for years, my closest friend moved to Europe for work, and I hoped to make a friend again nearby. I planned to invite myself in for tea and get to know you." She grinned, reminding Andie of Zack. "Imagine my surprise when I came home from buying ingredients to find you already here, being doctored by my favorite brother."

Andie didn't know what to say at first. "It would be nice to have a friend who lives close."

"Two friends," said Val as she readied a second to-go container filled with cookies. "If I read my brother right, he likes you. He's not usually one for dating either. I'm surprised he asked you out."

The feel of Zack's warm hands and an image appeared in her mind, of his blue eyes twinkling as he teased his sister. A date one day soon sounded... fun.

"Is there anything else you need to settle in?" said Val. "I can show you the best places to walk and if you need anything else for your house, I'll help you shop."

"Actually," said Andie, trying not to bite her tingling lip. "I wondered if you have a typewriter. It's a long shot, but I wanted to type my resume and drop it off somewhere Susan mentioned. I need a summer job, since my teaching position doesn't start until September."

"I'm a teacher too," said Val, stopping with a direct stare for Andie. "I teach fourth grade. You?"

"Fifth, usually," said Andie. It seemed she and Val had a lot in common.

"The typewriter part is easy," said Val, picking up Andie's earlier question. "I have an electric one in the basement, but I'll bring it up and dust it off. Why don't you come back Friday afternoon and you can type your stuff then. We can decide together on a movie and out-vote my brother." She hesitated, glancing down at Andie's knees. "Maybe you'd like to go for a walk on Friday, too. Now that it's spring, it's lovely. I could use a new walking partner. I promise, not only will it be good exercise, but it'll be safer than running."

"I'd love that," said Andie with a smile. It was more than an offer of a walk, but an overture of friendship. She would see where it led.

•   •   •

Saturday morning arrived and with it, more torrential rain. Andie winced as she checked her front window. Outside was dismal and gray. The trees tossed their branches, and the wind rattled the glass panes with gusts of wind from the west—a perfect day for hanging out at the movie theater. When Andie had returned Val's empty cookie container yesterday, she'd typed her resume as planned and they'd chosen a movie for Saturday at three p.m. They'd also walked along a path lined by cherry trees trailing pink petals like snow. It had been gorgeous.

Though Val was more than a decade older than her, Andie discovered they had a lot of similarities. Val was both an avid reader and a teacher. She also hated a hectic life and was a devout baker and walker. Spending time with her new friend was easy, and so much different than most friends Andie had met before. Val was authentic, which allowed Andie to be herself as well.

The movie they'd chosen was one Andie had seen once years ago, but not on the big screen. Val had a crush on the actor, Judd Nelson, and Zack had been convinced to watch the movie they'd chosen—*The Breakfast Club*. Andie remembered a story she'd read years ago about Judd Nelson being a method actor. He'd gone undercover at a high school and hung out with troubled teens much like that of his character in the movie. His performance as the burgeoning criminal was so convincing, it upset the director, who wanted him to stay away from the young and impressionable Molly Ringwald, who was only sixteen during filming.

Andie touched up the medication on her lower lip, dabbing some onto her cold sore. She'd talked to the pharmacist on Wednesday afternoon after lunch with Val and Zack. The pharmacist had suggested taking antihistamines to keep the swelling in her lip to a minimum and guided her to a topical gel which stung like fury when applied but seemed as effective as anything she might have used in the future. She couldn't wait for the sore to be gone.

Though her cold sores still made her self-conscious, they were common enough most people didn't stare. People didn't have time to worry about how a stranger looks, and Andie was fine with that. She hated attention. Andie picked up the page with her resume and slid it into a protective plastic cover as she headed to the video store, braving the nasty weather. She also had the VCR to return, plus her second set of rental movies that included the original version of *Ghostbusters* and *The Karate Kid*.

She'd watched the 2020s TV series, Cobra Kai, in high school with some of the same characters as *The Karate Kid*, set over thirty years after the original movie. Because of that, she found herself more sympathetic to the young Johnny Laurence than was probably intended. In this movie, he was the villain. Even with that change, there was something comforting about watching movies which connected to her original time.

Andie drove the few blocks and parked. Flipping up her jacket's hood, she unloaded quickly. She shivered as the wind whipped her bare legs, making her wish she hadn't worn a skirt after all. She'd chosen it so her sore knees wouldn't rub against her jeans. The more serious one had broken open several times this week and required daily dressing changes. Thanks to Zack's expert care, nothing seemed infected, just sore.

Once under the store awning, she took a deep breath and smoothed the stray hair that had escaped her ponytail before picking up the VCR case again and heading into the store. She'd arrived a couple of minutes early, but it was too cold and wet to wait on the sidewalk. Better early than late.

Once inside, she set the machine on the floor at the end of the counter and deposited the movies on the counter. The same unfriendly young man who'd worked both times she'd chosen shows was here again. His eyes didn't leave the screen where, once again, *Return of the Jedi* was playing. Still, he couldn't be all bad if he loved Star Wars.

"Hello," she said, clearing her throat. "Is Rick here? I'm a little early, but we have an appointment."

The clerk didn't answer aloud. Instead, he slithered off his stool, maintaining eye contact with the overhead TV. He walked backward to stand beside one of the bookcases filled with rows of video cassettes and yelled. "Hey, Rick. There's someone here to see you."

A thick, burly man emerged from a back room carrying a large, covered tumbler. Old food stains sprinkled the front of his worn gray shirt, and he stumbled across the carpeted floor. Though only eleven a.m., something about his deliberate manner suggested he was well on his way to being drunk. A look she was familiar with, after growing up in her mother's household. What was in his cup? Probably not coffee. He didn't smell like alcohol. Vodka? The choice of many closet drinkers.

"I'm Andie," she said. "I called a few days ago about a summer job." She kept her eyes on his face, watching for how he would react. Given her past, alcoholics got her guard up—even possible ones.

"I didn't expect you to be a chick with a name like Andie." His gaze traveled up, then down, giving her a greasy feeling. She disliked him on sight and would keep her distance. Still, she needed to make money and with only temporary ID and no other leads, this job would have to do. For now.

She smiled, pasting it on to seem friendly but not flirtatious. "Here's my resume." She passed him the paper she'd typed at Val's. It had taken several attempts and her new friend's formatting assistance to make it look right. While working on it, Andie had secretly lamented the absence of her laptop with its high-speed printer. She'd also wished for the online job applications she was used to. It seemed computers here were still too expensive for most homes. Long ago, her mother had mentioned her family had owned one by the time she'd finished high school in 1990. So, computers would soon spread everywhere.

Rick barely glanced at the resume and set it on the counter. "You're pretty and here on time." She clenched her jaw at the mention of her looks. What did her appearance have to do with her job performance? He glanced at his watch. "Five minutes early." His red-streaked bleary eyes looked her over again, and he took a swig of the mystery contents of his travel mug. Some of the neon pink liquid splashed onto his chin. He swiped it away with the back of his hand. Charming. "Can you start training on Monday? We need someone right away."

"Yes." The sooner the better.

"Do you have experience using a computer?" Why didn't he read her resume? She'd mentioned keyboard skills, data entry, and the use of computers.

"Not the system you probably use, but yes, I've used a computer." She spoke with confidence. She probably had a hundred times the experience he had, but it would take time to adjust to the limited abilities of 1980s technology.

"We'll train you this week. Nate here wants fewer evening shifts and I'm not available most nights. Are you good with working five or six shifts per week? Sundays off?"

She nodded, hoping Rick wouldn't be here while she worked.

"You'll have to run the store on your own, though sometimes I stop by on Friday and Saturday nights during the pre and post-dinner rush. If it's busy, I might help for an hour or so."

She'd prefer working alone, but she couldn't chance offending him. "I understand. Thank you. What time should I come in for training on Monday?"

"11:00. You can help Nate open and get the lay of the land." He turned toward Nate. "If you want time off to practice with your band, cooperate and train her properly. You hear?"

Nate met first her gaze, then Rick's. "Yes, boss."

"I'll be here at 11:00. Thanks again. I'm looking forward to working here for the summer." It wasn't a total lie—she was looking forward to having income and she'd like being around so many movies. She nodded toward Nate. "Have a nice day. See you Monday."

She left, both sets of eyes drilling into her as she stepped out into the buffeting wind which pelted her with icy drops of water. A shiver ran down her spine as she climbed into her car and drove away.

# CHAPTER 14
## ANDIE

"Screws fall out all the time, the world is an imperfect place."
-John Bender, The Breakfast Club (1985)

On Saturday at two-thirty, Andie peeked outside when a silver sedan honked outside her house. Must be Zack. Like all the cars in this time, his had sharp edges and square corners that looked odd. Would she get used to the dozens of all the tiny details that jarred as different? At least until she returned to her time, of course. She shoved her feet into her sneakers, grabbed her jacket and purse, and headed out to meet Zack and Val for the movie. Butterflies swooped around her insides as much as if it were a proper date and not just friends. No matter who it was, talking to someone new wasn't easy.

Val had already claimed shotgun while Zack sat in the driver's seat, but she jumped out of the low two-door vehicle and snapped the seat forward for Andie. Good. She exhaled. She wouldn't have to feel awkward sitting next to Zack in the front. Andie had expected to make small talk, something even more difficult. She slid into the back seat and groped for the seat belt, finding only a lap belt without a shoulder harness. She clicked it together and adjusted the strap.

"Thanks again for picking me up. I've wanted to see this movie at the theater for a long time." She bit her tongue. Why did everything she say sound awkward?

Val spun in her seat after she'd resettled in the passenger seat, her poofy hair bouncing. "You must have seen the previews at the theater for another movie. I read a review in the paper. I think the show is aimed at a slightly younger audience than we are, but it's supposed to be rad."

"I just like movies," said Zack. "All sorts. I know nothing about this one." He shot Andie a friendly smile, which had the butterflies back in action. Something about him made her pulse race. It wasn't just he was broad-shouldered and fit. He exuded a quality which made her feel safe and calm, her anxiety melting away. She wasn't used to that when she was around other people. Usually, she remained on guard.

Andie leaned against the cold vinyl backseat. She couldn't let on *The Breakfast Club* became a classic—required viewing for teenagers, as were most of the John Hughes flicks. It would be fun to see it again, especially on a big screen. Somewhere far across the country, would her mother watch it too? Or perhaps she was too young.

Maybe Andie could relate to her mother better if she experienced some of the same things her mother had growing up. The usual deep well of anger, which thoughts of her mother brought, threatened to overflow. Or maybe it wouldn't. In this time, her mother was just a teenager and not deserving of these negative feelings.

When they reached the theater, one of the biggest surprises was the marquee facing the parking lot listed only two movies—four showings for each title, at three, five, seven, and nine p.m. on weekends. On weekdays, only two evening shows existed. Andie was used to places with ten screens or more and movies running all day, every day. This seemed so much more moderate.

Besides *The Breakfast Club*, the second movie playing was *Mask*, starring Cher. While Andie had heard of the pop icon, she hadn't seen her movies. Her fingers itched for her phone to look up Cher and check what other shows she'd starred in. Could she ask Zack and Val how to get more information without giving away that she didn't belong? They might think she was stupid. Perhaps she could just check out the movie boxes at the video store when she started work. She fidgeted with her seatbelt, at last unclipping the stiff buckle and hopping out.

Andie sighed. Without the internet, she needed another way to find out all the things she wanted to learn. She hated not knowing anything.

When they reached the sidewalk near the theater, Zack hurried ahead and held the door open for a pair of little old ladies with clunky purses and pastel sweaters. One got her umbrella stuck on the door frame, and he untangled it for her with a heart-stopping smile.

"Thank you, young man," the old woman said, heading into the cinema. Her friend patted his arm on the way past as she followed.

Andie's gaze lingered on them. They didn't look like John Hughes fans, but you never knew. In Andie's imagination, her grandmothers would have been like those two. Maybe the old women were best friends and had been bridge partners for fifty years. Or secretly were lovers. That must have happened in the past, even if being openly gay or lesbian hadn't been common until much later. On the other side of the glass door, they continued across the lobby.

"Earth to Andie," said Val, giving Andie's shoulder a nudge. "Where'd you go?"

Andie smiled when the old women made a beeline for the concession. "Just making up stories."

"Are you a writer?"

Andy nodded, glancing sideways at Val.

"That's so cool. If you need me to read anything to give feedback, let me know." Her offer seemed sincere.

"Thank you. I might take you up on that," said Andie.

Val tucked her arm through Andie's.

Andie didn't cringe or pull away as she often would have in the past as they strolled across the parking lot. In fact, the feeling of camaraderie filled her with a sense of belonging she had rarely felt, so she enjoyed the sensation as they entered the theater.

"I just dabble with writing," said Andie. She should write more now, since she wasn't teaching—she had time. She'd be surprised if working at the video store would be as exhausting as teaching. As much as she enjoyed working with her students, the constant barrage of noisy children left her drained. She sighed. She wasn't sure how she'd keep track of her documents without a computer. Notebooks perhaps? Another 1985 challenge.

For a time that had seemed idyllic on TV, it wasn't living up to its billing as simple. Teaching would be weird without devices for the students, too. They must spend so much time writing. She might ask Val for tips closer to September. Part of her looked forward to overcoming these unforeseen minor complications.

"What kind of stories do you write?" Zack must have been listening as she and Val caught up at the entrance.

"Fantasy," Andie said, prepared for the typical look of surprise or disinterest.

"Like David Eddings and Raymond Feist?" He quirked an eyebrow and his eyes lit up.

She froze. Those names meant nothing. "I haven't read those." None of her favorites, like V.E. Schwab, Rebecca Yarros, or Sarah J. Maas would exist.

"I can lend you mine or you can check them out at the library," Zack said. "They're my favorite fantasy writers. I'd start with the *Rift War Saga* or the *Belgariad*."

"Thanks," she said, once more adding the library to her mental list of places to visit. Tomorrow. At the last second, an old series she'd borrowed from her mom's bookshelves came to mind. "I like *The Dragonriders of Pern*." She'd read them and the related Harper Hall trilogy half a dozen times, her favorite being *Dragonsinger*.

He smiled. "Those are good too. Would you consider them fantasy or sci-fi?"

"Both," she said. "Dragons are fantasy, but they're on another planet, so that's science fiction."

"Correct," he said with an approving nod. "Plus, the time travel aspect could be either."

"If you two are done with your book club, let's go in." The side of Val's mouth twitched.

Once inside the main lobby, the familiar scent of buttery movie popcorn filled the air. Andie inhaled, filling her lungs with the amazing aroma, making her mouth water. She'd never been able to afford the theater growing up, but there had been times she had attended with friends' families. Those had been some of her favorite childhood memories.

As a teenager, she'd had fewer friends, and movie invitations became rare. It was hard to be close to others when she couldn't bring them home—to their dump of an apartment. She also hadn't trusted her mother's erratic behavior to be appropriate. Sometimes she'd seemed friendly and energetic. Other times, she'd been surly and rude.

In recent years, Andie had only gone to a movie theater every year or two. She wracked her brain for the last title she'd seen. Perhaps the latest Mad Max. She always felt conspicuous sitting on her own, as if advertising she didn't have friends.

"I love movie popcorn," said Zack, striding toward the counter. He rubbed his hands together. "My treat."

Val and Andie exchanged grins and followed.

"Two large popcorns." Zack turned to them. "With butter?"

"Absolutely," said Val. A crease appeared between her eyebrows. "Do you think two tubs are enough?"

Zack laughed. "I figured we could share two between the three of us. If we run out, I'll sacrifice myself to get the free refill." He turned to Andie and repeated his question. "Butter?"

"Yes, please." Andie's eyes widened as the cashier with enormous fluffy blonde hair filled two giant buckets. 1985 sizes were also larger and a free refill? Unheard of. Nothing in 2033 was free.

The attendant punched in the order on her register. She looked up, snapping her gum. "You want drinks with that?"

Andie's gaze swung to the concession prices—they were cheaper now, too. She was used to gouging movie prices, and she seldom ordered anything except water, but here, sodas were listed under the heading "Pop" and were only $1.50 for a regular drink.

"I'll buy the drinks," she said, wanting to chip in because friends took turns. She was sick of holding herself apart—in this time and her own.

"Nope. I'm buying," said Zack, blocking her from the counter by spreading out his arms. "Cokes?" He glanced over his shoulder.

At Andie's nod, he placed the order. "Three Cokes."

"You're okay with new Coke, sir?" the cashier said.

Zack shook his head. "Regular Coke, please."

The youth shook her head, her giant bangs swaying. It was difficult not to watch the girl's hair. It stood upright in front, like a solid wall over her forehead. "I'm sorry, sir. We only have the new formula now."

"Guess we'll take new Coke then." Zack grimaced like it might be poison.

What was new Coke? Hadn't Coke been around forever? Andie kept her mouth shut on the issue, so she didn't expose her ignorance. While waiting for the snacks to be ready, she tabulated the total cost of their trip to the theater.

$3.00 per movie ticket, three $1.50 drinks, and two large popcorns for $2.50. It almost took her breath away. The three of them, with everything included, cost less than twenty dollars in total. With no snacks, she was quite certain she'd paid that much for her last movie for the ticket alone. Even adjusting for inflation, 2033 prices seemed excessive. No wonder she hadn't gone to the theater more. Still, she'd be making a whopping three dollars per hour at the video store. She'd need a lot of hours to pay for essentials.

Collecting their popcorn and drinks, the three of them headed for Theater One.

Inside, Andie stumbled at the sight of the bright velvety-purple rows of tiny seats. There were so many more than the large recliner chairs she was used to, with close to half filled.

"I want to sit near the middle," said Val. "That okay?" Her gaze turned to Andie, who nodded.

They had their choice of seats, so at only five foot two, Andie was glad she didn't have to sit behind someone tall. Val filed into the row first, then Andie, with Zack at the rear. They settled on a three-person gap between two couples in the row ahead on one side and groups of teenage girls on the other. Andie hoped nobody came to sit in front of them. The three of them sat and stared at the empty screen, waiting for the movie to start while crunching their popcorn.

Zack and Val each held a bucket with Andie sandwiched between them. She fidgeted in her seat, trying to find a comfortable position so she could sit without her feet dangling—a hazard of being petite. With nothing on the screen, the silence stretched, becoming awkward.

Andie pitched her voice low as she tried out a joke. "Looks like I get to share popcorn with both of you. This is a great deal." She reached for a handful of popcorn with each hand.

Val snorted. "Good luck. I'll probably hoover half of this one by the time the previews are over. You're better off sharing with Zack."

Previews? It was the second time they'd used that word, and it took Andie a second to process. They must mean trailers for upcoming movies.

"I'll share," said Zack, holding the bucket closer to Andie. "Val always hogs the popcorn. Have as much as you want. Remember, I can get more if we run out."

Val flipped him a middle finger and kept crunching.

"Thanks again for bringing me," Andie said. "It's a real treat. I haven't been to a theater in years, even if I watch a lot of movies." Her voice had a wistful tone she hadn't meant to share.

"No problem. With your teaching job not starting until the fall, it seemed like the least I could do." Zack angled himself in his seat to face her slightly while holding the popcorn steady.

"I got a job today," she said. "At a video store." It didn't sound like it would be glamorous, but at least it would help pay the bills. "I'm pretty much full-time for the summer."

"That's fantastic," he said. "Must be a relief not to worry about earning money until your fall job." He tossed a couple of fluffy bits of popcorn into his mouth.

Andie's chest constricted. Teaching would be different without computers, devices, and the internet. She would need to adjust her process, assuming she was still here in September.

Zack and Andie reached into the popcorn tub at the same time. When their hands met, a zing shot through her at the contact. His startling pale gaze met hers as he withdrew his hand. She could swear his eyes twinkled.

"Ladies first." He let her scoop a handful of popcorn before he dove in again. Before their next handfuls, the overhead lights dimmed and the purple curtain rose, uncovering the movie screen. The upcoming movies included a couple she'd love to see, including *St. Elmo's Fire* with many of the same actors as *The Breakfast Club*.

The next preview made her heart race.

Opening in July was *Back to the Future*—another classic, one that took on additional meaning, considering her last week. She held her breath through the entire trailer. She'd always wanted to see that one.

"That one looks totally rad," said Zack, whispering in Andie's ear, his breath warm on her cheek. A flush of heat spread downward. She was in so much trouble. She couldn't help being attracted to Zack, but it didn't seem smart to get involved with someone in the wrong time. It would go nowhere if she got back to her future.

Still, she couldn't help responding as she nodded. "Michael J. Fox is awesome."

"Standing date?" In the low light, she caught a gleam from Zack's eyes. Andie glanced toward Val, who sat munching popcorn, her expression transfixed by the third preview, a James Bond movie Andie had never heard of called *A View to A Kill*.

"Val too, if you'd like," said Zack, his gaze flicking to his sister. Andie couldn't read how he felt about the idea of another group outing.

Val shrugged. "I'll come if you want me to, but I won't be insulted if you want to go on your own. I'm more interested in the new Bond." She nodded at the screen and the ongoing chase scene with a different Bond than Andie was used to. This one looked old and frumpy compared to the slick modern one.

Suddenly, Andie wasn't sure why she'd been worried about going on a date with Zack. When sitting next to him in the darkness of the movie theater, he didn't seem intimidating. "I'm in." She swallowed. "Either way." Probably not prudent, but she didn't care. She was single, and Zack seemed nice. Plus, it would be pleasant to have something to look forward to if she was stuck in 1985. It wasn't like she was promising anything besides a date to a movie.

The idea of being stuck here wasn't so terrible, but she missed the comfort of the familiarity of her time. She still hadn't figured out how to search for Dr. Maeve Fossey since she hadn't been listed in the phone book.

Andie made up her mind. She would drive to the doctor's former address tomorrow. There was a slim chance the woman already worked at that location, even if it was a long shot.

Andie glanced at Val and then at Zack. It might not be so awful to be stuck in this time—at least for a while.

Zack's grin widened. He leaned closer and whispered. "I knew I'd wear you down."

Andie's stomach fluttered. To cover her wave of nerves, she grabbed another handful of popcorn, eating one piece at a time, and she focused her gaze on the screen as the movie started. Soon, she was immersed in the story. Not only was the movie better than she'd remembered, but the music was terrific. Maybe she'd need to buy another tape with the soundtrack once she had additional funds.

After the show, Zack dropped off Val first. Val checked with Andie as she got out of the car, raising an eyebrow in inquiry. Andie nodded. She'd be fine.

"I'll call you about dinner one day this week," said Val to Andie. "Maybe we can meet on Tuesday or Wednesday afternoon after I get home from work? By then you should know your schedule. You can tell me about your job and your writing." She turned to her brother. "Bye Zack. Have a good night."

Zack waited until his sister entered her house after unlocking the door and waving goodbye, before he drove away. Further up the block, he parked behind Andie's yellow car and stopped the engine. She wanted to invite him in, but the words froze on her tongue. Andie wanted to hang out some more. She'd had a fun time at the movie and didn't want it to end. Still, she didn't want to give him the wrong impression. She cracked a couple of knuckles as he flipped the front seat forward so she could escape the backseat.

She reached for the door handle. "Thanks for inviting me. I had a great time."

Zack ran his hands through his wavy brown hair. "When does your video job start?"

"I'm training on the computer system on Monday." Her heart pounded.

"Any idea what your schedule will be? I work four days, four nights, then have four days off." He touched her hand, still on the upright seat, warmth shooting through her at the unexpected contact. "Maybe we could do something before that other movie in July."

"I think I'll be working most afternoons and evenings. I'll have Sundays off."

He rubbed the back of his neck. "Would it be okay if I called you?" His voice lowered. "If I don't want to wait a whole week to talk."

"I'd like that." She paused. "Oh. I don't remember my new number yet. Would you like to come in and get it? It's written beside the phone." She wasn't used to sharing contact information this way. The phantom limb of her phone still plagued her every move.

He smiled. "I didn't want to make a big deal of it, but I thought maybe I could check your wounds. I notice you've still got the worst one bandaged, so I assume no ER meant no doctor check-in either."

She nodded. "Let's go." She reached for the handle again and exited the car. Zack leaned over, locked her door before getting out, and slammed his with a bang that made her jump.

Andie remained aware of him on the way to the door and inside. He kept his hands in his pockets and when she removed her shoes inside, he followed her example. She appreciated he didn't comment on the stack of boxes at the side of the living room. She still needed to get to those.

She grabbed the notepad and pen from beside her phone, copied her number on a slip of paper, and handed it to Zack. His smile took her breath away when he folded it in half and put it in his pocket.

"Let's look at those scrapes."

Andie sat on the couch and pulled the hem of her skirt aside while he crouched in front of her, his manner shifting from friendly to professional.

He lifted her left leg and examined the road rash. "This side looks like it's healing well. I'd guess no long-term scarring even if they'll take a while to fade." His finger traced the edges. "The scabs are good."

She lowered her leg and lifted the other, wincing. "It's probably time to change the dressing on this one." She'd left it uncovered at night, keeping a towel on her bed so she didn't ruin her sheets. The rest of the time, she had it bandaged. It still hurt.

Zack peeled the tape from the bandage on two sides, pulling it back to look. "This is still a mess." His intense gaze met hers.

She shrugged at his frank assessment. "It still bleeds and oozes every day. I try to keep the Neosporin on it or Vaseline, so it doesn't crack, but it weeps anyway. I bought gauze, the non-stick pads, and tape like you used. They're on the kitchen table."

He collected her first aid supplies, then resettled in front of her and poked at the reddened edges of the wound. She sucked in her breath at the contact. "No sign of infection. It's just deep. Do you have a doctor you can check in with? Maybe get a second opinion."

She shook her head. "I haven't lived in the Seattle area for long. I was back East before that."

"What brought you to the West Coast? The teaching job?" He slathered more Neosporin on her raw knee.

"That was a separate arrangement, but I came because I needed a change." Even if she didn't mention the timing or Dylan, it was still true. After university, she hadn't known what to do with herself. She'd taken an extra year to get her teaching certificate and found a job right away. Teaching had occupied her time, but she had felt desperately lonely outside of work—years with oceans of spare time. She'd felt adrift and started to write, though she'd given it up once Dylan monopolized her time.

The low-key West Coast Video job was a bonus that would hopefully keep the past from repeating. She'd be sure to use the time for her interests.

Dylan and the move had come along as a chance to do something different, to reinvent herself. While the relationship had been a bust, moving here had given her a fresh start. Not 1985 fresh, but new geography where she could try again. Another positive thing to result from this shift to the past, was it had given her a chance to make friends and be less alone.

Zack changed the dressing using her supply and re-taped the bandage. His hands were warm and gentle.

"Can I give you a tour of my soon-to-be house?" he said, surprising her with his change of subject as he stood. Perhaps he sensed she didn't want to talk about her past.

"I'd love to see it," she said, gathering the soiled bandage and throwing it into the trash on her way toward the door.

They put their shoes on and headed outside once more. The rain clouds had cleared, leaving a cool breeze and crisp spring air. Andie shivered and zipped her hoodie. It shouldn't be dark until nearly eight p.m., so they had time to wander his site. Knowing what the finished house looked like from 2033 gave her a different perspective. Usually, a foundation and concrete-covered hole wouldn't be enough to help her visualize the final construction. A surge of satisfaction filled her. The house would be beautiful and one day, Andrea would live there.

# CHAPTER 15
# ZACK

Harry Burns: "Would you like to have dinner?... Just friends."
Sally Albright: "I thought you didn't believe men and women could be
friends."
Harry Burns: "When did I say that?"
Sally Albright: "On the ride to New York."
Harry Burns: "No, no, no, I never said that... Yes, that's right, they can't be
friends. Unless both of them are involved with other people, then they
can... This is an amendment to the earlier rule."
–When Harry Met Sally (1989)

Zack watched as Andie gazed from the sidewalk at his future house.

"Who designed your house?" It was just the excavated hole with its concrete foundation and chunks of metal rebar poking upward. She turned toward him, her face alight with interest.

Zack pictured how it would appear to someone who hadn't seen the blueprints. The site didn't look like much yet, just a muddy pit with some concrete, still in forms while it cured.

"My cousin Xander," said Zack. "He's a contractor and has his own business. This is the first full house he designed, though." What was he doing? Zack had never brought women to his place, but he couldn't seem to help himself around Andie. He kept getting in deeper despite his intention to play it cool. This crazy want pervaded every interaction. Something about her called to him, leaving him aching to know her better.

Of course, that thinking would lead to disaster and heartbreak. He wouldn't go there. It might be easier to decide she was off limits.

They filed onto the property along the temporary wooden walkway through the mud. A faint scent of lemon and vanilla trailed after her. He exhaled, trying to remove the last trace from his lungs.

"We're just waiting a couple of weeks for the concrete to harden before the crew moves on to the next phase." There was no hint of desire in his voice, and he was proud of locking it down. Still, walking around together at night wasn't making it easier. Why had he asked Andie to see the house site? The answer hit like an anvil—to spend more time with her. First the movie, then he'd asked for her phone number. Now this. It had to stop. He didn't want a girlfriend to break his heart.

"Soon they'll strip the forms and start the studs for the walls. Then you'll be able to see the bones of the house." He kept his comments strictly about the construction.

"That must be so exciting," she said. "Seeing it from the beginning and watching your house become a home." She shivered as she turned toward him.

Zack slipped off his lined jean jacket and wrapped it around her shoulders over her thin sweatshirt. Due to their size difference, his jacket engulfed her, making her look small and in need of protection. She smiled up at him and his heart almost slammed to a halt. A tight panicky heat rose in his throat. It would be so easy to kiss her, but he didn't do girlfriends.

The question remained. Was he already leading her on? Did she think he wanted to be more than friends? He would need to be clear before he headed home to his quiet and uncomplicated apartment that he wasn't looking for a romantic relationship.

He walked behind her, ready to catch her if she slipped off the wood, but she balanced with no problem, keeping her sneakers clean. Andie was the kind of woman he could lose his mind over—smart, fun, and beautiful. Too much potential for heartbreak. The image of his father—lost and broken without Zack's mom flashed through his mind. Love brought pain.

Wandering the site with Andie, questions continued to loop through his mind. Was asking out this attractive young woman a way to evade Aunt

M.'s machinations? Not entirely. He found Andie attractive in her own right. Zack enjoyed her quiet demeanor, her unexpected sharp comments, which made him laugh, and the hum of electricity buzzing between them. He hadn't felt that attraction in years, if ever. Was something wrong with him? Shouldn't he want this feeling?

When they reached the edge of the construction, he pointed out sections of the future house. "This will be the kitchen over here. Over there, the dining room. The master bedroom will be on the main floor and there will be three more upstairs." He pictured the plans and outlined the rest of the living space. Unbidden, the image of Andie in his kitchen, in his bed, watching TV with him passed through his mind.

"That's a lot of house just for you," she said, tucking her hair behind her ear. "Are you planning to sell it when you're finished?"

He followed her slight movement and swallowed, hoping his feelings remained hidden. "I don't know," he said, surprised he'd admitted his uncertainty. He had a habit of forgetting to be cautious around Andie. The whole time he'd baited Val when she was baking earlier this week, he'd watched Andie. Something about her had made him want to flirt and get her to laugh. He'd wanted her to feel included and be happy. Oh god. He was already half in love, and they'd just met.

Tonight, they walked around the edge of the foundation, staying far enough back from the pit they wouldn't slip. "This section with the curved concrete will be a sitting room on the main floor and a library on the second." Xander had designed built-in bookcases on the house side and a bay window with a window seat along the curve. Zack shared these details, too, pride welling up as they toured. The house would be stunning.

"I've always wanted a library," she said, her brown eyes shining. "Your house sounds like it will be beautiful." They took a few more steps before her voice resumed. "Your library will be in a turret, like for a castle."

Surprised at the delight in her image, he laughed. "Much smaller scale than a castle." Despite his laugh, he enjoyed her imagination. He'd originally thought Xander's plan was overly grandiose, but perhaps a library wasn't such a wild idea after all. Her excitement made the plan more real, and he enjoyed sharing the details more than expected.

Without warning, Zack's breathing grew constricted, like a vice clamping his chest. Was he showing this to her because he hoped she should be a permanent fixture in his life? He needed to slow his roll.

He swallowed. "Look, I'm sorry if I came on too strong today. I don't know what got into me. I'm not looking for a girlfriend." He shot her a sideways glance, hoping he wouldn't make her upset. He hated tears. "Maybe we can be friends." Though the word hung in the air between them, he longed to cross the new chasm between them, take her in his arms and kiss her senseless.

She bit her lip and stopped, staring back toward the street. Had he offended her? Her shoulders dropped. Was it defeat or relief? "I'd like that," she said at last, turning back toward him. "I don't know how long I'm staying here, anyway. My lease is month-to-month."

Despite his previous declaration, disappointment furled through him like smoke. "What about your teaching job? The one starting in September?" His voice came out rougher than he'd intended.

She shrugged. "I took the job, but I don't know anything about the school. I have no idea if they'll be interested in me long-term. Besides, I haven't been on the West Coast long and I'm not sure I'll stay." Her gaze turned toward her place, and her downcast eyes looked sad. There was something mysterious about her answer that called to him. He wanted to solve her puzzle and bring back her smile.

Zack tamped down the traitorous thoughts as a further wave of disappointment broke over him and he stumbled. Why would he push away someone like her? Aunt M.'s choice couldn't be better than Andie, even with all her soulmate talk. Maybe Xander would have some insight. Most guys didn't talk about their feelings too often, but his cousin was engaged to a wonderful woman, and he wanted Zack to be happy, too. It would be better than asking his sisters for advice. They'd just tease him, tell him to get over it, and the next thing he knew, he'd be dating someone they chose. Plus, he had a feeling, even though they'd just met, Val would be pro-Andie.

They finished up at the site and he walked her back to her door, his hands once more jammed deep in his pockets so he couldn't change his mind and do something foolish, like kiss her after all.

"Goodnight." She returned his jacket, unlocked her door, and disappeared inside.

Once the door closed behind her, he was sorry their evening had ended. Zack took a deep breath, spun, and left, more confused than ever.

•  •  •

Monday afternoon, Zack and Xander sat overlooking the ocean from the pub window, watching the gray clouds hugging the water. More infernal rain on the way. This was the wettest, most dismal spring on record, and it was wreaking havoc with Zack's mood. They'd ordered and were sipping drinks while they waited for their lunch.

"What's the timeline for the walls being up on the house?" said Zack, swivelling his Coke half a turn on its coaster. He'd asked his cousin to meet for lunch but hadn't dared to bring up the real reason he wanted to talk.

"You in a hurry to have it built all of a sudden?" said Xander, leaning back in his chair. "Do you have an interested buyer already? I thought you were going to wait and see how the house turned out." His tone hinted at disappointment.

Zack shook his head. "I am waiting." He adjusted his drink again. Why was it so hard to ask for advice? He cleared his throat. "So. There's someone I like, and I can't decide what to do," he said, flicking an eye toward Xander. If his cousin laughed, he'd punch him. Well, he'd drop the subject like a hot potato and resume bottling up his feelings—as most men did.

"She hot?" Xander's flippant comment made him seem shallow, though he was probably fishing for information.

Zack shrugged. "I enjoy talking to her."

"So, keep talking. Why do you have to stress? They're just words." Xander was so helpful.

Maybe Zack should have kept his mouth shut. He glanced up. "Is it dating if we just hang out?"

"You kiss her?" Xander made smooching noises. His cousin wasn't making this any easier. Zack almost gave up on the conversation, but he didn't have anyone else to talk to.

"No." The sudden image of Andie's full pink lips gave Zack bad ideas. He shifted in his seat. Talking to Xander had been a rotten idea.

"We should do lunch more often." Xander took a long drink of his beer and sighed. He met Zack's eyes over the top of his glass. "You could fuck her. See if you suit one another."

Zack sliced the air with his hand, hard and sharp. "No," he growled. "Why do you have to make this about sex? She's just nice." And ridiculously smart and awkward—and impossible to get off his mind.

"Sorry. I was being a dick. Is she the one who bailed off the sidewalk last week, and you patched her up?" Xander's smile disappeared. He must know he'd pushed the teasing too far.

Zack lifted his drink and sipped. "That's the one." He sighed, staring at the boats docked at the nearby marina as they bobbed along the floating pier. What if Aunt M. was correct about soulmates? Maybe there was someone out there meant for him.

"It shouldn't be this hard, dude," said Xander. "What's the worst that happens? You hang out, decide she's not that great, and stop calling. That's the usual pattern."

Zack's heart sank. That had been the pattern. It sucked.

"She's also Val's new buddy. If it doesn't work out, I might wreck that, too."

"Na. That's not on you. Val can befriend whoever she wants. But you're still going to end up seeing this woman if she turns into Val's new bestie." Xander laughed. "You're screwed. Damned if you do and damned if you don't. Good luck."

Zack covered his face with both hands and groaned. This shouldn't be so difficult.

"I've never seen you like this before. What's the real problem?" said Xander. "You aren't still worried about Aunt M.'s set-up, are you? Like this girl will get in the way?"

"Maybe," said Zack, drawing the word out. "Aunt M. is always right. What if the girl she's chosen is the one and I'm not available because I like Andie? She set up you and Cindy."

"Has Aunt M. given you a name? Has someone called?" Xander wiggled his eyebrows.

"No." The pressure in Zack's chest lessened. Good point. Perhaps it had just been an idea or suggestion, even if it had seemed like more.

"Then don't worry about it. Either the chick she had in mind doesn't want to call you or Aunt M. got her wires crossed. She can't *always* be right. At her age, she might forget stuff or get something wrong."

"How old do you think she is, anyway?" Zack had always wondered.

Xander shrugged. "My mom mentioned M. has always looked the same—for as long as she's known your dad and his aunt. Like forty years. She's our grandfather's sister, right? It sounds like she's always been quirky."

Zack frowned, his forehead tight. "So, she must be close to eighty. She doesn't look that old." Her youthful enthusiasm and bright colors often made her seem younger.

"Tell you what," said Xander. "Why don't you ask M. about the lady in question? See what she says."

"You mean," said Zack, slowing his words. "Be direct? No way."

They both laughed.

"Your loss," said Xander as the server slid their sandwiches and thick-cut fries onto the table.

Zack picked up the ketchup and poured a red puddle for his hot fries, their salty scent making his mouth water. He dipped a fry into his ketchup and popped it in his mouth, his mind whirling.

"Maybe Andie and I can be friends." He sighed.

"Do you want to be just friends?" said Xander. "It doesn't seem like it."

"Yes. No. I don't know," said Zack, continuing to pick at his fries.

Xander pointed a fry at Zack. "Look. As long as I've known you, which is your whole life, you've never seriously dated anyone. You're thirty-three. That's unusual. Why is that?" He ate the pointer fry and picked up the first triangle of his BLT.

Zack bit into his clubhouse, chewing giving him time to think. Without answering, he took a second bite, then a third. At last, he said, "I don't date because I work a lot." Would Xander call bullshit?

Xander nodded. "You and everyone else. That's the lamest excuse yet. I don't have an answer for you, but maybe you need to figure that out first. Get your shit together. If she's still single at that point, ask her out then. Stick with your friends thing until that time, or it probably isn't fair." He returned to eating.

Xander was right.

Zack tucked into the rest of his meal. The next time he spoke, it was to ask questions about the building timeline and the work site. Providing details, Xander was in his element and the time sped past.

After they'd eaten and were waiting for the bill, Xander leaned back in his chair. "I have a serious question, too. Will you be my best man?"

Warmth filled Zack. While he and Xander were the closest thing either of them had to a brother, the request was still unexpected. Zack had booked off the wedding weekend in October, of course; he wasn't missing his cousin's wedding.

"Cindy's got her heart set on a small ceremony, so we don't go into debt for just one day; about thirty or forty people, and a dinner in our backyard. No church. No dance. Not a bunch of speeches. Just celebrate with our closest family."

It sounded simple and amazing.

"I'd love to," said Zack. "Does this mean I get to plan the bachelor party?"

"No offense, but I want something casual, like a steak dinner with you and a couple of buddies. I'll give you their numbers. Nothing crazy or expensive. I'm too old for the whole strippers and night of drunken debauchery thing. I'm asking you because I trust you to listen to my wishes." His usual levity had vanished. "Bryan will push for strippers. Tell him, 'No.'"

Zack nodded. "I'm honored. I'm your man."

Xander grinned and pushed back from the table, throwing down a twenty. "I've got a job site to get back to. The owner keeps riding my ass for updates." He winked and headed toward the door, stopping three strides from the table. "If you sort out what's going on, bring Andie as your plus one to the wedding."

Zack couldn't tell if the rush of heat was embarrassment or stress. He mechanically finished the rest of his fries and paid before he followed his cousin. He headed home to change, stretch, and allow his food to digest before hitting the gym.

Despite the chat with his cousin, Zack remained conflicted. How did one go about being friends with a woman?

# CHAPTER 16
# ANDIE

"You can be my wingman anytime."
–Maverick, Top Gun (1986)

Andie took the time on Monday morning before her first training shift at the video store to drive downtown to the address where Dr. Maeve's office had been in 2033. It should have been her first mission, but she'd avoided the inevitable as she'd feared what she'd find. For good reason. Checking the street address for the third time, her heart sank.

The four-story brick office building where she'd met Dr. Maeve didn't exist.

In its place stood a run-down apartment building with peeling paint, matching the shabby ones on either side of the street. At some point between now and Andie's original time, the neighborhood became more commercial. This had been her last idea about how to find the elusive doctor.

She pounded the steering wheel several times with the heel of her hand. While she sat in her car waiting for the pain to subside, she stared at the building for ten minutes. Her vision blurred. Now what? She couldn't ask Susan how to get a hold of her "aunt." Her land lady might think Andie was crazy and kick her out.

How would she ever get back to the future?

•   •   •

Andie stood on the cracked sidewalk outside West Coast Video late Thursday morning—the first sunny day in over a week. Too bad she couldn't stay outside, but she needed this job. She ran through the checklist she'd made during training and gave herself a mini pep talk. This job was temporary, and she could do it. She sucked in a deep breath and unlocked the door with her shiny new key. Her hands shook as she walked in and flicked on the overhead lights for her first solo shift.

She would open the store in fifteen minutes and needed to be ready. With a twist to relock the door, she dropped her purse behind the counter and started the opening checklist. She powered up the computer and stepped away while it woke—a slow task. The side of her stomach twinged. Not this again. She'd been having intermittent pain all week. Nothing serious and she chalked it up to nerves.

During her training sessions, Nate had stressed the importance of immediately dealing with the overnight returns and checking them for unrewound movies—a chronic nuisance. Once cleared, requested videos needed to be placed on the reserved shelf. A small neighborhood store like this one was successful because of customer service, or so Nate had said. They handled reservations and kept their customers loyal. She'd noticed a massive video store near the grocery store and was pleased she'd be working at this smaller location. This one should be less hectic and more personal, also the kind of place she'd prefer to shop.

Andie unlocked the return bin from inside with a twist of a separate key, grabbed the foam-lined cardboard box, and unpacked the videos from inside, making three trips to the counter—each with an armload. She stacked the cases in several neat piles.

She switched on the monitor, biting her lip as she entered the password on the rudimentary computer system like she'd been shown. The cursor blinked and the computer whirred, grinding noises emerging from a separate disc drive below the counter. She shouldn't ever have to touch the weird floppy disc inside. A small light flashed red, then green, and the drive grew quiet. She crossed her fingers. The video rental checkout system came on and she entered her name. So far, so good. She checked the time. Two more minutes until she opened.

At the stroke of eleven, she unlocked the door, tugged on the chain on the neon pink "Open" sign, and closed the overnight slot. Any other returned videos would be brought into the store so they wouldn't be missed. She checked her list and the machine rentals to remind herself what else to do this morning. The store listed four VCRs out last night, with two of the machines due back today, and the other two tomorrow. She'd have to watch for those and check all the cables, attachments, and instructions came back inside the case. She worried about messing up, but as these tasks became more familiar, her anxiety should decrease.

Andie went through the returns one at a time, scanning each barcode and determining the video was in the correct case before restocking the shelves. She placed the reserved movies on the shelf to her right. Customers who requested them could pick those up after five. Because most of the overnight returns were not rewound, she placed them one at a time in the high-speed rewinder on the counter. Like so many items in the 80s, video cassettes seemed archaic and almost absurd. The technology was simpler, just awkward.

The same as during her two training shifts with Nate on Monday and Wednesday, the store remained empty while she continued to scan, rewind, and restock the tapes onto the shelves. Today she worked the day shift, tomorrow and Saturday she was on nights, freeing up Nate to play with his band. Evening shifts would be much busier, and Rick said he'd come by to help her close the first time. She was grateful for the slow start today and the time alone, allowing her to work through her list in peace.

When she finished with the rewinder, she checked to see if anyone needed help. The store's interior seemed too quiet and time crawled, so Andie grabbed one of the new releases with a PG rating. Andie loaded the movie to play on the overhead TV. She didn't care what it was; she needed something to break the silence. At this time of day, and for the next few hours, many customers would be quick, dropping off returns, or at least that's how it had gone during the other day shifts.

She might also serve seniors or those who worked shift work and wanted movies at atypical hours. With little to do, her mind wandered to Zack. What shift was he working today? They hadn't spoken all week. He hadn't called despite asking for her number—which was disappointing. Maybe he'd just asked to be polite. While he said he just wanted to be friends, it had seemed like there had been more to it, but it wouldn't be the first time she'd misread someone's intentions.

After scanning in all the videos, she printed a list of overdues and skimmed it for newer titles the store needed back tonight. She called those clients first, often leaving a message, which was her preference. In the 80s, most people seemed to work at offices and not their homes, and without cell phones, she left messages on their landline answering machines. She hated calling about lates, but she followed the script Nate had used when he'd called on Monday and survived the nerve-wracking chore without a hitch.

While the store used another archaic corded phone, at least it had push buttons instead of a rotary dial like the one at her house. If she'd had to use a dial, it would have taken all day to call about the lates.

She spent the rest of her day watching bits of shows, tidying the shelves, replacing tags on returned movies, and handling additional returns as they came in. In the first three hours, she only rented out four videos and made reservations for three more. The afternoon became busier, peaking between the time school got out and before dinner. Weeknight rentals would be slower than on the weekend.

Near the end of her shift, she grabbed a glossy catalog from under the counter and flipped through the ordering information for the upcoming movie releases. The price of most videos was a staggering hundred dollars per copy. Mind blown. What expensive chunks of brittle plastic. No wonder video stores had a limited number of the newer titles. The odd popular movie was cheaper, at only twenty-five dollars to purchase. That likely explained why most titles had only one to three copies and a few had more. She enjoyed finding out these bits of information, as it made her feel more like an insider.

Nate arrived ten minutes before his shift started at five-thirty and transferred the computer sign-in to him. He checked her work. "Looks like you handled things right." He stowed his backpack out of sight in a cupboard behind the movie shelves near the hall with the staff washroom and Rick's office.

"The reservation list is complete," she said, pointing to the shelf.

"Nice. You feel okay about your first night shift tomorrow?" He was much friendlier and helpful when Star Wars movies weren't playing.

Andie wished she could've worked a night shift as training first, but Rick didn't want to pay double for another session. She nodded. Though she and Nate weren't friends, he'd been polite and had explained things well when she'd trained with him. He hadn't seemed to think it strange she'd taken detailed notes and made a list; she'd probably written more than necessary, but she felt more confident with the reference. "Is there anything else I should know before an evening shift?"

His mouth scrunched, and he ran his tongue over his lips. "This is just something the last few women mentioned." He hesitated. He glanced toward the back hall.

"Yes," Andie said, her spirits sinking. She had a bad feeling about where the conversation was headed. It must be about Rick.

"Well. Rick will probably stop by in the evening, though he seldom helps. He comes in the back door near his office. Most of the time, he stays back there."

She nodded. She hoped she wouldn't need to call on him to help.

"He'll arrive after dinner," Nate said, his dark eyes intense. He waited. What was she missing? His eyebrows rose and the silence stretched. "That's late for him."

Andie frowned. She still didn't understand what Nate meant. "I know. The after-dinner rush."

Nate glanced around the empty store and blew out a heavy stream of air. "Rick drinks. You're a smart woman. You noticed he was drunk as a skunk for your interview and that was at eleven in the morning. That wasn't a one-off, but an everyday occurrence. Evenings can be bad. He's often slurring and unsteady. Watch him. He gets sloppy and all hands. Just be careful. Stay out here near the counter where customers might be, not in the back. Don't go into his office until he leaves."

She nodded, her eyes widening. Surely, Rick wouldn't touch her, right? But it sounded like he'd been inappropriate with others, so she needed to be on guard. It must be serious if Nate mentioned it. "Thanks. I will. See you tomorrow just before five-thirty." If she didn't need the money so desperately, she'd leave. Luckily, with the teaching job on the horizon, she wouldn't have to stay long. Gathering her purse, she walked home.

• • •

Andie sat curled on her couch, sipping tea and staring out the front window on Friday morning while the sun streamed inside. Today's weather might be more blue skies and sunshine. The phone's loud ring echoed through the quiet house. She jumped at the unfamiliar sound and grabbed the receiver.

"Hello." This was the first call she'd received since arriving in 1985. Talking on it was a novel experience—her old phone had been a mini computer and for texting more than conversing. Even in her time, she hadn't had many contacts, other than a few colleagues and Dylan. She no longer ached without her cell phone, but she still missed the convenience of texting and access to information about books, music, and movies.

"Hey. It's Val. I took the day off. The sunshine and gardens were calling me. After all, 'Subs need money too,' so I declared today a 'me' day."

"You're so brave to take a sick day when you aren't deathly ill." Andie would have been terrified of being caught. Guilt and paranoia would have ruined her day off.

"I use them sparingly," said Val. "Plus, like all teachers I know, I drag myself in so many days when I should stay at home sick in bed." Andie could relate. "Sometimes preparing for a sub is more work than going to school. A fabulous day like today is my reward."

Perhaps this was a policy Andie should adopt next year when she was teaching again. If she took care of herself more, she'd be better equipped to handle the ten-year-olds in her class with patience.

Val continued, having no idea she'd rocked the foundations of Andie's teaching. "Do you want to go for a walk? We could stop at my place after to have tea?" Without a doubt, she had whipped up a batch of cookie dough or muffins to pop in the oven upon her return.

Andie smiled. "I'd love to. When are you thinking?" Walks and tea with Val were becoming a pleasant habit.

"Five minutes?" said Val. "I want to enjoy this incredible sunshine. I felt cooped up half the winter and trapped by the rain ever since. Now I want to be out."

Andie could relate. "I'll be right there." The line went dead, and she hung up the plastic receiver with a satisfying click. This was the third time she and Val had made impromptu plans. Val had done all the asking, the other times, by arriving on Andie's doorstep after dinner, but so far, that didn't seem to be a problem. Still, she'd try to reciprocate soon.

Andie shoved her feet into her shoes, double-tied the laces, and headed out. Just as she turned where her walkway met the sidewalk, a dusty gold pickup truck drove up and parked at the curb. It was one she'd seen parked at Zack's work site every day this week—must be one of his laborers. She was about to continue up the street to Val's when a bulky man with long, greasy hair jumped out of the passenger side. His scowl in her direction stopped her in her tracks, though he continued toward the worksite, pausing by the gate.

Her mouth dried like a Kalahari summer and her hackles rose. He looked eerily familiar. It was the man from the navy-blue car who'd reminded her of Dylan. Up close, the resemblance between this man and Dylan was uncanny, despite the man's age and the year. Could he be Dylan's father or grandfather? She hadn't met either, but the chances seemed too farfetched to be possible. Still, a chill slithered down her spine.

"Tom," said a voice from the other side of the truck as the driver's side opened as well. The long-haired man stopped. "Go ahead. I'll meet you on site to go over your assignment today. Please wait for the next set of drawings. I'll be right there." A man with short dark hair turned toward Andie and rounded the front of the truck to stop near her on the sidewalk. "Hey. I'm Xander, the contractor next door. You must be Andie." He stretched out his hand for her to shake.

Andie's face burned as she shook it. Had he heard about her from Val or Zack?

"I am," she said. "You're Val's cousin, right?" He had the looks of their family, though his were muted compared to Zack's. His hair was browner and his eyes a solid, more typical blue than Zack's band of azure surrounding icy blue.

"That's right. Their favorite cousin." Xander grinned, a dimple popping on his right cheek. Still, handsome as he was, he didn't make her heart race like Zack.

"I'm on my way to meet Val for a walk," she said, edging away. She didn't want to make Val wait. She'd said she'd be right there.

"Say 'hi' to her from me." Xander turned toward the job site and then spoke over his shoulder. "Say, my fiancée and I are planning a barbeque in June to celebrate our engagement. You're invited to join us. Tell Val I said she should bring you. The more the merrier. I'll introduce you to my Cindy." He winked and strode off, a thick roll of blueprints tucked under his arm. She watched as he grabbed a hard hat from a stack inside the gate, plunked it on, and entered the site with a quick wave.

Andie turned for Val's, still thinking. Summer. It was daunting to think about still being here when the barbeque happened. No harm in thinking about what if? She still hadn't found a way home. She allowed her mind to wander. If she accepted Xander's invitation, she might see Zack. They hadn't spoken since the evening tour after the movie last weekend. Large gatherings weren't her thing, but if her time here was going to be any different than her old life, she needed to make an effort to meet and interact with people. Spending time with Val reminded her how often in the past she'd been lonely. If Andie was still in 1985 and Val was going, Andie would go too, as long as it didn't interfere with work or bother her new friend.

With a smile, she picked up the pace down the sidewalk, her skin warming from the sun as she walked. What a beautiful day to spend with a friend.

# CHAPTER 17
# ANDIE

"That's why they call them crushes. If they were easy, they'd call 'em something else."
–Jim Baker, Sixteen Candles (1984)

Cheeks flushed, Andie tapped the numbers of the client's phone number on the store computer, pulling up their account, her bottom lip between her teeth. She glanced upward, assessing the line of customers. It was bogging down because everyone in the store seemed to want their rental movies at the same time. Now. She glanced up again and stifled a groan, counting the people waiting—six so far and several more wandering, with multiple tags in hand. Being new, she couldn't process customers any faster. She finished her transaction and turned her attention to the next customer.

"Your membership card or phone number, please?" she said, trying to sound pleasant. At least she was used to faking emotions in many situations—all part of masking. She hoped she was projecting calm despite her mounting anxiety inside wrapping her stomach in knots.

"555-4902," said the gruff man at the counter. He wore a frown and a leather jacket with what looked like a motorcycle club patch. Under his arm, he carried a matte black helmet.

She punched in the numbers on the keypad and hit *Enter*. The account loaded and she skimmed through the videos already listed. Shit. There were already four movies rented. All overdue new releases. She flicked a glance at the overflowing stack of videos waiting to be checked in. Should she ask about his?

The man must have seen her glance. "Yeah. I returned the others. You gonna charge me the late fee for a few hours?" He glared.

Her chest grew tighter, though she maintained eye contact, difficult as it was. "Did you return all four?"

"Yeah," he said, pointing to four cases in the disorganized pile near her elbow. "Those." None looked to be rewound, but the titles matched the list on her screen.

Andie took a breath and flicked a glance at the analog wall clock—only seven-thirty. She might still rent out all the returned movies if she could just check them in. "Only one was reserved tonight. I'll let it slide this time, but please try to have your rentals back by five." Her voice quavered on the "please."

"Uh-huh," he said, sliding three more tags across the counter. He glanced at the street.

`She grabbed them and fumbled for cases behind the counter, checking the numbers to ensure she had a match. She'd already given someone the wrong movie once.

"Can you hurry already?" He tapped the counter with a blunt, grease-ingrained finger. "I'm parked in the loading zone."

"Give her a break. She's new," said a familiar voice from farther back in the line. Andie's spirits soared, then crashed while her face burned. Zack was here, witnessing this fiasco. She'd thought about him all week, and though she would have loved to visit, she was harried and too busy to talk.

"Yeah. Where's Nate?" said another customer in line. "It's about time something other than *Star Wars* played on that TV." Several other customers laughed. They must be regulars. The mood lightened.

Andie glanced up to address everyone. "Nate's playing with his band tonight. This is my first evening shift. He'll be back Monday to Thursday evenings and Fridays during the day." Maybe she hadn't needed to give so much information, but having something to say felt right.

"That will be twelve dollars," she said to the man with the helmet at the counter.

He paid without speaking and departed with his movies.

She bit her tongue, suppressing the words that begged to come out. *You're welcome for waiving the late charges.* Pressing her lips together, she collected the movie tags from the next customer. She grabbed their videos, scanned the next membership card, and took payment.

"I wanted a copy of *Ghostbusters*," said the next person. "There's no tag, which means it's out, but you have a mountain of returns." The woman ran her fingers along the counter and nudged one movie aside to check the title below.

Andie's spirits plummeted. There were probably twenty to twenty-five cases in the jumble, waiting to be checked in. Her chest grew tight. She wasn't keeping up. Where was Rick? He was supposed to be here to help with the evening rush. She'd expected him by seven, but he hadn't arrived.

"I can check." She took a breath. This wasn't much different from a busy classroom. She just needed to tackle each issue in turn; the customers would just have to be patient. Everyone would have to understand she was doing her best.

With another deep breath, she lined the tapes up on the counter, turning the clear plastic cases on edge so she could scan each barcode. "I have a copy of *Ghostbusters*," she said, catching sight of the distinctive red and white title. "But it isn't rewound."

The woman shrugged. "I'll do it at home." Her next words surprised Andie. "I appreciate you checking when you're so busy."

Andie completed the transaction and moved on to the next. A peek confirmed the line had grown again. No wonder streaming services had caught on. No late returns, long lines, or missing movies—something simpler in the future, or at least on the surface. Still, choosing a physical copy of your movie for the night was more satisfying. She stumbled again.

Zack slid behind the counter, and her eyebrows raised. He wasn't allowed back here. She was working.

"Zack," she said. "Hi. Um. You shouldn't be back here."

He winked. "I'm not. You are. Tell me what I can do to help. You're doing fine. It's just slammed right now. I've never seen this place so packed. I blame the rain."

The mention of rain set a smile to her face, remembering her fun morning hanging with her new friend. After a stunning morning hike with Val, the clouds had rolled in once more. They'd had tea and muffins from the safety of her kitchen, laughing about arriving home in the nick of time.

"You could rewind the tapes I just scanned if they need it, shelve them, and take the tags back out. If you find a copy of *The Muppets Take Manhattan*, it's reserved. It can go on that shelf." She pointed and turned back to the line. She took a deep breath and met Zack's eyes. "Thank you." Some of the tightness in her chest lessened.

Andie dealt with the next few customers while Zack rewound movies and ran two dozen tags back to the display shelves. He seemed to know where many of the movie boxes were located. Either he was a quick study or was familiar with the store. Whichever was appreciated. Without watching the crowded store and focusing on the checkouts, Andie worked faster. They kept up this rhythm, working their way through the crowd.

"Thank you. Enjoy your movies." She looked for the next person in line, only to realize it was Zack. He'd waited for everyone else to go through the checkout. Now, he leaned on the counter and her pulse raced. Behind him, the metal bell over the front door rang as the last of the other customers filed out. She'd done it—gotten through the rush. She exhaled and rotated her tight shoulders.

"You're welcome," Zack said with a crooked smile, sliding a white plastic, numbered tag across the counter. "I'll take this one."

"You must not be working tonight." She stumbled as she turned, and her face felt like it had caught fire. "Obviously." Why couldn't she act naturally around him?

"I worked day shift today and I work again tomorrow, but not until afternoon. I tend to stay up late on the changeover to nights, so I can sleep in before my shift at four." He nodded at the movie playing overhead. "That's a good one. How late do you work?"

She grimaced. "Until just after eleven. I'm closing." She glanced at the clock. Somehow, over an hour had passed since she'd last checked and it was almost nine. Still no sign of Rick, but maybe the worst rush was over.

"Thanks again for pitching in. I was drowning." She should have said that right away.

"I hadn't realized you were working tonight," said Zack. "I didn't see your car outside."

"That's because I walked," she said. "My car wouldn't start." Back at her house, she'd been on the verge of tears when she discovered her car had died. At least she'd given herself ample time, so she'd been able to speed walk and still arrive on time. "When I tried to start it, it made an odd clicking sound and the engine wouldn't turn over." She shrugged. Though she could speak about it now, with no money, it was devastating. She had utility bills, rent, and food to buy, which took precedence.

He frowned. "Maybe it just needs a new battery. I can help you pick one up. The situation's unacceptable."

"What situation? My car dying? It's not like I planned it." She couldn't keep the edge from her voice.

"Without your car, you're stuck walking home tonight after work." His lips pressed in a straight line.

"Yes." She'd debated whether she should call a cab, but she didn't have the cash. She hadn't seen a bus stop outside, nor figured out how to find out about public transit without access to the internet. Every cent she earned was for her June rent, since everything she had now was for May's, due in just a few days. With her hopes of returning to the future beginning to look further and further away, she had to be practical. Her house wasn't far, and she'd brought an umbrella. She'd be fine.

The intermittent pain in her side stabbed, and she tried not to crumple. It must be the stress of knowing she was stuck in this time and trying to figure out how to juggle her expenses. She'd have to be frugal. There was no way of knowing if, or when, she'd ever get back to the future.

"You all right? You look pale." Zack's brows drew together.

"Just stress, I think." Her pain seemed to come and go.

Zack's frown deepened. "After eleven's late to walk home on your own. Especially if you aren't well."

She shrugged. "I'm okay. It doesn't seem like a rough neighborhood." What was his problem?

He laid a hand flat on the counter and his eyes grew frosty. She inched backward, his intensity frightening her. "It isn't terrible, but you have to pass the billiard hall and two pubs. Plus, there aren't many overhead lights along the stretch by the park. It's never smart to walk alone there at night. Especially for a beautiful young woman."

She blushed at his compliment. She hadn't considered the details about the neighborhood and how different the area might feel at night. The businesses might be busy on a Friday night. Perhaps it wasn't a smart idea to walk home alone in the dark without a cell phone. She'd forgotten that technicality. What if she had trouble?

"I'll be fine," she tried to infuse confidence into her statement because she didn't have a choice. She passed him his movie. "I watched *Terminator* last week and loved it." The action scenes had seemed low-tech but gritty and dangerous. Her heart had raced, and she'd been terrified for Sarah Connor's life. The time travel aspect of the movie was very different from her situation, but interesting. "I hope you enjoy your movie. That's four dollars, please." His pale stare made her more nervous about walking home. Her hands grew damp.

Zack slid a five-dollar bill across the counter. "I'll be back at eleven-fifteen. I'll drive you home. I'll come by tomorrow with jumper cables to check if we can start your car."

"You don't have to do that," she said, "but thank you for the offer." She handed him a floppy dollar bill in change. "I don't mind the walk." She would figure something out for tomorrow night. "Or maybe I can find a bus?"

"There's no transit in this part of town. Honestly, picking you up is no trouble. I should be finished with my movie by that time, and I can return it. It'll save me a trip tomorrow before my shift." He smiled, this one not reaching his eyes. Was he worried?

Andie didn't believe it was convenient for him to return tonight. He would barely have time to watch the show, but he seemed insistent. Besides, after his comments, she didn't want to walk home alone in the dark.

"Okay. Thank you. I'll see you later." She smiled as he turned and left, holding the door open for a couple entering the store. Tonight was busy. At least lots of customers made the time speed past.

At eleven o'clock, with the store deserted, Andie locked the front door and turned off the Open sign as well as half the lights, as Nate had instructed. A sense of relief filled her. One active shift down, a bunch to go. Weekends would probably get easier over time as she became more familiar with juggling all the different aspects of running the store. She opened the overnight return slot and ran the end-of-day report as shown on the computer. The printer was so loud, she jumped at the high-pitched sound in the hush of the quiet store.

While she waited for the report to finish, she counted the money—separating it by denominations. She filled in the tally and wrote the final amount on a cash slip. She'd done this after her shift on Thursday too and was, once again, correct. Her money matched the shift's take to the cent. This might not be her profession, but she was competent.

She placed the bundled money and the report in a Ziploc bag and carried it to the back. When she entered the musty, cluttered office, she found Rick. He'd either fallen asleep or passed out at his desk. Sprawled backward in his office chair, his chin slumped against his chest. She hesitated, remembering Nate's warning. She narrowed her eyes, watching Rick's sleeping form. He showed no sign of waking—no change in breathing or eye twitches. Keeping an eye on him, she punched in the code, opened the small wall safe, and slid the Ziploc inside.

Andie pressed the safe's metal door closed without a sound, tiptoeing out of the office, shutting Rick inside once more. She exhaled and returned to the computer station, shut off the monitor, grabbed her purse, and headed for the door. She glanced up at the clock. Eleven-fifteen. She checked outside where Zack leaned on the hood of his car, parked in front of the store in clear view. The rain had stopped. Her heart leapt. He'd come, as promised.

When he spotted her through the glass, he dropped his movie into the slot, where it landed in the box with a thud.

She unlocked the door, exited, and relocked it.

"I hoped you were still here," he said. "With the lights dimmed and the sign off, I wasn't sure. I guess it takes a few minutes to get everything squared away." He yawned.

Guilt shot through her. She was keeping him up. He must need to go to bed soon. "Thank you. You didn't have to do this, but I appreciate it."

He gave her a tired smile and opened her car door. "That's what friends are for."

She climbed in and he closed the door.

# CHAPTER 18
# ANDIE

"You know what? I'm not afraid anymore. Not with you guys here."
–The Goonies (1985)

Andie knocked on Val's front door at five-thirty on Sunday afternoon. She'd been told to bring nothing but herself for dinner, but hadn't quite been able to comply. It seemed wrong to show up empty-handed, so she'd baked spice cake cupcakes and frosted them with browned butter icing, hoping her friend would appreciate the gesture.

From inside, measured steps approached.

Zack opened the door. "Andie, you're right on time." His inviting smile lit up the front hall.

She hadn't expected him to be there, and a warm heat suffused her body. Last time she'd seen him had been when they'd failed to jumpstart her car last weekend. "Zack. What are you doing here?" He raised his eyebrows. She winced. What was wrong with her? "Sorry, I just meant, what a pleasant surprise."

He laughed, smile lines crinkling next to his eyes, which made her insides swoop. He was so damn sexy. "Nice recovery." His gaze drifted to the container she held. "Dessert looks amazing. Can I take those?" He held out a hand for her cupcakes, which she passed to him. His arm grazed hers, though she ignored the zing, and her eyes turned toward the floor as she toed off her shoes. Val didn't like shoes being worn in the house, either. Maybe it was a West Coast thing, so they didn't track in water or mud.

Andie followed Zack into the kitchen where Val leaned over, checking something in the oven while a fruity aroma filled the kitchen, making Andie's mouth water.

"I hope you like apricots," Val said as she closed the oven. "I've got apricot chicken with water chestnuts baking, the rice is on, and I wanted to check with you before making the salad."

Andie inhaled the delicious smells. "It smells amazing. Do you need help with anything?" She hopped onto the bar stool at the island she now considered "hers." She'd visited several times and always sat in the same place.

"Can I get you a drink?" said Zack. He crossed the kitchen to the fridge. "There's water, juice, cider, Coke, and Sprite."

"Or tea," said Val with a smile. "I filled the kettle already."

"Just water, please," said Andie. "I'll save tea for after dinner with dessert."

Val set a cutting board and knife in front of Andie while Zack filled a glass with ice, poured water, and set it beside her, the ice cubes clinking. Andie liked that Val would give her a job, even just chopping vegetables. It made her feel useful and included.

"Thanks," said Andie, lifting her water glass.

"How about broccoli?" said Val, as she crossed to the cupboards where she removed a green pottery salad bowl.

While Andie didn't love the tree-like vegetable, she could stomach broccoli just fine. "Sure."

"Good. I wanted to try a new salad," said Val, who kept moving. She reminded Andie of a hummingbird, always in motion. "Zack, can you grab the broccoli from the fridge? The drawer on the right. And the plain yogurt, lemon juice, and feta cheese?" She tossed orders over her shoulder while she set the round kitchen table off to the side.

He retrieved the requested items.

"Thanks." Val showed Andie what size of raw broccoli chunks she wanted cut, then mixed a dressing with the yogurt and lemon juice. As Andie chopped the broccoli, Val prepared the rest of the ingredients.

Once Andie had filled the salad bowl with bite-sized green chunks, Val added a healthy amount of crumbled feta, a handful of raisins, a few sunflower seeds, and poured the dressing over the top. Across the kitchen, the oven timer beeped. She removed the rice from the stove, the chicken from the oven, and set the salad on the table. Everything looked wonderful.

"Let's eat," said Val. "Zack, you can take the far side.

The three of them dished up and Andie's nervousness faded as they ate. As expected, Val's dinner was delicious.

"Have you been writing much?" said Val, directing her question to Andie.

"I have," said Andie, shooting a glance at Zack, unsure whether she wanted to talk about her writing in front of him. "Almost every day. I wasn't sure about writing longhand, instead of typing. But it's oddly productive. I swear sometimes, it seems like my hand comes up with the ideas instead of my brain."

"I'm totally jealous," said Zack. "I used to draw, but with how busy I am at work, I never seem to find the time."

"The gym always wins, doesn't it?" said Val. "I've never heard of anyone exercising as much as you do unless they're planning to be in the Olympics or training for a marathon."

"Hey. Working out is relaxing. At least, when I'm done." He pointed his fork at his sister, perhaps tired of being teased for staying fit. Zack dished up a second helping of chicken and rice, scooping additional sauce onto both parts, just how Andie liked it too. Saucy.

"I enjoy running," said Andie. "At least, when I manage not to trip off curbs and damage myself. Running makes my head quiet." She glanced up to see how her new friends took her comment. She seldom mentioned the vortex of thoughts and emotions constantly spinning in her brain.

"Me too," said Zack. "That's what I liked about sketching. The peace."

"We all need something to help us relax," said Val. "I like crocheting, baking, and reading." She looked at Andie. "Maybe one day, I'll be able to read a book you've written."

"You write fantasy, right?" asked Zack as he reached for additional salad.

Andie nodded. "I'm working on a portal story about an unexpected heroine who's transported to a parallel world to fulfill their prophecy." The plot sounded silly out loud, but neither of the others said anything of the kind.

"Does anyone at home notice she's missing?" Zack took a mouthful of chicken. "You know, after she slips through a portal and vanishes?"

His question hit closer to home than he probably intended, as once again, Andie's mother's obituary flashed through her mind. As far as Andie knew, her mother and sister had never searched for her when she'd left for university. The guilt for abandoning her sister bubbled to the surface. She continued to chew to avoid an immediate answer, which might come out too emotional.

Perhaps Zack sensed she needed a moment to collect her emotions as he turned to Val. "Sis, this is one of the best dinners yet." He smiled at Andie. "She's always trying out terrific new recipes. I'm lucky she loves to share. We both are." His expression warmed her inside, though his piercing blue eyes were difficult to meet for long. He raised his eyebrow and prompted her to continue. "Your story person?"

Her throat still constricted, Andie reached for her ice water and drank the ice-cold water. "Nobody noticed she was missing."

"That's not realistic," Zack said, pushing the issue. "Her family must have noticed."

"She didn't have a lot of family," said Andie, somehow defensive.

"Not everyone has constant family underfoot like ours," said Val, with a frown for her brother. "Us Mirabelli's are always up in each other's business or betting on the outcome of each other's lives. If you hadn't noticed." She turned to Andie, her face alight with excitement. "Oh, I have an idea. Did you want to take my typewriter to your place? To borrow." When Andie hesitated, Val said, "You mentioned you're used to typing, and I never use it anymore. That's why it was in storage until you used it for your resume. I've taken to using the computer at work if I need something typed."

They would be amazed to know about the personal computers of the future. Andie bit her tongue, to avoid accidentally saying something that would only garner looks of disbelief. No good would come of telling them about her time.

"I can carry it down the block for you after dessert," said Zack, perhaps noting her hesitation. "It's no problem."

"Thank you," said Andie. "I'd like that." While a handwritten rough draft was fine, it would be easier to edit once typed.

Throughout the rest of dinner, the three of them talked about movies and made plans to meet for dinner the following Sunday. Andie decided to bring pie after hearing it was something they seldom had. She hadn't made one in years, but she used to have a touch for nice pastry. The secret was not to touch it more than necessary.

When she left that night, walking beside Zack with the typewriter in the quiet evening, contentment percolated throughout her. She couldn't remember a better evening. Delicious food and wonderful company made a great combination, both of which had been lacking in her old life.

•   •   •

Andie left Val's after another Saturday morning walk along a sheltered beach. Hanging out with her neighbor was becoming a welcome habit. No matter how much time she spent with Val, she never felt uncomfortable and could be herself. That had so seldom been the case in Andie's life, but she and Val fit and always had a pleasant time with easy conversation.

With Val getting out of school for the summer next week, they had plans for several daytime excursions, including berry picking to make jam and several day hikes. With warmer temperatures as May sped past, becoming June, soon they'd be walking in shorts and T-shirts.

Andie glanced down. Her knees were still a mess, even if they no longer caused her pain. They'd finally healed, leaving large purple scars which had yet to fade. Maybe she should go for a run tomorrow, the first since her accident in April. She would have extra time on her hands tomorrow, as

Sunday was her day off. The forecast was for sun and, with flowers emerging everywhere as bright pops of color, it would be stunning.

She continued up the block where the hood of her bright yellow car was lifted. Her steps accelerated and her jaw grew tight. Who was messing with her car? She squinted, trying to see better, but the raised hood blocked her view. As she approached, she passed Zack's car and her shoulders dropped with the release of anger. He must be trying to fix her still-sidelined vehicle. Her throat constricted. He'd been concerned she'd left it immobile for over a month and he had picked her up several times after work when he was off. She kept telling him he didn't need to, but he always showed up to drive her home.

Zack was only trying to help, but while kind, she didn't have money for car repairs. She wasn't just being careful; she had no savings and not enough income. Her paychecks were earmarked for necessities, like rent and food. Her gut churned. She hoped he wasn't doing something expensive.

"Hey, Zack. How's it going?" She said, stopping beside him, worrying her lip again.

Zack shot her a sideways glance that made her stomach flip-flop. It would be easier to accept his friendship if he wasn't so gorgeous—his T-shirt molded to his solid muscles and broad shoulders. Today, the pale blue color matched his eyes. His mouth moved, but Andie missed whatever he said. When he waved a hand in front of her face, she tuned in again. What had she missed?

He shot her a look she couldn't interpret before he said, "Earth to Andie. I lost you for a sec." He grinned. "I'm just about done. I picked up and installed a new battery. You have perfect timing. Why don't you grab your key and see if it starts now."

"You didn't have to do that," she said, tucking loose wisps of hair behind her ear.

"Yes, I did," he said with an amiable smile. "You work again tonight, right? So, you'll have the same problem as the last few weekends and I'm still not comfortable with you walking home at night. I'd do the same for Yolanda or Val."

She hoped he didn't see her as another sister.

"How much do I owe you for the battery?" She hoped the amount wasn't too dear. How would she pay him back? As usual, discomfort caused a wave of heat. Her face burned like it was aflame, adding to her embarrassment.

"Let's try to start it first. No guarantee a dead battery was the problem. It's just the cheapest and easiest attempt at a solution. Cross your fingers." He wiped his hands on a rag from his back pocket.

She admired his efficient movement, trying not to stare at his capable hands or wonder how they'd feel on her skin. Andie produced her keys from her pocket with a faint jingle.

"Okay. I'll give it a whirl." She unlocked the door, stuck the key in the ignition, and turned. Once again, a clicking sound was the only result. Damn. There must be something more serious than a dead battery. Her shoulders slumped, and she blew out a large breath. Now what?

She shook her head as she exited. "No luck." She slammed the door in disgust, the sound filling her with an odd satisfaction, like swearing.

"I have a friend with a garage. I'll get him to look next week." Zack frowned. "I work tonight and can't pick you up after your shift." He rubbed the back of his neck. "Could Val collect you again?"

Val had done it three times previously when Zack had been working and she'd already offered to do it tonight. Andie counted the days ahead—two of the next three weekends would be a problem. Andie couldn't ask Val for so many favors either, even if they were friends. It was too much. It had already been six weeks' worth of rides.

Andie flushed. Time had flown. She felt like she was taking advantage of them, even if she didn't have another option besides walking. Asking Zack to continue wasn't fair. She would have to get her car fixed—credit card debt be damned. She sucked in a breath. Maybe she could wait for the next bill, which would only be another week.

Even to collect her the following Saturday night, Zack would have to work all day, go to bed, and set an alarm to pick her up before going back to bed. She'd been horrified when she'd discovered that's what he'd done a month ago.

Confirming her thoughts, Zack counted on his fingers. "I'm off next Friday, so that's fine, but I start days on Saturday, so I can't pick you up. It would be great if your car worked by then." He grimaced, then continued. "My friend John's auto shop is pretty busy, so if your car isn't fixed by the week after next, I can drive you home again. Month's end is when it becomes impossible, as I'm on nights and will be out in the ambulance."

"Are you sure picking me up a few more times isn't a problem?" she said. "I don't like to be a burden."

He grinned. "I told you, anything for a friend." He dropped the hood with a bang that made her jump back to the sidewalk.

Friend. There was that word. Again. Though it shouldn't, she couldn't help it if it made her unhappy.

Andie tried not to wilt from his continued use of the "f" word. It appeared she'd been punted deep into the friend zone with no sign of a way out, especially since she hadn't been brave enough to show she was interested in more than friendship. The more time she spent near Zack, the more she appreciated his kindness. He was so much more than another pretty face.

# CHAPTER 19
# ANDIE

"I'm making this up as I go along."
–Indiana Jones, Raiders of the Lost Ark (1981)

Friday morning arrived, overcast and gray, but the weather report on the news last night had forecasted that the skies would clear throughout the morning. Which meant it should be fair for Xander and Cindy's engagement barbeque this afternoon. The idea of the party made her nervous, so Andie looked around her living room for a distraction—the boxes were still there. She sighed. At least she could be productive and stop the procrastination.

She'd put off this chore long enough, but with plans this afternoon and better weather ahead, she needed to unpack now, or the moving boxes might sit unopened for months more. It had already been too long, but at first, she'd hoped to return to her time. If she left, the contents would be irrelevant anyhow, but now, with no contact from Dr. Maeve and no way to locate her, Andie wanted to deal with whatever had been left for her to find.

It was time to admit she might be here to stay.

She dragged the first heavy box off the top row of three, set it on the floor, and scraped the flaps open. Inside, she found stacks of battered paperback sci-fi and fantasy novels, including the entire *Belgariad* series Zack had mentioned. Her heart raced at the idea of so much new reading material in her genre.

After reading the back of Book One, *Pawn of Prophecy*, she shoved the pile of five books aside to read soon, even if she'd rather start now. If she had time before she left, she would shelve the rest of the books.

Two more boxes of books followed, keeping her excited about her upcoming late-night and summer reading. Another stellar find was a stack of coil-bound notebooks with lined paper. They'd be handy for writing, and better than the loose-leaf sheets she'd been using. Her heart fluttered as she extracted an envelope sticking out of the top one. Her hands shook as she read the brief note.

*Dear Andie,*

*I hope you aren't missing your computer too much and have worked out a system for writing. Your stories deserve to be out in the world. One day you just might be a published author. Keep at it!*

*I believe in you.*

*Andrea*

*P.S. Now that you're in the 80s, without a cell phone, I thought you might like to have my old watch.*

Andie tipped the still-heavy envelope. A familiar silver watch fell into her hand. With shaking fingers, Andie fastened her neighbor's slim watch around her wrist. She stared at the faded ink of the note. It was difficult to be angry with someone who seemed to be on her side, even if she'd worked with Dr. Maeve. Andie had barely mentioned her writing to Andrea, but her neighbor had thought of terrific gifts. Not to mention words of encouragement. Andie was past wondering how the future and present intersected.

She would enjoy writing in the notebooks; it wasn't quite like a computer and saving to the cloud, but it would get the job done. She glanced toward the kitchen table where Val's typewriter sat. This process would save her time in the long run as her drafts were often quite scrappy and needed organization and polishing. Several times she'd gotten into a flow writing longhand, discovering she enjoyed that part of the process. Yes. Notebooks were perfect.

At the bottom of the next box, one filled with miscellaneous household junk, Andie discovered a large yellow envelope packet that crinkled as she extracted it from the box. From its weight and thickness, it contained a stack of paper. She turned it over. Her name was written in Sharpie on the outside.

Andie's hands shook as she removed the first document from the packet—an authentic-seeming birth certificate for Andie Sterling. She'd be able to apply for a new permanent driver's license. Her birthday remained the same, but this document had the birth year as 1955. It seemed having valid ID wouldn't be a problem. How in the world? More of Dr. Maeve's magic?

Andie huffed out a breath. That woman owed her a world of explanation. Too bad there was no way to call her on her decisions and her unorthodox therapy, if that's what she called sending someone to another time. Still. The birth certificate was excellent.

Andie traced her restored name on the thick paper. Strange as it was, she liked having an official document with her name and birthday. Though a mystery, the find filled her with satisfaction. The papers settled the issue of how she could prove her identity moving forward in this time, including applying for an updated driver's license with her photo. With a lighter heart, she examined the rest of the envelope's contents.

Another stapled sheaf of papers appeared to be an employment contract with Northwest Elementary for the 1985-1986 school year. She scanned the document. She would teach fifth grade, starting September 3rd, 1985, and finishing June 13th, 1986. The school had an option for an additional two years at the same salary plus two percent each year if they wanted to retain her services.

Her jaw gaped when she flipped to the last page. Her starting salary was much higher than expected. Perhaps carrying a little debt would be okay this once—just until her life settled. Private schools often paid better than public ones, but she hadn't expected to be so well-compensated for teaching—that hadn't been her experience. She would pay to fix the car with her credit card.

September seemed distant. Almost another world distant, though it was only two months away. Maybe she would call the school before the summer ended and request curriculum materials so she could plan before the fall.

Most schools opened a week or two early for administrators and the office staff. She didn't even know what topics she would be teaching. With advance prep, she would feel more confident about teaching in such an unfamiliar environment than what she'd done at her previous job.

The gravity of remaining in this time settled, and she didn't fear the idea anymore.

Andie would just have to survive until her first paycheck in the fall. She sighed and glanced out the window. Her car still sat abandoned by the curb, undrivable. Even with Zack's friend's help, she hadn't been able to afford the cost of a new alternator. He'd quoted four hundred dollars for parts and labor, telling her he would replace it at cost plus his time. The price wasn't a ton of money and was more than fair, but she didn't have any excess. A driveable car wasn't worth more than a month's rent.

Everything always came back to money and her lack of funds. She hadn't even been able to cancel her car insurance because if the car was uninsured, she couldn't park on the street. But there was no alternative; she didn't have anywhere else to store it. At least while she hadn't been driving, there hadn't been the additional expense of fuel.

For her last several weeks' worth of trips to the grocery store, she'd allowed price to dictate what she chose, falling back into old habits from growing up on a limited income. She shopped the specials, avoided junk food, and stuck to healthy, filling options, even if her diet might lack variety and had become monotonous. She walked to and from the grocery store, going twice a week to keep the trips manageable, light enough for everything to fit in her backpack and one additional bag.

Last week, she and Val had coordinated, taking Val's car, and Andie had stocked up on a few things that were heavy to carry while walking. Traveling on foot worked for some things, but work nights remained the main issue. Her pride struggled with being so dependent on anyone.

Last Saturday night, as Zack had suggested, Val had picked her up. Her friend had arrived bleary-eyed and yawning. Guilt still pricked Andie's conscience as Val usually went to bed by ten—even on the weekend. Andie wouldn't ask again, even if that meant she would walk home and not tell anyone. She grabbed the important documents from the yellow packet and stowed them in her bedside table to keep them safe.

She didn't want to dwell on her temporary money problems, so she returned her attention to her immediate task of unpacking. The last few boxes held clothes, jackets, and shoes. Andie sorted through them, stacking them in categories by season. When everything was folded in neat piles spread across the floor, she smiled. She was set for a while now. Some of the clothing styles were ones she'd seen people here wearing, though she never would have chosen stirrup pants and shirts with shoulder pads. At least she didn't need to shop—costly and a form of torture.

Andie made toast with peanut butter, smearing it with Val's homemade raspberry jam for breakfast. She carried her plate and sat on the couch, staring out the front window as she took stock of not only her discoveries this morning, but her life.

Tonight might be busy at West Coast Video and she hoped Rick continued to stay away. She'd gotten through the evening rushes without his help so far, preferring it that way. It was difficult to believe she'd already been here for two months. Her routine had become weekdays of working at the video store during the day and walking home to cook dinner. After dinner, she wrote for a couple of hours, then switched to reading. On weekends, she typically spent part of Saturday with Val and Sundays were spent writing all day unless she, Val, and Zack ate together for dinner.

On average, twice a week, she ate dinner with Val, and they often walked afterward, enjoying tea and dessert when they returned from their evening ramble.

Andie loved having a friend who lived so close. It made getting together convenient and easy, though that wasn't why she liked Val. As much as they got along, part of Andie waited for Val to tire of spending so much time together, as had happened with previous friends. But that was her own insecurity rearing its ugly head. Her new friend genuinely seemed to enjoy Andie's company, and Andie intended to repay the dinners when she received a real paycheck.

She'd be embarrassed to serve Val Hamburger Helper, ramen, or mac and cheese, with carrots sticks, even if that's what Andie could afford.

Andie checked the time and jumped to her feet. She grabbed the remaining stacks of folded clothes and ferried them to her bedroom. Val was picking her up in about an hour for the barbeque at Xander and his fiancée's house. Val had invited Andie to join her, mentioning she'd run into Xander, who had re-invited Andie for today.

Since Zack had seemed annoyed with her after their encounter the other day, she probably should have mentioned to him she would be coming to the barbeque, but she'd forgotten. She'd intended to, but he'd been quiet when he'd picked her up last Saturday.

He'd asked if she'd gotten her car fixed, and from the way his mouth flattened, he'd been disappointed when she'd answered in the negative. He'd probably hoped she'd taken his friend John's offer. After that, Zack hadn't spoken. Still, he'd waited until her front door was open before he'd driven away. He might be grumpy, but he was still a friend looking out for her well-being.

Andie stared out the window facing the construction site. She didn't want to keep being a nuisance. Surely, Zack had better things to do than drive her home after her night shifts. Next weekend he was working both Friday and Saturday nights. If her car wasn't fixed in time, she might have to walk. Her friends might not like her choice, but Andie would take her chances.

Still, she had to get things in motion for the rest of the summer. She picked up the business card Zack's friend, John, had given her when he'd stopped by to check out her vehicle. She inhaled, picked up the phone, and dialed, releasing the dial after each number only after circling the proper distance. Andie waited while the phone rang several times at the other end of the line.

"J.M. Autobody," said John's voice. At least she thought it was him.

"Hi. This is Andie Sterling, Zack's friend." She bit her lip, hoping John remembered her.

"Right. Honda Civic with a dead alternator," he said. "You might need a new serpentine belt too, just to be safe."

Relief flooded through her at his memory. It would save her an explanation. "Yes. How soon can you replace it? Are you still willing to tow it to your shop for no charge?" That had been something Zack had asked, and John had agreed to.

"I've been thinking. No tow required. I can fix it at your place. I'll bring my tools and can place the order for the parts today. I'll fit you in for the installation on..." His voice trailed off, as he must be checking an appointment book. "Next Friday. Does that work?"

"Yes, please." The timing for finishing the repair would be close, as she had a shift that evening and hoped to drive, but it should work. She rattled off her phone number so he could confirm the appointment.

"I have your address and will come by Friday noon. No later than one."

Her chest loosened a little. "It's okay if I pay with Visa?" Using her card still didn't feel real, though the previous bills had arrived, and she'd mailed a check for the minimum amount each time.

"Of course. The bank pays on time. Zack said you're good for the money. Just stop by the shop once the car is operational and I'll run your card."

The call had been easier than expected, even the part about payment had been handled in a way that would never happen in 2033.

"Thank you. See you Friday." Andie hung up, dropping the receiver into the cradle. Her shoulders felt a thousand times looser. It had been a productive morning—mystery boxes unpacked, employment details located, important papers read, and the mechanic called. What a relief to have dealt with things instead of avoiding them. No decade seemed without complication, but if she didn't let everything stack up, she could handle things.

She stood, promising not to stress and worry about money anymore, or at least not, until after the barbeque. She'd never be able to relax otherwise. Val had promised to leave the party long enough to drop Andie off at work, and Zack had already confirmed he'd pick her up after eleven tonight. Her side stabbed again, and she rubbed at the ache in her temples. She'd had a low-grade headache since last night. The constant stress about funds wasn't improving her health.

Andie stowed her new clothes in the antique dresser and sparsely filled bedroom closet. She surveyed the hanging tops, now arranged in rainbow order. It was exciting to have more than the three pairs of pants and half a dozen T-shirts she'd found upon arrival. She tried on a few new things which looked nice but casual, including a pair of jeans with a mottled appearance. She'd overheard someone call a denim jacket with a similar pattern, acid washed. Choosing a lilac top with buttons and a collar that flipped up, Andie prepared for the barbeque and for work afterward.

Though she didn't have fluffy hair, she combed out her waves and left her hair down for a change. Loose, it reached mid-way down her back and though she didn't tease her bangs upward or spray them with hair spray, she didn't feel too out of place. From a still unsorted box filled with shoes, she grabbed a pair of black and white Converse sneakers. Size Eight. She frowned. They looked like the same as a pair she'd left in 2033—even with identical scuff marks on the toes. Though the rest of her new clothes were unfamiliar, everything seemed worn enough to be comfortable.

She found it interesting how everything fit. Dr. Maeve had pulled off incredible magic. Maybe if Andie found the woman, instead of just yelling and demanding she be returned to her own time, she'd thank her for a job well done. It seemed Dr. Maeve had thought of everything.

•   •   •

Val and Andie exited the car on Xander's street at a quarter after one. The promised sunshine warmed the pavement while the blue sky spread overhead. Andie inhaled, so the warm air and scents of summer filled her lungs. What a stunning afternoon, one that hinted at the rest of summer to come. A few remaining clouds scudded across the sky, chased by the mild breeze. Andie could live without gray and rain for some time. Plus, the sun improved her mood, making it easier to ignore her headache. She'd felt off all week, though no cold had developed, and she didn't seem sick.

Andie checked out Xander's block. Peonies and rose bushes, in brilliant magenta, fuchsia, and pale pink blooms, decorated most yards. Their bursts of color seemed perfect for late June. Though the flowers were stunning, they bloomed for such a short time. Peonies always reminded her of her mother's yard in the house they'd lived in for three years, from age ten to thirteen, one of the few places she'd considered a proper home and the only location they'd lived that long. She'd been able to attend the same school for three full years.

Andie carried a salad bowl while Val held a large plate of cookies as they walked up the sidewalk toward their destination. As they approached, Andie's steps faltered. The neighborhood was more upscale than where she and Val lived, the houses grander. Otherwise, it seemed much the same, though most properties had driveways and garages in which to park instead of curbside street parking. Did coming today make her an imposter? She hoped she fit in and it wouldn't be awkward.

At Xander's, the double driveway held four parked cars, including his gold pickup she'd seen at Zack's worksite, and Zack's silver sedan. Her heart fluttered. He was already here. She glanced down the street, discovering most of the street parking was also full. From the backyard, the sound of music played. From this distance, Andie couldn't recognize the song. What had she gotten herself into? She wanted to bolt.

The backyard barbeque might be louder and more hectic than a simple family gathering—more like a party. Xander had made it sound casual. She bit her lip, coming to a full stop. She inhaled, then forced herself to move. Val continued for another ten feet, toward a tall, wooden gate at the side of the house. She reached over the top, unlocked it, and motioned for Andie to proceed. "You ready?"

"So, who all is supposed to be here?" whispered Andie, stopping in front of her friend. Her voice sounded strained.

"Just the family and a few of Xander and Cindy's closest friends. Nobody will bite, though they might hug you. You'll get to meet Yolanda and her husband Mike. Plus, Cindy. My dad will be here. Xander said Wanda and their parents, Aunt Jen, and Great-Aunt M. will be here." Val's list was daunting.

"I hope you won't be offended if I want to leave early?" Andie rolled her shoulders. "Sorry, I'm just nervous."

Val rested her free hand on Andie's arm and spoke in a soothing tone. "You're just panicking. Xander and Cindy are kind people, and you'll like my sister. Plus, you know Zack. He's here. If you get too overwhelmed, tell me and I'll run you home. It isn't far. My family can be a lot, but their hearts are in the right place." She waited for Andie's reaction.

She nodded and took a deep breath. She trusted Val enough to explain her sudden reluctance. "My family included three people. A few times we joined an elderly aunt, but I've been on my own for ten years. This might be a lot to handle." It was the truth, other than her time with Dylan, which was already becoming a nightmarish blur—like something far away. She'd done her best to block out the previous year. Without constant reminders and billboards plastered with his smug face, or drop-ins at her house and work, he was fading into an unpleasant memory.

"You've got this," said Val as she squeezed Andie's arm. "Stick to me like glue. I like to have someone to talk to, too. If any of my aunts get too nosy or make you uncomfortable, I'll put them in their place. You ready?"

Andie nodded, clutching her salad bowl closer. They headed into the backyard.

# Chapter 20
# Zack

"I'm scared of everything. I'm scared of what I saw, I'm scared of what I did, of who I am, and most of all I'm scared of walking out of this room and never feeling the rest of my whole life the way I feel when I'm with you." –Frances Houseman, Dirty Dancing, (1987)

Zack stood in a patch of sunshine on the deck near Xander's pool by the sizzling barbeque, where billows of steam poured from the grill, the mouth-watering scent of cooking burgers filling his nostrils. He gazed at the expanse of brilliant green lawn; his cousin probably had the grass mowed twice a week to keep it trim. Zack hesitated to join his family inside, enjoying soaking up some rays on his own outside.

He surveyed the space, admiring the extensive backyard and planning how he'd use his own, if he kept it. Zack's backyard wouldn't be quite so large, and he didn't have room for a pool, but a hot tub might be just the ticket. His usual distraction teased him at the idea, this time the lilac bikini-clad image of a hot tub evening with Andie. She was seldom far from his thoughts.

He dangled a long-necked bottle of beer at his side, but it was mostly for show. Today was about celebrating Xander and Cindy's engagement, but Zack couldn't remember the last time he'd had more than a single beer. It wasn't just because he was driving later to collect Andie from work—that was hours from now.

Like Xander, Zack wasn't interested in partying anymore. He never discussed the decision, which was mostly a by-product of seeing all the disasters caused by excessive alcohol through his job. Though today was his last day off, he'd been unable to relax and unwind. A certain friend remained on his mind far too often. Pretending indifference was a torment.

He remained separate from the natural-occurring groups scattered across the yard, monitoring the grill while Xander checked in with his guests. The older generation gathered inside, while the younger crowd milled outside. The patio held several couples who were Xander and Cindy's friends. Wanda and her boyfriend chatted with Yolanda and her husband, Mike.

Zack was one of the few single people in the group. Single by choice.

It seemed nothing had come of Aunt M.'s mystery girl. No wonder his aunts continued to try to rectify the situation. They were probably inside plotting. He suppressed a sigh. They would ask who he was dating over dinner when they emerged from the air-conditioned house for food. He wished he had an answer that would make them cease and desist. Maybe he should tell them he wasn't interested in women and let them draw their own conclusions.

He hadn't felt self-conscious about not bringing anyone to family get-togethers, until now. He took a tiny sip of his beer. Beside him, Xander opened the grill, releasing the scent of roasted meat into the yard.

Across the lawn and patio, movement by the gate attracted his attention as Val arrived with Andie in tow. Both had dressed up, and he couldn't help admiring Andie's firm ass in her stylish jeans. With her pretty light purple top, she looked springy and attractive. He glanced down at his faded jeans, wishing he'd at least worn a newer pair. He shouldn't be surprised she was here—every time he spoke to Val, she mentioned Andie's name.

Xander bumped the lid down and nudged Zack's shoulder. "She's a bodacious babe."

"Who?" said Zack, turning to face his cousin. "Andie?"

"Your 'friend' over there who has braved our family. I can't believe you haven't made a move on her. As the one who invited her, I'm going to say hi." Xander strode away. When had he invited Andie? As he neared the house, Cindy appeared at the sliding glass door with a large wooden bowl, so Xander detoured toward her, taking her burden. She stepped outside beside him. He leaned over, whispered in her ear, and then she tucked her arm into his.

A pang shot through Zack as the two of them headed for Val and Andie by the food table. Xander and Cindy looked like they fit.

Zack's eyes swiveled back to Andie, drawn like magnets. A force he was unable to deny and inevitable. If he was trying to guard his heart, he wasn't succeeding. He'd wait two more minutes before joining her, so he didn't seem too eager. His stomach flipped when Xander and Cindy greeted Andie. Zack wished he was already at her side, his arm wrapped around her—the way Xander was with his fiancée.

It took tremendous effort for Zack to wrest his gaze away. He had no business getting weird about Andie. What had changed? Today, he felt too tongue-tied to speak to her without worrying she'd discern his secret. If he'd known she'd be here, he might have prepared himself, like he did for every dinner at Val's. On those evenings, he'd exhausted all the innocuous topics and common interests, like books and movies. He wanted a heart-to-heart in a dim corner, somewhere he could get to know her better. Not going to happen. He worried he'd give in and kiss her delectable mouth.

She was sweet and smart. It was becoming more difficult to remain indifferent.

He shifted again, unwilling to follow that line of thought. Instead, he circled back to the call he'd received from his buddy John this morning. Andie had finally booked an appointment to have her car serviced. High time. It had driven Zack crazy that she hadn't taken her car in sooner. It was her car and her choice, but if he'd had a say, he'd have had it fixed weeks ago so she wouldn't be dependent on anyone. He couldn't help worrying about her walking home alone in the dark.

Now that he thought about it, she never asked for help. He and Val had always insisted on helping. Perhaps she'd grown up in a world where nobody looked out for her. If that was true, Zack wanted to take on some of her burdens. He'd been holding himself back for weeks, afraid to overstep or give himself away. Instead, he'd probably come off overbearing when he just wanted to protect her and provide assistance.

Andie was so independent and self-contained. She didn't like owing him when he picked her up from work. He could tell by the way her voice changed when she thanked him—like she was swallowing something gross. Sure, she appreciated the rides, but clearly wasn't comfortable accepting more. While there were no strings attached, it seemed like she wanted a way to pay him back—which wasn't required.

While Zack didn't mind collecting her from work, he couldn't tell her he looked forward to seeing her—that he enjoyed knowing she was safe. It might give her the wrong idea about having a relationship. He'd been clear. Still, seeing her here now was a bonus. A bonus and a torment.

Zack had just decided it had been long enough, and he could wander over to join Val and Andie, when Aunt M. stepped over the threshold from inside. Her eyes lit up and M. made a beeline toward the two young women. From across the pool, he watched her thread her way among the groups on the deck, her brilliant clothes and flaming hair drawing the eye. What would Andie make of his eccentric great aunt?

Andie's cheeks flushed pink, then pale, grabbing the edge of the table as though for support. He loved how expressive her face was and how easily she blushed. He tamped down the fleeting thought. His eyes narrowed and a frown tugged at his face. Why was her reaction so extreme?

Did she know his aunt? Like lightning, the truth struck. Could Andie be his aunt's choice for his future partner? Watching them from his vantage, he'd bet on it. The puzzle piece clicked into place. He didn't know how they could be connected, but they must be, even if Andie hadn't mentioned therapy. Unable to contain his curiosity, he stepped toward the group.

His aunt's words confirmed they'd met before. "Andie, dear, I was hoping you'd be here," said Aunt M. "I'd love to chat."

"Aunt M.," said Val, a line appearing on her forehead as she glanced from one to the other. "You know my new friend? She just moved in down the street a couple of months ago."

"We met earlier this spring. I'm old friends with one of her former neighbors," M. said, waving her hand as though the answer was obvious.

Not a client then? Or was her answer a cover? Today, his aunt wore rings on each finger and her thumbs. The colored stones winked in the sunlight like jewels, though they were probably polished crystals and semi-precious stones. He took a breath. The rings were a distraction, and he needed to concentrate.

"We've only met once before," said Andie, a slight crease between her brows. She nodded to Zack as he joined their group on the patio.

If he hadn't been scrutinizing her, Zack wouldn't have seen her jaw flare. Was she upset?

"Actually, I'd love a chance to speak with M. about something." Andie glanced down, cracking her knuckles. Was it his imagination or had she hesitated before his aunt's name? "In private?" She turned to Val with her explanation, swallowing. "It's about my ex."

"The one that hit you," said Val, her concerned expression replaced with a scowl. While his sister was usually calm, she was fierce when it came to protecting those close to her.

Rage spiked through Zack. How dare someone hurt Andie? She must have opened up to Val enough to talk about her past. Why hadn't Andie mentioned an abusive ex to him? The burst of envious ripples faded, replaced by common sense. Just like other women, Zack had kept her at arm's length, not giving her a chance to confide. He inhaled, tracking her movement as Aunt M. and Andie strode across the lawn to the far corner of the backyard.

From this distance, he couldn't hear their words, so he remained beside Val. They looked at each other, mirroring their expressions with raised eyebrows. Curiosity rose off his sister in waves. If anyone learned what was said, it would be her. Trying not to stare, he used his peripheral vision to interpret the conversation across the yard by observing body language. Andie's fists remained clenched while M. looked like her usual, easy-going self, unperturbed by Andie's anger, her hands waving. One of M.'s generous laughs emerged.

Zack forced his eyes away to give their conversation the privacy they wished for. He switched his attention back to his sister, finding her thoughtful eyes trained on him. Damn. Busted.

Val's gaze held several questions he wasn't ready to answer.

He needed to distract her. "It was nice of you to bring Andie. She doesn't know many people besides us." While he didn't spend time with people, other than colleagues, at least he had his family. He met up with his cousins and sisters more than anyone else. Without them, he'd have been on his own. If it wasn't for Val, Andie's life would be lonely.

"Xander ran into her outside your house site, and he invited her. He thought she might like to get to know more than just a neighbor or two. She could use friends." Val's gaze was direct.

Guilt suffused Zack's chest. He'd said he wanted to be Andie's friend, but he hadn't called or spoken to her, other than driving her home from work or running into her at Val's. He'd been too scared.

His eyes flicked back to the conversation in the corner. Had Aunt M. promised Andie he would ask her out for a date, and he hadn't cooperated? He didn't date, and he'd been clear with them. Or maybe their discussion was unrelated to him. Still, their meeting here was quite a coincidence.

His mind staggered back through his early interactions with Andie. They'd met because of her fall, which hadn't been staged. She'd been in pain and covered in blood. Besides, M. wouldn't have known he'd be biking that day, let alone which route. Meeting Andie must have been a fluke. His face felt tight, and he rotated his shoulders and neck, forcing his muscles to relax. Maybe M. hadn't interfered.

Zack opened his mouth to speak, and Val shoved one of her famous chocolate chip cookies into his mouth. Chocolate melted in his mouth and his eyes almost rolled back in his head. So delicious. He chewed, forgetting what he'd been about to say.

"It's okay if you like her." Val's eyes twinkled.

He took a second bite of the cookie, breaking off the final chunk in his hand. "Pardon?" He hated to be so transparent. "She's just a friend."

"Right," said his sister, raising one eyebrow. "You only pick her up from work late at night on both Friday and Saturday if you aren't working, just so she doesn't have to walk home. They have these things called cabs. Besides, I see you checking her out. What does that mean?"

He ignored the second part of her statement. "I'd also give you a lift home if you needed one." He glanced toward Andie and Aunt M. again. They were still talking. Andie's cheeks were red, and he caught the word "time." He turned his head, but he'd already seen Andie whirl away from the conversation. She was heading in their direction.

With her face flushed and her eyes shiny, she was struggling not to cry. When she stopped in their small circle, she crossed her arms. Zack wanted to scoop Andie into a hug. She was so obviously upset.

"Are you okay?" He set his beer bottle on the table and jammed his hands deep into his pockets. Maybe he should have a word with Aunt M. Sometimes she could be a bit much.

"I'll be fine," said Andie. "I just got some unexpected news."

"I'm sorry if my aunt upset you," said Val, squeezing Andie's arm. "She means well, and we love her, but she's kind of an interfering meddler sometimes. She's quirky and generous, so she gets away with saying all kinds of things that are sometimes rude." Her frown remained.

"You must be talking about Aunt M. I'd say her eccentricity is part of her charm," said Xander, reappearing with a platter of hamburger buns, which he set on the table. "Cindy said to tell everyone to get your plates organized. The grub's ready. Grab what you want and meet me at the grill." He sauntered away, picked up his spatula, and struck a pose, poised by the sizzling burgers.

He looked happier than Zack could remember. Being engaged suited his cousin, more evidence of Aunt M.'s interference. Panic shot through him again. He definitely found Andie attractive, but friendship was better than nothing. He had to protect himself from the pain his dad and Val had lived through. They'd chosen to be alone after losing their true loves. He could skip the middle part and save himself a world of pain.

He turned from the others. "I'm starving. Bring on the food." He collected a plate, grabbed two pre-cut hamburger buns, slathered them with ketchup and mustard, and set cheese, lettuce, tomato, and pickle on the top buns.

A waft of vanilla and citrus struck him. Andie stood beside him. "You like your hamburgers the same way I do. Sloppy with sauce and lots of pickles."

He cleared his throat. "I love a good cheeseburger." He left with a nod, heading for Xander and the hamburger patties. He added how she liked her burgers to a tiny list of her likes and dislikes.

"Smooth," said Xander, dropping meat onto the buns. He waggled his eyebrows.

"Shut up." Zack's words lacked his usual zing. His cousin was right. He was a mess. A sliver of jealousy toward his cousin returned. Xander's life seemed a lot fuller than his own. His cousin's life had changed enough that Zack now felt the difference between them. Perhaps living for work wasn't enough. It was like a punch to the gut, a betrayal of everything he'd strived for throughout his life.

Was it too late to change everything?

# CHAPTER 21
# ANDIE

"You're not thinking fourth dimensionally!"
–Doc Brown, Back to the Future (1985)

The rest of Andie's afternoon at the barbeque passed in a daze. Val's Great-Aunt M. was Dr. Maeve. It had come at her out of the blue like a lightning strike on a clear day. One minute she'd been getting her bearings at a family barbeque, the next, she was on her ass and trying to recover. After giving up on finding the doctor, seeing her this way had stolen all of Andie's oxygen. Her brain had frozen, and she hadn't even asked most of the questions burning inside her since her arrival in 1985.

She bit into her cheeseburger, letting the delicious taste defuse her anger. Despite two months of frustration with Dr. Maeve, Andie hadn't yelled. She'd maintained her calm until just before the end. Though grateful for her new life, as soon as she'd seen Dr. Maeve, that all went out the window. Unable to let the turn of events go, Andie replayed the incident for the third time while she ate.

When she and Dr. Maeve reached the far corner of the yard, Andie turned. Seeing the woman had brought a fresh wave of homesickness washing over her. Her bottled-up anger seeped to the surface and unleashed.

Through clenched teeth, she said, "What the hell am I doing in 1985? I want to go home." Her furious words had sluiced off Dr. Maeve without seeming to make an impression.

"Aren't you having a good time, dear?" Her tone was pleasant but concerned.

"When I traveled through time, I left everything I knew." Andie struggled to keep her volume down. Her pent-up feelings were difficult to contain.

"You wished for somewhere safe to belong, somewhere simpler than where you lived. Isn't life here more to your liking?" Dr. Maeve's hands waved through the air as she spoke, her multiple necklaces clicking with the motion of her body, distracting Andie from her anger, which infuriated her more.

Andie couldn't formulate an answer as her thoughts ground to a halt. She had made that wish. She loved the freedom from Dylan, and despite her monetary woes, she'd adjusted to many aspects of life in the 80s—even the lack of computers, cell phones, and internet. Her mouth opened to protest, but Dr. Maeve carried on.

"Are you planning to tell Val and Zack you come from the future?" Dr. Maeve pinned her with a mesmerizing stare, fixing Andie in place.

She glanced toward her friends across the lawn. They must be curious about this unexpected conversation. "Not a chance," she hissed. "Why would they believe such a ridiculous claim? If I told them I'd slipped back in time because of a wish made on a magic stone you gave me, they'd think I'd lost my mind." What they didn't know couldn't harm their relationships— Andie would continue to be careful not to let her secret slip.

"That's probably for the best. They're lovely people and Zack might believe you, but Val." Dr. Maeve had laughed, then wrinkled her nose and shook her head.

"Will I ever go home? To my time?" Andie asked.

To which the infuriating Dr. Maeve replied, "But why would you? There was nothing for you there. Nobody to miss you, except maybe your students, who would have left for summer break by now. You'd be back to having no one. You fit better in this time, with these people. Give this life a real chance." She patted Andie's cheek and returned to the house, passing Val, Zack, and Xander with a small wave.

Andie took another bite. Now that she'd had time to settle down and her brain resumed proper function, there was another problem. Shouldn't Dr. Maeve look younger in this time? She'd appeared to be the same, despite a forty-eight-year time difference between their conversations. Had she also time-traveled?

That possibility was a new idea. Either that or, if there was such a thing, was she a witch?

With Dr. Maeve returning inside the house carrying a plate laden with food, it was easy for Andie to ignore her. Instead, she talked to Val, Xander, and Cindy for most of the afternoon. Zack remained nearby, but he spoke little. Still, when she went inside to use the washroom and snag a piece of carrot cake, she sensed his eyes tracking her movements. What was with him today? He wasn't usually this quiet or serious.

Andie finished her glass of lemonade; he brought her another without being asked. She took it and said, "Thanks." Hoping she wasn't off base, she whispered, "Are you okay?"

He smiled, this one not reaching his eyes. Something must be on his mind. "I'm fine." He tapped his plastic cup against hers. "To Xander and Cindy."

Val leaned over and said to Andie, "I forgot to ask. Do you need me to run you home to change before work? After I drop you off, I'm going to come back and talk to my sister for a bit. We haven't connected yet today." She frowned slightly. Yolanda and Xander's sister Wanda had been drinking wine for a few hours and had gotten loud, their voices carrying from across the patio.

Andie shook her head. "I planned to wear this, and I'm ready to go whenever is convenient."

"I'm going to head, too." Zack turned to Andie. "I can drop you at work and save Val a trip. I have a few things to do this evening."

Val raised her eyebrows toward Andie, probably checking the change in plan was okay.

"Are you sure?" Andie asked. "You're already picking me up later. It's too much."

"It's no bother. I'm going to the gym, and the video store is almost on the way."

"That's why you didn't drink," said Andie. "You're going to go work out."

Val and Xander looked at each other, perhaps confused. They may not have noticed Zack had abandoned his single beer half full, but Andie had. He'd set it on the table hours ago and drank water for the rest of the afternoon. Was that something she shouldn't have mentioned? Drink counting had been ingrained in her during childhood, but Dylan had always gotten angry if she mentioned a number. She braced for an argument.

Instead, Zack smiled, a genuine one, and nodded. "Someone's observant. I'm not a big drinker."

That was something he and Andie had in common. Her mom's alcoholism had caused endless problems throughout her childhood. She figured it was best not to imbibe and had never developed the habit.

Her shoulders dropped, glad her comment hadn't caused an issue. Something about Zack set her so much at ease, she'd forgotten her usual rules for socializing. She hadn't remembered to be careful and had just been herself. That might not sound like much to some people, but for her, it was everything.

"You're ready now?" said Zack, checking his watch.

Andie nodded. She turned to Val. "Thanks for bringing me. I had a nice time. Enjoy the evening with your sister and cousins. I'm going to take Zack up on his offer and I'll see you next week for dinner one night. Let me know if I can bring anything." To Xander and Cindy, she said, "Thanks for inviting me. All the best for your engagement. You have a lovely home."

"You're welcome anytime," said Xander. "Thanks for coming."

Then Andie left with Zack.

He was quiet for the first several minutes in the car. His first words must have been on his mind all afternoon. "It was quite a surprise you'd already met our Aunt M."

"It really is a small world," Andie said, keeping her tone even. How else would she explain something so surprising?

"Val mentioned you had a boyfriend not long ago. Is that why you aren't interested in dating anyone?" His comment seemed to come from left field. Wasn't he the one who didn't date?

"In part," she said, her eyes fixed ahead. "I moved across the country to be with Dylan, but he wasn't what I expected." She couldn't explain they'd met online. "I got caught up in being part of his busy world. He hit me, so I left. I wasn't about to give him another chance. I'm not that girl." She hoped that sounded strong and reasonable.

"Leaving takes guts. Do you still talk to your ex?" Zack shot her a sideways glance.

"No. He isn't around anymore." Since in 1985 Dylan hadn't been born, it was adjacent to the truth.

Andie bit her lip before forging ahead. "He's the reason I don't date. What's yours?" She hadn't meant to be so blunt, but the words popped out. She'd wanted to ask for as long as she'd known him. Someone like Zack should have been taken long ago.

"Dating seemed kind of pointless," he said, shooting her another sideways glance, mostly watching the street. "It wouldn't have gone anywhere."

At last, he was talking about himself. Pointless was strong language. If she waited him out, he might say more. She clamped her lips together.

Zack continued a block later in a quiet voice. "For a long time, I wasn't interested in ever getting married, though Xander wears his engagement well. I just couldn't see myself that way." He paused and his voice deepened. "My mom died when I was young, which wrecked my dad. He took years to recover to the point he's at now. I didn't want to end up like him if something happened to my partner."

"That sounds pretty lonely," said Andie. She rested her hand on his shoulder, a zing of current racing through her. He was so warm and solid that she forgot herself. "I'm not trying to be rude or change your mind about going out with me, but in my opinion, your reason is such a waste. For me, a potential hurt is worth it if it means not being lonely and being with someone wonderful. You're never going to date anyone in case you fall in love, because they might die, and you'd be devastated? It's sad you might lose out on happiness because of a remote chance of being crushed."

She removed her hand when he didn't reply. The tension in the car grew thicker, and she stared out the side window, watching the stores they passed as he drove across town. The silence stretched like an elastic band, and she waited for the snap. He turned down the street where West Coast Video was located, and she glanced across the vehicle.

Zack's jaw was set. He didn't speak as he parked outside the store. Was he sorry he'd been real? Maybe he rarely talked about his mother. Should she have been more sensitive? Andie felt like an idiot. She'd probably misread the situation. Uncomfortable sweat made her shirt sticky. Had she overstepped or possibly struck a nerve?

"You don't know me at all," he said, his voice leaden. "Whether or not I date is none of your business. We're never going to be together." Both of his hands gripped the wheel as he stared out the windshield. His knuckles turned white when he stopped in front of the video store.

Andie stifled a gasp, like she'd been struck. At the least, she'd thought he liked her. "I'm sorry," she said. "You're right. Your love life is none of my business. I'm sorry I said anything. Thank you for the ride." Her words came out as stiff as cardboard while she fought her impending tears.

He didn't reply.

She rested her hand on the cool metal of the door handle. Her chin wobbled as she spoke in a wavering voice. "I'll figure out another ride tonight. Now that school is out, Val can get me tomorrow, so I don't inconvenience you. Your friend is coming on Friday to install the new alternator so I can drive myself next weekend. You've been extremely kind." Her words sounded overly polite, as if for a second, they hadn't connected about something more important than getting a ride.

Zack's lips twitched upward, but his expression seemed strained, his smile not reaching his ice-blue eyes. His tone was frosty and detached. "I'll be here tonight at the usual time. I'm glad you're getting your car taken care of because you need wheels. I'd have given a ride to anyone in your position, but driving your own car is better, more convenient."

She nodded. "Don't worry. I didn't think the rides had anything to do with me. You're just a nice guy. Usually." Right now, he was an asshole. Tears pricked behind her eyes. She hated that she'd read him wrong this afternoon. "Enjoy your workout. See you later." She lifted the handle and fled, rushing inside to start her shift.

# CHAPTER 22
# ANDIE

"Since the invention of the kiss there have been five kisses that were rated the most passionate, the most pure. This one left them all behind."
–The Princess Bride (1987)

Andie stared around the hushed store Friday night after the barbeque. The quiet came from one of the odd lulls between customers, the first in hours. She'd learned to stay on top of the action, even when it was busy—which often occurred in spurts. She checked in the returned movies, shelving them as soon as possible. Andie kept the customer line to a manageable level if she emerged from behind the counter to make movie recommendations and replace the movie tags.

After the last couple of months, the regular customers no longer made her flustered. Even the gruff biker no longer left her off-kilter. People seemed the same in every time, friendly if you had common interests, and this was her domain—she spoke "movie." A perk of working here was she could take anything home that hadn't been rented for the evening—for free. She'd sometimes taken movies to Val's for Sundays, leaving her an expert on many of the current titles. If only she'd been able to afford her own VCR.

She'd also worked here long enough to develop a work persona, not unlike the one she wore when teaching. Smile, be courteous, be knowledgeable. Some men gave her flirtatious comments or glances, but she ignored them all. Their looks and words were probably just habit, and not meant to be taken seriously.

"So, is that guy who picks you up your boyfriend?" Rick's slurred voice startled her as she swiveled to face him. Her heart thumped hard against her chest, slowing when there was no defined danger. She'd thought she was alone in the store. He must have come in the back door, as usual. This was the first time since she'd worked here that he'd made it beyond the office and the back hallway.

"No," Andie said, reaching up to replace a movie tag. She kept Rick in her line of sight as she stuck on another handful. He wouldn't surprise her again. "Just a friend." The word seemed wrong. Maybe she and Zack weren't anything, despite what seemed like mutual attraction and interest. Apparently, it had turned out to be one-sided. She swallowed. He'd made that clear this evening. They weren't even friends, just acquaintances. The word seemed hollow, like they'd missed an opportunity.

She edged farther away from Rick, pretending movie boxes were out of place, she straightened the top row. The usual tumbler was in his hand and his eyes seemed hard, unpredictable. She didn't know her boss well, so it was difficult to get a read on what was going through his head. Her headache throbbed, and she wiped her damp hands on her jeans. She didn't like the way he was checking her out. She hoped he wouldn't be a problem. Perhaps Nate's warning made her suspicious when it was unnecessary.

"You're managing the store just fine. Any questions?" Rick stumbled to his left and caught himself on the edge of the counter. Sweat beaded on his forehead, trails rolling down his face. Maybe he was sick. She'd been feeling under the weather all evening.

She shook her head. "I've got the hang of it." She strode back behind the counter, giving him a wide berth. Andie hoped customers would arrive soon and he would disappear. She didn't want to be alone with her boss. Maybe if she didn't need help, he'd leave.

To her dismay, Rick dragged the stool behind the counter to the far corner, leaving her to work in front of the computer. He stared at the overhead TV, seemingly engrossed in the current movie. His continued presence at the front remained off-putting, but she ignored him, pretending she was alone through the next several customers. Their eyes cut to Rick, but he just watched the TV and didn't engage. Perhaps this was customary when he was in the store.

His gaze bored into Andie's back, but she had a system and stuck to it, refusing to let him affect her performance. She greeted each customer, loaded their account on the computer, collected their movies, scanned them, and answered questions they had before telling them the total and taking payment. Each customer who left wished her good night or said something personal. She always replied and thanked them for their business. It was much friendlier than the anonymous, impersonal world of 2033, where everyone ignored each other like strangers.

As the end of her shift neared, the store emptied, and still Rick sat on the stool, drinking and watching whatever movie was playing. She didn't ignore him, but she moved around without speaking to him until the store was empty. "Can you watch the front for a minute while I use the washroom?" As usual, she timed her bathroom break for when the store was deserted.

"Sure," he said, taking a swig from his covered mug. His eyes were heavy-lidded. Maybe he'd leave and go sleep it off in his office. She crossed her fingers.

Hurrying, she wound behind the shelves of movies, turned down the dim hall, and rushed into the bathroom, locking the door, which she didn't normally do. She took an extra second afterward to straighten her hair in the mirror. It must be late enough she could start some final jobs, even if she left the front door unlocked. She often stayed open a few minutes late for people who ducked in just before closing.

The last time that had happened, Zack had come inside to wait while she closed, ran the report, and counted the cash. Despite how they'd left things when he'd dropped her off, she found herself hoping for the same tonight. She disliked being alone with Rick.

However, Zack might notice the boss hanging around, which might convince him to stay outside.

Andie opened the bathroom door and ran into Rick in the dim hallway. She stumbled.

He grabbed her arm. Instead of steadying her, he spun her toward him. His other hand grabbed her ass and squeezed. "This is a nice handful." He leaned closer, alcoholic fumes assaulting her face. "What're you doing after work?"

Heart pounding, she shoved away, somehow extricating herself from his grasp. Her voice shook. "My friend is picking me up soon and taking me home."

"I'll slip you an extra twenty bucks if you give me a blow job. Cash." Rick licked his lips. "Fifty if you come back to my place and let me fuck you."

Bile rose in her throat as he grabbed her arm again. "I'm not interested." This time, his grip was hard enough that he might leave bruises. "Get your hands off me." She'd give him one more chance before she pushed the issue.

"You're broke. I can tell you could use the cash." He leaned toward her.

She froze. How had he guessed when he was seldom here or sober? Perhaps her limited wardrobe or lack of a car.

The bell above the front door rang. A customer. Thank god.

"Just a minute," she called, her voice the friendly one that didn't sound like anything was wrong. She lowered her voice. "No matter how broke I am, I'm not interested. Don't touch me again or I'll report you to the police." She couldn't be clearer. Her stomach churned. What if Rick fired her for refusing his advances?

Rick's eyes narrowed, but he said nothing as she wrenched her arm free and hurried out front.

"I was afraid you were closed," said one of the regular customers, a middle-aged man who often rented two or three new releases each time he came in.

"We're open until eleven." Andie glanced at her watch. Five more minutes. "But if you need an extra couple of minutes, don't worry." From down the back hall, a door slammed. Hopefully, Rick had returned to his office. Or better yet, left. She hoped it was the latter. She didn't want to face him again when she locked the money in the safe. Her stomach churned at the thought of working here if he continued to harass her. She'd have to quit.

Did she have to stay until school started? Maybe she should look for a different job. Her heart sank. She couldn't afford to be without work; nobody seemed to be hiring, and even then she didn't have references.

Before she checked out the first customer, a young couple joined him in the store.

The young woman squinted at the clock on the wall. "Oh good, you're still open. Don't you close at eleven?"

"We do, but go ahead and find something. I don't mind staying open a few extra minutes." Andie glanced around. She'd done everything she could to straighten the store. All the movies were dealt with, so she just needed to run the report, cash out, and lock up.

Andie handled the customers and followed them to the door when they left at ten minutes after eleven o'clock. She flipped the lock, peering outside. There was no sign of Zack's car yet, though it was past closing time. Maybe she had offended him so much he wouldn't come. Or he might have forgotten.

She immediately dismissed the idea; he must just be counting on her needing the extra time. Angry or not, after all these weeks, he wouldn't strand her here when he'd been so concerned about her safety. He seemed like the kind of man who followed through with his commitments.

She turned off the pink neon sign and opened the overnight drop slot. With a last glance outside, she watched headlights approach until she identified the car. Zack. Her breath whooshed out. He parked outside in front of the door, and she gave him a small wave. Even if it might get her in trouble, she opened the front door.

He rolled down his window and leaned out of the car. "You ready?"

She shook her head. "Not quite." If Rick was still here, would she be fired for letting Zack inside? No matter how much she needed the money, she didn't want to be alone with her boss again. Especially not tonight, not when the feel of his groping hands hadn't faded. His slimy offer still lurked in her head. She needed money, but she wasn't that desperate.

"The last customer just left, and I need a few more minutes. Would you like to wait inside?" Her voice sounded high and odd.

Zack turned off the engine and stepped out. "Everything okay?"

She half-turned toward the back office but caught herself. Zack couldn't do anything about drunken Rick. She shook her head. "I'm just running late." Her hand shook as he walked past her, and she relocked the door. She kept her gaze from straying. It had been quiet in the back for several minutes. Maybe Zack could come with her to the office, just in case.

She'd no sooner let Zack in past her and relocked the door when Rick lurched out from behind the tall shelving. His eyes widened when he saw she wasn't alone. She needed to make it clear to Rick that she had friends and support and wouldn't be intimidated into submission.

Andie froze. "This is Zack," she said. "He's my ride. I'm almost finished closing." She hurried forward, passing Rick, making her way to the computer. Her cheeks burned, and she swallowed, her mouth parched. She ran the report and counted the money with sweaty hands while Zack waited near the door. She lost track of the total twice and had to start over. He didn't say anything but stood, jingling his keys. He appeared to be watching the movie on the screen overhead, so she left it on until she completed everything else. This TV at least had a remote.

Rick stayed in the store, leaning against the movie shelves, and it took all of Andie's control and concentration not to fumble through her closing tasks.

She ripped the printed pages off the printer roll, folded the pages into sections, and slipped it into the Ziploc with the counted stack of money and the cash slip. Instead of taking it to the office, she handed it to Rick.

"Everything is accounted for." She made a point of looking him in the eye.

Rick nodded. "Have a good night. Lock the front door on the way out." His eyes flicked to Zack once more. "You're a decent guy to pick her up so late."

"Just looking out for her." Zack's tone was unfriendly.

Her cheeks remained hot as she grabbed her purse. "I'm ready."

Outside, she gulped the cool night air while she locked the metal-framed glass door. Zack unlocked the passenger side of the car, and she said nothing as she slid into the car. She folded her shaking hands into her lap and focused on breathing. If she didn't have to speak, everything might be okay.

Zack slid behind the wheel and closed his door. He backed out of the parking spot and drove her home. They remained silent, and she stared at the blur of bright city lights as he drove. He pulled up at the curb behind her still-deceased yellow car.

The ride was over already?

"Did that asshole do something?" His voice emerged as a growl.

Andie burst into tears, her hands covering her face.

Zack unbuckled his seatbelt, slid closer, and tugged her toward him. She leaned into him, letting his clean fresh scent calm her. His powerful arms wrapped around her, holding her while she sobbed. Upset as she was, his warm, solid presence made her safe.

She didn't cry for long, but her tears were a tremendous release. She'd been terrified and angry with Rick at the same time. Zack rubbed her back and held her until she pulled back, just enough to see his gorgeous pale blue eyes at close range. He tracked her slight movement as her breath caught.

Zack cupped her jaw, his thumb stroking her cheek. Jolts of heat shot through her, chasing her previous fear. He smoothed her hair back from her eyes with his other hand. He stared at her a moment and inched forward. Capturing her lips with his, one hand tangled in her hair, he held her close. Zack was kissing her.

Oh, my god. Zack's lips melted problems like popsicles in the sun.

Andie kissed him back, scooting closer on the uncomfortable seat. For the first time in months, her brain stopped whirling, the world peaceful. She could kiss Zack forever, their lips sliding, their breath mingling. Safe in his arms, everything chaotic stilled and time ceased to have meaning. Being with Zack felt right.

Until Zack wrenched himself back, his breath heaving.

Dazed and with a buzzing head, she took a moment to regain her senses. Why he had stopped?

"Oh shit," he said, his pale eyes wide. "I shouldn't have done that." He didn't give her a chance to speak. "Your boss is such a jerk. I don't know what got into me. I guess I turned into some Neanderthal, all set to prove you're my woman, not his. I had no right to kiss you. I'm so sorry. It won't happen again."

"I don't mind," she said, one hand touching her bottom lip. It throbbed. "I kissed you back."

"I mind," he said, turning his head away. "You're a friend, and kissing you was a mistake. You don't have to worry about me kissing you again."

His words staked her heart, turning it to dust.

A red haze descended, and her words came out clipped. "I appreciate your help with Rick. He had too much to drink tonight and made me nervous. I'll be fine. And, with my car being ready soon, I won't need your help anymore after tonight." She opened the car and stepped out. "Thanks for the ride." She slammed the door, hard—the sound satisfying as she turned. What the hell? She was too old for these games of hot and cold.

Andie ran for the front door, fumbling with the lock until the key turned. Once inside, she slid down the wall, rested her head on her knees, and gave in once more to tears.

•   •   •

Saturday morning, Val picked up Andie, and they spent the day hiking along the coast, enjoying the rocky beach with the pervasive scent of salt and seaweed, and the soothing sound of the waves as the tide came in. The fresh air and sunshine chased the shadows from Andie's thoughts, adding much-needed distance from last night's problems. Though they didn't talk about Zack, Andie remained confident her friendship with Val was separate and secure.

The morning passed, and they reached the car afterward, windblown and despite the shade from Andie's ball cap, possibly sunburnt. Her stomach grumbled.

"Let's stop for fish and chips and have a late lunch," said Val, removing her hat. She fluffed her hair, combing it with her fingers. Her dark curly hair billowed, wild, and loose in the ocean's breeze. "There's still time before your shift."

Andie took off her hat and smoothed her hair, using the car window as a mirror. She pulled it into a ponytail and re-twisted her elastic. "I shouldn't." Half a dozen times that day, she had almost told Val about what had happened with Rick the night before, but her friend would tell her to quit her job. She would say that no amount of money was worth the risk. But Val had a decent job and benefits. She didn't need money the way Andie did. Her face burned as the memory of kissing Zack flashed through her mind. If he hadn't pushed her away...

She also didn't mention the kiss.

"It's my treat," said Val, perhaps misinterpreting Andie's flaming cheeks. "There's a great place in Fairhaven. Plus, a rad bookstore we can hit before going home. I wanted to look for the new John Irving book, *The Cider House Rules*. You can borrow it as soon as I'm done." With her hands shoved into her pockets and her wide smile, she looked younger and less stressed than Andie had seen at any point in their friendship—summer vacation working its magic.

Andie couldn't disappoint her friend, so she nodded, and they drove to Fairhaven.

A streak of rebellion grew as she ate her crispy piece of halibut on its bed of thick-cut fries, smothered in vinegar, enjoying every bite. If she found something she was interested in at the bookstore, she would buy something too. Finances be damned. She was so sick of being broke and just as tired of playing everything safe. Part of her itched to go wild, just this once. Maybe if she were someone less predictable, Zack wouldn't have shut her down last night. On the other hand, he had issues that were more likely to blame.

After lunch and the bookstore, which lived up to its billing, Val dropped Andie at home about an hour before her shift at the video store. She clutched all three books of the Rift War Saga in her hands. She'd read the first two chapters of the first book in the store while Val had shopped, and Andie was hooked already. Tomorrow would be a reading day.

"I can't wait to have a bath and read all night," said Val, stroking the cover of her new book. "I only read like this in the summer, so I plan to enjoy it. You know how it is." She smiled. "I have plans Sunday, but maybe I can tear you away from your new books on Tuesday night for dinner?" Her eyes danced.

Andie nodded. She could relate. Teaching was a rewarding job, but draining, often sucking away her creative impulses and all her energy. As much as she enjoyed teaching elementary school, summer was where she found herself again.

"Dinner sounds great."

Andie pushed down the urge to ask if Val could pick her up after work. She would manage. Andie just said, "Thanks again for a great day. Enjoy your book. I'll talk to you tomorrow. Can I bring anything on Tuesday?"

"Just yourself," said Val, as she always did, before she drove away.

Andie watched until her friend was gone before she entered the store to take over from Nate.

Andie's Saturday night shift was uneventful and Rick-free. When the store was quiet, she pulled out her book and read a few more chapters, though she was careful to tuck it under the counter and out of sight when customers circulated through the store. Time passed more quickly than usual, and she closed without incident and on time.

When she left the store on foot at eleven-ten, the surrounding streets were quiet. At first, the dark section by the park freaked her out, and she startled with every noise, but she set a brisk pace as she walked home, reaching her street without incident. She didn't see what all the fuss was about. Sure, the billiard hall had been noisy, but nobody had paid the least bit of attention to her as she marched home. Who needed overprotective men?

When she reached home, she unlocked the front door and slipped inside, a rush of adrenaline coursing through her because she'd taken control. She'd done something risky and gotten away with it. She hadn't bothered anyone and had looked after herself. She'd been in control of when and how she got home. Neither Val nor Zack would have approved of her coming home alone in the dark. While she appreciated their worry, perhaps they'd been overreacting.

Andie would keep this minor act of rebellion quiet. What her friends didn't know wouldn't hurt them, and while she liked the rush she got from being independent, she valued the connections she'd made and didn't want to upset her friends. She headed for bed, her book in hand. Though it was approaching midnight, she would read as late as she wanted and sleep in tomorrow.

# CHAPTER 23
# ZACK

"You're not a guy. The world is full of guys. Be a man. Don't be a guy."
–Corey Flood, Say Anything (1989)

Zack leaned on the front counter of the Rec Center, talking to an attractive woman he'd noticed working there on several previous occasions. She'd called 9-1-1 this time. He'd always guessed she wasn't his type, but perhaps that was for the best, as he was only interested in something casual. He wasn't looking for his soulmate. What a crock. He needed Aunt M. and Andie out of his head. He wanted to ask this woman out before he spent too much time thinking. Or before he talked himself out of this course of action.

"Want to meet me for a drink one night this week?" He blurted. While asking someone out, especially at work, was a radical departure from his usual, he needed to change it up. Perhaps the reason he'd mauled Andie had been because his hormones were out of control from long-term abstinence. Maybe he'd try to be like the other guys at work and get laid from time to time. Blow off steam.

"I'm free tomorrow evening," said the receptionist, flipping her short brown hair away from her face.

Zack and Cole had checked the patient inside and let the woman go, not needing to transport her to the hospital. She'd collapsed, probably from dehydration, after working out too hard. While she sipped a water bottle, he and Cole had run through their full health check. Her vitals had been stable, her heart sounded fine, and she had no known underlying conditions. Since it seemed she was fine, her friend would drive her home. They'd recommended she follow up with her regular doctor afterward to get the all clear.

The receptionist had checked him out before, but not obnoxiously. This was the first time he'd acted on it. "Sounds good. What time?"

"I get off at six," she said, leaning forward. "Where would you like to meet?"

He named a nearby pub. At her nod, he said, "Six-thirty? I'll give you my number in case something comes up and you need to cancel." He grabbed a business card from a holder on the counter, flipped it over, and scrawled his number on the back. He pushed down the nagging voice telling him this date was a horrible idea.

She smiled, showing her teeth and gums when he slid the card to her, dimples popping on both sides. "In case you've forgotten, my name's Jamie." She was more cute than pretty, unlike Andie, but she seemed friendly.

Zack turned. "See you tomorrow, Jamie." He walked out, heading for the rig. Cole trailed him by several feet.

Zack jumped into the passenger seat and waited for his partner. Cole grinned as he clambered into his usual seat at the wheel. Zack stared out the side window. "I don't want to hear it." It had been unprofessional, and he wouldn't do it again. Already he regretted the invitation.

Cole chuckled. "Never thought I'd see the day you asked out a woman on the job. Took you long enough. That Jamie's had her eye on you for some time." He had every right to give Zack a hard time.

"Shut up." Zack's response came out sharper than intended. He forced a smile to take the edge off his words. It wasn't Cole's fault Zack was breaking the rules. "Sorry." He sighed.

"You've been like a bear with a sore tooth all day," said Cole. "Something happen?"

Zack glanced at his partner as he started the engine, heading back to the dispatch center. "I kissed someone. My sister's best friend." He rubbed his face, noticing stubble for the first time. He'd forgotten to shave this morning—almost unheard of.

"That's what's got you tied in knots?" said Cole, turning onto the main street.

Zack nodded.

"Then you asked out the wrong woman," said Cole. "We've been here half a dozen times this year alone and you've never given this Jamie a second glance."

"It's complicated." Though he'd started it, Zack didn't want to have this conversation. He was an idiot. Maybe two bad ideas didn't equal a good one.

As if reading his mind, Cole said, "Just don't be an ass and hurt someone else because you're confused."

"I'm not canceling," said Zack, though his partner's words triggered the return of his common sense. He would go out, have a drink, be friendly, and go home. Alone. That still didn't solve the problem of Andie and what he'd said and done. He'd been an ass. Twice. Three times if you counted not apologizing.

He shouldn't have been so offended by her words after the barbeque. They'd been accurate and close to his own thinking. His solitary life was unsatisfying and possibly misguided. She'd only told the truth when she'd said avoiding love was dumb. That was something a friend should say. He shouldn't have been rude and iced her out.

He'd planned to apologize later that night when he picked her up, but her reaction to her boss had catapulted him into a different mode. His tongue paralyzed, Zack settled for holding Andie while she cried. His protective instincts had screamed at him to take care of her. To take away her fear and sadness. That had scared the shit out of him.

Then, seconds later, Zack had wanted to devour her. He'd gone from knight in shining armor to savage beast in one move. He'd seen the look of betrayal in her eyes when she'd gotten out of the car afterward. She'd worn the tight-jawed look she'd displayed the first time they'd met. He was a heel. While it might have been because he'd kissed her, from her reaction, he was sure it had been because he'd stopped and announced it was a mistake.

After watching her leave on the verge of tears—ones he'd caused—he'd driven home and tossed and turned for hours, replaying those moments in the car a thousand times, tormenting himself. He should have asked what the asshole boss had done. Andie had been apprehensive about being alone with him, that was clear. This morning, Zack had woken up, more muddled than ever. He'd been the bigger jerk, but he didn't know what to do about it. He'd torched that bridge.

The radio crackled, and a call came in. Work. Something cut and dried.

He waited for dispatch to finish. "Unit Two. Ninety-year-old male collapsed at the Bellevue Green Home. Unconscious and unresponsive. Respond. Over."

Zack answered. "Unit Two. En route. Code Three. Over." He hung up and flipped on the sirens as Cole completed a U-turn, headed for the old age home. Too often these cases resulted in a call to the coroner. With work to focus on, Zack thrust his personal issues aside as they rolled up to the main doors of Bellevue Green. Though it was probably too late, they grabbed their kits, hustled out of the rig, through the doors, and past reception to where they were met by one of the staff. He waded back into the certainty of being a paramedic. Here, things made sense.

• • •

In the dim lighting at the bar, Zack ordered a Coke. Beside him on a tall stool, Jamie twisted back and forth, studying the drink menu before ordering some fancy fruity drink, her voice partially drowned out by the crowd. He should have chosen somewhere less busy. The bar was hopping with customers everywhere, and these had been the only available seats.

A TV screen over Jamie's shoulder replayed golf highlights, and another further left showed baseball. Zack refocused his attention on his fidgeting date. As she moved, the potent scent of her perfume wafted over him. His nose twitched. She'd changed after work into white stirrup pants, legwarmers, and a low-cut shirt she probably wouldn't wear to work. He kept his eyes firmly on her face.

A surge of guilt filled him. Fifteen minutes in, it was clear this date wasn't going anywhere. Cole was right. Still, Zack had to be polite and pretend to be interested in her conversation. He'd asked her out. The least he could do was be kind and attentive.

"So, I said to my sister, 'Girl, you just have to go after that.' That's been our motto ever since. Do you have a motto?" She twirled her short ponytail around her finger.

"I do not." Zack wasn't sure what she meant, but he was pretty sure he didn't have one. With the background noise, he also didn't want to ask for more details. "How long have you lived in the Seattle area?" Her accent indicated she might have lived farther south at some point.

"I've been working at the Bellevue Rec Center for about two years. Before that, I lived in Texas and worked at a preschool, but the kids were so annoying. Children sure want a lot. I mean, the kids were all so demanding, I don't know why anybody sane would want to even have them. Do you want kids?" Her mind zipped from one thought to the next like a clumsy bumblebee unable to land.

"I do," said Zack. He hadn't meant to say that, since he wasn't planning to marry. But at least he liked kids and looked forward to being an uncle.

"Ew." Jamie grimaced, crinkling her nose. "I don't want kids. I thought they'd be really fun because they look like it on TV, but in reality, they cry and they're like mess-orama. They're always sticky and smell grody. And besides, can you believe how fat some women get when they're pregnant? I don't think I'd be interested in looking like that. Do you think pregnant women are sexy?" She touched her hand to his arm. "You don't have to answer that."

He closed his mouth, and she flitted to the next topic.

"Don't you just love hair bands, like Twisted Sister and Dokken?"

He struggled not to tune her out while he answered. "I prefer the Smiths, Tears for Fears, and R.E.M."

She grimaced, then shrugged. "Never heard of those. My other motto is 'Rockin' like Dokken' 'cause they're gnarly. You should try listening to them. You'll love them."

His date occasionally slowed enough to ask Zack a question, but his answers didn't seem important. Half the time, she prattled on without waiting for his reply. He sipped his Coke and kept his eyes on her face. Asking her out had been an error.

Zack lost track of what she was saying as she ordered a second drink. His lukewarm Coke was still more than half full. He'd stayed more than an hour and escape beckoned. He struggled to follow her conversation and stifled a yawn. At eight, he signaled for the bill. He'd had enough. This had been the longest ninety minutes of his life.

He waited for a break in Jamie's latest babble, then said, "I don't go out much and I appreciate you being willing to meet me. But I'm sorry, I need to cut this short. I have to wake up at three for my next shift." It was a small white lie as tomorrow he switched to nights, but he'd been here long enough.

She pouted; her lower lip thrust out like a child. "Aren't you going to ask me back to your place?" She did a double take as his words sunk in, her eyes opening wider. "Like, you get up at three a.m.?"

He nodded. "I'm sorry. It isn't you. It's me."

"Let me guess," she said, jumped off the bar stool, and stuck one hand on her hip. "You just want to be friends."

"Okay." He hadn't been thinking about being friends with Jamie. They were too different. He missed Andie's quiet conversation and how she chose her words carefully, not filling the world with nonsense. She read interesting books and watched all kinds of movies, things they had in common. Jamie just liked to talk. He hated that he was comparing the two women, but it helped him realize how being around Andie made him happy.

"I've heard that line a million times," she said. "Oh well. I tried." She narrowed her heavily made-up eyes covered in thick peacock-blue eyeshadow. "Can I give you some advice?" Her voice dripped with sickly sweet syrup.

Startled, Zack nodded and waited for her advice.

"Don't ask out women when you're not interested. I wore my best going-out outfit and my lucky shirt, and I still didn't catch you staring at my tits. Not once. Have you considered that maybe you're the boring one?" She pivoted on her heel and stormed out.

With a sigh of relief, Zack threw down cash to cover their drinks. He finished his Coke in peace, giving her time to leave the parking lot before he headed home. It was still early, and he wasn't ready to sleep. Andie wouldn't be at the movie store this late on a Wednesday, but it seemed a reasonable time to stop and pick up an action movie. Something fast-paced which wouldn't require thought. This date had been a failed experiment, one he had no intention of repeating.

An insistent voice inside, one sounding strangely like his late mother's, told him dating would be different if he went out with the right woman.

•    •    •

Thirty minutes later, Zack unlocked the door to his apartment, slipped off his shoes, and headed for the living room, video in hand. He tossed his keys into the bowl on the desk in the front hall, when his phone rang. He didn't feel like talking to anyone and continued toward the TV, letting the answering machine pick up.

*"This is your dad. It's been a couple of weeks since I've seen you and I just had this strange feeling that we should catch up. Nothing urgent but call me back sometime if you have a few minutes."* His dad's voice cut off and the machine clicked as he hung up.

Zack hung his head. With the mood he was in, he didn't feel like talking to anyone, but his dad seldom called. The last few days had been rough—maybe his dad could help. Zack crossed the room and picked up the phone, immediately returning the call.

His dad answered on the first ring. "Screening calls now, son?"

Zack forced a brief chuckle. "No, sorry. I just got in. I had a date." Almost right away, he wished he could take his words back. Still, he wanted advice, and it was a relief to start the conversation instead of dancing around it for several minutes. Better to get to the point. He was home alone not long after eight p.m. It was clear it hadn't been a terrific date.

"Oh?" said his dad. "Anyone I've met? Perhaps that nice Andie girl who is Val's friend?" His voice sounded hopeful.

Zack wished that had been true. "I think I screwed that up." He sighed, leaning back on the couch.

"I doubt that. From what I observed at Xander's, she likes you, too."

"I like her too much to date her," Zack said, his throat scratchy and raw.

"I don't understand," said his dad.

Zack pictured his father's confused expression. "If Andie and I dated and fell in love, what if something went wrong? Or what if something happened to her? I'd be devastated. I saw what Mom's death did to you."

When his dad didn't reply, the silence stretched. Had they been disconnected? "Dad?"

"I'm here," his father said. "I'm trying to articulate my thoughts. Do you like Andie?"

"Yes." The word escaped like air from a balloon. Zack liked her a stupid amount.

His dad continued. "Then I have a follow-up question. Is fear of losing someone why you seldom date?"

Of course. Duh. He couldn't say that to his father. "I guess. I don't want to lose the most important person in my life. Better not to have anyone matter."

"Aren't you lonely?" His dad knocked another difficult question out of the park.

Startled that his dad asked so bluntly, Zack answered. "Yes." Had it been obvious? He took a deep breath and asked the million-dollar question. "Do you ever regret marrying mom?" An image appeared of her laughing in the kitchen, her dark hair swirling when she danced. His mom had been wonderful, and he still missed her. So did his father.

"Son, I have a few regrets about my life, but loving your mother could never be one. If I hadn't met your mother and allowed myself to fall in love, I wouldn't have you or your sisters. She was my best friend, and marrying her was the best thing I ever did. Without her, I wouldn't have my most precious memories. I'd never wish you kids didn't exist. You're worth every bit of pain from her loss."

Speechless, Zack stood, pacing the small room, the phone in one hand, the other pulling at the cord while the receiver balanced between his shoulder and aching jaw. This conversation wasn't going the way he'd imagined. He always thought his dad's advice would be to play it safe, be smart, and guard his heart.

"So, no regrets, even though you're alone now?" His dad hadn't been himself for years after her death and had never dated.

There was no pause. "Not one. I regret letting you kids raise yourselves for a few years. I regret letting you deal with her loss on your own. But regret my Carola? Not for a second."

His dad's voice rang with truth that struck like arrows in Zack's chest, making it ache. Was he willing to be alone forever? Months ago, he'd been willing to go that route. But now? Hell no. A vivid image of Andie popped into his mind. This time, it was of the two of them strolling hand-in-hand along the beach, sunshine making her hair glint like gold—her inviting smile just for him.

It was too late to safeguard himself from Andie. His heart was already hers.

Zack needed to fix his mess. There was more to life than playing it safe.

"Thanks, Dad. Your timing was impeccable." Zack had needed this conversation. Why hadn't he asked years ago? He swallowed. Perhaps he hadn't been ready to hear what his dad had to say. Or, maybe, the difference was Andie.

"You're welcome. Anytime. Will I see you on the Fourth of July?" After giving Zack so much to ponder, his dad was astute enough to change the subject.

"I'll check if I'm working and let you know," said Zack, his heart less heavy. Maybe he could ask Andie for forgiveness and to accompany him to the next family dinner. He would give love a chance.

# CHAPTER 24
# ANDIE

Han Solo: "You said you wanted to be around when I made a mistake,
     well, this could be it, sweetheart."
Princess Leia: "I take it back."
          –The Empire Strikes Back, (1980)

Tuesday morning, Andie woke sticky and overheated. She kicked off her covers and lay still, staring at the water-stained ceiling of her bedroom as she gathered her strength. She needed more than a fever to miss work. So what that her bones ached, and she didn't feel well. A dull pain throbbed in her head, matched by a faint one on her side.

The sensation was sharper than the intermittent ache she'd had for the last couple of months. Had she'd given herself an ulcer with all her stress? It wouldn't be the first time her anxiety had given her physical symptoms, though usually a headache and upset stomach were the extent of the damage. Her tried-and-true strategy was to ignore the cause and treat the symptoms with Tylenol and Tums. She'd make sure to go to bed early the next few nights. If her fever was caused by a virus, sleeping should also help it pass.

She rolled out of bed, showered, and got ready for work. Just before she left, she downed two Extra-Strength Tylenol, tucking two more tablets into her pocket for later. She walked to work, the fresh air helping her to forget about her headache. Upon arrival at the video store, she took care of the opening chores, keeping busy. The activity provided an excellent distraction from her slow start.

A door slammed in the rear section of the store, causing her to jump. She shuddered. Rick was the only one who had access to that entrance.

Andie left the counter area and patrolled the display shelves with a dust cloth, cleaning and straightening as she walked. With the odd glance toward the back office, she continued until she had no more active tasks. Though they didn't need it, she rearranged several of the movie boxes into categories by release date, with the newest ones on the top shelves.

It wasn't until there was another faint bump of a door closing that she slid behind the counter. Had Rick come and gone without speaking? Like yesterday. Maybe he was embarrassed about his actions on Saturday or what he'd said. He should be. She peeked into the back hall to double-check he'd left. His darkened office and the bathroom doors stood open. Both were empty. Only when his absence had been confirmed did her breathing return to normal.

At a quarter after five, Nate arrived, and they switched over the computer while Andie counted her shift money. Just as she finished, a wave of heat swept over her. She raced for the bathroom, flung up the lid of the toilet just in time, and then threw up the contents of her stomach. After several more heaves, she finished and wiped her mouth with shaking hands. This must be the flu, but similar to times in the past when she was too busy to be sick, she would suck it up and pretend she was fine.

She stared at herself in the mirror. Sweat beaded her face, her pale skin looked pasty, and her hair was disheveled. Tiny red and purple dots sprinkled her swollen eyelids. She smoothed her messy hair, doused her face with cold water, and rinsed her mouth, trying to appear more presentable.

She took her second dose of Tylenol, sipping the water while sitting on a stool in the corner, pretending to watch *Star Wars: A New Hope* for half an hour. Once the meds had kicked in, she felt steady enough to leave.

Though it was a beautiful June evening, with flowers blossoming everywhere in vibrant shades of pink, yellow, red, and purple, Andie didn't enjoy it as much as usual. The walk home took longer than normal because twice more she stopped to be sick in the bushes. Could she have food poisoning? Unlikely on a steady diet of ramen, crackers, apples, and carrot sticks.

At last, Andie reached her house, stumbled inside, stripped down to her underwear, and slipped into bed. A nap would be incredible.

No sooner had she settled, when her phone rang, causing her to flinch. It would just keep ringing. She shuffled to the living room to answer on the fourth ring. "Hello."

"Andie, I'm going to have to cancel dinner and our walk this evening," said Val. "I'm sorry, but my dad is under the weather, so I'm heading up to his place to make him some homemade soup. I know it's last minute, and I'm sorry. My plan is to stay at his place for a few days."

"Thanks for letting me know," said Andie. "I've got a bit of a cold or something too, so it's probably best I stay away. I'd hate for you to catch what I've got." Their dinner plans had slipped her mind. Her appetite had disappeared anyway.

"A cold? Are you taking care of yourself?" said Val.

Andie pictured her friend's frown. "I'm drinking lots of water and going to rest. I still plan to work tomorrow, but it's a straightforward job and I can just sit when I need to on the day shift. Not like teaching." Of course, teaching she could order a replacement when sick.

"What about Friday and Saturday?" said Val. "Your nights can be so busy."

Andie didn't want to worry her friend. "I'm sure it's nothing serious. By Friday, I'll probably be back to my normal self. Don't worry about me. Go take care of your dad."

"You're sure?" said Val. "I'll check in with you when I get home. Talk later."

"I'm sure. Talk to you soon." Andie hung up the phone and shuffled back to her bedroom to collapse into bed.

When next she woke, hours later, her legs tangled in the blankets, she was sweltering hot and covered in a sheen of sweat. She glanced at the clock. It was three a.m. After a quick trip to the washroom to brush her teeth, she swallowed two more tablets, then once more tucked herself into the covers. She'd already slept eight hours, but she couldn't keep her heavy eyelids open. A fever always left her exhausted.

The next morning, Andie got up with her alarm and showered. Feeling as though her shaky legs might not hold, she leaned against the cool shower wall as the icy water pelted down. Her skin broke out in goosebumps. She shivered and checked the temperature dial. The water was set to her usual warmth, but it seemed too cold. She turned it hotter, washed her hair, and stepped out, still shaking as she towel-dried her hair and dressed for work.

In the kitchen, she surveyed her groceries. She'd shopped on Sunday and had several options. Her stomach churned at the thought of eating, but she made toast, spread it with margarine and forced each bite down. She made a peanut butter and jam sandwich to take for lunch. The end of her shift seemed an eternity away.

Wednesday and Thursday passed in much the same fashion. Her fever came and went, somewhat controlled by Tylenol, but never completely vanished. She only eaten toast and sandwiches since Monday, but it was tough without an appetite. Most of the time, she didn't feel awful, just low on energy and easily drained.

Friday, she slept until eleven a.m. because she didn't have work until after five. After an extended shower, she felt more human—almost normal. She must be on the mend. She glanced out the window at the overcast skies and ominous gray clouds, so different from the blue skies and warm summer weather they'd been having. The browning, patchy lawn could do with some rain.

At least today was the day she had an appointment with John to fix her car, and she looked forward to driving to work again. The walks had been torture while she'd been unwell. Rain would have made them unbearable. She didn't want to catch a chill to go with her fever.

Time ticked by while Andie sat at the kitchen table, writing her story in her current notebook. Twice she scribbled out everything she'd written and started over. She kept an eye out the front window, watching for when John arrived. She checked the time and frowned when she noticed it said 12:30. The mechanic still wasn't there. He'd said he would be there just after noon. He was late. She returned to her writing, becoming absorbed in the story once more as it flowed.

By 1 p.m., John still hadn't come, so she called his shop.

There was no answer, and her call went straight to voicemail after the first ring. His machine must be full. She hung up, unable to leave a message. Maybe he was on his way.

At two o'clock, there was still no sign of the mechanic. How long would installing an alternator take? He'd said a couple of hours. She tried calling again at three and four, but still no one answered. Not knowing what was going on almost reduced her to tears. She would walk again after all.

To top it all off, when dressing for work, Andie threw up twice. She rested the back of her hand on her clammy forehead. Her hand was like ice. Her fever had returned with a vengeance. It was too late to call in sick. Besides, who else could work in the shop? Nate was busy Friday nights and Rick was always drunk, so he avoided customers. Last week, Nate mentioned a customer had found Rick passed out on the floor on Sunday.

When it was time to leave, Andie took an extra Tylenol and headed out the door, scanning the street for a last-minute reprieve. She sighed. Still no John. Something must have happened. He seemed reliable, like he'd follow through with a favor. So much for driving. She headed down the sidewalk, passing her inert car.

On the way past the park, a chill came over her and the stabbing pain in her side worsened, so she slowed her pace. A fever and chills, rotten luck. Maybe tonight, at the end of her shift, just this once, she would splurge and call a cab instead of walking. She'd gotten home last Saturday without incident, but tonight she didn't have the energy. Zack was working tonight and was unavailable, plus she didn't want to see him, anyway. With Val staying in Snohomish with her father, Andie couldn't call her either. Val's father had the flu.

Andie probably had the same problem. Perhaps they'd both been exposed at the barbeque last weekend. This illness was more than nerves or stress. It had also persisted too long to be food poisoning.

Andie's legs trembled from exertion by the time she arrived at the video store. She was sweaty and unsteady. At least this time, she hadn't thrown up en route. She focused on the positive.

The bell above the door rang as she entered, and Nate glanced up from the computer. His eyebrows lifted as he stared. "You look like shit."

"Sorry," said Andie. "Give me a minute to freshen up, then I'll sign in."

"Do you need me to stay?" His mouth turned down and he paused his Star Wars movie.

"Don't you have practice tonight?" It was difficult to focus, but she remembered that much. "I thought your band could only meet for rehearsal on Fridays?"

"Yeah, but we don't start until eight," he said with a shrug. "I could hang around a little longer. If you want to go home and come back in a bit."

She couldn't face walking home to return in a couple of hours. Better to stay and suck it up. She was here, so she might as well work. "It's okay," she said. "I'll tough it out tonight. If I don't feel better in the morning, I'll call in sick then."

"The band has a gig tomorrow." Nate sounded apologetic. "We're getting some referrals. This one is in Tacoma and will pay actual money." He grabbed the back of his neck and shifted sideways. "I need to be there tomorrow night. The band is counting on me."

"That's great," said Andie, trying to infuse energy into her voice. "I'll be here tomorrow unless I'm at death's door. Don't worry about me." If she could joke, it must not be too serious.

"Alright. Thank you." Nate took a deep breath and held up both hands and crossed his fingers. He gestured toward her with both hands. "Don't come tomorrow if you're sick. It's Rick's problem and I won't answer my phone. You have his number and can call him at home."

"Good idea," said Andie. "I'll be right back." She cleaned up in the back and returned while Nate cashed out.

Before Nate left, he gave her another long look. He pursed his lips. "Tell you what. I'll write the number for my buddy's place, where we're rehearsing tonight. If you change your mind about staying, leave a message and I'll come back." He scrawled the phone number on a Post-it note and handed it to her, his eyes filled with concern.

"Thanks," she said, slipping the paper with the number into the front pocket of her jeans. She was committed to finishing her shift. Surely her fever would break, and she'd feel better soon.

# CHAPTER 25
# ANDIE

"Whoa, whoa. You better watch what you say about my car. She's real sensitive."
–Arnie Cunningham, Christine (1983)

The Friday night video store shift was mostly a blur. Andie completed her job on autopilot, going through the motions of being courteous and efficient. She took more Tylenol at eight and somehow made it through the busy rush. She couldn't close on time at eleven as half a dozen customers lingered until after eleven-forty-five, coming to the counter to pay at last in a final rush.

At midnight, she sighed, locked the front door, dimmed the lights, and turned off the neon sign. Finally.

Ten minutes later, Andie had just thrown the money in the safe, when with a sinking sensation, she realized she hadn't ordered a cab. Her exhaustion was bone-deep, and she couldn't face another walk. Returning to the front of the store, she pulled out the phone book with the yellow pages. Just as she was about to dial the Yellow Cab number, the hair on her nape rose as the back door creaked open.

Her heart galloped, pounding against her chest. Rick had arrived to collect the day's take. She wasn't staying to be intimidated or groped, and she didn't have the energy to deal with him. He'd been avoiding her this week, or at least they hadn't crossed paths, and she didn't want that situation to change. Without a sound, she slid the phone book back under the counter and bolted, locking the front door behind her with a faint click. Even sick and tired, she'd take her chances outside.

A freezing gust of wind hit her, the awning above rattling. With a deep breath, she zipped her jacket and glanced around. Her regular walk was only about twenty-five minutes and she'd done it dozens of times in the daylight, plus once at night. She'd be fine. Zack was the one who'd made a fuss about walking after dark. She strode out, calling on unexpected reserves, trying to appear confident.

Even wearing her jacket, Andie shivered as she walked, the breeze tossing the branches on nearby trees. An empty chip bag blew past, while roadside dirt sprayed into the air with the next gust. She jumped as an empty beer can rolled past, smashing into a trash can with a metallic thud. With her hands jammed deep in her pockets, she hunched against the chill wind that seemed to blow through her, her bones aching again.

She passed the busy billiard place, receiving a couple of catcalls and a wolf whistle from the crowd of young men milling outside in the parking lot, smoking. The comments might not have been aimed at her, but she didn't slow her pace to investigate. She maintained her steady gait, keeping her eyes focused ahead, striding faster than she had all week.

A dark-colored muscle car with a growly engine drove past, slowing as it pulled alongside. From an open window, a man's deep voice called, "Hey, baby, you look cold. Want a ride?"

"We can keep you warm," said another voice. Laughter floated through the windows. The car rolled beside her as she walked, the tires crunching on the gritty asphalt.

She kept her gaze fixed straight ahead, ignoring the men. The second voice sounded youthful. Maybe it was a car full of silly teenagers. A lump filled her stomach when bottles clinked from the backseat. The guys were likely drunk, dredging up her ingrained fears of unpredictability and violence.

When Andie didn't respond, the car spun its tires and accelerated up the street, its brakes squealing as it tore around the corner, the bright lights disappearing.

Only then could she breathe. With the immediate threat gone, tears filled her eyes, but she willed them away. She wouldn't cry. Nothing had happened, but she needed to get out of here. With her heart in her throat, she kept walking. She couldn't wait to be home.

Two minutes later, the same car passed, once more slowing alongside her. Only turning her head a fraction of an inch, she squinted, trying to make out the color and model. Was the car black or navy blue? This time she counted the shadows inside—four occupants. Not great odds. If they got out, she might not outrun all her pursuers. When she ignored their shouted remarks, the car spun out and drove away again.

The tight squeeze of her chest remained. The pit in her stomach became heavier as she grew certain they would return.

With so many businesses closed at this time of night, traffic was non-existent. Twice more, the same car passed, each time with rude shouts and whistles. Her chest grew tighter, each breath almost painful. The car must be circling the block. Each time, it came from behind. When she spun to check, the headlights almost blinded her, her eyes watering. Raising her arm to block the glare, she hurried on, hoping to shake her pursuers. Maybe the punks would give up and leave her alone. Maybe they just thought it fun to give her a scare.

Halfway home, Andie reached the deserted park where she had to choose which path to take. Following the sidewalk would double her travel time, increasing the chance of discovery. The direct route through the park would be faster and keep her out of sight from the road. Still, without overhead lighting, the path was as dark as soot. She glanced down the empty street. She hadn't seen the car in a few minutes. Had the guys abandoned the chase to seek other prey? She hesitated.

The sooner she made it home, the better. She bit her lip.

The trail through the park beckoned, but anything might lurk, concealed in the dark. Zack's words about vagrants sleeping there replayed in her head. She opted for the sidewalk with its occasional lighting—the safer choice.

Andie hadn't gone far when it became clear she'd miscalculated. Even with the odd light overhead, the scant glow hitting the sidewalk left the concrete so black she could barely see where to walk. Storm clouds must have covered the moon, which had lit her journey last week. Worried about slipping off another curb and rolling her ankle, her pace dropped. Lights emerged from behind and the muscle car reappeared, this time creeping along at a crawl. A hundred yards up the road, it stopped, its brake lights gleaming like demon eyes. The engine revved, but nobody emerged.

She stopped and waited for it to leave. It didn't. Shit.

She glanced over her shoulder. She contemplated returning to the store; Rick might still be there, but he might be the lesser of the two evils. But she was more than halfway home. Better to push on and act confident, so with her heart drumming and mouth dry, she continued. A few sprinkles of rain landed on her face. Great. Rain was all she needed.

Just before Andie reached the spot where the car sat, the driver's side door opened with a grating metallic sound. A tall, sturdy man stepped out, his boots crunching on the gravel on the edge of the parking area by the park. Though his face remained in shadow, she could tell he wasn't a teenager. Her steps faltered as the rear doors of the car opened and two more figures stepped out, silhouetted by the headlights.

"You need a ride, sweetheart," said a deep male voice as a fourth person exited the car. "We'd like to give you one."

Someone snickered and her blood ran cold.

Another voice said, "That's what you're calling it now?" Derisive laughter followed. Her hands became icy. She stopped. If she got any closer, she'd be out of options.

"I'm fine." Her voice emerged too high and thin. Hardly the confident image she wanted to project.

"Get in. We'll take good care of you," said the driver. "A pretty little thing like you shouldn't be alone out here at night." His deep voice grated like a rusty hinge.

"No, thanks," Andie said. "I'm expected at home. If I don't arrive soon, my boyfriend will come looking for me." She hoped they would believe her lie.

The men spoke amongst themselves, and one snorted, then laughed, but she couldn't make out their words, which blew away on the wind. Her hackles rose again as, one by one, the men closed the remaining car doors behind them.

They started in her direction.

Taking a painful deep breath, Andie pivoted and dashed into the park. She hopped the low wooden fence and sprinted down a paved trail snaking left, away from the car. She wasn't familiar with the trails, but this should take her away from the threat.

Behind her, the men cursed and pounding footsteps came after her. Indecipherable shouts followed but blew away with the gusts of wind. She panicked, sprinting deeper into the park where the trail forked. She hesitated at the next branch, not knowing where she was. Behind her, something crashed in the bushes. Chest tight and heaving, she bolted again. Once her eyes adjusted, she discerned several shades of gray and avoided the blackest patches. Those must be bushes or rocks.

Andie alternated running and walking, leaving the sounds of pursuit behind, but lost her bearings. She slowed and crept along until another trail intersected her current one. She turned around, squinting at the trail marker in the dark. Even in the dark, it looked familiar, like she had already been here. If she wasn't so scared, she might have burst into tears.

Something crackled in the bushes on her left. She froze, heart pounding.

A chittering raccoon emerged and stood on its rear feet, peering at her, the white around its dark mask highlighted by a flash of lightning. With the crash of thunder, the critter dropped to all fours and disappeared into the thick bushes on the opposite side of the trail.

Her strength depleted, Andie hunched down at the side of the wet trail and waited while her heart rate slowed. Just a raccoon. Her chest heaved. Shivering, the cool night air pressed in while icy droplets trickled down her neck. Her canvas shoes were drenched. Something rustled on the left again and she startled. She didn't know where she was or what was out there.

In the distance came the loud revving sound of an engine. She stood up, teeth chattering, hesitating until the distant noise faded. Probably the muscle car leaving. She hadn't run as far as she'd thought or the trail had curved toward the road in an arc, but the sound helped her regain her bearings.

Andie crept out of the bushes, a warm patch on her cheek where she'd gotten scratched. In the open, the rain bucketed down in an icy torrent. Her jacket and pants were soaked through to her goose-pimpled skin and her chest ached from holding her breath. She retraced her steps toward the road, on alert for any indication the car had returned. The stitch in her side throbbed with her movement as she shivered. She massaged the pain, hoping it would lessen.

After several tense minutes, she reached the edge of the trees. She was two blocks closer to home than when she'd left the sidewalk, but she still had the long side of the park to traverse before she reached the well-lit neighborhoods and her street.

She glanced around, taking in her new surroundings. Across the street, the small, rundown houses were dark. If there'd been lights on inside, she might have approached to ask for a ride or to call for a cab, but this late at night, they were silent.

She slipped back to the sidewalk and marched a little farther, her shoes squelching with each step. Ahead, a car turned onto the far end of the street, its lights blinding. She almost burst into tears of frustration. The roaring engine sounded the same as before as it approached. Fuck. Why wouldn't they leave her alone? Without further thought, she trotted to the nearest house, up the stairs, and pounded on the door, praying someone answered.

The car revved its engine and paused just beyond the driveway.

Andie stabbed the doorbell. Once. Twice. A third time, each press harder than the last. She tucked her icy hands into her pockets while she listened to the loud ringing inside. She prayed someone was home and would answer. Glancing over her shoulder, the men from the car still watched.

Andie couldn't leave. Fear lent her strength as she beat on the door with her fists.

She held her breath. At last, from deep inside, a light flicked on.

Hope surged within. "Please. Help me," Andie called, her voice shaking.

"I've called the cops," said a tired voice from inside. "I'm not opening the door."

"Thank you. If the police come, they'll help me," Andie said. "The car out front followed me. There's four guys who won't leave me alone."

"Explain it to the cops," said the gravely voice. The porch light flicked on, flooding Andie with light. She winced, trying to block the harsh, stabbing light. Her eyes stung. At least she was partially protected from the downpour by the overhang.

"That's her all right," said a slurred voice from the car. "Doesn't seem like she wants to go for a drive."

"That's not her house," said the deep voice of the driver. "She's still outside. Plus, I've seen her somewhere else."

Did they know her from the store? She didn't recognize their voices.

"Come play with us," called one of the other creepy men. He took a swig from a bottle and opened his door.

The driver stepped onto the street, joined by the others, who headed toward where she huddled on the stairs. Their footsteps crunched on the gritty sidewalk and onto the gravel beside the road. The headlights from the car made the rain appear bright white where it streamed through their path. The prowling men were too close, and her energy was gone.

Andie made a final effort. "Stop right there. The cops are on their way." Her throat hurt.

They hesitated where the sidewalk met the walkway to the stairs. She squinted. The car wasn't black, but navy blue, and vaguely familiar. Her blood turned to slush, and chills slithered down her spine. The driver was the man who resembled Dylan and worked at Zack's construction site. She replayed the afternoon she'd met Xander when this man had stepped out of Xander's truck. What was his name? Tom.

In the distance, the faint wail of a siren broke the silence.

"Shit. No fun around here tonight. Let's go," said the driver with his deep raspy voice. "We can find something better." He sauntered to his car, his pace even and unhurried.

The others crunched through the wet gravel, joining him at a faster speed. They jumped inside. Car doors slammed, and the massive engine roared to life—extra loud in the quiet night. The wheels spun out, spraying gravel that ricocheted off the nearby parked cars and the picket fence. A heavy smell of gasoline hung in the air as the sirens grew louder.

The car disappeared at the end of the street, turning right with a screech. A police cruiser with flashing red and blue lights appeared from the opposite direction, pulling up curbside in front of the stairs where Andie crouched, shivering.

Her legs sagged, and she crumpled to the wet stairs.

"Excuse me, miss. Are you the one causing a disturbance?" said the voice of an officer from beside the police car.

Andie lifted her head and tried to answer, but before she managed, the front door of the house opened with a grating creak.

A tiny, elderly woman, wearing a fuzzy red robe, peeked her head out. "I'm the one who called the police. This one here was pounding on my door and woke me up." She glared at Andie, and then her tired expression softened. "But some men climbed out of their car out front and yelled at her. They followed her to the edge of the yard. They drove off when y'all arrived."

The explanation helped Andie, and for that she was grateful.

"We'll take it from here, ma'am," said an officer. He exited the patrol car and stood halfway between the sidewalk and the stairs. "Excuse me miss, are you okay?"

Andie raised her head. She tried to stand, but her legs wouldn't obey. With her head swimming, she vomited in the gravel beside the stairs as she clutched her side. The pain in her side stabbed again. "I don't feel well."

"What happened?" One of the officers approached while the occupant of the house slammed the door. The light inside vanished.

She told the short version. "I was walking home and some men in a car followed me. They pulled over and I ran. They found me again, so I tried to get help here."

A flashlight shone in her face, and she winced, too weak to hold up her hand.

"Have you been drinking?" The officer's question made sense at this time of night.

She shook her head, the pounding in her temples almost deafening. "I work at West Coast Video and got off work late. My car is broken, so I was walking home."

"It isn't safe out here alone at night, miss," said the closest officer. "It's well after midnight."

Andie squinted to avoid his piercing light. "I'm aware."

"Is there someone we can call to collect you?" the same voice asked. "Or we can drop you off if it isn't far. We can't leave you here."

"I don't have anyone," she said. "That's why I was walking."

"You should have called a cab." The officer's words came from a distance as she struggled to stand.

Everything grew dizzy. With a cough and a sharp side pain, she gasped for air. She descended two steps and then lost her balance, slipping down the last three stairs on her back. She fumbled behind, checking the damage. Her hand came away bloody from where she'd scraped her spine on the concrete stairs. When she tried to stand, the world faded to black.

•     •     •

When Andie opened her eyes, she was sprawled on the wet cement, unable to move. She closed her eyes to keep out the rain. The pain in her side throbbed. Maybe she could stay here until it passed.

"Miss, are you okay?" Someone shook her shoulder. She couldn't focus on his face and her mouth wouldn't work. "She's burning up. This isn't from alcohol or drugs. Or from being chased. She's sick."

"Fever," she muttered. "All week. My side hurts." She curled onto her side, trying to lessen the intense pain. At least the rough walkway was cool on her fevered skin.

"Call it in. Get an ambulance," said the distant voice.

"Don't bother Zack," she said, thrashing one arm. "I'm in the friend zone."

They ignored her. Had she spoken aloud?

A police officer spoke into his walkie-talkie. "Dispatch an ambulance to our current location at 722 Parkside Ave. Medical assistance required.

Female mid to late twenties. In and out of consciousness. Feverish and delirious." His voice faded again.

The hard ground was frigid, and she couldn't remember the last time she'd been warm. Cold rainwater pooled around her. Andie kept her eyes closed, as unfamiliar sounds came and went. Someone covered her with a waterproof blanket and held an umbrella over her head, providing a respite from the slanting rain. At some point, the ambulance arrived, flooding the area with swirling red lights.

People lifted her off the solid ground onto something dry and softer. She couldn't stop shaking and her teeth chattered.

"Andie," said a familiar voice from afar. "Andie." Zack was here! "What happened?"

She tried to sit up, experiencing a swimming sensation in her head as she opened her eyes. It was too much. She closed them to lessen the spinning.

Zack squeezed her shoulder, the other resting on her sternum, keeping her flat. When she stopped struggling, he moved a hand to her forehead. She leaned into his cool fingers.

"You know this woman?" Another calm voice came from a distance. Was that a police officer or Zack's partner?

She fluttered her eyes, struggling to open them again. "Zack." Her voice was too quiet. He didn't turn his head or look at her.

"Yes, she's a friend." Zack's voice sounded strained. Wrong. They weren't friends. He almost sounded annoyed. "Do you know what happened?"

She clutched his rigid arm. "I'm sorry." Her voice caught.

Zack glanced down and covered her hand.

"She told us she got off work, headed home on foot, and some creeps in a car followed. She woke the homeowner who called us. Upon our arrival, she vomited, then collapsed, slipping on the stairs. The blood is from her scraped back. Her head looks fine."

Zack's chilly hand touched her forehead again. "She's burning up. Let's load her into the rig. Get her out of the rain."

"I can't go to a hospital," she said, struggling once more to sit, her eyes flying open. The faces hovering nearby wore expressions of confusion, perhaps at her protest. She must have garbled her words. "No hospital. Not without insurance. I'm broke."

"Andie, honey," said Zack, still at her side. His voice was soothing. "You're sick. We need to transport you to the hospital."

Tears leaked from her closed eyes, too exhausted to fight any longer. She slumped back, no longer struggling. It was easier to just give in. Zack and his partner loaded her into the ambulance, out of the rain. Without meaning to, she yelped as the stretcher wheels hit the floor. Why did her side hurt so much? Zack jumped in the rear of the ambulance beside her and took her hand as the door slammed. She grit her teeth as the hot pain radiated through her body. Someone spoke, but she could no longer focus on making sense of the words.

She drifted while the motion of the ambulance put her to sleep.

# Chapter 26
# Zack

"I love that you get cold when it's 71 degrees out. I love that it takes you an hour and a half to order a sandwich. I love that you get a little crinkle above your nose when you're looking at me like I'm nuts. I love that after I spend the day with you, I can still smell your perfume on my clothes. And I love that you are the last person I want to talk to before I go to sleep at night."
–Harry Burns, When Harry Met Sally (1989)

Zack clutched Andie's frozen hand as the ambulance rushed toward the hospital—a quick trip at this time of the night. He couldn't let go, but she needed to be treated for exposure and shock, plus whatever was making her sick. Andie lay on a stretcher unconscious, covered by dry blankets, pale and shivering. One hectic splash of heat remained on each cheek while her lips were dark blue, almost purple. They needed to get her temperature up. He grabbed a nearby towel and wiped the water from her face.

His jaw clenched. What had she been doing walking home? She knew that was dangerous. Of course, being told and experiencing things were different. She must have believed no one would cause her harm. His gut churned. Or she'd believed she had no alternative. He wished he'd realized before tonight how much her money troubles preyed on her.

At the ER, Zack hopped out of the back of the rig, accompanying her into Emergency, maintaining his hold on her hand.

"What have you got for me?" said Dr. Jones, one of the familiar faces at this hospital.

Zack didn't answer, shooting Cole a panicked glance. He'd been so focused on Andie, he'd almost forgotten he was working.

Cole jumped in. "Female. Mid to late twenties. In and out of consciousness. Not drug or alcohol related. Fever of 105 degrees. Heart rate is elevated. Right side is tender and reactive. No visible injury. Eyes equal and reactive. No head injury suspected."

"Exposure?" said the doctor, taking in her wet hair and purple lips.

Zack gathered himself. "Not long term, though she was caught in the downpour. She's sick. Flu maybe? She should have stayed home in bed." He kept his grasp on Andie's hand, unwilling to let go. He should have taken better care of her. His gaze flicked to her on the stretcher. She looked young and vulnerable, and she didn't have anyone else to stay.

The doctor gave him a long look with his eyebrows almost at his hairline. "You know her."

Zack gave a sharp nod, staring the doctor down. He didn't need a lecture about not treating friends or family. It hadn't been intentional. Zack hadn't known when the call had come in that the person requiring assistance would be Andie.

"We need her name for the paperwork. A nurse hovered with a clipboard.

Zack panicked. "Andie."

"Her full name," said the nurse.

Andie could be short for anything, so he invented a name. "Andromeda Sterling." *Andromeda?* He wished he'd picked something more ordinary, like... Andrea. Too late now. He took a breath. "Can I stay with her?" His voice broke. He panicked, shooting Cole a glance, hoping his partner understood Zack's dilemma. It wasn't fair to leave his partner short-handed, as they still had a third of a shift to work, but leaving Andie alone at the hospital wasn't an option.

"I'll clock you out." Cole clapped a firm hand on Zack's shoulder. His volume dropped. "You take care of her. Don't worry about your shift. We'll get someone to cover the next few nights, too. They owe you two hundred vacation days you never take."

Zack swallowed the hard lump in his throat. "Thanks, man." He glanced toward the pay phone on the wall. Should he call Val and let her know about Andie? He took a deep breath. Tomorrow would be soon enough. Not only would his sister have been asleep hours ago, but she'd been staying at Dad's this week, looking after him. She couldn't have picked Andie up, either. Zack's jaw flared. What the hell had happened with John and fixing her car? He'd have to give the man a piece of his mind. He exhaled. There was probably a reasonable explanation his friend hadn't got the car on the road.

On the gurney, Andie clutched her side and moaned. He'd seen that movement a few times in the last couple of months. Some kind of chronic condition, perhaps. Pieces clicked. The intermittent pain, the extreme fever. How could he have missed the signs?

"Possible appendicitis. Inflamed or even ruptured." Zack's voice cut through the hubbub in front of the busy nurse's station in the ER. They would need to keep her under close observation, and he could help. An untreated rupture guaranteed sepsis and death.

The doctor pursed his lips. He gently tapped Andie's side, and she groaned again. He shot another glance at Zack. "Good pick up. Appendicitis is a strong possibility." He waved to a hovering orderly. "We need to get her out of these wet clothes and monitor her fever. Get some warm fluids into her." He motioned to two more hospital employees. "We'll have her monitored at all times."

They moved her from the ambulance gurney to a narrow hospital bed on wheels. The doctor turned to Zack. "I'll order a surgical consult to confirm. There's someone on call." He wrote something on the clipboard and hung her chart on her hospital bed. "Has she mentioned her appendix?"

Zack shook his head. "Just a hunch, but she's had intermittent pain for months. Nothing severe." His stomach churned. If her appendix ruptured, she could be extremely sick. The high fever or pain may have caused the vomiting. She hadn't called him because he'd been at work. His brain looped through the facts.

He rubbed his temple where a tension headache was spreading. And because he'd been a jerk, avoiding her all week. She'd felt like she had no one and walked home, cold and sick in the torrential rain. She'd sounded so alone at the bottom of those stairs. He'd just wanted to scoop her into a hug and make everything better.

Zack had screwed up. No friend would have let this happen. He needed to do better. Her collapse had made something else clear. Maybe she was his soulmate—the way Aunt M. insisted. He felt like he'd been run over, all the air squeezed from his lungs. Was it too late to fall in love? He hoped he hadn't lost Andie.

*   *   *

Zack jerked to awareness, his mouth dry and sticky, tasting like something had crawled inside and died. He must have forgotten to brush his teeth after work. Memories of the night before came rushing back as he opened gritty eyes, expecting to see his living room. He was at the hospital.

Yawning, he looked around the dingy room. He'd stayed overnight with Andie in Observations. She was sleeping. He stretched, cracking his aching back. A blue curtain separated Andie's bed from several others where she was being monitored. His neck ached from sleeping in a hard plastic chair beside Andie's bed while he waited for the on-call surgeon.

Zack took Andie's hand and her eyes fluttered open.

She stared into his eyes. "I don't feel so good." Her voice was raspy and judging by the heat in her cheeks and the glassy look in her eyes, her fever raged.

He checked the time. She must be due for more pain medication. He'd asked twice last night, but her chart said they'd given her Tylenol when she'd first been admitted. They hadn't. He'd argued with the first two nurses and insisted they hook her up to an IV. He'd also forced the issue to make sure she was monitored to be sure her appendix hadn't already ruptured. They took blood to be analyzed also at his suggestion. Then, afraid they'd force him to leave if he persisted, he shut up to wait for the surgeon.

Once she'd been admitted, he'd drifted off—about three hours ago.

"Did I come here in your ambulance?" Her voice was weak.

He squeezed her hand. "You did. The police called. Cole and I were the ones who arrived on the scene. Do you remember what happened last night?" He kept his voice gentle, so he didn't scare her as the memories cascaded back. She must have been terrified.

She nodded, shifting her position to sit higher. He pressed a button on her bed to elevate the top section behind her back. He stood and rested the back of his other hand on her forehead. Yep, still too damn hot.

"I haven't been well. Some flu, but I seemed better yesterday than I had all week. When your friend didn't arrive to fix my car, I walked to work. I meant to take a cab home, but Rick showed up at the store just after I closed. I didn't want him to find me there alone, so I bolted." She stared at the bed, picking at the blue fuzzy blanket. Her voice dropped. "You warned me not to walk home. It wasn't my best decision."

"Hey," he said, forcing a lump back down his throat, hating how she wouldn't meet his gaze. "This isn't your fault. You wanted to be independent and were in a crummy situation, upset and sick. It should have been fine to walk and I'm sorry it wasn't."

She glanced upward. "You're not going to give me a lecture?"

He swallowed what he'd been about to say. "I understand your motivation for walking."

Andie still wouldn't meet his eyes for long. She seemed concerned that he was angry. Best to be clear about the reason. "Hey. I'm angry at the creeps in the car. Not at you." He smoothed her hair and kept his voice soft. "Can you tell me what happened?"

"I closed late because it was busy, and I was a little spaced out. I probably should've nudged the customers to leave sooner." She told him about the car that followed from the billiard place and how it kept circling the block. She glossed over her fear in the park and focused on her dash up the stairs to the park-side house. "I woke an old lady who called the cops. When the police came, the car took off. Everything else is a little foggy."

Before Zack asked additional questions, a nurse scraped back the curtain, her eyes widening. Maybe they'd forgotten Zack was here. "The surgeon is here."

"Andromeda Sterling," said a doctor coming through behind her.

Andie turned toward Zack and raised an eyebrow.

"I'll explain later," he mouthed.

The doctor acknowledged Zack, then retrieved the chart from the bed's foot. He ran through the questions the other doctors had tried to ask earlier. Andie hadn't been coherent enough to answer, so they'd given her an electric blanket and let her sleep, hooked up to an IV. They must have given her more medication for her fever that way. Zack's brain seemed to have resumed function.

This time, she gave them her medical history and ran through her allergies, etc.

Her elevated temperature remained the biggest concern.

"Appendicitis crossed my mind a couple of times," Andie said. "But I didn't have the classic pain. I kept thinking I must have a stress-related ulcer."

Zack's heart went out to her. If only he'd paid better attention.

The doctor asked questions about the pain's location, if she'd had trouble sleeping, or nausea.

"A fever, lack of appetite, and some vomiting." She didn't look at Zack.

The doctor noted her answers, updating her chart. "I'd like to perform a relatively new procedure, a laparoscopic appendectomy," said the surgeon. "This can't wait. I'll schedule one for later this morning. It's best if we take out your appendix if it's inflamed. I believe we're in time because your condition is remaining stable. Hopefully, it hasn't ruptured."

His "yet" hung unsaid in the air.

"I don't have insurance." A tear trickled down Andie's cheek.

Zack wished he could help. He squeezed her hand.

"This is an emergency," said the surgeon. "If we don't remove your appendix and it ruptures, you could die. The biggest cost is always staying in the hospital. If there are no complications, you'll be free to go home soon, provided you have someone to care for you. We'll do our best to keep the cost down and your stay minimal. With this less invasive procedure, you can be released in two days instead of five." He raised an eyebrow at Zack, still in his paramedic uniform. It paid to be recognized. It might save her an extra night or two's stay.

Zack nodded and sat up straighter, his cramped muscles protesting. Already, plans spun through his mind. He didn't have space for a recuperating patient at his cramped apartment, but there was no reason he couldn't stay at Andie's on the couch. Or better yet, they could stay with Val. She had three bedrooms, so there would be ample room for him to stay too. He wished to be where he could be close to Andie. It didn't have to mean more than that, but he needed to show he cared.

He kept Andie company until she went into surgery at ten a.m. Once she was out of reach, he used the time to race home, have a quick shower, pack a bag, and call his sister. He had a few hours until Andie would wake after surgery, and he wanted to be there when she came back from Recovery.

Val answered on the second ring. Good. She was home and not in Snohomish.

"Hey, it's me. Andie had trouble last night," he said. "She collapsed on the way home from work and the doctors suspect appendicitis. She's in surgery right now." He didn't mention the creeps in the car. They could get to that later.

"Oh no," said Val. "She mentioned not feeling well, but I didn't know she was this sick. I wish I hadn't been out of town."

"Don't blame yourself. She's used to having to do everything on her own." Even as he said the words, he realized they were true. "I wanted to ask for a big favor," said Zack.

"Bring her here," said Val, anticipating his question. Her tone was decisive. "I'll help look after her. She could use people taking care of her for a change."

He exhaled. "Thank you. I was hoping I could stay as well." Let her interpret that how she wanted.

"It's about time," said Val. "It's obvious you're crazy about her."

"Well, I'm an idiot," said Zack, feeling the need to come clean with someone who wouldn't judge. "I drove her to work last Saturday after we left Xander's and when I picked her up that night, I kissed her." He ignored his sister's quiet "yay." "Then I freaked out and didn't talk to her for the rest of the week."

He took a breath, pinching the bridge of his nose as he exhaled. "Last night, she tried to walk home while sick, in the downpour. With you out of town, and me working, she didn't have anyone to ask. Which reminds me, I have one more phone call before I head back to the hospital."

"Andie told me her car was supposed to be fixed on Friday," said Val.

"That's the call. John was supposed to have taken care of it. I'm going to find out what happened." Zack hoped his friend had an explanation. It wasn't like him to bail.

"I'll cook comfort food for dinner the day she gets out," said Val. "Homemade chicken soup and biscuits. Andie might eat that. If not then, the next day."

"Good idea. Thanks." Zack hung up. The light on his answering machine was blinking. He pushed *Play*.

*"Yo, Zack. It's John. I'm stuck working a different job that's taking much longer than expected and can't make it over to your friend's place until Saturday. I must have written her number down wrong, as the one I tried is out of service. If you can pass along my message, that would be appreciated."*

Zack checked the time of the message. He'd been running yesterday when John had called. Zack had come home, showered, and gone to work without checking his messages. Though it was just poor timing and bad luck, he wasn't to blame for her accident, but he wished he'd known about her car. It was too late to say he'd have done something about it, but at least John not fixing the car had been explained. Zack also wished he'd known about her fever.

If he hadn't been so afraid, a lot would have been different.

# CHAPTER 27
# ANDIE

"I found out what the secret to life is: friends. Best friends."
–Ninny Threadgoode, Fried Green Tomatoes (1991)

A high, whimpering sound disturbed Andie's deep sleep, her foggy brain slow to wake, her weighted eyelids impossible to open. As greater awareness returned, the high-pitched noise became an annoying distraction. Memories trickled back to her. She was in the hospital. Why didn't the nurses come to help that poor patient? The sound put her on edge, but she couldn't move her hands to cover her ears. The intensity lessened as her eyes fluttered open. She squinted at the brightness of the overhead fluorescent lights.

Oh, my god. She was making the noise. Andie clamped her lips shut. With the whimpering contained, she took stock of the rest of her body. She ached all over, her mouth was as dry as sand, and the back of her hand stung. She moved it and tubing followed, tugging on the end attached to her skin— an IV. Additional memories came flooding back as a series of movie-like images. The panic and the rain. Zack and the ambulance. Surgery. Tears welled up in her eyes. How would she pay for a hospital stay? She would be in debt forever.

Her thoughts flipped to her upcoming job in the fall and her potential earnings. At least she had over a month to recover before she needed to teach—the paycheck more essential than ever. Her muscles tensed as she spiraled, but her body's needs became more pressing than her worries. She broke out in a sweat and retched, attempting to sit up. She clapped a hand to her mouth, endeavoring not to gag again.

Immediately, someone with a soft voice and gentle hands appeared, holding a basin with one hand and rubbing her back with the other.

"It's okay. Let go. Patients are often sick in recovery as a side effect from the anesthesia." Her voice was soothing. "You'll feel better once you throw up."

Andie heaved. When finished, the nurse whisked away the container, and gave her a warm, wet cloth to wipe her face. "Here you go."

"Thanks," Andie croaked, glancing at the young nurse.

"If you're more settled, now you're awake, I'll wheel you up to your room. You've got two roommates, but they both usually nap in the afternoon." The nurse's kind eyes were sympathetic.

Andie nodded, and the nurse transported her through a labyrinth of hallways. They passed a bank of windows as they neared the elevator. The sky indicated that it was probably mid to late afternoon.

"I guess I slept the day away," said Andie, breaking the silence.

"Your boyfriend's been anxious about you," said the nurse. "He's asked for updates several times. We gave him your room number and he should be there already. I hope that's okay."

Boyfriend? The nurse must mean Zack, who'd stayed with Andie all night. Though she flushed, she didn't have the energy to correct the nurse's assumptions. "It's fine. Thank you."

Andie wasn't feeling her best or most attractive, but it was sweet of him to want to be around. Since he wasn't interested in her romantically, he wouldn't be dissuaded by her less-than-stellar appearance. Their talk earlier came back to her. He hadn't blamed her for trying to walk home and running into trouble. She frowned. Something about the incident last night had surprised her, but her memory was fuzzy and parts of last night remained murky.

"Did the surgeon remove my appendix? He said it was a possibility." Andie licked her dry lips. She needed to get ChapStick or Vaseline. With her queasy stomach, she wasn't sure she was ready for water. Perhaps some Sprite. That's what she'd liked for an upset stomach since she was little.

The nurse glanced at Andie's chart before pushing the elevator button for the fourth floor. "Yes, the laparoscopic procedure was successful. The note says your appendix was severely inflamed." The elevator doors opened. "You're lucky it hadn't ruptured to leak toxins all over inside."

Perhaps the incident with the creeps in the car had a silver lining. Without them, Andie would have gone home alone, as usual. Again, there was a sense of an important detail that had been forgotten. She shook her head as if clearing it. If her appendix had ruptured, she could have collapsed and not been found for days. She shivered at the idea of that narrowly missed possibility.

They entered a room with three beds, the long baby blue curtains pulled, screening off three separate sections. The dimmed room was quiet, and faint even, sleep breathing from the far back. Andie and the nurse stopped at the first open section. A pang of disappointment shot through her. Zack wasn't in the room, though a steaming cup of coffee sat on the moveable table tray, as did an unfamiliar Anne McCaffery novel. He must have just stepped out.

Two nurses helped Andie to transfer over to the ward bed. Her legs shook and her body ached. The insides of her mouth felt odd, too. Raw and rough. Maybe it had something to do with the pain medication.

"You've got three incisions," said the original nurse as she helped Andie settle. "Only one has stitches. Another has a drain we'll remove just before you're discharged. The longest cut is only an inch and below your bikini line." She winked. "You're lucky. An appendix scar is usually three times longer and thick, more if a rupture occurs and it leaks into the abdominal cavity." She supported Andie with an extra pillow, tugged up the covers, and repositioned the IV stand, ensuring nothing pulled on the tubes in the back of Andie's hand.

Seeing her glance, the nurse said, "Antibiotics and morphine for the pain, plus Gravol to prevent additional vomiting." She adjusted Andie's pillows. "Have you had morphine before?"

Andie shook her head and leaned back on the pillow, closing her eyes.

"It might make you feel strange, but it should help with the pain and allow you to rest so your body can heal. If you're dizzy or develop a rash, tell us immediately. Questions?"

"Is that why my mouth feels weird?"

The kind nurse smiled. "Yes. Be careful you don't bite your tongue. It might seem numb, but you can do damage."

"Thanks for everything." Andie leaned back, allowing herself to sink into her soft pillows. Suddenly, her eyes flew open, her heart racing. Nate's gig was tonight. He couldn't work and nobody would know why she didn't arrive for her shift. They might think she was unreliable and had blown them off. She needed to call someone, but there wasn't a phone in the room.

Maybe she could get Zack to call her boss. This early in the afternoon, Rick might even be coherent. Where were her clothes? Nate's number was in her pocket, and she needed to reach him in the next hour, while he was still there.

Unaware of Andie's rising panic, the nurse finished up. "Your fellow should be back soon. If you need anything, just push the button." She held up a cord with what appeared to be a handle with a red button on the end. "Your dinner tonight is clear liquids only. Tomorrow, you can eat regular meals with soft food. Get some rest." She smiled on the way out, passing Zack in the doorway.

He hesitated at the threshold, then crossed to sit beside Andie's bed. He was out of uniform now, wearing his usual jeans and T-shirt combo. His eyes were ringed by dark shadows, and he seemed paler than usual.

"Hey," Andie's heart lurched, thunking her chest with a familiar ache. "You look like you're the one who needs a nap. You stayed here all night, too." She went for a joking tone to keep it light, but from the serious look in his eyes, it came out flat.

"I zipped home for a few hours once you went into surgery, but I left my number in case you needed someone right away."

Had his pale eyes always seemed to see through her? No secret was safe.

"Thank you for staying last night. If I didn't say it before." Andie chewed her lip. The pauses in their conversation seemed awkward, and she struggled to fill the void. "You didn't need to come back so soon." But it was nice that he had.

"I wanted to. I had a quick shower, changed, and grabbed a bite. I'm good." He leaned back. "I don't have anywhere else to be."

"No work until this afternoon," she said, her forehead tightened.

"I took a couple of days off," he said.

"I'm surprised you aren't at the gym." She stifled a yawn. Then another.

He leaned forward again, and to her shock, he picked up her hand. "I'm glad you're okay. You scared me."

She blinked, fighting tears. She was fine now. "I was frightened too. Thanks for taking care of me. For staying with me because that's a lot more than just your job." She needed to reciprocate his kindness. Maybe she'd bake him an apple pie once she recovered and was home. She also needed to learn how to be his friend and to stop wanting more. Friendship was also a genuine connection. She stared into his gorgeous blue eyes and disappointment flared in her gut. She'd figure it out.

Zack cleared his throat, dropping his gaze first. "Is there anything I can ask Val to bring or anything I can do to make your stay here less boring?"

"Oh." She'd almost forgotten again. "Can you please call the video store? It isn't long until my shift. Nate can't work tonight, but at least he can let Rick know I'm unable to come in." She rushed on, "I hope I don't get fired. I'm already so broke I can barely buy groceries, let alone pay my hospital bill or fix my car." She pressed her hand to her mouth. Her eyes widened as she stared at Zack. The morphine might have loosened her tongue. She needed to be more careful.

He nodded, his forehead creasing. "Sure. I can call the store right away. Then Val. Do you need anything for here?"

Thank goodness he'd changed the subject before she blurted something about her unrequited crush. She'd already said too much.

"Maybe something to read." Zack picked up the Anne McCaffery novel on the table—*Moreta: Dragonlady of Pern.* "It's a newer one. I wasn't sure if you'd read it, but I brought it for you to try. It's got dragons and time travel. Two of your favorite things." The tips of his ears turned bright red.

Andie's throat tightened. "How did you know I like time travel stories?" Her question emerged as a croak. Had she let something slip when she'd been sleeping?

"From when we saw that movie preview." When she shook her head, he said, "I haven't forgotten *Back to the Future* opens next week. I bought two tickets." He grinned, the hint of an answering one tugging at her lips. "It will take more than recovering from surgery to get out of accompanying me."

Her mouth dropped open, speechless.

"Anything else you need?" He turned to leave.

"A hairbrush and an elastic?" she said, licking her dry lips. Andie wanted clean underwear, a toothbrush, and a way to tame her scraggly hair, but it was her turn to flush at the idea of Zack rummaging through her belongings to find the necessary supplies.

"Easy," he said. "Val can pick those up. I'll phone her after I call your store."

"Val doesn't need to come today," Andie said, dismayed at being so much trouble. It seemed odd to have two people concerned enough to visit. Not that long ago that she had no one in her life. They were true friends.

"Val wants to visit. She's worried about you because you matter." Zack checked his watch and winked. "Actually, I'm surprised she isn't here yet." His grin this time was crooked. "Though, even she can't drive that fast. I called her from the pay phone by the nurse's station when they told me you were awake." He stood, releasing her hand. "I'll be back soon." He ducked out the door, this time taking his coffee.

Andie let her eyes close, intending to rest just while he was out making calls. Though it seemed like she'd only shut them for a few minutes, the light outside was dimmer when she opened them. There was no sign of Zack, but Val was ensconced in one of the two chairs, crocheting. A ball of variegated yarn trailed down from her project to her craft bag.

She must have caught Andie's movement, as Val lowered her crocheting. "How are you feeling?"

"Groggy," Andie said, her tongue thick. "Like I'm not quite awake. I slept longer than I meant to. I'm not a great napper. You should have woken me when you arrived."

"You've been sick and just had surgery. Of course, I should let you sleep." Val's tone was teasing and full of care.

Andie's throat thickened. She pushed herself to a more upright position with a wince. "My mouth feels funny and is all ragged inside. Probably from having morphine. Do I sound normal?"

"You do," said Val with a gentle laugh. "I brought a few things I thought you might need."

"Thank you." Andie would have frowned, but with her face numb, she wasn't sure she was successful. "How'd you get into my place?"

"I talked to Susan, and she let me inside. I hope that's okay." Val raised a tote from the floor where she'd tucked it behind her craft bag.

"You're extremely resourceful," said Andie. "I hope you brought my toothbrush." She grimaced at the horrid taste in her mouth. "That's what I want most."

"And toothpaste," said Val. "I figured you'd need all those things. Plus, pajamas. I've always found hospital gowns to be drafty." Her eyes twinkled.

"Good call. Thank you," said Andie. Tears pricked her eyes at her friend's thoughtfulness. "I'm sorry," she said. "You and Zack have both been so kind. I don't mean to cry."

Val waved her hand, brushing off the thanks. "I'll chalk it up to morphine this time. Don't let it happen again."

Andie laughed, as intended, swiping away her remaining tears.

"I have a proposal," said Val. "And to be clear, I won't take no for an answer."

Andie raised her eyebrows. She could be in trouble. It was almost impossible to say no to Val. "Shoot."

"You're scheduled to be released the day after tomorrow, but I don't like the idea of you going home alone. I worry you'll overdo it and hurt yourself, so I'd like you to stay at my place for a few weeks. Maybe longer." Her direct gaze said she wasn't joking. "What do you think?"

Andie's face heated, and she shook her head. "That's too much."

Val leaned in. "I'm off for the summer, and you need to relax and take it easy. Please let us take care of you." Perhaps noticing Andie's hesitation, she continued. "I'd love the company, plus you know, I love caring for people. Please come to my place instead of your empty house. I already prepared my best guest room."

The metallic taste of blood flooded Andie's mouth. She stopped chewing on the inside of her numb cheek. "Okay." She didn't want to go to her empty house, either. Besides, it was pointless to argue. Val wore her determined face, and Andie loved the idea of staying with her best friend.

Val glanced at the open door and lowered her voice. "I also checked your fridge when I was at your place, wanting to make sure nothing would rot while you were gone." She cleared her throat. "Your fridge was practically empty, so I snooped a smidge. You have almost nothing to eat at your place. Your cupboards are bare."

The time for Andie's confession had arrived. She inhaled. "I'm barely scraping by. That's why I haven't invited you to dinner or suggested we go for lunch on weekends. My paychecks only stretch so far, and I've been saving every cent for rent." Her cheeks felt like they were on fire, but she maintained eye contact. "Until my end of September paycheck, I'm strapped."

"That's three more months," said Val, shaking her head. "You can't live like that all summer."

"I can." Andie lifted her chin. "I grew up poor. I don't need much."

"Would you like to live with me for a couple of months?" said Val. "Not just while you're recovering, but at least until after you've saved up rent money this fall."

"I can't take charity," said Andie. To her horror, more tears escaped, rolling down her face. She brushed them away from her hot cheeks. Damn morphine.

"I didn't say it would be free," said Val. "How about $100 a month?" She held up her hand when Andie tried to protest. It wasn't enough. "All you get is a room. Pitch in for groceries. Whatever amount you think is fair." Val probably wouldn't accept much, plus she would do ninety percent of the cooking and act like Andie was doing her a favor.

"You're too nice," said Andie.

"This is what friends are for," said Val. "We take care of each other. I'll call Susan and let her know you're staying with me. While I'm at it, I'll convince her not to charge the July rent so you can keep some cash. Zack and I can move your stuff before the first. It doesn't look like you have much." Val rested her hand on Andie's arm. "I'm sorry I didn't pay better attention. I should have noticed you were struggling. I want you to know you can share anything with me."

Andie swallowed before nodding. She still planned to keep the secret of her origin, as there was too much danger in revealing something so outlandish, but she was done hiding the rest. "I didn't want anyone to know. Especially you and Zack. It's embarrassing that someone my age, with my education, has so little. I guess that happens when you start over three times before the age of thirty."

"No more secrets," said Val. "Don't worry about a thing. Zack and I will take care of everything until you're recovered."

"Thank you." Andie swung her feet to the floor, taking care not to tangle anything on her IV stand. Val appeared at her side immediately, supporting her wobble-legged walk across the room to the bathroom. At the door, she passed Andie the bag with her collected belongings.

"Take your time. I'll be here until Zack returns. We're taking turns until visitor hours are over, and don't be surprised if he sweet-talks the nurses into staying longer." She sniffed. "He looks rougher than you do, so I sent him home for a nap."

# CHAPTER 28
# ANDIE

"Wait a minute, Doc. Are you telling me you built a time machine...out of
a DeLorean?"
–Marty McFly, Back to the Future (1985)

Monday afternoon, Andie examined Val's living room from her comfortable position on the couch, settling in after being released from the hospital. It didn't have expensive or designer furnishings, but that suited her just fine. Instead, it had a cozy feel, reflecting Val's interest in the West Coast, indigenous art, and birds.

She'd picked up Andie from the hospital and was making tea and rhubarb muffins in the nearby kitchen. Their sweet, fruity, mouth-watering aroma already filled the space. She might need two. She'd discovered how much she loved this recipe shortly after arriving in 1985, when Val had harvested the first tender shoots of rhubarb and used them for baking. The muffins must be almost ready.

"That's the last of it," said Zack, bounding down the stairs. He had so much energy. "You don't have much stuff."

"Thank you for packing and moving everything," Andie said. Val had helped Zack box up Andie's possessions yesterday, in between taking turns visiting at the hospital. "It was a lot of effort for a move down the street."

Zack shrugged. "It was easy without furniture or nine thousand knick-knacks. It was also handy you kept your moving boxes from a few months ago. They weren't even broken down yet."

"I wasn't quite that organized," said Andie with a chuckle. "I only unpacked the last six boxes the morning of Xander's barbeque." She couldn't believe she'd have to find homes for everything again so soon. Some of that must have been communicated in her expression.

"Well," said Zack. "I hope you don't mind, I put most of your clothes away and the books on the bookcase. There wasn't much else, so I left your paperwork on the desk."

"Thank you," said Andie. Had he snooped?

He flopped onto the recliner beside her, his long legs sprawling before him. "Have you figured out what to do with your unexpected time off?"

"I shouldn't stay off for too long," said Andie. "I'll have to call Rick in the morning and tell him I'm out of the hospital." She dreaded the conversation, though she'd run through it in her head several times.

Zack frowned. "How long did the doctor say you should stay off your feet?"

Andie hesitated. Should she tell him the truth? She shrugged, then freed her jumbled thoughts, the words picking up speed. "Three weeks, but I'm not sure I'll have a job if I wait that long." Zack lifted one eyebrow. He would have excelled as a teacher with that look. "Besides, I have to quit at the end of August. Rick might have difficulty finding someone for such a brief time. He might prefer to hire someone now to replace me."

"But you're trained already," said Zack. "I bet he'd rather you work as soon as you can and through August, even though I rather you not have to work with that creep."

Andie understood most of Zack's mumbled final words. She smothered a grin.

"Maybe." She wasn't so sure. She'd rather avoid Rick, but even with her change in circumstances, she still needed money to pay Val.

"Are you going to rip the Band-Aid off and call today?" said Zack. "You'd probably rather get it over with. Hear what he has to say so you don't stress about the uncertainty any longer than necessary."

Warmth shot through her. Zack seemed to know her well.

Andie checked the time on the wall clock. 4:00 p.m. She shook her head. "He's already had too much to drink. I have his home number for emergencies when I'm working. I'll call him tomorrow morning."

"Is he always drunk?" Zack turned toward her, his posture stiff.

"Seems like," she said, biting her lip. Where was Val with the muffins? Andie could use a distraction.

"You didn't say, but did your boss come on to you last week?" Zack's eyes were now a piercing, frosty blue, like snow on ice.

"He grabbed my ass and offered to pay me for sex," said Andie, shocking herself by telling the truth.

Zack's eyes blazed as he stood up, fists clenched. "He can't get away with that."

"Sit down," she said. "I told him off. We avoided each other after that. I don't expect any more trouble." She was telling the truth. Rick seemed to avoid her, hopefully out of embarrassment.

"That took guts." Zack sat once more. "Him being your boss and all."

"He understands I won't let him push me around." Andie kept her tone even, and she met Zack's gaze. Perspiration seeped onto her forehead.

Zack snorted. "Good. He'd better not lay hands on you again." He still looked fierce, but he exhaled and changed the subject. "Any plans for your spare time?"

"I've got my notebooks for writing," she said, nodding toward the coffee table. "I'll probably write for a couple of hours most days, then read."

"John fixed your car on Saturday when you were in the hospital," said Zack. "He hadn't flaked, he just had the wrong number. He called me Friday and left a message, but I didn't get it until Saturday when it was too late. I'm so sorry. If I'd listened to it, I would have at least known you didn't have a ride. I would have figured something out."

"I should have called a cab. It wasn't your fault. Really. Please, stop tormenting yourself. I'm trying not to dwell or to feel too much guilt. I've learned for next time."

Andie bit her lip before continuing. "I'd forgotten about the bill for the car. I've got that to pay, plus the one for the hospital." Tears threatened again. Get a grip. She inhaled and exhaled, trying to dispel the tension in her shoulders and chest.

"I paid John," said Zack.

Her tears overflowed at his kindness. Since she was off the morphine, she couldn't even blame the painkiller for her emotional state. These days, her raw feelings lurked close to the surface.

"I was an ass for pushing you into the repair, not realizing you were strapped for cash. I also should have consulted you first, instead of jumping in without being asked. I'm sorry for putting you in that position."

"I didn't want either of you to know. It'll be better once my teaching job starts." She tried to infuse her voice with confidence, but the truth was money concerns plagued her late-night tossing and turnings. No matter what plans she made, the hospital bill of hundreds of dollars per night would take months to pay. At least, in this time, it wasn't thousands.

"You said you'd explain why I was Andromeda to the hospital?"

He laughed. "I panicked and couldn't remember if Andie was a nickname. I made it up. You're lucky you weren't Andretti or something like that."

She chuckled, being careful not to jar her stitches. "I like them. It's nice to think I can have multiple names. Thank you for everything you took care of. I wasn't at my best."

"I admire you and Val." Zack shifted. Perhaps uncomfortable with praise. "Working with children all day would drive me up the wall. I don't have the patience."

Somehow, Andie doubted that, but she wasn't going to argue. "Sometimes, I'm shocked by my restraint. I don't particularly like children." Andie laughed at the expression on Zack's face as his eyebrows shot up. "But I just think of them as younger people and I enjoy their company once we get to know each other. They listen better when they know I care and am interested in their lives. I'm sure I'll like my own someday."

"Are you looking forward to teaching again?" He leaned forward, fidgeting with one of Val's coasters.

"I am," she said. "I'm going to call the school in the morning. I meant to do it before the summer break but didn't get around to it. However, Val said the private school office still be open. It's common for the office staff to be around longer than the teachers. I want to pick up curriculum materials and textbooks so I can plan lessons and units."

"My sister is smart that way. It must have been a lot different back East if you need all new materials," said Zack.

He had no idea. It would be a whole new job—one that made her sweat if she thought too hard.

"The school curriculum is different from where I taught last," she said. To say the least. No computers, tablets, or internet for starters. She faced significant adaptation challenges. Funny how the importance of technology diminished when it was no longer useful in day-to-day life. She had stopped reaching for her phone, and then out of the blue, she'd forget, and her hand would twitch. She missed it much less than expected.

Val entered the room balancing a wooden tray with a pottery teapot, three cups, a sugar bowl, a stack of side plates, and another carrying four muffins topped with crispy brown sugar and chopped walnuts. Andie's mouth watered. They looked scrumptious.

"Tea anyone?" Val placed the tray on the coffee table and looked at them. She laughed. "You both sat up straight like puppies on your best behavior, trying to get a treat." She sat beside Andie on the couch, reaching for the plates.

Before Andie stretched for a muffin, Val handed her a plate with two and poured tea into three cups, sliding one within Andie's reach. She set another muffin on a plate for herself.

"How come Andie gets two?" said Zack, grabbing the final muffin. His fake scowl fooled no one.

"Because if you want more than one, you can fetch another from the kitchen. You have two working feet and can serve yourself. She's supposed to take it easy for a couple of days." Val picked up her muffin, peeling the paper. She turned to Andie. "Even odds he gets another two when he goes into the kitchen."

Andie smiled, enjoying their banter and feeling part of it.

"I get it. It's okay. Preferential treatment for your new roommate. I can handle it." Zack winked. He stirred a teaspoon of sugar into his tea and leaned back while he took his first sip of the steaming liquid. Only then did he bite into his muffin.

The conversation shifted as Val and Zack discussed their plans for the summer—lots of walks and picnics, that included Andie. Her calendar was shaping up to be full, even without employment.

An hour later, when Val left the room, Zack said, "Are you still up for going to a movie next Sunday? I figured that gives you the week for your stitches to heal, plus that's when I work my last day shift, so I can sleep in before my first night shift."

He'd taken days off for her, helped her move, and stayed with her in the hospital on top of all the other kind actions. She hadn't forgotten the movie tickets. "A movie sounds wonderful," said Andie.

"I'm off the next two days and was hoping you wouldn't mind if I hung around." He shot her a look she couldn't interpret. "I haven't been the best of friends, and I intend to do better."

"I'd love the company," said Andie, "even if I'm just planning to read and write."

"I brought a book for me too," said Zack with an easy smile. He grabbed his third muffin and took a bite.

•　•　•

The parking lot was busy as Zack parked in front of the movie theater.

"Wait just a sec," he said as he jumped out. He trotted around the front of the car and opened Andie's door, extending her a hand.

Andie accepted his help in getting out of his low-slung car. The usual buzz of current raced through her at his touch. She'd gotten better at ignoring the sensation. Her incisions were healing well, but she moved gingerly. Her body was still sore, even if she was on the mend. She had two tiny scars that hadn't needed stitches and one longer, thicker one just over an inch where her stitches had dissolved.

It was difficult to believe the small surgical cut had been enough to remove her appendix. She was thankful the "new" procedure had been available. Laparoscopic surgery was commonplace in 2033, but Andie hadn't been conscious enough to be nervous about undergoing something so recent to this time. Her scars were small and hidden, unless someone saw her naked.

Andie flushed. Where had that thought come from? Biting her lip, she glanced at Zack. She still had lingering feelings there, but she brushed them off. She cherished their friendship—lately he'd been wonderful.

When Zack held open the theater door upon entry, the aroma of buttery popcorn once more assailed her. She breathed deeply, holding the delicious air in her lungs. Theaters should bottle the scent. They'd make a fortune.

He strode toward the concession counter. "It's on me. Movies are better with popcorn."

"It will be my turn to pay in the fall," she said, glancing toward the huge cardboard display of an action-comedy she'd never heard of starring Michael Douglas, Kathleen Turner, and Danny DeVito called *Jewel of the Nile*. She nodded toward the life-size ad. "That one looks fun."

Zack smiled. "I can't wait. It's a date."

The words thrilled her, but she sobered quickly. It must be just an expression.

His friendliness made her stomach flip-flop and her palms damp, but Andie tried not to read too much into his words. They'd already been down that road and it was a dead end. He didn't want a girlfriend, and she respected that now. She'd done better since the hospital at reining in her hopes, though he'd been sweeter than ever. He'd even stopped by the library, taking out several battered fantasy paperbacks, guessing what she might like.

The stack beside her bed included *The Summer Tree*, *The Blue Sword*, and the first three Shannara books. She'd loved reading the one he'd bought for her from the hospital gift shop, *Moreta: Dragonlady of Pern*. He had great taste.

Once the transaction was complete, Zack handed her the gigantic bucket of popcorn. "This shouldn't be too heavy."

"I'll help lighten it," said Andie with a toothy grin she seldom displayed in public. She picked several buttery bits off the top to pop into her mouth. Another handful followed.

"I'm glad you've got it covered," said Zack with a matching smile. He headed toward the theater, carrying two drinks. He tucked one into the crook of his arm to hold the heavy door at the entrance of Theater Two.

Her eyes adjusted to the dim hall while they entered the familiar movie theater with old-style seats, the purple curtain over the screen, and the gentle slope. She couldn't wait for reclining seats to become the norm.

"Where would you like to sit?" Perhaps sensing her indecision, he said, "I prefer the middle of the back rows, but I'm tall."

"Maybe we could choose seats near the back behind short people." She scanned the crowd. The theater, though not full, bustled with activity. The movie must be popular, plus it was a new release, having only been showing for less than a week. Viewers ranged in age from about ten or twelve-year-olds to seniors, and everyone in between. This movie must appeal to all ages, which made sense for a film about to become a classic.

Her heart drummed as she got into the spirit of excitement about seeing this brand-new blockbuster movie—one she'd heard of forever but never seen.

Zack leaned in, his breath warm on her cheek as he pointed to a row about three-quarters of the way back with two seats near the middle, behind a family with children in the middle, ones about ten or eleven, the age she was accustomed to teaching.

"How about there?" His voice being so close sent goosebumps skittering across her skin.

She took a deep breath, determined not to let his nearness fluster her or inhibit their friendship. The family shouldn't be loud or distracting during the movie, and the kids were short enough not to block her view.

"Perfect. Lead the way."

Zack smiled and headed up the shallow concrete steps beside the rows of seats. Before he started down the chosen row, he waved and caught the attention of the couple near the empty seats. "Are those two taken?" He spoke over excited voices and chatter from the waiting crowd.

The young man sitting next to a young woman, holding hands with her while they ate popcorn from a bucket placed strategically between them, shook his head. Zack and Andie shuffled down the aisle and settled in the seats.

"These are terrific," she said, taking another handful of the buttery popcorn. "Thanks again for inviting me."

He grabbed a handful of popcorn. "You eat that like my sister does. I'm not sure I can keep up." He moved the bucket closer to her. "Have you read any of the books I picked up? One looked like it was intended for younger readers, but I liked the picture of the warrior riding her horse with a flaming sword."

"I love *The Blue Sword*," she said. "I might have already read it twice this week." She almost clapped a hand over her mouth, but at the last second halted the motion. Zack wouldn't think less of her for being herself. She didn't need to hide her quirks, like rereading.

Zack grinned and set the popcorn between them, bracing it against his body. Suddenly, a ripple of energy buzzed throughout the room when the overhead lights dimmed, while smaller ones along the wall lit the sides of the room with a faint glow. At the front, the plum-colored curtain bunched at the bottom and rose toward the ceiling, revealing the widescreen beneath.

Butterflies filled her stomach as Andie glanced at Zack. He grinned and whispered. "I'm so glad you're here with me to watch this. It's better with you here." He draped his arm across the back of the seats, above her shoulders.

Despite herself, his thoughtful words warmed her throughout. She'd never been told anything of the kind. Her chest tightened with powerful emotion. Friends was also a nice connection, and she was glad to share this experience. They oohed and aahed over the previews for upcoming movies, none of which she'd heard of before, though *The Journey of Natty Gann* looked interesting, and Michael J. Fox had another movie called *Teen Wolf* releasing later this year. He'd been busy.

The room hushed as the feature began—the only remaining sounds the film, crunching popcorn, and laughter.

"The flux capacitor is a fabulous name for a time travel device," whispered Zack, lowering his arm as he leaned. He grabbed a handful of popcorn.

While Andie was conscious of his warm leg pressed against hers, she read nothing into the contact. He needed more space than the small seats allowed. Still, she liked his solidity. She so seldom had anyone in her personal space. Not to get distracted, she directed her attention back to the movie, entertained by the unfolding story. When Doc was shot by the terrorists, Andie grabbed Zack's arm with a gasp. He grinned and her skin went up in flames as she released her grasp. They laughed together when Marty McFly impersonated Darth Vader from Planet Vulcan.

"It's heresy to confuse, or even combine Star Wars and Star Trek," said Zack with another quiet comment for her ears only. He shook his head.

Andie loved that he shared his thoughts during the movie. Some people might dislike the quiet talking, but she enjoyed it. It made viewing a movie a shared experience instead of a solitary activity in a darkened room.

Throughout the movie, Andie couldn't help comparing the young Michael J. Fox on screen to the older man he'd been in her time. She'd watched a documentary about him called *Still* eight or ten years ago. For her whole life, Michael J. Fox had been an advocate for Parkinson's research, and she'd only seen his work on TV after he'd been affected by the degenerative disease and no longer hiding his diagnosis.

Andie and Zack stayed until the end, watching the credits roll. There would be sequels, but she wasn't sure when, so she locked that knowledge inside. She was reluctant to leave when they'd had such an enjoyable evening.

The idea of changing the past through time travel wasn't something she'd thought about much—though perhaps she should have been more aware of her actions. The idea of ruining her future made her blood gurgle like rivers of ice. Perhaps the concept held some truth. Marty had improved his life by making his parent's relationship stronger and their lives better. By altering the way they'd met and how they'd gotten together, he'd given them confidence. Was she changing the future somehow by her presence in 1985?

Unlikely. One thing she could learn from the movies. If she stayed in this time forever, she'd be sure to invest in tech companies like Apple, Microsoft, and Amazon.

"What are you thinking about so hard?" said Zack as they filed out of the empty theater, tossing their garbage into the bin by the exit. His hand strayed to her lower back as they walked, the protective gesture warming her as much as the heat of his hand.

"About the similarities and differences in how this movie and *Terminator* portrayed the concept of time travel." She may as well tell her true thoughts. Zack wasn't likely to mock, or if he did, it would be friendly teasing; she could handle that. Only with Val, and now Zack, did she feel safe enough to be genuine.

"They portrayed time travel more the same in the two movies than different, even if one was an action flick, the other a comedy," said Zack.

"I agree," she said. "In both movies, the future was changeable." What if she lived long enough to catch up to her former self? Forty-eight years wasn't that long.

"The future is not set." He imitated the voice of Kyle Reese, the time traveler from *Terminator* who'd traveled back to save John Connor's mother. Reese had fallen in love with Sarah Connor and become his idol's father, proving he was supposed to come back.

"Didn't Doc Brown say something similar in the movie we just watched?"

"He did. Something about making your own future."

Andie couldn't recite the exact quote either. She'd have to catch it the next time she watched the movie. She chuckled inwardly. Of course, there'd be a next time.

Maybe by staying here in 1985, she was choosing her own fate, like in the movies. Instead of viewing time travel as a punishment, it was a gift. Maybe Dr. Maeve was correct, and she should accept the happiness and friends in this time. Was this her intended destiny? Andie could make this be the future she'd dreamed of, one where she was finally happy even if it wasn't always simpler.

Zack held the door open as they left the air-conditioned theater and crossed the dry heat of the parking lot toward his car. "You up for a stroll on the way home? It's a shame to waste such a gorgeous evening."

The light outside had softened, with the sun still above the horizon, but dipping downward. In an hour, the sunset would be stunning.

"I'd love to," said Andie. While it would delay eating dinner, she'd consumed enough popcorn that she wasn't hungry. "Maybe we can go somewhere overlooking the water."

"Great idea," said Zack, starting the car. "I know just the place."

# CHAPTER 29
# ANDIE

"We came, we saw, we kicked its ass!"
–Dr. Peter Venkman, Ghostbusters (1984)

Andie pulled up to the three-story brick building which housed the private school where she would teach in the fall and parked in the almost empty lot—two other cars had parked close to the main entrance. She had a positive first impression of the place. Lofty trees, well-manicured grounds, and shady pathways surrounded the school. In the distance, neighborhood kids played soccer in one of the three verdant soccer fields, their shouts filling the air.

She'd be teaching at a fancy school—unlike anywhere she'd attended or taught before. With luck, she could stay longer than a single year; she'd love the stability. Unlike the intimidating atmosphere of her previous job, she felt positive about this place, where she felt she belonged.

She stepped out of her car and headed for the main door, waves of summer heat rising from the asphalt, though a breeze blew in from the west, tossing her hair as she strode.

In almost the exact words Val had suggested, Andie had spoken to the school principal and made an appointment for this morning. With her head held high, she marched up the front stairs without worrying more about being hired through a recruiting company and having never met her future employer. She opened the front door and strolled inside. The temperature dropped immediately. Her footsteps echoed in the open entryway with high ceilings and cool tile floors. A colorful mural filled the entire end wall.

Andie didn't have time to gawk more as she was on a mission. There would be other opportunities to soak in the atmosphere. She released a deep breath.

The office was on her right.

"Excuse me," she said to the older woman stuffing folders into a wide four-drawer filing cabinet. Several stacks of additional folders waited on the floor, while papers were strewn on the desk, the counter, and several chairs.

"How may I help you?" said the woman, straightening up and removing her glasses, letting them drop to her ample chest via a chain lanyard.

Andie bit her lip. "I'm sorry to interrupt, but I called earlier..." Her voice trailed off when the secretary nodded.

"You must be Andie. How can it be eleven already? My morning has flown." The gray-haired woman smiled. "It's nice to finally meet you in person. We're looking forward to having you join the staff this fall. Mr. Griffiths is expecting you." She waved Andie forward into the outer office and led her down a short hall, where she stuck her head into an opening. "Wayne, Ms. Sterling has arrived." She beckoned Andie forward.

A gangly man with silver hair stood, straightening the front of his crisp navy-blue suit. "Thanks, Marge."

He had to be well over six feet in height and composed of all angles. He towered over Andie, but when he smiled, his craggy face seemed kind. "I'm the principal, Wayne Griffiths," he said, holding out his hand.

Andie shook his warm, dry hand. "Andie Sterling." She made a point of maintaining eye contact.

"It was a smart idea to come in this summer," he said. "The recruiting agent who found you for us mentioned you might be in contact once you'd settled on the West Coast. I'm glad that turns out to be the case."

Recruiting agent, Aunt, Dr. Maeve, and all-around meddler—a full-service therapist. At least Dr. Maeve was thorough—providing ID and a profession in 1985. Without these, Andie wouldn't have been able to support herself long-term. These gave her a chance.

The principal patted a stack on his desk with five, one-inch, three-ring binders. "I got the head teacher to pull these for you after you called. It should be sufficient to get you started. I haven't changed your grade assignment so you can feel confident planning for fifth grade."

"Thank you." Andie kept her face composed, but the amount of reading material in the binders for each subject made the lump in her stomach expand. She'd told herself it would be different than viewing a few pages and links online. It was so much more. However, this was her boss, so she kept her feelings to herself. She had all summer; she could do it by breaking it into manageable pieces and Val would help if asked.

Funnily enough, for once, Andie was confident she wasn't in over her head.

She forced a nervous smile. "I appreciate you taking the time to meet with me so I could collect these." She slid the stack of binders, one by one, into a tote bag she'd brought. Each was labeled on the front with a subject area title page protected in a plastic sleeve on the cover. Now she could make units for Language Arts, Math, Science, Social Studies, and Art. A peek inside of the top one showed it contained information for all grades, not just hers, which decreased her anxiety.

"Will I be teaching any other subjects?" said Andie. Maybe she'd better read up on the other areas of the curriculum as well.

"This should do the trick," said Mr. Griffiths. "We have dedicated gym and music teachers. That's how we'll provide you with prep time."

She nodded. No curriculum for social-emotional learning, core competencies, work habits, skills, or technology. Another difference from her old time. In her old time, she'd taught school, but at times, she felt more like a counselor than a teacher. In 2033, she'd often been overwhelmed by her role and the massive load of expectations.

Her thoughts buzzed with the possibilities of her upcoming planning. She planned to create integrated units that worked together for multiple subjects at the same time. She loved that type of teaching and learning, when one area bled into another and connected.

"Oh. I have one more question," Andie said, before leaving. "When will I be able to set up my classroom?"

"The school will be open the last week of August before Labor Day," said the principal with another friendly smile, this one making the skin by his eyes crinkle. "Many teachers come in for a day or two. I hope to see you then. I'd take you upstairs to your class now, but the custodial team hasn't cleaned yet, so the furniture is in disarray and stacked in the hallway. You wouldn't get an accurate picture of the space where you'll be working, but you have a stunning view of the mountains from your windows." He waved toward his windows, where the jagged coastal mountains with snowy peaks jutted toward the blue sky.

Andie smiled. She had this. "Thanks again for letting me pick up the materials. I'll see you at the end of the summer." She strode out of the office, waved to the secretary, and headed out the main door. The binders were heavier than she should likely carry so soon after her surgery, but she only had a short walk before she stowed them in her car.

While she drove back to her home at Val's, she made a schedule. She would designate a few hours every day for school-related work until she had enough ready for the first term, maybe beyond. Whatever she created, she could always adapt once she met her students and learned their level. The best activities were open-ended anyway, to meet the needs of struggling learners, those in the gifted range, and everyone in between. For the first time, genuine confidence infused her feelings about this position. She would be a terrific teacher.

Buoyed by the positivity, she cranked the radio, belting out "Everybody Wants to Rule the World." Tonight, she also had plans with Zack to watch a movie—something he'd rented for the three of them. Everything was looking like aces.

●　　●　　●

Andie and Zack strolled outside in the cool evening after another delicious dinner at Val's. They'd invited her to join them for a walk, but she'd declined, saying she was looking forward to quiet time in her own home. Andie bit her lip, hoping she wasn't overstaying her welcome. Maybe she should talk to Susan about the old rental.

When Zack guided her outside, he whispered, "Val's happy you're here, and she's been putting up with me, too. She just needs an hour of peace." He tucked her hand against his arm as they headed out.

Andie remained silent as they walked, side by side, along the sidewalk for a few blocks until they reached the quiet park. There they ambled along one of the paved paths. In the daylight, it seemed a welcoming place.

Andie broke the silence. "Why are you still staying at Val's? You have your own place." She clapped a hand over her mouth and her eyes rounded. Since the surgery, it seemed she couldn't keep her thoughts to herself. "I'm sorry. I seem to just blurt whatever's on my mind these days." If only she could suck the words back inside. They sounded appallingly rude. Heat rose to her skin. She must resemble a lobster.

Instead of being offended, Zack laughed. He grabbed Andie's other hand, lacing his fingers through hers. In shock at his bold move, Andie froze, her feet dragging to a stop like anchors.

"I wanted to be where you were, silly. I wanted to help take care of you." He squeezed her hand and tucked an errant lock of hair behind her ear with the other.

She was so hot she felt she must have gone up in flames, and her clothes stuck as she became drenched in sweat. "As a friend," she said, swallowing. She stared into his pale blue eyes. Electricity buzzed through her, spreading from her hand in seconds. Even her toes tingled.

Zack shook his head. "When Cole and I responded to that call in the rain, and you were the one lying on the concrete, it broke my heart. You were sick, alone, and had been in danger. In that moment, I made a life-changing discovery." His earnest blue eyes met her steady gaze. "I want to be clear. At no time did I want to be just your friend. From the moment I saw you falling off the curb, I've wanted to get to know you. Considering some of my actions, this might be difficult to believe, and I hope you'll forgive me."

"You like me." She bit her lip, noting his eyes tracked the movement. Her stomach fluttered and her heart rate spiked. This couldn't be real. "As more than a friend." She couldn't keep the incredulity out of her voice. He'd insisted they keep their distance all this time. Even though he had kissed her that night, she'd convinced herself it was a mistake made in the heat of the moment.

"I do," said Zack. His thumb pressed harder on the back of her hand. "I didn't want to admit it, but I've felt like I was supposed to be with you. I resisted, even when seeing you was the best part of any day or week. Even late-night pick-ups from that stupid video store when I was an exhausted zombie. I've been an idiot." He rubbed circles on her skin with the pressure of his thumb. He glanced down at their joined hands with a smile.

"I wouldn't go that far." She shot him a sideways glance. "Maybe a slow learner, though." Her heart galloped as he stepped closer. He tugged her against him, and she went willingly.

"Can I kiss you?" he whispered. "I've spent a thousand hours imagining your lips."

Drawn forward as though caught in a tractor beam, she tipped her face upwards and he captured her lips with his own, tugging her against his hard frame. When he wrapped a muscular arm around her, it was as though a missing piece of herself clicked into place. She lost track of time, enjoying the sensation as he deepened the kiss. She draped her arms around his neck and tightened her hold, suddenly desperate to be as close as possible.

When at last they broke apart, quiet while they caught their breath, he rested his forehead on hers.

"I don't know how my Aunt M. did it." His voice was soft and filled with wonder. "She told me she'd found my soulmate, but I didn't believe her. I never imagined it could be true, but here you are. I don't understand how she could know about you, but she did."

For half a second, the truth about traveling through time sat on Andie's lips, but she restrained her tongue. Her time-slip could remain a mystery; a secret she would hold close forever.

"Tell me what you're thinking." Zack straightened and tipped her chin upward, so she once more met his gaze. Staring into his eyes, a sense of peace and calm infused her being.

"About this is how it is supposed to be," said Andie. They kissed again, losing themselves in the moment until a barking dog from around the corner returned them to awareness.

"There's something I've been meaning to ask." Zack sounded out of breath. "Will you come with me to Xander and Cindy's wedding in October?"

"I'd love to," said Andie, as they resumed their walk in the park. "Will they be okay with you bringing an extra person? They want to keep it small."

Zack shot her a look. "Last spring, Xander told me I could bring you. I'll let him know you said, 'yes.'"

She raised an eyebrow at the mention of the timing, but didn't question him further. A yawning pit opened in her gut. "How will Val react to our dating? She's important to me, too."

"When I asked to stay at her house, she said 'It was about time I came to my senses.' She's good with us being together. She saw we fit long before I admitted the truth."

Breathing easier, Andie said, "Val's smart like that."

On the way back to the house sometime later, a navy-blue muscle car—the one that haunted Andie's nightmares—roared past. She clenched Zack's hand hard enough it could have hurt.

"What?" he said, following the direction of her gaze.

"That's the car. The one that followed me the night I was sick," said Andie. "The driver works for Xander at your job site. He's an asshole."

Zack stopped, his eyes narrowing as he gazed up the street at the now-distant car. "You're sure it's the same guy?"

"Yes. His name is Tom." Her voice was tight enough to make her throat ache. If her suspicion was true, that he might be related to Dylan, she worried about interfering. He might be fired, but he also shouldn't get away with harassing women. He might hurt or scare others, and that was unacceptable.

"Leave it to me," said Zack. "Xander won't have him on his crew once he knows."

A wave of disquiet settled over her like icy mist. Was this the action that trickled down to make Dylan who he was? But she refused to blame herself for the horrible actions of another.

# Chapter 30
# Zack

"Life moves pretty fast. If you don't stop and look around once in a while,
you could miss it."
–Ferris Bueller, Ferris Bueller's Day Off (1986)

Two weeks after Zack and Andie's relationship status changed, she completed her follow-up with her doctor from the hospital where she received a clean bill of health. Zack held her hand as they walked outside, heading for his silver car parked in the shade. They glanced at each other, smiling. She was cute when she blushed. It was like she was reading his mind. Finally, no more restrictions on her physical activity.

Zack had been careful and patient, but he yearned for more than kissing. He ached to express his feelings on a deeper level. Well, that and he was tired of going to bed with blue balls every night after their heated make out sessions.

They piled into his car after her appointment, and headed north, driving an uneventful hour north to his dad's house for a family birthday party. Excitement flared through Zack. Today was the first time Andie would be present at one of his family gatherings as his girl. He couldn't wait to witness the shocked expressions on Aunt Sarah's and Aunt Jen's faces. Given an opportunity, he might also thank Aunt M. for finding Andie. However unlikely his great-aunt's involvement, he suspected he owed her for his current happiness.

Zack glanced at Andie, sitting beside him, eyes shining as she sang along with the radio. God. She was stunning. He admired her natural beauty and the way the sun glinted in her hair with its multitude of gold, copper, and blonde hues. Not to mention her brain. Smart chicks were the best.

He reached across the center console and took her hand. She was everything he'd always wanted. His fear of losing someone had been a lousy reason to be alone. He was damn lucky she'd helped him figure that out before he lost her. He remained haunted by that night in the rain. If she hadn't made it to the hospital in time, or if she'd recovered and moved away, he would have regretted the loss for the rest of his life. But he had figured his shit out before it was too late. No point in dwelling on what if's, even if he'd been close to having nothing.

Needing the reassurance of her touch, the reality of loving someone at last, he squeezed her hand. That earned him a breathtaking smile that fired his blood.

They needed to head home early tonight—to his apartment. While their relationship was new, and he had a few regrets over wasted time, he had no qualms about moving forward. His throat thickened. With Andie, he was all in.

His future had never looked so bright.

Reaching his dad's house, they parked in the shade of a tall pine. He squeezed Andie's hand again, as they stepped up to the front door. She nibbled her lower lip.

"You good?" He kissed her temple.

With her nod, they headed in—time to face the Mirabelli clan.

•  •  •

Zack stepped out of his dad's downstairs bathroom by the guest room. The other had been occupied, a hazard with an extra dozen people milling around the house. Before he returned to the group, Andie's voice caught his attention. She wasn't in the kitchen where he'd left her a few minutes ago. Someone must have asked for a word in private.

"I'm not sure I'm comfortable having this conversation." She must be in his dad's study further down the hall, away from the party.

He stopped. Did he need to rescue Andie from whoever had dragged her away from the birthday gathering? His family could be so overbearing.

"Is there anything else you've learned in this time?" Aunt M.'s clear voice carried down the hall.

"I've thought a lot about my sister. I'm not to blame for abandoning her like I'd always thought. It took coming here to realize I was allowed to attend university and carry on with my life. I was eighteen and needed more than staying home. Staying in touch was a two-way street and we both failed."

"Good for you," said Aunt M. "She can't find you here, but there might come a time you can help her in the future. She might need someone."

"I'll look for her later," said Andie. "Can I get back to the party now?"

"Just one more thing," said Aunt M.

Andie seemed fine, but Zack wasn't sure he understood the conversation. He lingered.

"About staying, I just wanted to determine if you'd made a final decision," said Aunt M.

Zack frowned, his forehead tightening. Maybe he shouldn't eavesdrop. Still, his feet remained stuck in place, the hall carpet like quicksand.

"I don't want to go back to 2033, even if it was an option. You were right. There was nothing for me there. I choose to stay and make my own fate."

Zack cocked his head to the side. Did she say 2033, as in the year 2033? He shook his head. That couldn't be right. All the discussion about fate and the future was messing with his head. He rested his palm flat on the wall, leaning closer.

Andie's assured voice continued. "Val and Zack are better family than I ever had on my own. They're good for me."

"I thought so." Aunt M.'s pleased comment broke Zack's trance.

He stepped back. This was a private conversation, and he must have misunderstood about Andie being from 2033. Perhaps the number was part of an address, not a date. Whatever. What mattered was she planned to stay.

They could make long-term plans. The kind where if all went well, she could move into his new house and help make it a proper home.

He crept away from the study, not needing to hear anything else so he could respect her privacy. If she wanted to talk to him about helping her sister, she'd share. If not, that was her prerogative.

A few minutes later, Andie reappeared in the kitchen, her cheeks flushed. He couldn't take his eyes off her as she crossed the tile floor. Even her walk was sexy.

He tucked her against his side and kissed her forehead. "I'm glad you're here," he whispered.

She smiled up at him. "It looks like I'm back in the nick of time. I'd hate to miss cake."

Overhead, the lights dimmed. Zack turned his attention to Val as everyone broke into "Happy Birthday." She placed a homemade birthday cake in front of their dad, a white candle, shaped in a sixty-five, aflame on top.

His dad smiled, sucked in a huge breath, and leaned forward, blowing out the flame. "Thanks, everyone. I'm lucky you didn't stick all sixty-five candles on one cake, or I'd have worried about burning down the house." The surrounding family laughed. "I can't believe how fast the years have gone."

"It's too true," said Aunt M., the colorful stones of her homemade jewelry clicking with her movement. "We have to live our best life every day and make the most of our time." She seemed to stare through Zack where he stood, his arm around Andie.

"Happy birthday, Dad. To living our best life," said Zack, raising his glass.

"Our best life," echoed the family's voices.

Zack glanced down at Andie, and his heart swelled. New as this relationship was, she was an integral part of his best life. He'd have to make damn sure she knew how important she was. Time around them seemed to slow as everyone accepted plates with chocolate cake and ate the rich dessert. They stood in the bustling kitchen, surrounded by family. He let the content feeling settle over him, basking in togetherness, and then the presence of his family faded.

He only needed one more thing to make his life perfect.

"Come with me," said Zack, glancing around the crowded kitchen. They set their empty plates on the counter. Andie didn't hesitate to follow when he slipped into the hall, away from the noise. With the background of cheerful chatter and the quieter scrape of forks, the sounds ceased to matter.

He couldn't keep his hands off her much longer. Time to go.

Zack pulled her against him and kissed her. A low moan escaped his lips. The lingering chocolate taste and her sweet scent made him almost forget where they were. He wanted to devour her, but the front hall at his dad's wasn't the ideal location.

"Can I take you back to my place?" he said. "Now."

Her brow creased, on the verge of a frown. "Won't people expect us to stick around? We just ate birthday cake."

"I want you," he said, his voice low and intense. "To make love to you for hours, and I don't want Val to hear or interrupt. I've been burning for months, and I couldn't do anything about it. You're part of my best life and I want to touch all of you." He couldn't wrest his eyes from her beautiful face.

"Let's go," she said, tugging him toward the door.

They slipped outside. Behind them, the plates clinked as Val and Yolanda worked together, loading them into the dishwasher. He closed the front door, and the sounds faded.

"We didn't say goodbye," she said with a last glance over her shoulder.

He shook his head. "They'll delay us another hour, just saying goodbye. They'll get over it if we just go. Let them wonder when we left." He grinned. His family would understand. They would tease the two of them for years about escaping so early and he looked forward to their ribbing.

•　　•　　•

Zack hadn't slept at his apartment for almost a month. He'd only stopped by to pick up his mail and collect new clothes when necessary. He opened the door, crossed to the kitchen, and cracked open the window to relieve the stale air.

He and Andie kicked their shoes onto the floor mat. They'd only taken two steps when they turned toward each other, unable to wait. He didn't pay attention to who grabbed who first. What mattered was the speed he had her shirt up, her bra off, and her pants undone. She stepped free of her clothes, standing before him in just her underwear.

Zack pressed her against the wall, his hungry kisses on her lips, caressing her soft skin. He nibbled at her neck, inhaling. He couldn't get enough of Andie's delicious scent. Up close, it was intoxicating.

She fumbled with his T-shirt, which he yanked over his head, tossing it aside. From the glint in her eyes, they burned for each other; this passion wasn't one-sided.

Zack took a breath and slowed down, his kissing becoming more leisurely, his hands gliding instead of groping. He laced his fingers through hers and led her down the hall to his waiting bedroom. This didn't need to be rushed. He wanted to savor every moment now that he was no longer afraid of caring. He was more afraid of feeling nothing and regretting it forever.

He and Andie had their whole lives to love one another and could take their time.

# Chapter 31
## Andie

"I thought this was a party. LET'S DANCE!"
–Ren McCormack, Footloose (1984)

*Three months later...*

Andie glanced around at the seated reception guests scattered around Xander's backyard, now surrounded by brilliant yellow and blazing red leaves. She recognized most of Xander and Cindy's friends and family from the barbeque in June. The backyard ceremony for their wedding had been perfect, with fewer than forty guests. Strings of twinkle lights throughout the yard bathed the early evening wedding ceremony and dinner in soft light. This early in fall, despite being a stunning, cloudless day, Andie shivered in the chill spreading since the sun had set in a fiery glow.

Zack shrugged out of his suit jacket and draped it across her shoulders, tucking the edges around her. She leaned closer, grateful for his usual heat and the kind gesture.

Andie had never been in a crowd and still felt connected. For so long, she'd been alone, even in the company of others. That was no longer the case. She caught Val's eye as she stood up across the table.

"I'm going to mingle for a bit." Val headed for a group by the bar with Yolanda and Wanda.

Zack kissed Andie's temple, leaning her against him. He tugged her chair closer and wrapped his arm around her. "You still cold? I can zip out to the car and grab your sweater."

She shook her head. "Just happy. The ceremony was beautiful, wasn't it?"

He grinned. "Women. All of you. Fools for love and weddings, aren't you?"

She smiled up at him. "Someone has to be. We keep an entire industry in business."

Zack swallowed, glancing at his watch.

She checked the time on hers too. Nine o'clock. Was he going to suggest they cut out early again? As expected, his family had been merciless at every gathering since July and their abrupt exit from his dad's birthday. She shot him a sideways glance and grinned. It had been worth it.

The love theme from *Footloose* came through the speakers placed at the edge of the patio, and Zack stood. He wore an indecipherable expression as he held out his hand.

He cleared his throat. "Dance with me?"

Andie glanced around the wedding party. She loved this song, and even though nobody else was dancing, why not? She took Zack's hand, following him to a clear spot beyond the pool on the patio, following his lead. He tugged her against him while she rested her arms on his broad shoulders while he held her close, his hands on her lower back. As they danced, his hands slid lower while they turned in place.

She sighed. He was warm and sweet. He was her safe home. They swayed to the voices of Mike Reno and Ann Wilson, letting the lovely music wash over her until the song faded—another special moment for her memories.

As the last strains of music drifted away, Zack stopped dancing. He stepped back, took her hand in his, and dropped to one knee.

Andie's heart stopped, and she covered her mouth. He wasn't. He couldn't be. They'd only been together for a few months. She hadn't expected anything so soon, even if they'd talked about someday and their future.

"Andie. My Andretti. My Andromeda. I have a question to ask." His pale blue eyes once more pools of glacial water—startling, pale, and deep.

Transfixed, she couldn't look away as butterflies swooped through her stomach. She uncovered her mouth, returning her shaking hand to Zack's steady one.

"Yes," she whispered, tears welling up. She blinked to clear them.

"I haven't asked yet, Gorgeous." Zack's smile melted her inside, turning her into mush. "Andie, I didn't want to love anyone because I was too scared of losing someone to take a chance. Meeting you changed my life. You're irresistible and I can't help loving you. You're my everything."

Her lip trembled and her happy tears escaped, scalding her cheeks.

"Will you marry me? Love me for all our days?" Zack's icy hand remained solid in hers.

She nodded, unable to speak.

He beamed, his eyes sparkling, and her heart fluttered. "Is that a yes?"

"Yes. I love you," she whispered. "All my life, I've only needed you." She echoed the lines of the song that had just played.

Zack winked, probably recognizing the borrowed words. Standing up, he held her face between his capable hands and kissed her.

Somewhere behind them, Val yelled. "I called Xander's reception. I win twenty bucks from each of you. Everyone, pay up. Like those two would make it until the holidays without getting engaged," she scoffed. "Whoever took next summer, you pay double."

Andie and Zack broke from their kiss, laughing.

Of course, the Mirabelli's had been taking bets.

The family rushed in to hug them both, with Val first in line.

She whispered in Andie's ear. "Welcome to the family. Thank you for making my little brother so happy." She squeezed Andie's upper arms, then stepped back to allow others to offer their congratulations.

When Xander joined them for a hug, he stage-whispered. "I'm sure to win the pool about when you'll get married. I'm betting you aim for when the new house is done. As your contractor, your fate is in my hands." He rubbed his palms together.

Everyone surrounding them laughed.

"No fair," yelled Wanda from the back of the gathering. "Xander's cheating, again."

"Leave them alone," said Aunt M. "It must be time for wedding cake."

# EPILOGUE
# ANDIE

"As you wish."
–Westley, The Princess Bride (1987)

*2033*

Secrets. I've kept one close for almost fifty years. They used to say to keep a secret, you had to hide it from yourself. That's worked for me as I tried not to think about my old life, the different time in which I was born. Sometimes I thought Zack must suspect, but how could he? At those times, my secret burned within me, trying to escape, but I buried it deep.

Until recently.

The hardest test came today.

This morning, a once-familiar white Honda Civic parked in front of the vacant house next door—a house I lived in for a few months in my youth, when its siding was painted, and its yard maintained. A slim young woman with blonde hair emerged, carrying two suitcases, making additional trips to transport half a dozen moving boxes. I've watched every day this spring, waiting for my tulips to bloom, barely able to contain my excitement as each day of April progressed toward the date circled on my calendar.

I would meet her again. The other Andie. The young me.

My larger secret contains a series of smaller ones, nested inside each other like Russian dolls. We've reached the center, and I have another role to play. I've run through my lines several times during the last few weeks, as I walk around the house, muttering to myself. Zack must think dementia is kicking in all at once. Young Andie's secret belongs to the only one I've kept from him.

At times, he might have questioned my choices, including my confidence about certain lucrative investments or regarding a young woman named Jess in Canada with whom I've been in contact for several years. My "good feeling" about Amazon, Apple, Microsoft, and Walmart made us money. Jess is my sister, and I am her closest family. But he's trusted me, and I've provided answers close to the truth. She's kin and has no one else.

For forty-eight years, my secret has lived inside me as I've waited to see if everything will come to pass how it did once before. That afternoon, before going outside, I closed the door to the library, removing traces of my pen name—Andromeda Mirabelli—hiding my twenty-two published novels. To her, I will be Andrea.

I remember this day from the opposite side. When I was Andie, fresh-faced, determined, and lonely, striding chin-up and bruised into that dump, I'd been seeking refuge from my abusive and almost forgotten first husband. I'd shaken hands with the old lady next door and accepted an invitation for tea.

When she accepted, I breathed a sigh of relief. So far, her visit matched my memories.

I could give her advice and a nudge in the proper direction. Soon.

In the kitchen, I put on the kettle, watching her out of the corner of my eye. I'd strategically placed several Visa gift cards as props, left for a remembered conversation. Young me was so careful, so tactful not to say the elderly were often the victims of scams.

Her phone buzzed a dozen times as we drank our tea and got acquainted. When she left, I sat alone in the kitchen, thinking about myself so long ago. Another memory drifted to the forefront as I readied myself for what came next.

At dinner time, I popped two frozen pizzas into the oven and waited.

When the doorbell rang, I took a breath. "Can you get that?" I called. Long ago, she'd met Zack. I shouldn't change that moment.

My chest tightened. I risked him discovering my buried secret when he answered the door. Young Andie had come back that night with her camera, asking for photos of fist-sized bruises on her back and ribs. The current me was proud of that brave young woman for leaving that asshole Dylan Marks.

She stayed for dinner, and I kept my voice even as I slipped her Aunt M.'s name and number, trying to conceal the tremors in my wrinkled hand. So much depended on playing it cool and not pressuring her, just giving her options. I'd given myself the means to contact Dr. Maeve and set my wish in motion.

I smiled at the thought of Aunt M. The old lady still comes and goes, looking exactly the same. Time doesn't touch her as it does the rest of us. We'll never know why, but that's part of her charm.

When young Andie left, headed back to her lonely house, I squared my shoulders, hearing the hockey game click off. Zack sauntered into the kitchen, holding his empty plate.

"Did I do it right? She didn't recognize me." His pale blue eyes twinkled as he opened the dishwasher.

My jaw dropped.

"I remember that Andie," he said with a wink, the kind that makes my heart race even now, forty-eight years later. "That's the secret you've been harboring all these years. When you dug out your old wrist watch, I wondered if it was related."

"You knew?" My voice came out breathless, like I'd been running. Of course he would have recognized her, but I'd wondered if the hockey game might have distracted him, causing him to miss something so unlikely.

Zack shrugged. "Before we were married, I overheard Aunt M. say something about 2033. I never forgot, even if it didn't make sense. It's never mattered where you came from, only that you stayed." He pulled me into a tight embrace—after all these years, our bodies still fit together so well. "You had to know I would recognize you at the door this evening. You're still my beautiful Andie. I love you."

I tipped my head back and kissed him gently. "I love you, too. Yes, you did it right. She never suspects a thing." As well as I know him, his knowledge was a surprise. It seems I hadn't kept anything from him after all. I love how close we still are. How connected. Our life hasn't been perfect, but it's been wonderful. We have two grown children, six grandchildren, and Jess, who just finished her Master's degree and plans to teach college-level art classes in Vancouver. We're due for a visit.

Zack and I stood there, in our house, our castle, wrapped together in the warmth of our love. Whatever time we had together was still ours. Young Andie has so much to look forward to, time to live, and a successful life to enjoy. My smile remains.

I chose to stay in another time, the right one, the one where I belonged. The best thing that ever happened to me was my wish.

First, I met myself, then I met my soulmate and made my dreams come true.

If you ever meet our Aunt M., the renowned Dr. Maeve Fossey, be careful what you wish for because you just might get it, even if the outcome is unexpected.

# Acknowledgments

This story is dedicated to *my* Val. In *The Right Time*, I wanted to write a story about connection, which includes friendship as much as love. When I asked to borrow her name, she said I could, as long as her character was nice. I believe I met that criterion, even if the real-life Val is even better.

I met Val when I was 22, and I was her student teacher. She taught fourth grade, and I was placed in her class for my short practicum in the fall of 1994. Because we were a great fit, the university also assigned me to her for my long practicum the next spring.

Just before my teaching practicum ended, I ended up in the hospital with a fever of close to 105 degrees. Some of that fevered evening was a blur, including meeting one of my favorite hockey players and being dismissive, running into a university friend I'd lost contact with (because I was delirious, I lost her number that night too. Sally Ng, if you ever read this, I'm sorry), and not being able to eat my cheeseburger, an unheard-of circumstance for the bottomless pit I used to be.

Like Andie, I had laparoscopic surgery, and my appendix was removed. I stayed in the hospital for three days. My boyfriend stopped in once a day, but my surprise visit was from Val. She brought her husband and stepdaughter. They ensured the nurses gave me ice cream and visited for most of Saturday morning.

From then on, Val was not just my mentor, but my friend. When my boyfriend and I broke up a year and a half later, I moved into Val's basement suite. She invited me upstairs for dinner at least once a week and for dessert or tea several times each week. Val, her husband, and I all taught fourth grade, so she would often plan shared lessons while doodling on a napkin over cookies or muffins.

Val and I remained close when I got engaged and moved. She's the kind of friend who could pop by without warning, and I could do the same. No need to vacuum or tidy up for company. We could be ourselves.

Every time I went to her house, for tea, for a walk, or just to visit, she'd put the kettle on and whip up a batch of fresh-baked goodies. I borrowed some of her recipes that became my favorites for my story. They are now posted on my website under "Extras."

My first marriage took a turn for the worse when we had children. My husband preferred to be out of town, hunting. Before kids, I'd often accompanied him for the hiking. But with first one child, then two, I didn't want to sleep in a tent in the middle of nowhere. So, I stayed home, where I had a standing weekend dinner invitation at Val's. When he was gone longer than a weekend, she'd often stop by my house on the way home from work with cookies and a ready-to-heat dinner. She understood I was exhausted as a new mom with little help.

In return, all she wanted was tea and a chance to snuggle with the baby.

Val was my best friend for more than ten years when I really needed one. She was there through everything, including my divorce. She and her husband also set the standard of what I should look for in my next relationship. They became more than my friends—I consider them family.

Near the time I met my current husband in 2009, Val and her husband retired and moved to Vancouver Island. They are an expensive ferry ride away, and I don't see them often enough, but she remains in my heart. We text and call, and when we see each other, we pick up like distance and time mean nothing. I'm honored to have a friend as special as Val.

I enjoyed writing *The Right Time: Back to the 80s*, but parts were difficult. It was fun to revisit the 80s, including some of my favorite books and movies from that time. But, reliving pieces of my past was more challenging. While Andie's unfortunate childhood was mostly invented, a few specific instances were borrowed from my childhood trauma, including the late-night fights between my mom and her boyfriend in 1982.

I had no idea if they realized I could hear, but it made for difficult listening. To this day, I can recall the sound a fist makes going through drywall and what smashed, splintering furniture sounds like. Because my family moved away from this situation when I was ten, my life experiences and Andie's diverged. However, I want to acknowledge the strength it takes to leave an abusive situation and start over. Never settle for less than you deserve.

As always, I wish to thank the supportive writing communities I've found with the Vancouver-based online writing academy, The Creative Academy For Writers, and the Black Rose Writing authors and staff. Included in these groups are my beta readers, critique partners, ARC readers, review writers, and book buyers who have taken a chance on me and my stories. Special thanks to Reagan Rothe, David King, Mary Ellen Bramwell, and Justin Weeks of Black Rose Writing for their hard work in making my books successful.

I especially want to thank the BRW and TCA authors who I can count on to read and review my books, both before they're published and after. Finding people willing to write reviews is hard work. Most people, even family and friends who might be supportive in other ways, seldom write reviews, likening it to root canal work.

Included in this early reviewer's group are A.J. McCarthy, Anna Daughtery, Cam Torrens, Diane Hawley Nagatomo, Gail Ward Olmsted, Gary Gerlacher, Karen K. Brees, Keay Francis, Lucille Guarino, Michele Amitrani, and Travis Tougaw. Thank you immensely for reading and reviewing *The Right Time: Back to the 80s* and the positive things you wrote.

I also wish to acknowledge and express gratitude to the author friends with whom I sell books in person. The days at craft fairs and book fairs would be long, boring, and lonely without the company of Bonnie Jacoby and Kirsten Poll. I feel like we make a dynamic group with lots to say about writing, publishing, and friendship. May we maintain our partnership and, like the Whisky Chicks of SiWC, support and uplift each other in positive ways.

I also wish to thank my readers for their continuing support. I appreciate you reading and recommending my books and taking a chance on the next ones, even those outside your usual genre—since I can't stick to one kind of book.

Thank you, as always, to the best critique partner, friend, and editor combo ever, Tracy Thillmann. I'd be lost without her guidance and her ability to hear my author's voice, even in the scrappiest of drafts. She makes my books better every time. May our partnership continue indefinitely.

I also want to thank my family for supporting my writing, and buying and reading my books, even when I've had six published in two years, and have another three on the way, they continue to buy and read.

For cookie and muffin recipes, please see the 'Extras' tab on my website at https://lenagibsonauthor.ca/

Keep reading for the opening chapters of<br>
*The Wish: A Time Slip Novel,*<br>
where we see Dr. Maeve in action for the first time.

# Chapter 1

Sometimes change is infinitesimal, slow. You don't notice its icy fingers wrapped around your throat, stealing your breath, your beliefs, changing who you are until you don't recognize yourself. I was in the middle of such a change before the accident. The slow erosion of myself, into nothing.

I hadn't been behind the wheel in two years, not since the accident. I didn't like to be reminded of those dark days. Few career women in their early thirties don't drive, but walking kept me from another harrowing driving experience. Plus, I'd discovered that I enjoyed the fresh air and exercise.

I crossed the Museum lobby and nodded to the recent hires at the Information Desk, though I'd never spoken to any of their fresh youthful faces. I stepped into an empty elevator, heading up to the peace of my office and lab.

"Hold the elevator," came the call from across the lobby.

I ignored the request. Christopher, the conservator of our museum, raced toward the closing door, shoved his arm inside, and slid in beside me. I rolled my eyes. I'd almost escaped but hadn't been fast enough. Trapped beside him, his heat radiated toward me, and I scooched sideways. He wore running clothes and his dark, wavy hair dripped with sweat. His muscles looked hard, the kind only dedicated athletes or gym rats achieved. I hoped he planned to shower before work.

"Hey, Lizzie." He smiled, the dimple appearing in his cheek.

My teeth ached with the effort as I maintained a neutral expression. I was not, nor had I ever been, a Lizzie. I hated that nickname. My name was

Elizabeth, which suited me—serious, classic, and a little stand-offish. The latter may not have suited me when I was younger, but it did now. I'd been burned too many times to let people get close to me. Life had been filled with harsh lessons.

I nodded to be polite. Being around Christopher was a constant struggle to maintain professionalism. What I really wanted to do was yell, "Leave me alone. I don't need anyone." More than anyone else, he brought out the worst in me. Why wouldn't he take a hint and leave me alone?

"Cat got your tongue again?" He leaned across me and pressed the button for his floor. "My magnificent presence has once again rendered you speechless." He winked.

The elevator ride lasted an eternity. How long did it take to get to the fourth floor?

He smirked.

I raised one eyebrow, but he knew I wouldn't respond. Even before I stopped talking, I hadn't spoken to him. Not since his brother Brandon had disappeared without a word of explanation. Why start now?

"Oh, Christopher."

His mincing tone meant to mimic my voice as he clutched his hands to his chest, caving in his broad shoulders in an attempt to appear feminine.

"You're so handsome and strong." He batted the long dark lashes that fringed his ice-blue eyes. "I'd love to meet with you after work. I don't want to be around anyone, but I find your magnetic charm irresistible."

I cast a withering glance in his direction. Other women fawned over him. He'd probably been told those exact words last week. He could have been charming if he wasn't loud and annoying. Half the time, what came out of his mouth was so full of expletives that I had to filter them out in order to listen. If I spoke, I couldn't imagine it would be to him. He'd never told me anything I wanted to know, like where the hell his brother had gone. Not that I'd asked, I'd been too proud.

Our colleagues at the museum left me alone. They were content to send me emails and receive answers the same way. But not Christopher. Christopher intruded upon the peaceful setting of my office and harassed me for details in person. He was the only person in my professional life who cared that I couldn't speak. His ridiculous remarks seemed designed to elicit a response, but I didn't give him the satisfaction.

"I'll see you later, Lizzie. I have a couple of questions about the new shipment from the Middle East, and something personal." He stepped off on the fourth floor. "I'll come chat after I've showered."

I gritted my teeth. I couldn't wait.

His tall frame strode from the elevator, and he turned to blow me a kiss. Why hadn't I reported his outrageous behavior to HR? I didn't want him to know I'd enjoyed his attempt, though after he was gone, I allowed myself an amused smile. I continued to the sixth floor where my office and lab were located. Maybe I should install a punching bag in the corner and bring workout clothes. It might help after encounters with Christopher. I could work on my left-right-knee-roundhouse combinations.

I couldn't wait to get to the lab that had become my sanctuary. The lab access was through my office. One side of the room had a custom-designed, painted chart of the most recent theory of human evolution. The tree-like diagram of the origins of the human race and their relatives took an entire wall. Seeing it made me smile because it reminded me of the part of my life over which I had control.

They'd hired me fresh from grad school, where I'd received my PhD in Paleoanthropology, and three summers of co-op jobs at the Smithsonian. My job was to create and maintain a display at the brand-new museum here in Portland, meant to one day rival the famous exhibits at the Smithsonian in Washington, DC, or the American Museum of Natural History in New York City.

Scientists used to think Neanderthals in Europe and the Middle East had died out, replaced by more advanced, modern humans moving out from Africa in a single wave.

Now, scientists acknowledged that multiple waves of anatomically modern humans had interbred with Neanderthals and older populations of early humans in several parts of the world. It shouldn't have been a surprise. Anyone who'd seen certain hockey players in the eighties could have recognized a Neanderthal brow ridge. Who knew what DNA lurked within the human species, waiting for selective pressure to force the next wave of evolution? Part of my job was to bring these modern ideas into the new exhibits.

Once I would have discussed these ideas with my boyfriend Brandon over tea in my office after work or over dinner at the cozy restaurants with good food that he always seemed to locate. Or I would have chatted online with my friend Jeff. We'd been close in grad school, but my job was here and his was across the country, in New York. It had been easy to drift apart, through geography and circumstance. The biggest factor in my lost friendship had been my husband, Eric.

It was hard to maintain a long-distance friendship with someone you weren't allowed to see or talk to. I missed sitting and talking about men and movies. We'd had almost the same taste in both, but now it had been years since Jeff and I had a conversation. The gulf had become too immense to bridge. Without a friend, I talked to myself or to my cat. Ember didn't mind, she just purred. Now she was the only one to hear my voice.

After the accident, I hadn't set out not to talk. I just had nothing to say. I'd become lost in my thoughts, trying to cope with my snarled mess of feelings. Then I didn't want to speak. It took months before I realized I couldn't anymore. It had been two years, and I still hadn't spoken in the presence of another person. I hadn't been injured, but the trauma had inhibited my voice. It infuriated my therapist, Dr. Maeve Fossey. We'd been unable to find a solution. We were scheduled for another fruitless appointment tomorrow. She talks. I type.

I read my emails and replied to everything that needed attention. It took an hour, but it would ensure uninterrupted peace afterward. In my office, I was accessible, but in the lab, everyone recognized I was unavailable. Barring an emergency, everyone would leave me alone. Hitting *Send* on the final message, there was a knock at the door. Before I could escape, Christopher barged inside. He'd changed into dark blue jeans and a t-shirt, his work uniform unless he was meeting with the Board, which was the only time he wore a suit and tie.

"Lizzie, perfect." He closed the door and the room shrank. His big personality stole most of the limited space. "Glad I caught you. Downstairs took longer than expected because there was a problem with a water leak in the Modern Technology display. I expected you would have escaped by now."

I shot him a sharp look at his choice of words, so close to my thoughts when I'd heard his knock.

"I had an unusual phone call last night. Once I would have talked to Brandon, but I want your opinion."

At the mention of Brandon's name, the world closed in, and it became difficult for me to hear the rest of his words. Maybe there wasn't enough oxygen in the room. I had trouble concentrating and my vision blurred. My face burned and I willed myself to keep the tears at bay. Christopher continued talking but trailed off when he realized I wasn't listening.

"I'll pick you up at seven. I'll explain then."

I wanted to refuse his invitation, but I was too upset to protest.

His expression was thoughtful, as if I'd said something he hadn't expected, though I hadn't said a word. Maybe my discomfort was written on my face.

I expected him to mimic my daze or pretend to dab at imaginary tears, but he didn't.

"You okay? Do you need to sit down?"

I shook my head. My palms were sweaty, and I crunched them into balls and shoved them deep into the pockets of my white lab coat. I didn't want to go. I couldn't spend that much time with Christopher. Trying not to be obvious, I took calming breaths.

"Look Lizzie, I wouldn't ask if it wasn't important. Please?" All traces of his usual jokes were gone.

I'd have done anything for his brother at one time—before he'd disappeared from my life without an explanation. For Christopher too.

"I know you don't like me," Christopher said.

I looked up and tried to focus. Not that I didn't like *him*. I didn't want to like anyone.

His voice was quieter, less abrasive than usual. His pale blue, almost silver eyes looked sincere.

"But I'm out of options. Please eat with me."

I panicked again and shook my head. Eat? That wasn't a meeting. It sounded more like a date. I glanced down at my jeans, comfortable walking shoes, and lab coat.

"You don't have to change. It's not a date," he said, interpreting my glance.

He'd said *'Please'* twice. I couldn't recall hearing that word cross his lips before now. Maybe I hadn't paid attention. Despite my feelings, I was the slightest bit curious. I shrugged and nodded. Sighing would be rude, so I kept it to myself.

"Thanks, Lizzie. I appreciate your overwhelming enthusiasm. I'll see you at seven." His blue eyes twinkled—his good humor restored.

What had I gotten myself into? I already regretted my decision.

When he showed himself out, I moved into the lab and retrieved the most recent box of fossils to arrive. I wanted to forget Christopher, banish him from my mind. Dr. Maeve said my favorite coping mechanism was avoidance. With a hint of defiance, I opened the box and sorted the contents. Most were casts of bones or bone fragments, but one box contained original fossils from the Middle East that were close to a hundred thousand years old. The Middle East's proximity to Europe, western Asia, and Africa made it the perfect place to find evidence of mixed populations of early humans and some of the rarer species that became extinct. This Mesolithic study was for the next exhibit I was developing.

I stayed in my lab for the rest of the day, removing Christopher from my thoughts until my phone chimed with a notification.

*"Ready?"*

I didn't know he had this number. He'd never used it before, as far as I could remember. I'd changed my number because Eric used to scroll through my messages, looking for reasons to be angry. It had been easier to start fresh. This number had been for family and work only. How could I reply and get out of dinner?

Christopher tapped on the window.

He was in my office. There was no escaping.

I shrugged and rotated my neck, the muscles tight from the precision of measuring, labeling, and identifying the fragments of fossilized bone. I glanced at my phone—seven-ten. How did that happen? I was late. He'd been patient. Leaving the box, so I could resume tomorrow, I jotted a few quick notes, shut off my computer, and turned off the lights before I joined him in my office. I needed a few minutes for my brain to change gears.

As I locked the door and joined him in the hall, my unasked question about his brother returned to my mind. Something he'd said had stuck with me all day and I wanted an answer.

*"Why can't you talk to Brandon?"* I texted while we waited for the elevator. Once upon a time, he and Brandon had been so close.

A strange look appeared on Christopher's face. I couldn't decipher his emotions, and his usual smile disappeared.

"I thought you knew about Brandon." His voice was flat, without inflection.

He looked like he was working up the courage to tell me something difficult. My eyes narrowed. If I'd Googled his brother, I could have known, but I'd avoided even that temptation for the last five years, deactivating my accounts on social media.

"Fuck. I'll just say it. Brandon died. Four years ago."

My body sagged as though I'd been gut-punched, and I used the cold stainless wall to steady myself. The taste of bile rose in my throat. All this time I'd imagined Brandon married, living his own happily ever after across town. Successful and alive. I shook my head. I'd been a bitch for thinking the worst of him.

"After your breakup," Christopher said, "He disappeared from everyone. Worked all the time. Didn't talk to anyone. Kinda like someone else I know."

I couldn't look at Christopher, but his voice continued as though from a distance. It seemed calm, which was shocking considering the topic was his brother's death.

"A couple of months after you two argued, he slipped into a coma and never woke up. At first, we had hope, but he stayed like that for a year. By the end, there were no longer signs of brain activity. We turned off the machines. He wouldn't have wanted to stay like that on life support."

For Christopher, this was old news, and the pain would be more distant. Not forgotten, but squished down to a manageable level. Would my pain become dull, blunt? Today it was like twisting knives.

I rewrote Christopher's words in my mind. The argument that led to my breakup with Brandon had been minor. After that, his brother ghosted me, blocked my number, and vanished. I'd waited outside his house twice, but I hadn't seen him. Later, I'd been so wrapped up in my own problems with Eric that I hadn't heard about Brandon's coma or death. Tears pricked at my eyes and this time, a few escaped. Christopher could mock if he wanted. I didn't care. I'd cared about his brother. With partial success, I smothered my feelings so I could ignore them. Dealing with them all at once was too difficult.

The elevator doors opened at the bottom, and we stepped out. I reeled—his words like blows. Coma. Dead. I'd spent all this time wondering what would have happened if we'd stayed together. How things would be different. They'd have been the same. I'd be in mourning, and still voiceless, since that was my response to trauma.

With this new grief surrounding me, the memory of the accident hijacked my waking hours. I slipped back to my moment of crisis, the flood of memories overwhelming my mind.

There was a clarity in the headlights. I discovered that in the moment with the blinding lights, screeching tires, and jarring crunch of sound, that while I didn't want to die, I was resigned. White light rushed toward where I was frozen, and time stopped. When I'd viewed photos of the wreckage online, I didn't understand how anyone could have survived. As the driver, it was my fault. I shouldn't have been the one to live.

"Lizzie, are you okay?" Christopher's voice came from far away.

I nodded, numb. We walked out of the museum as I relived when I'd walked away from the twisted, mangled metal. My old life had died in that infinite moment, transfixed by the lights, and with it my voice.

# Chapter 2

Christopher and I strolled a few blocks to a restaurant, the air warm in the May evening. In this part of the city, most restaurants had outdoor sidewalk patios—so many interesting places to choose from. It was a beautiful evening, ripe with the promise of the approaching summer. Outside was better. I had more space and fresh air. I could tell from his frown that he was concerned, but he'd asked to talk, and I would try to listen, despite the shocking news that brought back my trauma. Once again, my mind flashed to Eric and the night that had changed my life.

As we walked through the door, I recognized where we were. I'd been here before when it had served Italian instead of Indian. The scent of rich spices filled the air, bringing me back to the present, and I inhaled their fragrance. I was starving. I couldn't remember my last hot meal. For convenience, I ate a lot of salads and sandwiches. Once more, I breathed in the heavenly aroma. I couldn't wait to eat.

A server in black pants and a white blouse led us to a quiet table in the back with dim lighting. It wasn't supposed to, but it seemed like a date. To a stranger, we might look like a cute couple, though Christopher and I were mismatched. But they say opposites attract. He's tall and I'm short. He's dark, I'm fair. His face was made to laugh, while mine was serious. I've always been the kind of person who everyone says would be pretty if only I'd smile—the worst compliment ever. Despite all those differences, from the outside, it might look like we fit. I glanced toward the door, wondering if I could bolt or if Christopher would follow.

"Still not a date," Christopher said under his breath as we sat.

The way his thoughts followed mine was uncanny. Was I so easy to read? Our server said, "Can I start you off with drinks?"

"A bottle of red," said Christopher. "Do you have a recommendation?"

I didn't drink alcohol, so I handed my wine glass to our server and shook my head. He inclined his head and accepted it without pause.

Christopher chuckled. "Never mind. What's on tap? I'll get a beer instead. Lizzie, you want a beer? A cocktail?"

I shook my head and held up my water glass.

When our drink order was settled, Christopher said, "I didn't know you don't drink. Was it the accident?"

I started. I had forgotten that he'd know about it, but I didn't want the conversation to be about anything personal—especially not the accident—so I shook my head. It took up too many of my sleepless nights. I couldn't let it take my days, too.

He lifted my phone from the table and handed it to me. "Tell me."

*My mom drank. She died. I don't. Why are we here?"* Impatience surged through my veins.

"Let's order first. I'm starving. If you're wondering what's good, it's all as delicious as it smells. Sometimes I want one of everything on the menu."

I dreaded the ordeal of ordering in person. Most of the time, I ordered takeout online to avoid the embarrassment of silent pointing, which made me feel so useless. Sometimes I wanted to talk, but when I tried, nothing came out. Dr. Maeve said that I wasn't trying. That deep down, I didn't want my voice. She said I needed to find the right incentive.

I studied my menu and flipped it closed almost right away. Christopher was staring, but I was determined not to fidget under his gaze.

"Well, Lizzie. What're you getting?"

He leaned back in his wooden chair, the picture of ease and relaxation, while I dripped with sweat, a side effect of extreme anxiety. I hoped it wasn't obvious.

I pointed to the two items I'd chosen.

When our server returned with ice water and a pint of his chosen IPA, Christopher ordered. "The lady will have the lamb madras curry, and I'll have butter chicken. We need two orders of vegetable samosas, an order of naan, and a side of basmati rice."

Grateful he'd handled my order with so little discomfort, I sipped my ice water. Why was he being so considerate?

*"Thanks,"* I texted. My tense shoulders loosened a little.

"I suppose I should explain." He took a long drink of beer, then set it on the coaster. He adjusted it to sit in the exact center before speaking. "I didn't know you were unaware of what happened to Brandon. I apologize. He'd said it was a rough breakup, and I respected both of you enough to stay out of it—give you space. It was none of my business. I thought you would've heard what happened to him through others at work. I didn't consider how little you interact with people and I'm sorry I upset you."

I shrugged, watching him play with his fork.

"I didn't handle it well at first, either. I had a rough couple of years. We all need to escape. Hence the women. Though, as you may have noticed, I quit some time ago."

I hadn't noticed. As usual, I'd only noticed things I wanted to see.

I nodded, suspicious of his motives for taking me out for dinner. He was the last person I'd date, if I dated. Which I didn't. That would require being close to someone.

Christopher took another sip. "Last night, I got a strange call. Someone called for Dr. Winters. I seldom use that name outside work, even though I have a doctorate. Then the man launched into gibberish about the serum and needing to restart human trials. He talked really fast. Something about genetic enhancement."

Startled into meeting his eyes, I grabbed my phone. *'He was looking for your brother.'* I couldn't type his name any more than I could say it. My fingers felt paralyzed.

"Yeah, I figured that, but he didn't let me explain. It was a brief call. He freaked out near the end. Said he had to go, that they'd traced his line, that it was too dangerous. In the background, there was a crashing sound, then a bang, like a door had been forced open. There was a scuffle, and the line went dead."

My eyes widened in surprise and my pulse quickened. Once, I'd overheard Brandon on the phone. He'd mentioned the pressure to start human trials. I'd asked him about it later. That conversation had been our last.

"I've tried calling back, but it goes straight to an automated voicemail with no name. I didn't leave messages."

I shook my head.

"What?"

*"They might come for you if they think you're him."*

"Who? Brandon?"

I cringed when he said the name but maintained eye contact.

"Give me some credit. I blocked my number. But I appreciate your concern for my well-being." He grinned, his dimple reappearing.

My heart lurched at the sight. I didn't want to like him. I'd rather ignore him.

"What I was wondering," he said. "Does any of that sound familiar? Brandon said you remember everything. So, if he mentioned anything odd like that, I figured you'd know."

I must have hesitated or looked guilty because his eyes lit up and he talked faster.

"I knew it. It's years later, but better late than never. The doctors say a drug overdose caused Brandon's coma."

I choked on my water and my hands shook as I set down the cold glass. I couldn't have heard right. Brandon had been career-driven, health-conscious, and careful. He'd never take drugs.

I shook my head. No way. The room became too hot as my cheeks burned. A tightness constricted my chest as it sucked the air from my lungs. The restaurant became too confining. I had to get out.

"I agree. He didn't do drugs. It wasn't an overdose. His coma had to have been caused by something else. The call may be a clue. I want to solve this mystery, and I need your help. Help me Obi-wan Kenobi, you're my only hope."

Ignoring the Star Wars reference, which in other circumstances I would've loved, I shoved back my chair, grabbed my phone, and ran.

Christopher called after me, but I didn't listen. I made it outside and two buildings over before I stopped to throw up. I wanted to be left alone, but, of course, Christopher followed. When I leaned forward, one hand on the rough stone wall, he held my hair away from my face as I heaved. He rubbed my back and made soothing sounds I couldn't understand for the roaring in my ears. What if I could've helped Brandon, and I'd let him down?

Christopher handed me a glass of water and a cloth napkin from the restaurant to wipe my mouth. My legs were rubbery, and I shook all over.

My eyes filled with scalding tears, but I didn't let them fall. I took a deep breath and barricaded my feelings away. Since my childhood, I'd taken upsetting thoughts or feelings and visualized them behind a barrier. Sometimes it helped.

He stepped back, his hands shoved deep in the pockets of his jeans.

"I have nowhere else to turn, and I need your help. I won't say another word about Brandon tonight. I had no idea how badly you'd react. I'm sorry. Come inside and eat. You're too skinny. Then I'll drive you home, leave you alone to think."

I was a coward. I didn't know how to help, but I let Christopher take my arm and guide me back to our table. He slid a piece of gum across the table and ordered mint tea to settle my stomach. I allowed him to take this much care of me while he chattered about books and movies. He made it easy for me to just sit. He didn't ask questions or make demands. I'd walked to work, so it was convenient to let him drive me home—I could avoid the darkening streets.

On the walk to his car, I pulled out my phone to text him the address, but he said, "I know where you live. The same place, right?"

I nodded. He'd picked up his brother a few times, long ago. My heart hurt. I wanted to curl up with a romance novel and escape.

At my darkened townhouse, I got out, texted my thanks, and climbed the stairs. I wished I'd left the porch light on. I'd known I might not be home until after dark as I often worked late. I raised my hand to signal that I was fine, but Christopher didn't drive away until I'd located my key and unlocked the door.

If I hadn't found being around him confusing, it could have been a pleasant evening. I hadn't expected to enjoy his company. I'd felt more normal than I had in a long time. The last two years had been lonely and had seemed like an eternity.

I put down dinner for my kitty and headed for the shower, wishing I could wash my feelings down the drain. It was getting too hard to keep them distant. I had so many regrets in my life and tonight only highlighted them. I'd spent years feeling sorry for myself about Brandon's disappearance, wondering what I'd done wrong. Afraid I hadn't measured up. That I hadn't been good enough. I regretted getting mixed up with Eric. Our marriage had been a disaster. I also regretted the energy I'd spent hating someone who, while over-confident and annoying, wasn't so bad.

Tonight, my house seemed quiet and too empty. My eyes grew tired from reading, and I shut out the light, but the silence pressed inward and wouldn't let me rest. I tossed and turned for another two hours. Too many thoughts tumbled in my head, like clothes in a dryer. Around and around, going nowhere. My mind went where it always did when I couldn't sleep— back to the same few jarring moments.

After the accident, my boss advised me to take some time—a leave of absence was usual in these circumstances. Instead, I threw myself into my work, which became my existence. I went through the motions of living. I attended Eric's funeral, but all I remembered were white flowers and the smell of lilies. After the funeral, I avoided my family. They meant well, but despite the tragedy, it didn't affect their lives the way it did mine. My family misinterpreted my wall of numb silence as shock or sorrow. They didn't know that guilt consumed me. Or relief. Or guilt about the relief.

I couldn't remember the last time I'd laughed. It must be years, but it had nothing to do with the accident. It dated back to the beginning of my marriage, when I'd let myself slip away, becoming a cringing, fearful husk without friends. I was ashamed that I'd made such poor choices. I didn't want anyone to learn what I'd hidden the last four years, locked in the prison of my mind. The real secret was now six feet under.

In moments like this, I believed that keeping secrets had led to one thing. I was alone. I didn't have anyone to lean on, to confide in. Alone didn't have to mean lonely, but I was. Nothing seemed to fill the gaping hole inside.

"I'm still ashamed, Ember." I stroked her soft fur. She didn't open her eyes, but a rumbly purr emerged. "Eric hurt me and before that, Brandon. When you let yourself care about people, they have the power to hurt you. I don't know how much more I can take. Being alone is too hard."

In desperation, I jumped out of bed and grabbed a piece of amethyst from the top of my dresser. A couple of sessions ago, Dr. Maeve had brought out a tray of stones and asked me to select a piece to be my worry rock. I'd thought her request silly, but harmless, and had complied. My gaze had settled on the purple crystals as if they'd spoken. I had expected nothing to come of it but had taken it home. I reviewed her words as I gripped the crystals in my hand.

"All my hardest clients choose something special," she'd said. "Stones have properties to heal our minds. This may relieve your anxiety. Hold it when you're sleepless and overwhelmed."

I didn't know how it worked, but she wanted me to think of better times and believe I could get through this rough patch. I'd tossed it there weeks ago, skeptical of its use. I'd been unhappy for so long, but news of Brandon's death was the last straw.

What did I have to lose? Something had to make a difference. It was worth a shot. Tears leaked from the corners of my eyes as I stared at the ceiling and clutched the purple stone to my chest, its sharp edges etching the palm of my hand. My feelings were impossible to keep at bay at night.

With Ember curled into a tabby-sized ball of fur near my hip, I whispered.

"I don't know how to change anymore. I'm so alone."

As I squeezed the stone in my fist, I shuddered and suppressed a sob.

"I wish I had a mulligan so I could redo my life."

# More from Lena Gibson

**The Train Hoppers Trilogy:**
*Switching Tracks: Out of the Trash*
*The Long Haul: Pursuit of Hope*
*Rebels & Saints: Catching Freedom*

**Time Slip Novels:**
*The Wish*
*The Right Time: Back to the 80s*

**The Love and Survival Series:**
*The Edge of Life: Love and Survival During the Apocalypse*
*Aftermath: Into the Unknown*
*No Home Without You: A Post-Apocalypse Romance* (July 2026)

**Love on Track:**
*Racing Towards Destiny: A Sports Romance*
*Racing Hearts* (2027)

**Also in 2027:**
*A Spell of Dance and Silence: A Dark Fairytale Retelling*

# About the Author

Award-winning author Lena Gibson is a storyteller as an elementary school teacher and keeper of the family lore. As an adult newly recognized with autism, she often creates characters that reflect this experience.

A voracious reader from childhood onward, Lena seeks wonderful books in which to escape. She loves interesting characters and fast-paced, emotional narratives, leading her to write genre-defying stories in multiple categories. While her books are disaster romance, time slip, dystopian adventure, and sports romance, all are about love, resilience, and hope.

When Lena isn't writing, she reads, practices karate, and drinks a ton of tea. She resides in New Westminster, Canada, with her family and their fuzzy overlord, Ash, the fluffiest of gray cats. You can learn more at lenagibsonauthor.ca.

# Note from Lena Gibson

Word-of-mouth is crucial for any author to succeed. If you enjoyed *The Right Time*, please leave a review online—anywhere you are able. Even if it's just a sentence or two. It would make all the difference and would be very much appreciated.


Thanks!
Lena Gibson

We hope you enjoyed reading this title from:

# www.blackrosewriting.com

Subscribe to our mailing list – *The Rosevine* – and receive **FREE** books, daily deals, and stay current with news about
upcoming releases and our hottest authors.
Scan the QR code below to sign up.

Already a subscriber? Please accept a sincere thank you for being a fan of Black Rose Writing authors.

View other Black Rose Writing titles at
www.blackrosewriting.com/books and use promo code
**PRINT** to receive a **20% discount** when purchasing.

www.ingramcontent.com/pod-product-compliance
Lightning Source LLC
Chambersburg PA
CBHW030612170726

48283CB00002B/569